Once a Month

by

NICOLE PYLAND

Once a Month

She has a fantasy she wants to explore and has the means to do it. Joining a monthly sex club was never part of her big life plan, but the desire to explore that part of herself is too intense, the pull – too strong. The first month she goes, she meets a woman who is every bit her type, but flees. Each month she returns to find the same woman working the event to enjoy one night with her. One night per month is all she thinks she'll ever get. Only she finds herself wanting more than one night, wanting to know her name, learn about her life, see her outside of their arrangement. Should she risk it, or keep things just the way they are?

In Once a Month, there's a Member and an Escort. Each month, there are two sides to the story of their time together, and over the course of the year, they discover the fantasies they've not shared with others before. They also discover that this might be more than just fantasy.

To contact the author or for any additional information, visit: **https://nicolepyland.com**

BY THE AUTHOR

Stand-alone books:

- The Fire

- The Moments

- The Disappeared

- Reality Check

- Love Forged

- The Show Must Go On

- The Meet Cute Café

- Pride Festival

Chicago Series:

- Introduction – Fresh Start

- Book #1 – The Best Lines

- Book #2 – Just Tell Her

- Book #3 – Love Walked into The Lantern

- Series Finale – What Happened After

San Francisco Series:

- Book #1 – Checking the Right Box

- Book #2 – Macon's Heart

- Book #3 – This Above All

- Series Finale – What Happened After

Tahoe Series:

- Book #1 – Keep Tahoe Blue

- Book #2 – Time of Day

- Book #3 – The Perfect View

- Book #4 – Begin Again

- Series Finale – What Happened After

Sports Series:

- Book #1 – Always More

- Book #2 – A Shot at Gold

- Book #3 – The Unexpected Dream

- Book #4 – Finding a Keeper

Celebrities Series:

- Book #1 – No After You

- Book #2 – All the Love Songs

- Book #3 – Midnight Tradition

- Book #4 – Path Forward

- Series Finale – What Happened After

Boston Series:

- Book #1 – Let Go

- Book #2 – The Right Fit

- Book #3 – All Good Plans

- Book #4 – Around the World

- Series Finale – What Happened After

CONTENTS

MONTH 1, PART 1, – THE FIRST TIME

(POV Member)

I pull up in my car. By now, I've read the instructions for how this is supposed to go so many times, I have them memorized. A man dressed in a tuxedo approaches my car. He pulls open the door for me and bows his head as if I'm royalty. He holds out his hand, and I do as the instructions explained – I hand over my car keys. He says nothing as he waits a moment while I reach back into the car for my purse. I wasn't sure what to bring, so I went with the standard lipstick and compact, just in case I need to freshen up. He motions for me to walk toward the house and climbs into my car. I wait because I need a moment to gather myself before I walk inside. I watch as he drives my car around the long half-circle driveway and down the street.

It's then that I realize I didn't get a valet ticket. A second later, I remember that the instructions said there wasn't any reason to worry about that. I turn toward the house, which was white with blue shutters over at least sixteen front-facing windows. The lawn was perfectly manicured. Lights were on in every window. I can hear people talking inside, but it's not overly loud so as to indicate a party. That's a good thing – no one is supposed to know what goes on inside this house tonight. That's why all their cars were taken to a location down the block and spread out.

I swallow hard as I think about how I got here in the first place. A friend of a friend of a friend recommended this to me after I got drunk one night and confessed some things I might be interested in doing one day. I'd mentioned something about a bucket list, and she'd suggested this. I'd thought it crazy for over six months. Then, one night, I'd gone to the website, entered three layers of passwords along with the name of the person who had referred me, and read the instructions and rules for membership. There were rounds of background checks and even a medical exam to ensure that everyone would be safe. I'd have to get regular tests after this if I choose to retain my membership, but that's a big if. First, I have to walk through the front door.

"Winter," a woman says as I approach.

She's standing outside the door now, looking at me with an expectant stare.

"Masquerade," I reply.

She nods and looks down at her hand, where she has different color bracelets. They are real gold and silver, but they're to be returned at the end of the event. She has a couple of other types as well. I know they're bronze and platinum because I read the instructions, but I can't really tell that since we're standing on the porch, the light above us is not lit, and it's after eleven at night with a new moon in the sky offering little to no light.

"Here you go," she says, holding out a gold bracelet. "First time?" she asks.

"Yes," I confess as I hold out my wrist for her to place the bracelet there.

This is the next layer of the experience. After turning in my car and giving the password for tonight's party that would change for the next one and the one after that, I receive my bracelet.

"You're on time, which is good. Although, you should know that since we rotate houses for safety, we can't always guarantee there will be rooms available if you're late."

"I understand," I say, taking my hand back.

"Rooms with open doors are available even if people are in them. Rooms with closed doors mean–"

"Privacy," I reply, having memorized the directions.

The woman nods again and looks me up and down before saying, "Well, enjoy."

"Thank you," I say back.

She moves out of my way, and the door opens from the inside as if there's someone standing behind it, listening or watching us, preparing for my entry. I walk inside, and my eyes squint instantly due to the change from dark to light. The house opens to a massive foyer complete with a chandelier hanging in the middle and an opulent staircase that curved around and up one side, leading to the second floor.

"Your bag?" a man says, nodding to my purse.

"I'd like to keep it, if that's okay," I say.

He nods and says, "Your jacket?"

"Yes, please," I reply and shimmy out of my long, black jacket that had been concealing my elegant little black dress chosen just for this occasion.

"To the right is the party," the man said, taking my coat. "To the left, you'll find refreshments. If you choose to imbibe, we do reserve the–"

"I know," I say, recalling the part about them conducting breathalyzers and providing designated drivers if necessary – anything to prevent a guest from drinking and driving and that getting back to the people at the party.

"Upstairs, there are eleven bedrooms along with other private and not-so-private spaces. If you need anything, just find anyone wearing this ribbon on their lapels, and we'll be happy to get it for you." He pointed to a green, plain ribbon attached to his tuxedo jacket.

"Thank you."

"Door knocking starts fifteen minutes before the end of the event at four," he said.

I nod. The party went from eleven to four in the morning, but I doubt I'll be here longer than an hour – I just want to walk around and take it all in tonight. I don't plan on actually participating. I don't know that I'll ever participate, but after six months of not being able to get it off my mind even before I did my research – and then more months of background checks and testing – I'm more than curious to see what all the fuss is about. Of course, the hefty membership fee is also keeping me here for at least an hour. The first night is fifty percent off. After this, if I want to come back, I have to pay the full fee, and it's an annual commitment. I can afford it, so that's not the issue, but it's a lot of money to give away if I don't end up liking it.

"Can I get you anything?" the same man asks.

"No, thank you," I reply.

He nods yet again. I take the hint that he likely has another guest to welcome right after he drops my jacket off in the coatroom, so I walk to the left, where he said the refreshments were located. It's then that I see nine or ten people standing around the large dining room, complete with a table that could seat at least twenty people. It's covered in various food platters, cutlery, and full champagne glasses. There's also a bar behind the food-filled table, with two bartenders pouring wine and cocktails. I decide to skip the drinks for now since I'm not sure if I'm staying, and I want to be able to drive myself home. I look down at the food that looks delicious and in perfectly small portions for an event like this, but my stomach is rumbling with nerves, so now is not the time to put food in it.

I take another second to look around and take in my surroundings. I'm not looking at the artwork on the walls, or the ornate woodwork of the molding, or around the window that had closed curtains for the night; I'm looking around at the people here – specifically, at the ones wearing no bracelets at all and the color of the bracelets the others are wearing. I know gold means women. Silver means men. Then, there are people wearing platinum, which means anything goes, and bronze, which means–

I lose my train of thought when I see a woman walk into the room. She's approaching a man who smiles when he sees her, as if they know each other. Maybe he's a regular, and they *do*. He's leaning against the wall, holding his glass of dark liquor, and she's reaching for him. My heart falls to the floor when her hand cups him roughly. He takes a slug of his drink, leaves the glass on the table for someone else to take care of, and off they go. I guess the party is starting.

I turn around to see a man with no bracelet leaning in to whisper something to another man, who nods. My head is now on a swivel. I see a woman with a silver bracelet approach a man without one. They speak for only a second before he gently presses her to the wall behind her and lifts her right leg off the floor, pressing into her.

Knowing what to expect and actually seeing it are two different things, and my heart is racing in my chest. I have to turn around and leave the room. Where is my jacket? God, where did he park my car? Can I ask him to bring it back? Then, I see the man slide his hand between the woman's legs. Her eyes are closed. He's kissing her neck, stroking her, and she's enjoying herself. She doesn't care that she's completely exposed to a room full of people; that I'm watching him slide his fingers inside her now. I'm watching a stranger ride another stranger's finger. Then, I'm watching her come undone at his touch, and I'm wet.

I turn to go, and I as I do, I end up blocked in the foyer as more people enter the party and are welcomed by the attendant. I wait for them to move, and with the attendant now off to the coatroom with their jackets and bags, I head to the other room to await his return. It's then that I see people couple off. Some of them are in groups of three. Two couples are already engaged. One woman is down on her knees, in front of a man wearing the male version of the gold bracelet, indicating his preference for women. Another woman is slipping her hand into the dress of a woman who's also wearing a gold bracelet.

That gets my attention. I lean back against the wall and watch, worried for a second that I'm going to get caught and asked to leave but remembering that this is what some people come here for. In fact, there's a woman in the corner of the room, staring at them as well, and she has her hand inside her pants. She's licking her lips, and I think there's no way I'll ever be comfortable enough to get myself off in a room with twenty people in it, like her. I return my attention to the same couple, who – I notice now – are both wearing gold bracelets, indicating they're both members. Interesting, I think.

It's almost too much for my senses, but I keep watching. I watch as these two women kiss each other deeply and sometimes roughly. I watch as the one pressing the other to the wall, reaches inside her own pants. I expect her to place the other woman's hand there so they can pleasure each other, but she doesn't. I can't see what she's doing now, so I move. I actually move to get a better look. Then, I see her pull out a flesh-toned dildo. The woman pressed to the wall, lifts her dress up and slips her panties off – just like that, in a room full of people. She tucks them into the other woman's pants pocket and spreads her legs. The other woman smirks, and the dildo slides between the woman's legs. I watch as she coats it in her desire before I see it disappear inside her. They're pressed together now, and the woman with the strap-on is thrusting slowly. The woman against the wall is pressing on the other woman's ass, silently begging her for more; and I am captivated by this. I lick my lips and actually think about reaching inside my own panties because now, I am completely turned on.

It's then that I notice it. There's music playing softly in the background, and it's something classical that I don't recognize, but that's not what I notice. I notice the other sounds. There are moans and grunts and gasps. I tear my eyes away from the two women having sex against a wall not even ten feet away from me and look around the room. A man now stands behind a woman. He's reaching inside her silk top, massaging her breasts, while another woman is going down on her.

"Fuck," I whisper.

I return my attention to the women at the wall just as the one pressed against it comes hard and yells out. She grasps her own breasts through her dress, squeezes them, and I can't believe I just saw that. I can't believe I'm still seeing it. I want to watch more. I want to take it all in, but part of me wants to explore further. I leave the room and see the attendant is back at the door – I can leave. I can let him know I need my jacket and my car, and I can go. I got what I came for – I know what these events are like now. I can go home, get myself off, and go to sleep, having checked this off my sex fantasy bucket list.

I head upstairs instead, taking the curved staircase one careful step at a time, feeling like I might fall from wobbly, uncertain legs. I arrive at the first room, which is an empty bathroom. When I turn down the hallway, I see open and closed doors. I remember the rules: open doors, even if occupied, mean that people don't mind being watched or joined. If I want to join, I just have to ask first. An open door means I can watch without making the request. I pass two closed doors, hearing some sounds through them but not focusing on what I'm hearing. I approach an open door and look inside. A man is going down on a woman who looks up when she notices me standing there. She holds up her hand with a platinum bracelet, indicating she's up for anything or, in this case, anyone. She closes her eyes without awaiting my nod or a headshake, and she comes, moving her hand to the back of his head to press him farther into her. She's completely naked, as is he, and I watch her breasts bounce as she moans and curses in pleasure. When she finishes, he stands, and I watch as he climbs on top of the bed and flips her over.

She says, "Yes, baby."

He enters her from behind, and I turn to go. Across the hall, there's another open door. I peer inside and see three women on a bed. This room has my attention. One woman is sitting behind another; her hands are on the woman's breasts. The woman in the middle is staring down at the third woman, who has her mouth pressed against her sex and fingers buried deep inside her. I watch. The woman massaging the breasts makes eye contact, and God, she's gorgeous. She's striking in her androgyny. Her eyes are dark either by nature or because of arousal. Her hair is short and equally dark. Her skin is just this side of tan. I watch as her hands with short fingernails massage full breasts, and I nearly come at the sight.

The woman she's massaging *does* come, but the dark-eyed woman doesn't take her eyes off of me. It's as if she's touching me, not someone else. I open my mouth and lick my lips. It's too much, though. I can't take it, so I turn around and walk down the hall. My heart is thundering, and I'm not sure how much more it can take before it just gives out. Part of me wants to flee, part wants to go back downstairs to watch the couple against the wall, and the other wants to go back to that bedroom and make eye contact with the sexy woman massaging someone else's breasts. It's then that I think about the fact that she's not wearing a bracelet – she's working.

I find more closed doors, including what I assume is a bathroom, because I'm pretty sure I hear a shower running, and I come across another open door. There's a couple in this room, and I smile when I realize it's the two women from downstairs. The woman who had been wearing the strap-on is on top of the other woman now. They're both naked this time, and they're covered in a light sheen of sweat. I watch as she slowly makes her way down the other woman's body, feeling like a total voyeur until I remind myself that the door is open. They want this. They like this. When she finally takes the woman into her mouth, I bite down on my bottom lip. Just from watching them like this, I can tell there's familiarity with these two, and I wonder if they're together and come here to spice things up or if they meet here monthly and have done this dozens of times.

"Hi," a soft, husky voice says into my ear.

I know better than to turn around and say, "Hi."

"Do you like to watch?" she asks, the sound coming a little closer, meaning she'd taken a step toward me.

I think about lying but realize there's no point and say, "Yes."

"Do you like anything else?"

I take a deep breath and just nod, not trusting my own voice anymore.

"Would you like anything right now?" she asks.

Then, I feel a hand on my hip. It's not possessive or demanding. It's gentle and tells me that she'll back off the moment I say no. I should shake my head – I only came here to watch. This was some stupid fantasy that I've now fulfilled.

"Yes," I whisper back.

"While you watch?" she asks, seemingly knowing the answer already as she wraps her arms around my waist and gently pulls me back against her.

"Yes," I say.

I feel her lips graze the soft skin of my neck, so I close my eyes for a second and wait. Nothing happens.

"I thought you were going to watch," she says after a moment.

I open my eyes. She's still behind me. This is crazy. I don't even know this woman. I'm going to let her touch me, and I don't even know her. I try to push away my own insecurities, my judgments, and just about everything else as I nod again.

"Can I touch you?" she asks.

"Yes," I say.

Slowly, her right hand slips down to the hem of my dress. She lifts it, and then her hand is on my bare thigh.

"Oh," I say softly.

"Oh, good?" she asks.

"Yes."

Her hand moves up, still slowly. She uses her fingertips to graze and drag before her palm presses down more firmly when the woman in front of us comes. I worry that will be the end; that by the time I'm touched, the two women on the bed will be done. But then, the woman on top moves until her sex is over her partner's mouth. Her partner pulls her down and sucks her into her mouth just as a tentative finger strokes over my panties.

"Fuck," I say a little louder than I intended.

"You're hard," the woman says as she kisses my neck. "Fuck, you're so ready."

I close my eyes and lean back against her. The way she said that last part almost sounded like she was turned on by all this, too; but since I don't see her wearing a bracelet, I know she's working tonight, and I don't expect anyone working the event to actually get turned on by doing this.

"Touch me," I say. I'm already far beyond the point of worrying about begging for it now.

Her lips suck on my earlobe, and when her hand slips into my panties, I realize then just how wet I really am.

"So good," she whispers, and for a minute, I think that she's trained to make these kinds of comments, but then I don't care because her finger is stroking my clit.

My hips are moving forward and back. Her free hand is holding me against her body. I want it on my breast, though. I think about not taking what I want at first but decide that I've come this far.

"Unzip," I manage to say.

Her hand moves to the zipper at my left side, and she unzips my dress. Thank God I'm wearing a strapless bra. I lower the strap of the dress first, then the cup, and she knows what to do. She cups me and strokes me while I watch the woman riding the other woman's face, and we come at the same time. God, I come so hard, the woman responsible for my orgasm has to stop squeezing my nipple to hold my waist in place. I come so hard, I nearly topple over, and she pulls me back against her.

"I've got you," she says, and she *does*.

She kisses my neck, licks the spots she's kissed, and slowly strokes me as I come down. The women on the bed pause, and both of them turn to look at us. They smirk. I flush even more.

"Want to watch again?" the one on the bottom asks.

I realize a second too late that she's talking to me.

"Do you?" the woman behind me asks me, returning

her hand to my breast and starting up her strokes again on my clit.

I know then that I'm not done coming. I can just go home and take care of it myself, though. I don't need to—

"Yes," I say.

"We like being watched," the woman on top says as she moves to stand. "Any requests?" she asks me.

"What?" I ask back, shocked by the question.

"Any requests?" she repeats.

"What do you want to watch them do to each other?" the sexy voice from behind me asks as she moves a finger just a little lower, close to my entrance.

"Anything," I manage to say.

The woman who is now standing up moves to the side of the bed, bends over, and picks up a harness with the accompanying dildo from before.

"I'm going to let her ride my dick."

I watch as she gets ready. The woman behind me continues to stroke me softly, and my legs get wobbly again.

"Do you want to sit down?" she asks.

"Huh?" I ask, knowing I don't want to move.

"I'd really like to go down on you while you watch," she says. "Would that be okay?"

"Go…" I don't say anything else because the other woman is back on the bed; her partner is moving to straddle her hips, and I watch the dildo disappear inside her for the second time tonight.

"Over here," the woman behind me says.

She removes her hands from my body, and I want them back immediately. I'm about to say something when she walks around beside me, and I realize who's just given me the best orgasm of my entire life – it's the dark-haired woman from the other room, and she's even sexier now. I open my mouth to say something, but nothing comes out. I want her again so badly. I want her inside me. I want her mouth on me. I want to keep watching the two women writhing on the bed in front of me. I want it all, but as I stare into her dark eyes, I can't move toward the small sofa in the corner of the room where I can tell she wants to me go.

"I…"

"It's okay," she says. "We don't–"

"I have to go," I say.

"You have to go?"

"Fuck!" the woman on the bed yells as her hips rock.

"I can do what I just did if you want," my dark-eyed goddess says to me as she moves back behind me again. "Is this what you want?" Her hand returns to my still exposed breast, and her other hand moves back under my dress to cup my sex.

Yes, it is what I want. I want this again and again. But something is telling me that this isn't *really* what I want.

"I have to go," I repeat and step away from her.

Her hands fall. I pull up my bra, covering my breast, and zip my dress back up quickly. I pick up my purse, which I only just realize is sitting on the floor next to me, and turn around. She looks almost disappointed, but that can't be right. She does this for a living; she'll find someone else to fuck tonight. She nods, and I know somehow that I'm right – she *is* disappointed. I nod, too, for some reason, and walk past her, out the door of the bedroom and down the hall. I practically take the stairs two at a time, and as I request my coat from the attendant at the door, I take a chance to look back up to the landing.

When I do, I see her standing there and staring back down at me, wearing a sexy tailored suit that doesn't look like it has a wrinkle on it and an expression that tells me she is contemplating something. I take my jacket abruptly from the attendant when he returns with it, and I walk outside. The woman from before is still standing there, by the entrance. She doesn't ask me any questions. I hold out my wrist, she takes my bracelet, presses some buttons on a phone, and within a minute, my car is pulled into the driveway by the same valet. I take back the keys, climb inside, and breathe for the first time since I entered that house.

"Oh, my God," I say to myself before I pull the car out into the street, vowing that this will be the only party like this I ever go to, but knowing deep down inside that's just not the truth.

MONTH 1. PART 2. – THE FIRST NIGHT

(POV Escort)

Well, here I am. I'm standing in front of my floor-to-ceiling mirror, trying to fix my hair and wondering how the hell I got here. I'm wearing a suit jacket – I never wear suit jackets. I feel like this isn't me, but I know it is at the same time. I know this is not something I'd planned for myself, but I'm doing it anyway. I signed a contract, and they've given me an advance. I won't get the rest unless I actually show up, and it's a lot of money. God, it's a lot of money, and I need it. So, I take one more look and decide I'm presentable enough. I grab my phone and wallet off the table by my bed, tuck them into my pockets, and leave my house.

As per my instructions, I pull up a mile from the location. A man meets me, and we wait for a few minutes in total silence. This is the part where they drive several of us to the very nice mansion in a much nicer car than the one I drove here in because, in this neighborhood, a fifteen-year-old car would stick out like a sore thumb – which is an expression I don't actually know the origin of, and I think about that as three women and two men pull up, and we all get inside a black BMW SUV that drives us the rest of the way there.

It's a strange ride. No one says anything, but there aren't any actual rules about not talking to the other escorts that I know of, so it must just be something they do. We're driven to the back of the house, and we follow the man who drove us there. He'll go back and pick up the late arrivals and bring them here, too, so he leaves us after we're inside and checked in. The woman at the door looks at me and another woman who's arrived with me, and she nods for us to follow her. We do.

"First timers," she says. "One more review of the rules before the members get here."

I listen as she rattles on about things I already know. I tuck my hands in my pockets, trying to appear cool and calm, but I'm a ball of nerves inside. My stupid friends had to suggest this to me as a way to make money… I can't believe I'm listening to a woman tell me that if a member approaches me and I'm not attracted to them at all, I have to feign interest. Obviously; I know why I'm here. I'm here because people paid a lot of money to join this secret club. They just go from house to house, month after month, and they sleep with people, watch other people have sex, and sometimes, they do a little of both.

"Consent is the most important thing," she says at the end of her speech. "Theirs *and* yours. If a member gets out of line in the slightest, you notify one of the people wearing this green ribbon, and they're gone. Understood?"

"Yes," the woman next to me says.

I nod.

"That goes for you, too. You do anything to piss of a member, and you're out, too. You make the advance, and that's all; no payment for the night."

"I understand," I say.

"Me too," the woman beside me says.

"The members are always punctual – they get five hours a month to explore their deepest sexual fantasies, and they want to take advantage of every moment. Your job, ultimately, is to give them what they want. If you do well tonight, we'll ask you back next month. If not, we'll part ways here. Each month, the members review our employees on the site after the event, and we take those reviews very seriously."

I nod again. I know all of this already, but honestly, standing in the kitchen while the caterers move about briskly is helping to calm my nerves. It all started three months ago. I needed money. My very successful friends offered to give it to me or loan it to me, at least, and I pridefully declined the offer. A week later, they told me about this place and suggested I could get what I needed after a few months of *work*. I had rolled my eyes at them and definitely took offense, but they told me how attractive I was and that the members here would love me. They assured me that I would only have to work with women and that I'd be able to indicate I only wanted to be with women ahead of time, so no man would even approach me. That made me feel a little better. Of course, it's still sex, and they told me if I wasn't okay with it, they'd drop it, but the money side of things kept coming back into my mind. I needed it. *We* needed it. Three nights of work over a few months, and that would be it – I'd be caught up, and I could stop this and forget it ever happened. We'd have what we need, and life would go back to normal.

***

"How are you?" she asks me.

"Are you supposed to talk to me?" I ask my friend.

"We can talk here; it's not just sex," she says, smiling back. "Do you want a drink for your nerves?" she asks.

"No. I think it's best that I don't," I reply.

"Okay. But, trust me, it helps."

"You're a member. Why would *you* need it?" I ask her as her wife approaches with two cocktails in her hands.

"The first time we came here was a big deal," she says. "We'd known for a while that we wanted people to watch us; that it turned us on like crazy. You know that."

"I do," I say, recalling the first time I watched the two of them have sex on their sofa while I sat in the chair.

At the time, it had been a complete and total shock to me. I'd already known both of them for three years, and they hadn't been married yet back then. One night, I was watching a movie with them while they were snuggled up on the sofa, and I heard a soft moan. I didn't turn then, and I heard a louder one. I think I squinted first, wondering what was going on, before I turned. When I did, I saw one of them lying behind the other. She had her hand inside her girlfriend's jeans. They were unbuttoned and unzipped, and my first reaction was to jump up, ask what the hell was going on, and leave. But something kept me there; kept me staring. They both looked at me then.

"Is this okay?" she asked.

"Is *what* okay?" I asked back.

"We want you to watch," she said.

And I did. None of us said anything else. It was an unspoken agreement. I watched as she got her girlfriend off on the sofa first. I watched as she rolled on top of her, and her girlfriend – my friend – removed her shirt and sucked on her nipples. I watched as they stood up after that. I followed them as they walked into their bedroom, kissing one another, and I couldn't stop my feet from moving. They ended up on the bed, and I stood at the side until they motioned for me to lie down next to them. So, I did. They were naked. I was watching one of them go down on the other, and I couldn't help myself. I reached inside my own jeans, and I took care of the ache I'd felt since I first started watching them.

Since then, whenever the mood called for it, they'd invited me over. They're married now, and they only touch each other, but they love it when people watch; and they love it even more when people get off next to them. It's definitely the strangest friendship I've ever had, but it works for us, and I admire the openness of their marriage and how they're so free with these things that turn them on. I envy them in a way. While I can get off while watching them sometimes, I've never been truly able to express everything I want with sex – which is one of the reasons I think I'm here tonight. The money is the reason I agreed, but there's a desire in there, somewhere, begging me to find a sexy woman here tonight and give her everything I can to make her feel that sexy.

"Are you okay?" my other friend asks as she hands her wife a drink.

"Yeah, I'm okay," I say.

"You know we'll give you whatever you need, right? You don't have–"

"I know," I interrupt. "I think I'm actually good with being here right now."

"Yeah?" my friend asks as she downs her drink in one gulp.

There's music in the room now, which is something I remember from the instructions I'd been given. The party was starting. Shit. It's time. I lick my lips and look around the room.

"You can watch us for a while if you want," my friend tells me. "We can always say we're using you if they ask; which they won't – they leave members alone."

"It's okay. I'm going to walk around a bit," I say.

"Okay," she says, taking her wife's hand and moving them toward the wall.

I walk out the back of the room, but I turn just as the other glass is placed on a table next to a chair, and she presses her wife to that wall and slips her hand in. I've grown to love watching them do this. There's something about watching two women who love each other touch one another like this that just gets me going, which is probably a good thing because my mind right now should be on sex. I leave them to it, though, and I walk to the stairs, which are curved, massive, and somewhat intimidating. I take them slowly, thinking that maybe I can just walk up the stairs for the next five hours if I walk slowly enough. Somehow, I make it up in under a minute, and I watch people as they walk the same stairs past me up and down toward rooms, hand in hand and giddy. I try to feel that giddiness, but I'm not there yet.

I pass a few closed doors, which means I'm not to en-ter, and come across an open one where a man is sucking on another man. Finding that of no interest, I turn to the room opposite this one, which also has an open door. They only told us to make ourselves look available until a member makes us unavailable, so I don't exactly know what to do. I peek inside the room and find two women undressing one another. It's not fast but slow; they're still just kissing, and it's nice. I think it's nice to watch them do this before I realize I should probably leave them to it.

"Come in," one of them says.

I swallow and say, "If you want me to."

"Yes," she says.

She's an attractive woman in her early forties, most likely. Her hair is dark and down around her shoulders. Her breasts are now bare to me, and the woman in front of her has her dark-pink, erect nipples on display, and her pussy is neatly trimmed. She's fit, but not overly so, and I like her curves. I like her eyes, too. They're beckoning me forward as the other woman lowers herself to suck on a nipple.

"Sit behind me," she says softly to me as she cups my cheek.

I nod, not knowing what's going to come next but being okay with sitting behind this woman.

"Clothes?" I ask.

"On. You look so fucking sexy in them," she says, running a hand down the middle of my chest possessively, and I know I'm more than okay with this now.

Her fingernails are long and bright red – she's not likely a giver in the bedroom; at least, not with her fingers. Then, I think that she might not even have sex with women outside of one night a month when she comes here. My friends have told me that many members use these parties to let other parts of themselves out that they usually keep contained, and there's even something sexy about *that* to me. I slide my back against the pillows, and she lies back against me while the other woman – who I know isn't a member – kneels in front of her and spreads the woman's legs for her.

"You know how I like it, baby," the woman says to her.

She picks up my hands and places them on her breasts. The woman in front of her lowers herself until she's between her legs. Then, I hear the sucking sound. Fuck, I can *hear* it. This woman whose breasts I'm playing with right now is so fucking wet, I can *hear* someone sucking on her clit.

"Yes," she says, cupping her hands over my hands on her breasts, begging me with them to squeeze her harder.

And I do. I squeeze until her hands fall away. Then, I twist and play with her nipples. It seems to be what she wants because her chest is moving up and down in time with her hips, which are already begging the woman in front of her for release. I look down at that woman, thinking about how much I'd like to get off myself right now. Then, I hear footsteps, and I look back up at the doorway.

There's a woman standing there, and I swallow hard – she's sexy. Oh, she's so fucking sexy that I feel wetness between my thighs that has nothing to do with what's happening on this bed. That dress she's wearing fits her like a soft, perfect glove. Her eyes are very dark, and they're looking right into mine. I stop massaging for a second, which is a mistake because the woman in front of me is coming now. I can't take my eyes off this new woman, though. I try to resume the massaging how I just was – which, I'm sure, is no longer as good – and I stare into this woman's eyes, wanting her to know that I wish I were going this to *her* right now. I have no idea where this is coming from, but I want her tonight. I just want *her*, and I know it.

She leaves. My eyes go wide because she turns and leaves without a word, and I'm stuck where I am, behind a member that's still coming down from her orgasm and might ask me to do something else now. I don't know what to do, but I stop massaging her breasts and sit back a little, waiting for her cue. Why couldn't I have noticed that other woman first? I could have ended up with her instead.

"Your hands are nice, baby," the member says, and I think she's talking to me because the other woman only used her mouth a minute ago. "You're pretty stiff back there." She reaches a hand around and cups my neck gently. "Any chance you packed something for me?"

I know what she means, and I try to think about how to answer so I can leave, but I don't know what to say. I look at the other escort, who gives me an understanding expression.

"Hey, baby? I brought mine," she tells the member. "And I have it in my bag right here." She stands and picks up a bag she'd left by the bed.

"Thank God! Can you take care of me?" the member asks.

"Of course," my unexpected savior replies.

The woman leans up, and I take that opportunity to slip out from behind her. I watch the other escort slip on the harness and dildo she'd packed, and I just stand there, looking like an idiot, because I don't know what to do.

"You can go if you want," the woman says to me. "She's so good with this thing; I won't need another for a while."

The other escort smirks at the woman and smiles at me. I nod, and I leave. I would have stayed. I don't think I'd have a problem getting that woman off, but I can't think about anything other than those dark eyes staring into my own. I need to find her. I need to be the one that touches her tonight. I walk past closed and open doors and only hope she's not in a closed room. Then, I find her. She's again standing in a room watching two women have sex. Not just any two women, either. My friends, apparently, wanted a room, and one of them is now moving down the other's body. It's something I've seen dozens of times now, but it never fails to excite me to watch them like this.

The one woman I'm here for, though, is facing them, so she doesn't know I'm here yet. I double-check the bracelet on her wrist and smile. Now, I need to figure out if this is something she wants or if she's only here to watch to-night.

"Hi," I say into her ear after stepping closer.

She doesn't turn around but says, "Hi."

"Do you like to watch?" I ask, moving even closer.

"Yes," she says, and her voice almost makes me melt.

"Do you like anything else?" I ask, feeling more confident now.

She nods in response.

"Would you like anything *right now*?" I ask.

I place my hand on her hip – not possessively, but in a way I hope conveys that I'll drop it if she tells me to, but that I really don't want to.

"Yes," she whispers.

"While you watch?" I ask, wrapping my arms around her waist and gently pulling her back against me.

She feels so good against my body, warm and soft; and I can't believe I actually *want* to touch someone tonight and not just because I'm getting paid for it.

"Yes," she says.

My lips graze the soft skin of her neck.

"I thought you were going to watch," I say after a moment when I realize her eyes are closed.

She opens them, and wanting the answer so badly to be yes, I ask, "Can I touch you?"

"Yes," she tells me.

I close my eyes this time and slip my right hand down to the hem of her dress. I lift it and place my hand on her smooth, bare thigh. I almost just want to keep it there, but there's heat emanating from her sex, and I need to move closer to it.

"Oh," she says softly.

"Oh, good?" I ask.

"Yes."

I smirk and move my hand up slowly, using my finger-tips to graze her skin before I press my palm down firmly just as my friend comes on that bed from her wife's tongue.

It doesn't take long for her to come down, and my other friend is now moving her sex over her wife's mouth. Fuck, I love when they do this – I love watching one of them ride the other's face like they can't contain their orgasm and need it out of their body right now. Before I realize what I'm doing, my finger is stoking my partner over her panties.

"Fuck," she says, and I'm gone.

"You're hard," I say and kiss her neck. "Fuck, you're so ready," I say, unable to stop myself.

She leans back against me and says, "Touch me."

I instantly suck on her earlobe. Then, I slip my hand into her panties and, realizing just how wet she actually is, I have to stop sucking on her earlobe to bite my own lip before I return to her ear again.

"So good," I say after a particularly strong suck.

My fingers are stroking her hard and wet clit. Her hips are moving forward and back, and my free hand is holding her against my body, wanting to keep her there as long as possible because I don't want to stop touching her.

"Unzip," she says.

I know what she wants, so I unzip her dress at the side. She lowers the strap, and fuck – she's wearing a strapless bra, and I can see the tops of her full breasts now. She lowers the cup for me, and I don't hesitate – I cup her breast and stroke her clit harder and faster. I lift my gaze to see my friend cupping her wife's ass as her hips rock forward and back. For a second, she lifts up, and I see a tongue dart inside. Now, I know I need to come myself. This is too much for me not to get off tonight. The woman in front of me is so sexy. Her sounds are building, as are the woman's on the bed. Fuck! *She's* coming. I can feel her. Her body is tensing. She moans, gasps, and then comes undone at the same time my friend does the same thing. The woman in my arms juts forward, and I have to stop playing with her breast to keep her from falling over. I pull her back against me.

"I've got you," I say.

I kiss her neck, lick the spots I've just kissed, and

slowly stroke her as she comes down. My friends pause, and both of them turn to look at us. I see their cocky smirks and roll my eyes.

"Want to watch again?" my friend asks.

She's not talking to me, though, so I wait.

"Do you?" I ask her when she doesn't respond.

"Yes," she says.

"We like being watched," my friend tells her as she moves to stand. "Any requests?" she asks *her*.

"What?" she asks.

"Any requests?" my friend repeats.

"What do you want to watch them do to each other?" I ask and move my index finger a little lower, indicating I want to be inside her.

"Anything," she says.

My friend picks up her favorite strap-on and says, "I'm going to let her ride my dick."

She gets ready, and I stroke. I want *her* again. I don't care if it's now or down the hall in another room we have all to ourselves. As I stroke, I feel her wobble a bit.

"Do you want to sit down?"

"Huh?" she asks.

"I'd really like to go down on you while you watch," I say, thinking I want my mouth on her and my fingers buried deep. "Would that be okay?"

"Go…" she starts but doesn't finish as my friend moves back to the bed.

Her wife straddles her hips, and the dildo slips inside her.

"Over here," I say, trying to focus on the woman in front of me and not the two women in bed.

When I move beside her, she opens her mouth to say something, but nothing comes out. There's a small sofa in this room where I can kneel in front of her and take my time if I want; if *she* wants. But the expression on her face tells me she's not sure about something.

"I…"

"It's okay," I say quickly, trying to keep her here. "We don't–"

"I have to go," she says.

"You have to go?"

"Fuck!" my friend yells at the worst possible moment.

"I can do what I just did if you want," I say as I move back behind her, trying to recreate what we just did. "Is this what you want?" I cup her breast again and move my other hand to her center and up her softly.

"I have to go," she repeats and steps away from me.

My hands fall from her instantly. I don't want her to think I'm pushing. She pulls up her bra and zips her own dress back up. Then, she picks up her purse, which I hadn't even noticed she'd dropped to the floor, and she turns around. I just nod at her because I can't think of anything else to say or do. She nods back and walks past me. I wait a second, take a deep breath, and then go after her. By the time I'm at the landing, she's already at the front door. She looks back up at me. Our eyes meet, and I can see that she's thinking about something. Is it whether or not to come back to me? She takes her jacket abruptly from the guy at the door, and just like that, she's gone.

I wait a whole minute just in case she comes back, but when she doesn't, I rush down the hall, find an empty bathroom, close and lock the door, and unbutton and unzip my pants. I slide my hand into my underwear and start stroking. I'm leaning against the glass shower door because I need something to keep me standing. I let my pants fall to the floor, spread my legs, and thrust my fingers as deep as I can, biting my lower lip to keep from yelling out. I thrust and thrust, and my free hand goes to my clit. I'm working myself up inside and out, head back against the shower door, and I come so hard. I come harder than I ever have on my own before, or with another woman, or while watching my friends. What has she done to me?

"Oh, my God," I say to myself.

MONTH 2. PART 1. – BACK FOR MORE

(POV Member)

I stare at the screen in front of me and consider what I'm about to do. I'd waited until the last possible moment. While membership guaranteed access, an RSVP was still required. Members had up until twenty-four hours prior to the event to respond to an encrypted email with a yes or a no. Before I can do that, though, I have to make the annual commitment and pay for the full year upfront. The amount I see doesn't worry me – it's more about what it represents. That amount represents me paying for sex – me paying to watch other people have sex and maybe even having sex with those people – and it's not something I ever thought I'd do.

Truthfully, I'm what most people would call attractive enough. I'm not supermodel material or anything, but I'm not bad, either. I come from old money, but I also have a successful career. I earn enough on my own to be able to afford something like this, but it's not like I can't get sex when I want it – I'm a well-known out-and-proud lesbian. I've wined and dined women, and some of them have also wined and dined me. Usually, the sex is okay. Sometimes, the sex is great. I've had a few long-term relationships and a lot of first dates that have led to good sex, but I've never had an orgasm as good as the one I've had just under a month ago by a stranger's hand while I watched two other women have sex on a bed.

It's always been there, I guess, my desire to watch others. And I don't mean pornography – that's all fake, often overly dramatic, and it doesn't appeal to me. Watching two people be intimate in person, though, has been something I've been thinking about for a while now. Sure, some people are paid to be there, but the two women I watched last month were both members, which means they wanted to give one another pleasure, and that was a turn-on I never fully understood I had until that night.

Since then, I haven't been able to focus on much of anything in my life. I think about that night constantly – that moment when I came and nearly tipped over, and strong, secure arms held on to me from behind, and soft, warm lips pressed to my neck before a gentle husky voice told me that she had me.

I enter my bank account information and click submit. A few seconds later, I get the payment confirmation, and the next screen that pops up asks me if I'm going to attend the next event. If I say yes, I'll be sent the location and further information; and if I say no, they'll message me about the next event in a couple of weeks, requesting an RSVP. I've spent this past month trying to deal with my issues about how much I actually want to say yes for the next eleven events and, likely, many more beyond that. I'm like an addict that can't think of a life that doesn't involve these parties anymore, and I've only been to one.

What happens if once a month isn't enough, and I want once a week? Or, if once a week is not enough, and I want one every day? Every time I close my eyes, I picture the party. In my mind, I can clearly see men and women pleasuring each other in various ways, and I know I want it again. I click the *yes* icon on the screen and take a drink of my coffee. I know I need to focus on work now because I have a long day ahead of me, but I'm squirming in my seat because I'm already wet, and I know that won't change for at least the next twenty-four hours.

***

This house is smaller, but not by much. It's also a little farther away from my house than the last place was, which, I decide, is a good thing. The farther away I am from home and people who might recognize me, the better. This time, I have a little more confidence as I hand my keys to the well-dressed valet. It's a different guy than last time, but I pay that no mind and walk to the front door where the same woman from the previous event stands. She recognizes me, nods slightly, and without words, she reaches for the gold bracelet and places it on my wrist. The door opens, and I enter. A different man greets me, and I hand him both my purse and my coat that's covering a red-and-black dress to-night. It's slightly shorter than my first dress, but only by an inch or so. It's also mainly black, but the hem of the dress and about two inches above that is red, along with about two inches at my waist. I feel confident when I wear this dress on dates, and it does give me confidence now.

It's just after eleven, and the music is already playing softly. People are milling about. It appears more crowded here than the last event, but that's likely due to this house being a little smaller. The man at the door tells me there are eight bedrooms and an indoor cinema along with other nooks and crannies. He repeats the rules, which, apparently, he's required to do, and I turn from the left to the right. Straight ahead is the kitchen where they've laid out the floor. The bar is to the left, and to the right is the living room.

In the previous house, sex on the downstairs furniture had been against the rules, but the instructions for tonight had said it was permitted. This house was a rental and not owned by any members, which meant we could do whatever we wanted, and it would just be cleaned well afterward. *We.* That's the first time I've used that word when referring to members. I am one of them; I'm part of this *we* now. It's a strange feeling, but also a welcome one. I make my way to the bar, walking past several people. They're all talking, laughing, and exchanging light touches, likely trying to find their partner or partners for the night, and I order myself a drink – something I can down quickly, something that will give me more courage than I had the last time I was here.

By the time I turn back around, after handing my now

empty glass to the bartender, I see a woman kissing another woman, a man unzipping his pants, and two people walking hand in hand in the direction of the staircase. I think about watching the two women until the alcohol kicks in but decide to go to the other rooms downstairs first to see what I might be missing. I'm met with the sight of a woman climbing on top of someone I can't see on a sofa and two men fondling one another through their pants.

"You came back," a woman says, and I recognize the voice, smirk internally, and turn around to see her standing in front of me, wearing a pair of tight but not too tight black pants, a white button-down, and a tailored suit jacket. Her bow tie is undone. Her hair is a little longer than it had been last time, but it is still short and dark, and I want to run my hands through it. She looks me over, but not blatantly and not in a way that makes me feel like she's a predator stalking her prey.

"I did," I say, licking my lips.

She doesn't say anything at first, and I wait because I want her to say something – I don't exactly know how to start this myself. She started it before, but maybe that was only because I was new, and she knew that. I don't know. What I *do* know is that I need her to start things this time as well because I can't find the right words I want to say.

"I have a room," she says. "It won't be there forever."

"Okay," I say.

She holds out her hand, and I take it. It's soft but, somehow, firm at the same time. She entwines our fingers, and I wonder if someone's trained her to do that, to do all of this. Is there some school they send them to? Is there a training course they complete and get a certificate they can hang on their walls? She leads me up the stairs and around the corner. We proceed down the hallway, which is darker than I expected, but it also suits my mood. I'm in the mood for sex. I know what I want, and I'm ready to ask for it. I'm ready to have this woman touch me again.

We walk past two open doors, and I don't stop to peer

inside this time – I'm only interested in the woman holding my hand. She's occupied my thoughts for the past month. When we arrive at a closed door, and she pushes it open, I nearly protest because that's against the rules, but when we get inside, there's no one in here. She must have somehow reserved the room. Had she done that for me? For us? No, I tell myself. She's done this for the person or people she knew she'd end up with tonight. This is her job. No matter what, she'd be having sex with someone tonight.

The door gets closed behind me, and I snap back to attention. She walks back around me now, and I take the opportunity to stare at her lips as she licks them. Again, I need her help – I'm not ready to be the one to take the lead here yet. I know technically they're supposed to respond to our cues, vibe from us, but I don't know how to tell this woman what I want her to do to me. So, I don't. I just bite my lower lip and run my hand through my hair that I left down. Thankfully, I didn't put any product into it tonight because I was hoping someone else's hands would run through it at some point. Hell… Who am I kidding? I was hoping *her* hands would be running through it tonight. God, I was hoping it would be her. I wasn't sure if it were the same people at each event or if she'd even be back, but I was hoping it would be her.

"You look beautiful," she says.

"You have to say that," I say back.

"No, I don't," she replies.

"Don't they tell you to–"

She moves into me, and I stop talking.

"We could stand here and debate this or…" She places her hand on the side of my neck and pushes my hair off of my shoulder. "We could do something else."

I swallow, and she moves even closer. I can feel her belt buckle against my stomach. She's not that much taller than me, but tall enough that I have to look up a little to meet her eyes now. There are no rules about what a member can or cannot do, but both or all parties have to consent to anything proposed or performed, and I want to kiss her. I don't know if she even does that or if it's too personal, but I want her lips on my own.

"Safeword?" she says, leaning in and placing her hand on my hip.

Oh, I forgot about that. Her intoxicating scent of something woodsy mixed with something floral has my brain all mixed up.

"Wall Street," I say.

She lifts an eyebrow at me, and it's sexy as hell.

"It's definitely not something I'd say during sex," I say.

She nods a little, and the hand on my neck moves down between my breasts over my dress and settles there.

"What do you want?" she asks, her eyes following her hand to where it settles.

"Whatever you want," I reply because I can't quite articulate what *I* want just yet. "I know you... I don't mean it like–"

"I want to take this dress off of you," she tells me.

I nod. She drops her hands from my body and walks behind me. A second later, I feel the zipper of my dress lowering slowly. Two hands separate the back of my dress until the thick straps are off my shoulders, and the dress falls smoothly to the floor. I'm standing in the middle of a bedroom I'm essentially renting for the night with a woman I know nothing about standing behind me. I'm now dressed only in the black lingerie I wore tonight. It's a one-piece, which I should've thought to avoid, and there's a corset number that isn't exactly comfortable and not at all very feminist of me, but this is my fantasy. I'm allowed to live a little, right? She walks around to take me in, and I watch her eyes darken as she licks her lips again.

"Did you wear this for me?" she asks.

I think that that's a pretty brazen question, but I know the answer.

"Yes," I say.

"It's fucking sexy," she says and reaches for me.

Her hands are on my hips. Then, they're around my back. She's pulled me in so close that her lips are at my ear.

"Can I take it off?" she whispers. "I promise, I'll help you put it back on when it's time to go."

I nod, and I have a feeling I'll be nodding a lot with this woman because I can hardly speak around her. She is everything I've ever fantasized about. In fact, when I told that friend of a friend of a friend that night I drank way too much that I had this crazy fantasy of watching two women have sex, and they want me there, and someone else is doing things to me, this was the woman I pictured taking me to places I've never been.

She skillfully undoes the corset from the back without moving from her position. And, of course, she does, I think. She's a professional. She's probably taken off the lingerie of dozens or hundreds of women. I try to not think about that because they don't matter. Tonight, she's mine.

Even though she clearly knows what she's doing, she takes her time, and I want her to. I don't want fast, like last time. I want all night. Her lips meet my neck. She kisses me there, and it's like I'm back in the bedroom of the other house where her fingers are stroking my clit all over again, even though she's not really touching me yet. When the corset has been undone, she backs up a bit and watches me as I pull it off my body. I drop it to the floor, remembering how hard it was to get it on in the first place, and I stand there now in my heels and my black thong. Her eyes fall to my breasts, but they don't linger.

For the first time, I take the lead, feeling more secure about this now. I walk past her and sit on the edge of the bed. She turns around, smiles a small smile, and moves to stand in front of me. I reach for her this time, and she lets me. I undo her belt. She takes off her jacket and tosses it onto the dresser behind her. Now, I don't know if I can do slow anymore. Things are blurring, and my lust for her is making my brain foggy. I unbutton and unzip her pants, slipping them down to her thighs. She kicks off her shoes quickly and lets the pants fall to the floor. Then, she picks them up and tosses them on top of her jacket, and she's left standing there in a white button-down and a pair of black bikinis. I lean forward and breathe her in, hoping she doesn't think me crazy. She cups the back of my head and pulls me against her. I reach for the bottom button of her shirt and start undoing them one by one. As I do, I reveal her skin beneath, and I kiss it. Without asking, I just kiss her. She steps even closer, and I continue feeling as if I've been given silent permission.

I let her take over with the rest of the buttons as I continue to kiss her tight abdomen. When her shirt is off and on the floor, I look up at her bare, perfect small breasts and gape a little. It's embarrassing, but she doesn't seem to notice or care. She looks down at me with her intense eyes, and I realize I could stare into them all night, but I don't want to waste our time together, so I tug at her bikinis, wanting all of her to be revealed to me. She steps back a bit and lowers them to the floor. She stands in front of me completely bare now, and I want her. I lower myself onto the bed and wait.

She stares down at me for a second, and then her foot kicks gently at my calf. She repeats the action with my other calf, and I spread my legs for her. She kneels, and... Oh, God. This is happening. She's going to touch me. I've waited for this for a month, and I'm so turned on right now, I'm going to come at the first touch. My chest heaves as I breathe in and out too deeply for someone that hasn't even been touched yet. She places her hands on my knees and pushes my legs apart even more, and now, I am fully spread for her, still in my black thong but ready for her in every way.

Her lips press to the inside of my right thigh as my legs hang off the edge of the bed. I bite my lower lip and close my eyes. Her lips dance softly across my skin. She nips at the soft, sensitive spots a few times. I gasp, but I don't give her my safe word, so after a brief hesitation, she continues.

She moves to my other thigh, and I want my panties off – I need her mouth on me. I need fingers buried deep inside. I need my hips lifting off the bed and my hand pressing into the back of her head, running through her hair.

"Oh, fuck," I say when she unexpectedly licks me over my thong.

She does it again, and my hand *does* go to the back of her head, but I don't press down yet; I wait. Her tongue presses firmly against my clit over the thong, and my head goes back. She swirls it and, with her tongue, moves the fabric around, giving me a little pressure and friction. My other hand curls in the comforter beneath me, and she finally pushes the fabric aside with her fingers. I lift my head and open my eyes so I can watch her as she stares back at me with strikingly confident eyes and licks my pussy. I think I'm soaking this comforter because a rush of wetness comes out of me. She looks down, probably at what she'd just caused, and then she's sitting back, and I'm watching her yank my thong off and toss it away somewhere. She pulls me back against her mouth, and she sucks.

"God, yes. Fuck!"

I hold her now. She sucks on my clit, and I run my hand through that hair I've so badly wanted to touch. I'm waiting for her to slip inside, but before I can ask, it's too late – I'm coming.

"Fuck. I wanted…"

I can't say anything else; I'm coming too hard. Her tongue is flicking my clit back and forth, her lips engulf it after, and I'm lost in my orgasm – too lost to think about the fact that I wanted her to fuck me hard with her long fingers.

"Yes. Please, don't stop," I say, and she doesn't until I tap her shoulder.

She slows first. Then, she stops entirely and looks up at me. I wait for her to wipe her mouth, but she doesn't.

"You wanted to take longer, didn't you?" she asks.

"Yes," I say, trying to catch my breath.

"Good. Me too. Lie back on the bed."

I slide backward, probably looking ridiculous in the process, but she moves over me, not making a comment about it, and my head hits the pillow just as her breasts press to mine. My nipples are hard, and the press of her body against mine only makes them harder; I'm craving her touch. She looks down at me like this for the first time, and something passes between us. I say nothing because this is just another night to her. It's different for me, but it's the same to her. She takes my hand and places it on her ass. Then, she takes my other one and places it over my head, leaving it there but entwining her fingers into mine. When she rolls into me, my legs spread farther apart. My clit just came, and I know that there's a window of time where I can easily come again before it would take much longer, so I press her ass down into me, loving how hard it feels against my palm. She knows I want this now, so she rolls a little harder and faster as her lips move back to my neck.

"That's good," I tell her.

"Yes, it is," she says.

"Can you come like–"

She lifts up and looks at me, rocking now – no longer rolling but rocking hard. I close my eyes and shut up.

"You're so slick," she says. "I love it."

I say nothing.

"I loved licking your pussy," she says.

I gasp.

"I want to suck on your nipples."

I nod. She sucks on one after the other as she starts to grunt, and I think I might pass out because this is too much. She feels so good. I notice it then – she's wet. She's fucking wet. I can feel her wetness mixing with mine, and that's it; that's all it takes. I go over the edge, and it's much too fast, but I can't stop it. And I wouldn't if I could anyway. My head rolls back. Her hand still tucked into mine over my head squeezes, and her rocks become a little more erratic, but I can't ask her if she's coming too because I can't form words. She rocks and breathes hard against my neck. I breathe hard into her ear. Our breathing slows at the same time, and she lifts up. She lets go of my hand, and I lower both of mine to my sides.

"You like to watch, too," she says.

"What?" I ask.

"Do you want to watch too tonight?" She kneels between my legs and rubs her hands up and down my thighs slowly.

"Oh," I say, still trying to get oxygen back into my brain. "I guess."

"We don't have to."

We, I think to myself? She wants to watch with me?

As a member, I'm free to enjoy myself however I please tonight. I can have as many people as I want in as many ways as I want, but I know that I only want her tonight. She has the right to refuse anything and anyone, and if a member makes even one mistake or gets one complaint, they're out. There are no second chances. I'm not worried about myself in that regard, but I know that she can technically leave me to be with another member tonight if she wants.

"Yes," I say.

She nods and climbs off the bed. I almost tell her to wait because I thought we could watch later – I want more of her right now – but she reaches for my dress and holds it out to me to slip into so reverently, that I can't. I stand and make no move to get into my corset or my thong. She slips into her pants, leaving her own underwear on the floor, and buttons her shirt up to her breasts, leaving her jacket on the dresser. She picks up the remainder of my clothes and tucks them into her jacket and then the jacket into an empty dresser drawer. I watch as she puts on her shoes, and I slip into mine. Then, she takes my hand, and we leave the room. We walk down and pass two closed doors. Then, we approach an open one. She looks inside, smiles back at me, and then we walk in.

"Sofa," she says.

I'm too busy watching the women on the bed to hear what she says. It's the two women from before. The one that had worn the strap-on the first time was also wearing it now, and she was behind the other woman who was on all fours. She was going slow with her thrusts, playing with her partner's breasts as her partner rocked back into her. I've been pulled over to a small sofa – a loveseat, really – but I don't mind. I'm sat down on the sofa, and I can't stop staring at the women who are clearly enjoying themselves.

My partner kneels in front of me, and I look down at her. Then, she spreads my legs, and I remember I'm not wearing any underwear.

"Don't close your eyes, okay?" she says.

I watch her head lower, and then I feel her. I close my eyes for a second, but I open them right back when I remember what she said. I keep watching the two women on the bed as *she* slides her tongue through my wetness. I slouch down and sink into her mouth, giving her better access. Then, I hear it. It's a soft buzzing sound, and I don't know where it's coming from. I assume it's someone's cell phone for a second before I realize that it's a vibrator. It must be inside the harness or the dildo. I look at that woman's face closer, and I can see it there – the intense pleasure. She's going to come. I stare at her and rock my hips against my own partner's mouth as the woman wearing the strap-on begins to thrust harder into the woman on all fours.

"Yes, baby. Fuck me," that woman says.

"God," I whisper.

I spread my legs farther apart. *Her* tongue slips down and inside just enough to drive me crazy, and I have to hang on because I want to watch these women come before I do. Her hands move to my breasts, and I know I can't unzip my dress from this angle, so I press her hands harder to my chest, encouraging her to squeeze as hard as she wants. She sucks on my clit as the woman wearing the strap-on starts to moan and grunt louder. I feel my nipples twist between a thumb and a forefinger. God, I feel everything. I feel like I'm high on a drug I never want to come down from.

They come. The woman being fucked comes first. Her partner is right behind her, and I'm closing my eyes because it's all too good. I press the head between my legs farther into me, and I rock against *her* face, lifting and lowering my hips quickly until I'm coming in her mouth and hear her moan loudly.

"Yes," I say, taking my pleasure from her and feeling totally unrestrained for the first time in my entire life.

When I finally open my eyes, I see she's kissing my inner thigh. I look up and see the two women on the bed are now lying on their sides, one behind the other, and they're both facing me. The woman who had just been thoroughly fucked is behind her partner. Her hand is under the harness, and the sound of the vibrator is gone; she's stroking her. Their eyes are all on me as their bodies rock together.

"What's next?" the woman on the bed doing the stroking asks, and I realize she's asking me.

"Don't leave again."

I look down at the woman still kissing my thigh – *she*'d said that. Her eyes were imploring me to stay, and I can't figure out why, but I don't think to ask.

"Can I watch again?" I ask the woman on the bed.

"Yes," she says, stroking her partner, who closes her eyes.

I look down and run my hand through *her* hair.

"Will you just watch with me?" I ask her.

She nods.

"Come up here," I say, nodding to the other half of the loveseat.

She stands and moves to sit down next to me. I don't say anything, but I give her leg a shove and move into her. She understands and spreads her legs. I sit between them. We watch together as she kisses my neck, sucks my earlobe, and unzips my dress enough to slide her hands around me and play with my breasts while we watch these women I don't know at all come once and then twice. I know when they need to take a break, *she* and I will disappear into a room again, and she'll make me come at least one more time before the clock strikes four. And I know I'm going to let her.

MONTH 2. PART 2. – FROM HESITATION TO HOPE

(POV Escort)

It's been thirty days. It's been a *long thirty days*. A lot's gone on in my life since that first night, but it's all I can still think about. With every bad thing happening right now, it's like I needed to remember that night to feel like things can get better, which doesn't even make sense because I was working. I was having sex for money. I wasn't supposed to want it just as much as the woman I was touching, but I might have wanted it even more. After I finally took care of myself in the bathroom, I went back to that room to find my friends. It felt weird confessing to them that I'd not only liked touching a stranger, but I'd loved it, and I wanted to touch that *particular* stranger again.

"I've never seen her at one of these things," my friend said that night. "Maybe she's new."

"She might not come back," my other friend said.

"Shame. She's hot," her wife replied as she ran her fingertips between the woman's breasts. "Anyway, we're taking a break, but you can stay in here with us if you want. We can cover for you if anyone asks if you were with any member tonight."

"The whole review thing," her wife said.

The review, I thought to myself… I'm expected to get at minimum one review at each party, and on the five-point scale, anything lower than a four meant they might not call me back. Since it was my first time, they expected a five, and the only woman I've touched ran out on me.

"She left. I don't know if she's going to even review me. Should I find someone else?"

"Do you want to?" my friend asked.

"No," I said honestly. "I'm a terrible escort, aren't I?" I laughed a little.

"It's your first time – you'll get the hang of it. But we'll review you, at least. You *did* give us what we like, so we won't even be lying."

"You guys were extra hot tonight," I said, smiling at them.

"*Were*? We're not done yet," one of them said.

"Besides, I don't think that had anything to do with us, sadly. You were all about someone else tonight," the other one said.

And she'd been right. I'd never just walked up behind a woman and asked her if I could touch her. Now, it's all I can think about. I play it over and over in my head as I drive to my day job, while I brush my teeth, and before I fall asleep every night. The number of times I've gotten myself off this month thinking about getting her off, is more than I care to admit. And I don't have an explanation for this; I only know I need to touch *her* again. I'm not surprised when the only review I get is from two members that are also my friends, but they both give me fives, which means I'm invited back for a second event. I'm grateful because I don't know the woman's name, and the company that puts on the events would never break confidentiality to tell an escort the name of a member. I can only hope she shows up tonight.

It's ten-fifty, and I can't wait much longer. My foot is tapping on the floor. It's like I'm waiting for my drug dealer to arrive with what I need, and just as I think that, I realize that it's true. She's both the drug dealer *and* my drug. One touch, and I need more; I'm craving more. By the time eleven o'clock strikes, I'm going crazy. I know there's a very good chance she won't be here and I'll have to pleasure someone else tonight. I see the woman from the first party and the escort she seems to favor. The woman is wearing a short green dress tonight, and the escort already has her hand up in it. It doesn't look like she's doing anything quite yet, just maybe some light grazing, but it's driving the member crazy. The escort turns her head and sees me. She winks, and I laugh silently. At the end of the first party, I ran into her, and she told me about this member – this woman is married to a man but comes every single month and seeks her out. Most of the time, it's just the two of them, but every once in a while, the woman asks for a third. The escort told me she loves taking the so-called 'straight women' to bed – it's something she uses to get herself off later. Knowing all that made me feel better about leaving her alone with the woman last time. I watch as she presses her lips to the member's neck and her hand disappears higher. The woman moans; it's no longer just grazing.

This is turning me on. Watching these two stand there in a room full of people, pressed to one another – and I can't even see what she's actually doing – is definitely erotic, but it doesn't begin to cover what I felt at the last party, with my stranger pressed to my front and my hand inside her panties. I worry nothing will ever compare and that I'll never feel like that again, but then I see her. I approach her probably too eagerly from behind.

"You came back," I say.

She turns around to see me standing in front of her, and I look her over. She's wearing a black dress with red highlights, and she looks so fucking sexy, I just want to take her right now.

"I did," she says and licks her full lips.

She looks nervous or maybe just a little anxious. Something tells me she wants to say something else, but she doesn't.

"I have a room," I say. "It won't be there forever."

I don't have a room. I lie because I'm hopeful I can find one if we hurry, and I really want to hurry – I want all night with her.

"Okay," she says.

I hold out my hand, and she takes it. I lead her up the stairs and around the corner. We proceed down the hallway, and I'm anxious to find an empty room. I want her all to myself – at least, to start. We walk past two open doors first, and there's a closed door that I remember the woman downstairs telling me is off-limits because they'd planned on storing stuff there. I take a chance. I push the door open, and thankfully, there's no one in the room. It's just a regular bedroom, and there's nothing out of the ordinary in here, so I guess they didn't need it for storage after all. *She* walks in front of me, and I close the door behind her. I walk around her and stare, licking my lips. I wait for her to tell me what she wants, but she doesn't. She just bites her lower lip and runs a hand through her hair. It looks so soft.

"You look beautiful," I say before I can stop myself.

"You have to say that," she says.

"No, I don't," I reply, which is the truth.

There are no rules that say I have to compliment the members.

"Don't they tell you to–"

I move into her, not wanting to waste time talking about that now.

"We could stand here and debate this or…" I put my hand on the side of her neck and push her soft hair off of her shoulder. "We could do something else."

I watch her swallow and move closer still.

"Safe word?" I say, leaning in and placing my hand on her hip.

"Wall Street," she says.

I lift an eyebrow at her.

"It's definitely not something I'd say during sex," she says.

God, we're going to do this again. I'm going to get to touch her again. I take my hand from her neck and move down between her breasts over her dress, settling it there.

"What do you want?" I ask, looking at her breasts and how they're moving up and down and up and down.

"Whatever you want," she says. "I know you… I don't mean it like–"

"I want to take this dress off of you," I interrupt.

She nods, and I walk behind her, hardly able to contain myself. I swallow as I see the red zipper on her back. She has amazing taste in dresses. I pull it down slowly and take in the smooth skin revealed to me. I separate the back of the dress until the straps are off her body, and it falls to the floor. She's wearing a fucking black corset, and I nearly bite my own lip off at the sight. I end up walking back around and lick my now somewhat sore lip.

"Did you wear this for me?" I ask.

"Yes," she says.

"It's fucking sexy," I say, and I reach for her.

My hands go from her hips to around her back, and I pull her in so close that my lips are at her ear.

"Can I take it off?" I whisper for effect. "I promise, I'll help you put it back on when it's time to go."

She nods again, and I take my time with the corset, wanting to revel in this. My lips meet her neck before I finish with the corset. Then, I take a step back, allowing her to pull it off and drop it to the floor. She's only wearing a pair of heels and a black thong now. I only saw one of her breasts for a moment last time as she was leaving, so I stare at both of them now, bare and perfect, with rosy nipples begging for my lips.

She walks past me and sits on the edge of the bed. I turn around to watch her and move to stand in front of her. Then, she finally reaches for me. She starts on my belt, and I'm just watching as she undoes it. I take off my jacket and toss it on the dresser. Her hands move to my button and zipper, and my pants are down to my thighs now. I kick off my shoes a little too eagerly, but fuck – I *am* eager, damn it. I let my pants fall to the floor and pick them up to toss them onto my jacket. I'm standing here now in just my white button-down and black bikinis. She leans forward, and I hear her take a deep breath. I cup the back of her head and pull her against me. She takes the hint and starts undoing my buttons from the bottom. She kisses the skin she unveils, and I step closer. I want more.

Impatient, I end up finishing the buttons for her and practically throw off my shirt. She looks up at my small breasts, which aren't as big as hers. I look down into her eyes and find lustful hunger there I hadn't expected to see, but maybe I should have. She pulls at my panties, and I step back and lower them to the floor. For the first time, I'm standing there completely naked in front of her. She looks me up and down. Then, she lowers herself onto the bed. Her legs hang over the edge of it, and I know what she wants.

My foot kicks her calf gently, and when I repeat the light kick with the other calf, she spreads her legs. I kneel, and I can see her now. The thong is still in the way, but it's black lace, so I can see her; I can see where my hand was buried before. Now, I want my mouth there, too. I place my hands on her knees and push her legs apart even more. I've wanted to see more, and now I can. She's wet. She's so damn wet, I can't wait to run my tongue through it.

I press my lips to the inside of her thigh and let them move across her skin, taking it all in as I go. I can't resist biting her lightly in a few places that seem to make her produce these tiny, sexy gasps. Then, she gasps louder, and I pause in case she wants me to stop. When she doesn't say anything, I move to her other thigh. I kiss around for a minute before I can't take it anymore. I can smell her; I know she's ready for me. I move my mouth to her sex and lick her through her thong.

"Oh, fuck," she says.

I lick her again. Her scent is intoxicating, and as I'm able to taste her through her panties, I want more. I press my tongue to her, and she's so hard. She's so ready. I swirl my tongue and use it to move the fabric. Fuck this, I decide. I bring my hand to her sex and push the panties aside. She lifts her head to watch me, and I stare back at her. Then, I finally get what I've been craving for a month – I lick her pussy. I feel more wetness on my chin and look down. She's wetter now. She likes this, and I do, too. I pull off her thong and toss it somewhere. Then, I pull her back against me, and I suck.

"God, yes. Fuck!"

She puts her hand on my head and holds me in place. I keep sucking. She runs her hand through my hair, and that turns me on even more. I suck harder. I want her coming under me, because of me. I'm addicted, and I need my high.

"Fuck. I wanted…"

She stops because she's coming. It was faster than I thought, but I don't care. There will be time for more. I flick my tongue back and forth before I suck her back into my mouth.

"Yes. Please, don't stop," she says.

Why would I ever stop this? That's what I think until I feel a tap on my shoulder – she's asking me to stop. I slow down, licking and sucking and helping her coax the rest of the orgasm from her body. Finally, I stop and look up at her.

"You wanted to take longer, didn't you?" I ask.

"Yes," she says, catching her breath.

"Good. Me too. Lie back on the bed," I tell her.

She slides backward, and I move over her. I'm on top of her now, pressing into her. She's so beautiful. And I know I shouldn't be thinking that right now – I'm here to make her come, I'm not here to tell her how gorgeous she is and how sexy she is – but I can't help but think it as I stare down at her. She's staring at me too, and I wonder what *she's* thinking. I don't ask because it's not my place, but I want to.

I swallow, realizing my purpose, and then take her hand, placing it on my ass. I place her other one over her head and join our hands together. Then, I roll into her. Her legs spread wider, and she presses my ass down into her, which is exactly what I wanted her to do. I roll harder and faster, moving my lips back to her neck.

"That's good," she says.

"Yes, it is," I agree.

"Can you come like–"

I know what she's about to ask, and tonight's not supposed to be about me, so I lift up and look at her as I rock now. There's no more time for patient rolls into her. She closes her eyes.

"You're so slick," I say as my sex presses to hers, and it feels so good. "I love it," I tell her. I know I can come just from doing this with her, and I will if I don't stop soon. "I loved licking your pussy," I add.

She gasps.

"I want to suck on your nipples," I tell her, knowing I'm about to come any minute and hoping that it's okay because if it's not, I don't know what to do.

She nods her head. I suck on one perfect nipple after the other, and I'm grunting now. I'm so fucking wet, I can feel it. I'm sure she can, too, but I can't exactly do anything about it. Oh, fuck. She's coming. She's coming, and I start coming, too. Her head rolls back, and I squeeze the hand holding hers to prevent myself from screaming out my pleasure. I know my hips are going crazy. She has to know what she does to me; this can't be a surprise. I breathe hard against her neck, and she's breathing into my ear. Our breathing slows at the same time, and I lift up. I let go of her hand and both of hers move to her sides.

"You like to watch, too," I say, needing to pull focus from the fact that I just had the best orgasm of my entire fucking life from rubbing my clit against her sex.

"What?" she asks.

"Do you want to watch too tonight?" I sit back and kneel between her legs, rubbing my hands up and down her thighs, craving even more of her.

"Oh," she says. "I guess."

"We don't have to," I say, wishing I could take back what I'd just said – I'd much rather spend all night in this room with her and *only* her.

"Yes," she says.

I'm not exactly disappointed. I have a plan, and it's one that will, I think, make us both happy. I climb off the bed and reach for her dress. I hold it up for her, indicating that I want her to slide into it for me. She does. I put on my pants but leave my underwear where it is, and I button my shirt until the middle button. She stares at my somewhat exposed breasts. I pick up the rest of our clothes and put them with my jacket into an empty dresser drawer. We both slip into our shoes, then I take her hand, and we leave the room. I close the door behind me, hoping we can have this place to ourselves again later. Luckily, no one is in the hall to see that it's now available. We walk down and pass two closed doors. Then, we approach an open one. I look inside, finding what I was hoping for, and smile back at her. Then, we walk in.

"Sofa," I tell her.

It's not a request, it's a command. I know how I want her again, and I know she likes me to take the lead, so it's a win-win situation. She's watching my friends on the bed. One of them is behind the other, who is on all fours, and I agree with my partner: this is sexy as hell, watching them do this. But I'm getting impatient, and I want her now. I pull her to the sofa, which is much smaller than a regular sofa. I know there's a name for that, but my mind can only process the woman I'm about to taste again. I sit her down and kneel in front of her. Then, I spread her legs and look at her. She's bare and ready for me again.

"Don't close your eyes, okay?" I tell her.

I lower my head and slip my tongue through her folds. She shifts down a bit, and I get more access to what I want. After only a moment, her hips start rocking against my face.

"Yes, baby. Fuck me," I hear one of my friends say.

"God," *she* whispers.

I smirk – she's loving this. Her legs spread farther, and I slip my tongue down and inside her. My hands move to her breasts. I squeeze them over her dress and suck on her clit again. Then, I twist her nipples between my thumb and forefinger. There are moans coming from behind me that I recognize – someone's having a pretty good orgasm. *She* presses her hand to the back of my head, and I'm pressed harder against her. She's rocking against me now, and all I can do is hold on for the ride. Then, she comes.

"Yes," she says, taking her pleasure from my mouth.

My hand slips down to my pants, and I know it won't take long. I know it's not what I'm here for, but I need it. I'm not wearing my underwear, so I slip inside my pants while she's slowing down her hips, and I press my clit hard, grunting against her sex. A few strokes, and I'm gone. I've closed my mouth, and I'm biting down on my bottom lip to contain my orgasm. My fingers slide around, I'm that wet. I'm surprised I was even able to find the spot I needed, but I continue to stroke until I feel like I can pull my hand away and focus back on her. I kiss her inner thigh.

"What's next?"

It's my friend. She must be asking *her*, so I look up at her.

"Don't leave again," I say, sounding desperate.

I kiss her thigh again.

"Can I watch again?" she asks.

"Yes."

She runs her hand through my hair, and I close my eyes for a second at the touch.

"Will you just watch with me?" she asks softly.

I nod my reply, grateful that she's not leaving.

"Come up here," she says, motioning to the other half of the… sofa?

Loveseat, I remember the word finally; it's called a fucking loveseat. I sit next to her, and she pushes at my leg. I get it, so I move to the corner and spread my legs for her. She moves between them, and we just watch my friends together. I kiss her neck and suck on her earlobe in that way I know she likes now. I unzip her dress and slip my hands under it to play with her breasts. My friends come once. I continue to play with her nipples and wrap one of my hands around her neck, bringing her head back against me to nibble on the soft flesh of her neck. My friends come again.

"We're taking a break. You're free to stay in here, though," my friend says.

"Come back with me," I whisper in *her* ear.

"Okay," she says.

"We'll see you later," I tell them.

"Have fun," one of them mouths silently to me as we walk out of the room.

I don't even notice that *she*'s the one pulling me this time until we're at the door of the room we left about an hour ago. She hesitates a second but opens it. We're lucky; it's still available. She takes her dress off before I can even say anything. Then, she turns around, naked and gorgeous, and presses me to the door, closing it behind us. In an instant, her lips are on my neck, and I'm simply holding her against me, loving how good it feels when her mouth is on my skin.

"You don't have to–"

"Can I?" she interrupts, reaching for my button, undoing it, and then unzipping my pants.

"You already have," I say.

She pulls back and looks at me, confused.

"Twice, technically," I add.

She tilts her head a little, and my pants fall to the floor. She looks down, and when she lifts her head, her eyes are even darker now.

"Can I again?" she asks.

There's a knock on the door.

"Fuck," I say, pulling up my pants.

"The door's closed. The rules," she says.

"Sorry," I tell her, nodding for her to pick up her dress.

She slips it back on quickly, and I open the door.

"This is for storage," the woman tells me.

"I know, but there's nothing in here, and the member needed a room," I offer in explanation.

"Look, a VIP member reserved it, okay? We say *stor-*

age when we mean that. No one told you?" she asks.

"No."

"I need to set things up – he just got here. You need to leave. Did you mess anything up in here?"

"No," I repeat.

"Good." The woman pushes open the door a bit and looks at my partner for the evening. "I apologize. There's some confusion about this room tonight, but it's reserved for an event."

"An event?" my partner asks. "Isn't this whole night an event?"

"Once you've been a member for three months with no issue, you're eligible for *special* accommodations at our monthly events. For a fee, of course," the woman explains.

"Of course," *she* replies.

"We'll leave," I say. "Can you give us a minute to get– "

She nods before I finish, and I close the door.

"I'm sorry. They told me this room was for storage. I thought it would be okay," I tell her with flushed cheeks.

"It's okay." She smiles at me.

I pull out our clothes from the drawer, and we dress quickly, with me helping her with the corset, as promised. I take a second to kiss her bare shoulder as she puts her dress back on.

"What now?" I ask her.

"It's after two," she says. "I didn't even realize."

"We have two hours," I say.

There's a knock.

"We have to go," she says.

"To another room?"

"I doubt there's another one available now."

"Right," I say.

"I–"

Another knock interrupts her, and I nod at her, already knowing what she's going to say. I open the door.

"After you," I say, motioning for her to leave the room

first. "I'm sorry. I really didn't know," I tell the woman waiting for the room.

"It's okay. Just don't let it happen again." She walks past me and closes the door, leaving us in the hallway.

I look down at the floor, suddenly nervous.

"Tonight was…"

"Yeah," I say when she fades out.

"Are you allowed to… I mean… can you get a drink with me downstairs, or is that not allowed?"

"No, I can do that," I say.

We head downstairs. There are people around, talking. Some are dancing to soft music. Others are still engaged in the activities that drew them here in the first place. We walk to the bar and order drinks. When we turn around in unison, it's awkward now. There's a woman getting fucked by a man next to the pool table, and it's not something I really want to see. By the look in my partner's eyes, she's not interested in this, either. Maybe she *is* gay or, at least, interested in women beyond one night a month.

"Come on," I say, taking her hand and leaving my half-finished drink on the bar.

She carries hers with her as I walk her to the other room, hoping to find what I end up finding – that woman with her favorite escort.

"Oh," my partner says to me.

"I know you want to go," I say to her. "But you can watch this first, if you want."

"I don't think I'm ready to do anything in front of an entire room of people," she says.

"I'm here for *you*, remember?" I say, walking around behind her and wrapping my arms around her. "We can always do whatever you want."

We watch them for a few minutes while she finishes her drink, and I breathe her in but make no move to touch her. It's nice, just holding her like this… My eyes go wide. As the two women finish in front of us, I pull back. I'm not this woman's girlfriend; I'm her fucking hooker. I shouldn't want to hold her like that; I'm here to make money.

"Is something wrong?" she asks, turning around to face me.

"No," I say, shaking my head.

"Oh, okay." She looks toward the door. "I think I'm going to go home early."

"I'll walk you to the door," I say.

And I do. I walk this woman that I can't get enough of to the man who brings her the coat and purse she gave him earlier, and I watch her leave. It's after two, so I find my friends and sit on the loveseat. We talk for a bit, and I fill them in on what happened. Later, they decide to start back up for one final round before the night is up, but I'm not interested in watching, so I find a spot downstairs in the kitchen where I can hide until four in the morning.

When I get home, I'm exhausted. I know I should shower, but I'm not ready to wash her scent off me, so I fall naked into bed and close my eyes. The next day, I wake up and check the website – I've been invited back next month. I also have three five-star reviews this time, and only two are from my friends.

MONTH 3. PART 1. – MISSED OP-
PORTUNITY

(POV Member)

"Can you book it for me for this weekend?" I ask.

"I thought you wanted next weekend," my assistant says.

"I did, initially, but I have plans next weekend now, so this weekend would be great."

"Sure. Full treatment, like last time?"

"Yes," I say, nodding.

"I'll take care of it and email you the info," she says.

When she leaves my office, I pull out my personal laptop because the website I'm about to pull up, I would never go to on my work computer. I even connect to my phone's hotspot so I'm not using my office's Wi-Fi network, as an extra precaution. I log in to the site and confirm what I already know. Yes, I have made my reservation, and I am confirmed for the event next weekend. No, they haven't responded to my request from this morning for a private room with my own personal dark-haired beauty. I've waited three weeks to submit the request because I went back and forth on whether or not I even should. Last time, the woman who interrupted us said I needed to be a member for a minimum of three months to be eligible for private bookings at events. Technically, *this* would be my third month. I just put the request in this morning, and I'm not sure how fast they reply normally, but I'm eager to know if they'll allow me to book a room just for the two of us for the entire night.

This time, I'm not willing to risk us being interrupted. While I definitely enjoy watching others have sex, as I've always thought I would, I'd much rather prefer to have a whole night with her hands and mouth all over me. I'm also hoping she'll give me the chance to have mine all over her.

She said something before we were interrupted... I was about to ask if I could make her come, and she said I already had. She said I'd made her come twice, in fact. I've been thinking about that comment alone day and night. I'd wondered if she came when she was on top of me, rubbing her sex against my own. She must have. That's so fucking hot. I don't know when she came a second time, but maybe she somehow came silently when she was behind me while we watched the two women pleasure each other.

I close my personal computer and tuck it back into my bag. Then, I check my calendar on my work computer and notice I don't have another meeting for an hour. I click the button on the remote that runs my automatic office door, locking it behind my assistant, and I know it's crazy, but I have to... Prior to meeting this woman, I'd never touched myself at work; I've even thought of it. But since meeting her and taking this step in my life to acknowledge what I like – what I need – I've locked that door at least ten times. Normally, I wear business suits to work. Sometimes, I wear pants, and other times I'm in skirts, but I've been wearing more skirts than usual lately because it's better to picture her head between my legs. I've only worn a dress when we've been together. I push my chair back a bit and spread my legs. I know it won't be as good as when she touches me, but I can't stop thinking about her, so I have to give myself some relief if I'm going to get through the next week until I can see her again.

My hand lightly grazes the skin of my inner thigh. I close my eyes and picture her kneeling in front of me with my legs spread for her, my feet still in my heels. She kisses my thigh. I run my fingers over those spots. I picture her eyes looking up at me just as I stroke my index finger over my hard clit through my thong. I've been wearing those to work now. I never did before, but I loved how easily it came off for her when she wanted to take me fully into her mouth. This feels so good, and I'm already wet, but I know what I really need, and it's not my own hand. It's her.

"Fuck," I whisper as I stand and reach down with both hands to remove my skirt and my thong.

I'm standing there in just my silk shirt now, but I don't care. Luckily, the window behind me is tempered glass, so no one can see what I'm about to do. I find my purse, which is in my bottom drawer, and I pull out the bullet vibrator I bring with me everywhere I go now. Standing with my hand pressed to the glass, facing the city below, I turn it on and press it to my clit with my non-dominant hand.

"Fuck," I repeat as I slip my other hand down and inside.

It's not the same as being fucked by her. Although we haven't done that yet, I know it's not the same. She'd fuck me hard, fast and deep, and then slow and steady until I came again and again. I want her to. I want her to take me from behind, from on top of me, with me on top of her, and in any other way she wants. I flick my two fingers inside my own body, wishing so badly that it were her fingers or her toy that she's wearing just for me. The bullet isn't the strongest vibrator I own, but it is the smallest one and, therefore, easiest to conceal. I start coming on my clit first. My hips buck forward, and I'm pressed to the glass without being able to stop myself. My fingers go deeper, and now I'm coming inside.

"Jesus, yes," I say.

I can hear the vibrator hitting the glass – I don't care.

"Fuck. Fuck. Yes," I say every time my hips buck forward again.

Finally, I remove the vibrator, pressing the top to turn it off. I slide my fingers out and press my forehead to the glass.

"What has she done to me?" I say when I'm finally able to catch my breath.

I clean up in my private bathroom, leave my thong in my purse until I can wash it, and put my skirt back on. By the time my meeting is about to start, I look presentable again. I click the button to unlock the door, and when there's a knock at it, I tell them to come in.

"I've booked the spa for this weekend. They have the masseuse you like and said they can give you the suite you had last time, too," my assistant says.

"Thank you," I tell her as she ushers in the two people I'll be meeting with today to discuss contracts. "Have a seat," I tell them, motioning to the small conference table in the corner.

"Oh, I need to get the staff to take care of that," my assistant says.

"Take care of what?" I ask as the man and woman sit down at the table.

"Your window. It's filthy," my assistant says, pointing to the window.

My eyes go wide – my wet spot is clear as day from where I stand.

"You know… don't worry about it. I'll take care of it," I tell her.

***

I need the trip to the spa. Despite the numerous, and I mean, *numerous* orgasms I've had over the past two months, I don't feel any long-lasting relief. My muscles are tight, and I can't stop thinking about sex. I knew this could happen, and now I'm worried that it's interfering with my life. Work is fine. I haven't dropped the ball on anything, but that could change. The longer I go without seeing her, without being there, the more I want it; the more I want *her*.

As my favorite masseuse tackles the tight knots in my shoulders, I think about what *she* might be doing right now. There's a chance she's having sex with someone else. It *is* her job. She could be spreading the legs of another woman, removing her thong, and licking her pussy, making her come until she can't hold on any longer.

"Are you okay?" my masseuse asks me.

"Sorry?" I say with my head in the pillow.

"You're moving a little," she says.

Oh, shit. I was moving. I'm naked under this sheet, and I'm also wet. For fuck's sake, I think to myself. Am I just going to be constantly turned on for the rest of my life now?

"I'm okay," I reply.

After the massage, I disappear into my room before my mud bath. I visit the messaging portal on the site again, and there's still no response. The party is in six days. How long are these people going to make me wait? I need to plan. If we have all night, there are things I might think about buying or bringing with me. I go to my favorite sex toy site and find a few toys to add to the cart. I'll just buy them no matter what, I tell myself. Then, I visit the site I normally go to for lingerie. She liked my corset so much, I consider wearing it again, but I like the idea of showing her something new, too. I find a few options and add them to my cart.

It's time for my next treatment. I enjoy the mud bath and the hot shower I take after. I haven't taken care of the swollen nerves between my legs, and they've been begging me for release. While I'm in the shower, I give myself a quick but not nearly good enough orgasm. Then, I decide to eat dinner in the resort's restaurant because I need to be in public – the more I sit in my room, the higher the likelihood I'll touch myself, and my body could use a break right now.

When I get back to my room, though, I can't help myself. First, I pull up the site and check for messages. Finding no response again, I go to my porn site of choice. Yes, I have a favorite website for lesbian pornography. I pay for it, too. It doesn't do nearly enough for me, but it can help me focus on other women instead of the one I can't stop picturing on top of me. I find several new videos I've never seen. I always go to the story section of the site, preferring as much realism as one can get with porn, and there are three videos that get my attention. I click on the first one and lie back with the laptop at my side. I roll to face it, press my thighs together and watch as the two women in the video meet under ridiculous circumstances. I roll my eyes but don't look away. I promise myself I'll make it at least through the first sex scene before I touch myself. When one of them goes down on the other, and I get a close-up of how wet that woman is, I think about how wet *she* was against my sex.

I'm supposed to be thinking about anything other than this woman, but I can't. I manage to resist touching myself, despite how much my body is telling me I need it. I watch the first video until the end, roll onto my back, and consider falling asleep early. I know I can't, though. That's not how it works when my clit is so hard, it hurts. So, I fire up the second video. This was a mistake. In this video, a woman with short dark hair is packing. The other woman cups her through the pants before she unzips the fly. Then, she strokes the dildo, and I watch as the woman wearing the thing closes her eyes, liking it, even though she can't even feel anything.

By the time she's fucking her over a table, I'm gone. My own dildo, which I'd packed for this weekend away, is buried inside me. My favorite vibrator is pressed to my needy clit, and I'm coming hard. By the time I'm done, I'm exhausted. I clean myself up and fall back into bed.

I cannot keep going at this rate. I feel like a horny teenage boy that just can't get enough, but I can't. I wake up the next morning and get dressed for my next treatment. I check the site again, and finally, there's a response.

Member,

Our apologies, but the escort you've requested will not be in attendance at this month's event, so we will be unable to book you a private room with her for the evening. However, we have many other escorts that we can make available to you, and we'll be willing to wave the ninety-day rule for you, given your first choice is not available. We'd also like to inform you that we are considering offering parties for women who are seeking women, only. We are currently in the process of gauging inter-est, but if there is enough amongst the members, we will offer you for your standard fee the choice to attend either event each month. If you'd like to attend both events, there will be a separate fee. Information for the possible changes is included in the attachment. If you are interested, please find the notification on the site where you can let us know. Please also tell us if you'd like us to send you a list of available partners for you for this coming event. We'd be happy to reserve one of the larger rooms for you for the entire night and make any arrangements you may require.

Member Services

"She's not going to be there?" I say to no one.

I'm beyond disappointed. I'd just assumed she'd be there. Why had I done that? Why had I gotten my hopes up? I'd assumed she'd be there and that she'd find me again; that she'd want me for the evening more than anyone else. All of those assumptions had been ridiculous. I don't want another escort, so I reply that I'm not interested, but I *am* interested in the possibility of only seeing women who want other women at these events. I've never particularly been interested in men, or watching men have sex with women or other men. I wouldn't mind making the switch to those parties, but I don't know if *she* will be there. And if she's only at the other parties, I want to be there with her.

I reply, expressing my interest in women-only events because I *am* interested. I tell them to disregard the request for the private room and ask a question. I want to know if my escort is no longer coming back or if it's just this party that she's missing. I go to my treatments for the day, have dinner at the restaurant, and return to my room to find the response. They don't know, but she is still employed and in good standing with the company, which means it would be her choice if she doesn't return. That brings me some relief, but not much.

I consider rescinding my RSVP for this event, but I don't know; there's still a chance she might show up, and if she does, I want to be there. Besides, it's not smart for me to tie these parties to her specifically. She won't always be there, and she won't always be with me when she is, so I need to go and see what a night without her is like there, and if I still want to be a member.

***

It's eleven o'clock, and I'm already here. I arrived fifteen minutes early just in case she shows because I want to be the first to a room if she does. I've made my rounds, and I don't see her. I also don't see the two women I usually watch, which is disappointing, but I decide to walk around and see where the night takes me.

People are heading toward rooms or just starting where they stand. I sit on the sofa in the spacious living room and watch two women who are on the floor in front of the fireplace. I'm not the only one watching, though, and it feels more like the porn I watch rather than something real, so I leave the room and head upstairs. I find only one open door, and it's not the women I was hoping for, but at least it's two women. I recognize them as the member and the escort I watched with *her* the last time.

"Come in," the member says, "If you want. We're just getting started. You're welcome to watch or participate if you choose to."

The escort is pulling off the woman's stockings until they snap off in her hand, and she smirks, tossing them to the floor.

"I'm happy to have you join us," the escort says, turning her head back to me.

She *does* look like she'd be happy to have me join, but I stand there and continue watching. The escort is naked now. The member is naked now, too. She nods at me, I think. Then, the escort stands up and walks over to me, or so I thought. She walked past me to close the door behind me.

"She wants it to be just us for now," I get the explana-

61

tion from the escort. "You can stay or go. Up to you," she says as she walks past me, but her hand lightly grazes my own, and that touch turns me on.

This is why I'm here, I tell myself. I can't just come here expecting to see the woman I want and expecting her to be able to spend each month only with me. I watch as the escort tops the member, and the member spreads her legs wide for her. They begin to rock as they kiss, and there's familiarity here. They know each other; they've done this before, and it shows. It's nice. It's sexy. The member begins to moan into their kisses. I watch as the escort slips her hand between them, and it doesn't take long for the woman beneath her to come at her touch. I want to come too now.

I haven't touched myself since that last time at the spa, and I know I need it. I've been holding out for tonight, hoping *she'd* be here, but if she's not, I still need to come. I take a hesitant step toward the bed. The member's eyes open as she begins to come down. She smirks up at me.

"Would you like to join us?" she asks.

"Yes," I say.

"Baby, would you let her make you come?" she asks the escort as she runs her hands through the woman's hair.

"That sounds nice," the escort says.

"Will you fuck her for me while she sucks me?" the member asks. "She has what you need, and I love watching her come – it makes me come harder."

I nod. The escort slips out of bed and finds the strap-on in her bag. She holds it out to me, and I don't hesitate. I strip out of my dress, baring my breasts to both women but leaving my thong on as I slip the harness on. It's been a minute since I've used one of these things, but I like the idea of using one tonight. I watch the member spread her legs wide. The escort moves back onto the bed and kisses the woman deeply. She lowers herself down to suck on the nipples, and I move to stand closer to the bed. I slide my hand into my thong as I watch the escort suck on the other nipple and the woman writhe beneath her.

"You like that?" the member asks me.

"Yes," I say.

"Turn it on, then," the woman says.

"Turn what…"

I realize what she means. I look down and see the bullet tucked inside the dildo. I turn it on and instantly start feeling the vibrations against my clit. The escort slides down, starting on the woman's inner thigh, and I get ready. I stand between her legs as she moves to me. I grip her hips when she starts licking the woman's sex, and I bring the dildo to hers, moving it up and down through her wetness. And she *is* wet. I push inside her, and she groans pleasantly. I press all the way into her, feeling the vibrations on my clit. I know I won't last long, but I want to be here, in this moment. I want to participate. I want to know if this is enough for me.

I begin to thrust slowly. One hand is on her ass. The other is on her hip, bringing her forward and back.

"Slap it," the member says. "Is that okay, baby?" she asks the woman between her legs, running her hand through her hair.

The woman mumbles. I slap her ass lightly.

"Yes," the member says.

The escort moans, and I slap her other cheek lightly. She moans again. I thrust harder and deeper.

"Fuck," I say, knowing I'm going to come from this.

"You should play with your nipples while you're buried inside my girl," the member says.

I choose not to listen. Instead, I reach around the escort and begin to stroke her clit.

"Oh, fuck," she says, pulling away from the member's clit. "Yes."

"Oh, yes," the member says. "Make her come," she says to me. "Baby, I'm going down on you after this. I want you in my mouth," she says to the escort again.

"Yes," the woman replies.

I remove my hand from her clit and grip her hips hard

now with both hands. Now, I'm really fucking her. She's moving back against me and then toward the other woman. She's sucking and licking her as I push deeper. The vibrator is too much, and I come as I continue to push into her erratically. I close my eyes from pleasure, and my head goes back, but I'm not sure I'm focusing enough to make *her* come, too. Then, I hear it – both women are coming.

I open my eyes and see the member pressing the escort's head down. I see now that the escort has her hand between the woman's legs. She's moving in and out of her as she sucks on her clit, and it's so sexy. The woman I'm fucking is coming, too. I keep thrusting. I have to turn off the vibrator because I can't take it anymore, but I keep thrusting until she finally moves so far forward that I fall out of her. She then slides up the bed to the woman beneath her, and they're kissing again.

I'm standing there with a strap-on, watching these two women kiss one another after they come, and suddenly, I feel like I'm watching something I shouldn't be. It's like I'm intruding. The member is holding on to the escort's face, silently asking her to keep kissing her. I pull off the harness and leave it on the bed. Then, I dress quickly, turn to go, and turn back to see that the member is now on top of the escort. The escort is running her hands up and down the member's sides. The member is massaging the escort's breasts, then moves down her body, and it's like they've both forgotten I was even in the room.

"You feel so good," the escort says when the woman licks her pussy. "God, don't stop, baby. I need you."

"I need you, too, baby," the member replies.

Now, I *know* I'm watching something I probably shouldn't be, so I turn back and leave the room. I close the door and press my back against it. It was sexy. I came hard. Those two things are true, but there's something missing. It's her. I close my eyes and picture her face between my legs. I picture what I just did to the escort in that room, and there's no comparison – I want *her*. I miss her.

MONTH 3. PART 2. – LIFE

(POV Escort)

"We're glad you could make it," my friend says as she invites me into the home she shares with her wife.

"Yeah, I know. Things have been a little crazy lately. I'm sorry I've been distant."

"We understand," she says.

We walk through the large foyer and into the kitchen, where the smell of roasted chicken, garlic, and lemon meets my nose.

"I'm heating something up for you since we ate already," her wife tells me as she pulls a plate out of the microwave. "We would have waited, but–"

"I was two hours late," I say. "I'm so sorry. I had to– "

"It's okay," she tells me and sets the plate on the kitchen table. "We haven't had our dessert yet. We thought we could eat that with you."

"I'll get it," my friend says, heading toward the refrigerator.

I sit down and pour wine for all three of us into the glasses on the table. When they join me, it's with pieces of home-made pie, including one for me. I start on the chicken first, starving since I haven't eaten all day, and they dig into their pie.

"So, we're a week away from *you-know-what*. Are you getting excited?" my friend asks.

"Why would I get excited? It's work," I say.

"Because of her," my other friend says.

"I'll admit, she's sexy, and I've loved touching her," I reply. "But it's still a job. You guys go there for fun."

"That we do," my friend says. "But I've seen you in

relationships with women, and you've never looked at them how you look at this one."

"I don't even know her name," I tell them as I finish the candied Brussel sprouts with bacon.

"So? You know a lot more about her that matters."

"I do?" I ask.

"Yes. You know how she feels when you touch her, how she smells, what she looks like, how she tastes, how she sounds when she comes," my friend replies.

"You guys know what she looks like and how she sounds, too. Are you excited about seeing her?"

My friend laughs a little and says, "We aren't exactly paying attention to you when you watch us, you know? It's more that we *know* you're there, but we're pretty focused on each other. Honestly, she's nice on the eyes, though, and yes, we would like to see her there again."

"You want to, too," her wife tells me, finishing her pie.

"I know," I admit. "I think I'm downplaying it because I'm trying not to think about it."

"Why?"

"Because there's no guarantee she'll want me this time. She can have her pick of anyone there," I say.

"She's chosen you twice, and a lot of people have their regulars."

"It's weird thinking of her as a regular… It's weird thinking about me being paid for sex, period."

"Well, you don't have to. We–"

"Not again," I say.

"Fine. But even if we don't give or loan you money, you said you only needed a few months."

"Things have changed. I think I need to keep doing this for a while."

My friend's eyebrow lifts, and she says, "And this had nothing to do with the gorgeous woman you get to fuck when you're there?"

"Babe…" her wife says.

I finish my pie quickly and push the plate away.

"It's both," I say.

"What happens when you've got the money you need? Will you stop coming?"

"That was the plan."

"*Was?*" my friend asks.

"I don't know." I sigh. "I want to… I've never just fucked someone before, so I don't know. And I've never been paid for sex before, so I don't know. I just know how it feels when I touch her, and everything else aside, it feels really fucking good."

"Then, do it again on Saturday," my friend suggests.

"I want to. If she wants me, I want to," I say.

"You guys are pretty hot together," she says.

"We *feel* pretty hot together," I say, leaning back in the chair.

"If we see her, we'll steer her your way."

"How are you going to do that with your tongue down her throat and your hand up her dress?" I tease.

"We could always try a little rehearsal just to be safe," she says.

"Rehearsal?"

"Yeah, I can make my wife come up against the kitchen island and try to keep my eyes out for your lady," she says.

"I like the sound of that," her wife says.

"Yeah? Rehearsal, huh?" I joke.

"We've been to the place before, the house for this weekend – our kitchen is comparable. It's the best location."

"Don't let me interfere with whatever you guys have planned for the rest of the night," I say.

"Can we ask you something?" she says, leaning over the table.

"Sure."

"When was the last time you had sex?"

"What?" I ask.

"When was the last time you had sex?"

"A month ago. Why?"

"With her?"

"Yes."

"And no one since?"

"No. I've been a little too busy worrying about everything else in my life to try to meet someone. Why?"

"Did you come with her?"

"Yes," I admit.

"How was it?" my other friend asks.

"Fucking amazing. Why are you guys asking?"

"Because we like to be safe," she tells me. "I'm glad it was good for you, but I was more curious if you've been with anyone since her. Members are safe; we're tested regularly, like you guys."

"Why would–"

"We want you to join us," she interrupts.

"What?" I say.

"We want you to join us."

"Tonight?"

"Maybe for more than just tonight," my friend says, leaning even farther over the table. "It could be a regular thing if we all like it."

"You mean... you want me to participate, not just watch?" I say more than ask.

"Yes."

"You've always been very clear that it's just you two, and that works for me. I'm not looking for more if that's what you're thinking."

"We're not," her wife says, smiling at me. "We love when you watch us. It's sex on a whole other level, and it's become part of our relationship, but we've seen you with someone else now, and it's..."

"A whole other level after that one," my friend adds.

"I thought you said you weren't paying attention to us," I tease.

"We caught some glances and a few sounds," my friend says.

"And I remember some slurping," her wife says.

"Oh, God," I say, embarrassed.

"She was that turned on for you," my friend says.

"I don't know if it was for *me*," I say.

"Oh, it was." She stands up and offers me her hand. "If you say no – it's no, and that's fine; nothing else has to change. But if you're interested, we could take this upstairs, and all enjoy each other tonight."

"This seems like a bad idea," I say. "It's one thing to watch and get myself off… It's a whole other thing to–"

Her wife stands up, walks over to me, then leans down behind me, bringing her mouth to my ear, and says, "We want to touch you."

"Oh," I say softly.

"If you want us to," she says, sliding a hand inside my t-shirt and over my bare breast.

I lean my head back against her body. My chair is pulled out from under the table with hands I don't see, and there's my friend kneeling in front of me now.

"Do you?" she asks, reaching for my fly and pulling it down slowly.

"You guys are really sure about this?" I ask.

My button is undone, and there are now two hands massaging my breasts.

"Yes," she whispers in my ear.

"You know I'm more of a giver than a receiver," my friend says as she pulls apart my pants, revealing my underwear beneath.

"And I love both," my other friend says into my ear before she tugs on my earlobe with her teeth. "I'd love to watch my wife go down on you while I sit on your face."

"Oh, shit," I say as I feel lips on my stomach now under my shirt.

"Oh, shit, we should stop? Or, oh shit, you want this as much as we do?" my friend says.

"Guys, I wasn't expecting this tonight. Can we just slow down for a second?"

"Of course."

Hands and lips pull away from me entirely, and I stand up.

"Okay. You're married, and I'm your friend," I say, breathing hard.

"And you're very sexy to both of us; you know that. We've watched you touch yourself before. This is just *us* touching you this time, and you touching us if you want."

"I want. I mean, I didn't think that I did before – just watching is enough – but I do want."

"Good," my friend says. "Then, we can go upstairs, or we can start down here if you want."

"Can we just maybe do something tonight?"

"Yeah, that's what–"

"No, I meant... I just want to touch you guys. Is that okay?"

"You don't want us to make you come?" my friend asks.

"I'll come, trust me, but I'd like to do the touching. Is that okay?" I ask, breathing hard. "A first step."

"You want to touch us?" my friend asks, kissing her wife's neck now as her wife holds out her hand to take mine and pull me in.

I swallow hard – I *do* want to touch them. I wouldn't mind if they touch me, either, but something's holding me back. This makes sense – it's the natural evolution of what we've been doing since the beginning: I've watched them so many times, and they've seen me touch myself. They've seen me touch someone else, too. It only makes sense now that we'd do this together; the three of us. Then, I think of *her*. My friend takes my hand and pulls me around behind her wife, who is now sandwiched between us. My hand slips into the woman's pants without me even thinking about it, and as my friend takes off her wife's shirt and bra and starts sucking on her nipples, I'm stroking her clit. Her head is back against my shoulder, and I don't even realize that I'm kissing her neck until I'm already doing it.

I'm wet. I'm getting turned on, and I want to come

myself. I look down and see that my pants are undone still. As I stroke her with my dominant hand and listen to her sounds, I reach into my panties and find my swollen clit. I nip at her neck as I stroke myself in time. My hips roll into her, and I look down to see that she's got her hand inside her wife's pants now, too. This is crazy…

She moans first. Her wife moans second and kisses her. I keep stroking her clit and my own at the same time. Then, I feel her hand on mine, and she pulls it lower – she wants me inside. I'm not ready for that yet, so I move it back to her clit and stroke her harder.

"Baby, I need you inside," she says.

I don't know if she's talking to me or to her wife. I stroke her harder.

"Fuck," she says. "Yes, make me come."

So, I do. She comes hard against my hand, and I come after her. Then, a third voice is heard in the middle of the kitchen, and we're all coming together. I stop stroking myself first and picture another woman in front of me for a second. I want *her*; I don't want this. This is definitely hot, and maybe if I wouldn't have met *her*, I'd want this, but I pull my hand out of my friend's pants and step back.

"What's wrong?" she asks me, still hazy from her orgasm.

"I can't," I say.

She removes her own hand from her wife's pants and turns to me. Now, they're both staring at me.

"Are you okay?"

"Yeah, I'm fine. This was…"

"Too much?" my friend asks.

"I think so, yeah," I say.

"We shouldn't have pushed you. I'm sorry," she says, buttoning up her pants.

"No, it's fine. I told you I wanted it, and I *did*. I *do*. I– "

"Is it because we're married or because we're all friends?"

"No," I say, buttoning up my own pants.

"Okay. Why?"

"Her," I say.

"Who?" my friend asks.

"*Her*, babe," her wife tells her.

"The woman from the party?"

"Yes," I say.

"She's a member," my friend replies.

"I know."

"Don't take this the wrong way, okay? You can totally leave now and come back for dinner or to watch us have sex anytime you want without this ever happening again." She points between all three of us. "This doesn't have to do with what just happened."

"What doesn't?" I ask.

"She's a member," her wife says. "You're… *not.*"

"She's there to have sex with an anonymous person she pays for, and you're there to work. So, the sex might be great, but it's only once a month, and she could leave at any time. We'd just hate for you to get all tied up in her. Besides, while regulars are common, the longer you work the events, the more likely it'll be that you have to sleep with someone else."

"Plus," my friend's wife begins. "We want you to be happy. This is a temporary thing because you need money. What happens when you meet someone for real? She's not real. She's… fleeting."

I know they're right. Everything they say is right, but I know I can't do this – at least, not tonight.

"Can we revisit this a little later? I'm just all mixed up with everything going on right now," I say. "I promise, it's not you guys. I love you, guys. You know that, right?"

"We love you, too. It's why we want you like this," my friend says. "It not just the sex. If it were, we could get that at any event. We know you. We trust you."

"I know. And I'm sorry I let it go a little far tonight. I probably should have said no so we could talk more first."

"I'm not sorry – your fingers were amazing," she tells me, closing her eyes and smiling.

"They were?" her wife asks, not in a jealous way, but in an inquisitive one. "Can you show me what they did?" she asks.

"Of course," she replies.

I lean back against the wall in the kitchen and watch them as they speak no more. Clothing is tossed aside. Lips meet lips. Hands play and roam. Bodies lower to the floor. Moans begin. I stand there, hovering over them and thinking about how I know I could make this work with them – whatever it would turn into – but that I want *her*. I want to see her on Saturday and have her beneath me, above me, in front of and behind me. I know it's wrong. I know it's not real, and it can't go anywhere, but I can't stop myself from licking my lips thinking about how I sucked on her clit while she watched these two on the bed and got so wet, I worried there would be a wet spot on her dress.

I watch them until they both come, and I don't touch myself this time, wanting the next time I get off to be because I'm with *her*. Then, I watch them walk naked upstairs, and I leave. It's a strange friendship we have that most people probably wouldn't understand, but it works for us.

When I get home, I head to my room for a shower first. After I clean up, I hit my bed and pull out my computer. My day job pays enough for just me, but not for what I need right now. Being an escort was never part of my life plan, and I know I can't and *won't* want to do it forever, so I've been checking for second jobs that would pay enough. None of them do, though. It's a futile exercise, but it gives me something to do, so I do it in the morning and at night every day.

Finally, I close the computer an hour later and decide to try to get some sleep. On Saturday, she'll be mine again. I plan to get there and wait by the damn door – I'm not taking a chance that I'll miss her or that she'll meet someone else and take them to bed instead. I know it's wrong and makes no sense given what my job is, but I don't want anyone I work with touching her.

***

I was even more excited for this event than I was for last one, and that's saying something. Now, that excitement is gone – I can't go to the party. I can't see her… I can't touch her… I know how wrong it is to be thinking about *her* when my life is in shambles, but I can't help it. Thinking about her gives me a break from thinking about everything else. And I can't even have *that* now because thinking about her makes me realize I won't get to see her, after all.

"Hey, we're here," my friend says, taking my hand as she sits down next to me.

"You guys didn't have to come here," I reply.

Her wife sits on the other side of me in uncomfortable waiting room chairs.

"Of course, we did."

"How bad?"

"They're still running tests," I say, leaning my head back against the off-white wall. "She'll be here for a few days, at least."

"What do you need?"

"Nothing. I'll be okay," I lie.

"Sweetie, when was the last time you've eaten something?"

"I think yesterday," I say.

My friend's wife runs her hand over the back of my neck and says, "Let's go to the cafeteria and eat some dinner, okay?"

"I shouldn't leave."

"I'll let the nurse know where we're going," my friend says. "She's right – you need to eat."

It's seven days later when she's able the leave the hospital, and they tell me it's only going to get worse from here. The doctor tells me some of what I can expect, and I don't even hear him. It's all a big blur. When we get home, I get her settled in her room, making sure she has everything she needs. Then, I go to my own room and cry until she calls for me to help her to the bathroom. I wipe my eyes, stand up, and help her because she's helped me my entire life, and I'm not about to let her down now.

MONTH 4, PART 1. – WOMEN ONLY

(POV Member)

They've called it a test event. There were enough interested women to host the first women-only night. I'm not sure what that means exactly. They've described it as 'women seeking women,' so that can mean any number of things, but the only thing I care about is seeing *her*. They're not offering reserved rooms or special accommodations for the first party, so I can't request it this time, but I did message to confirm that the woman I'm most interested in seeing will be there. Thankfully, they replied within a day of my email, letting me know that she would.

I can't wait to see her again. I breeze through work, trying to pay at least some attention to things I was signing off on and the emails I was sending, but it's Friday, and I'll see her tomorrow. When five o'clock hits, I'm out the door, despite still having work to do. And I normally stay in the office until well after six, and most nights, even seven.

I didn't want to take a chance with ordering my lingerie online, so I set it for pickup at my local store. I arrive around six-thirty and make sure to try everything on before I purchase. One bra feels a little tight around my breasts, and they'll only get fuller with arousal when I get near her, so I go up a size and try that on, liking how the see-through red lace makes me feel. The matching thong isn't something I can really try on, but I know it'll fit. I pay and head home to try on combinations of everything I just bought, deciding on what I'll wear tomorrow and next month, too. I take time to shave my legs and trim my pussy. Then, I pack the bag I plan to bring to the event with my preferred toys and some extra clothes, which I've never done before.

When I wake Saturday morning, I have two quick cups of coffee and do some work to help keep my mind from *her*. I don't want to come until she's the one touching me, but I'm already so damn horny that it's hard for me to resist. I decide to go for a swim in my pool to cool off and then lie out to get a little sun while I read, but I'm still thinking about *her*. I guess that means something because I'm not thinking about the two women I had sex with a month ago. That was my first threesome, and as sexy and fulfilling as it was – it was not enough. I can really only think about *her*.

I head inside and shower, making sure to get the chlorine and sunscreen off my skin. I want her to smell *me* tonight, so I wash my hair with my favorite shampoo and conditioner and my skin with my preferred shower wash. I also moisturize with my favorite lotion. I don't put any product in my hair, but I do pull it up with a clip that I'm hoping she'll remove. I feel confident in my choice of red lace bra and matching thong. I have a new red dress that I put over everything, with matching heels. Now, when I go to these things, I know what I want; I know who I am, and I dress like it. I'm there for sex. I'm there to watch people have sex. I'm there for *her*.

Once I'm ready and I have my bag, I'm out the door. I pull up to the parking lot, where I park my car this time. The valet approaches – well-dressed, as always – and takes my keys. He explains that I'll be driven to the location in an SUV, which I see lined up ready to take us to the place. I climb into the first one expecting to see more members, but I'm alone when the driver takes off. Apparently, we each get our own SUVs tonight – environment be damned for this company. It's a nice black BMW, too, and they've got a bottle of water and a card on the seat next to me. I don't want the water yet, but I *am* interested in the card.

Welcome to the first night for women only. While we know this is the first time we've done this, we're hoping to provide you with a memorable and pleasurable evening. We've

*done our best to ensure that our top-rated escorts will be here
to take care of your every desire. Please let us know at the end
of the night if you'd like to have more of these events. And if so,
we'll be happy to discuss the terms of an adjusted membership.
Tonight, let our people know what you want, and we will do
everything in our power to make sure you have it.*

Member Services

Well, they said they couldn't give me what I wanted
before, I think to myself. When the car pulls up to a mansion in a neighborhood about forty-five minutes away from
my own, I'm not surprised. I meet the woman at the front
door, and she recognizes me now, so I hold out my wrist.

"No need," she says.

"Oh, right," I say.

Tonight, I don't need a bracelet – we're all interested
in the same thing. She checks me off of her list, and the door
opens. When a woman at the door asks if she can take my
bag this time, I say no; I'm hanging on to it for the night. I
do give her my jacket, though, and then I'm off. I'm early,
so I hope I can find *her* before someone else does, and we
can make our way to a room. I hold my bag at my side and
enter the large living room where I see only women. I sigh,
hoping they do this every month because I would love to
get to *only* look at women at these events. I see the escort
and the woman I was with last time. They're on the sofa,
almost snuggled up, with the member's arm around the back
of the sofa, whispering something into the escort's ear. The
escort laughs, and I look away.

She's not here. I worry she didn't show up after all, but
this is only the first room I've seen, so I head to the dining
room, where there's food and champagne laid out along
with the bartender – who is also a woman – pouring the
drinks. I see *her* then. She's standing with a woman I've
never seen before, handing her a drink. I'm too late. The
woman leans in, and she's a member – I only know because
the employees tonight are wearing small silver buttons on

their clothing somewhere, and I don't spot anything on her dress. I watch *her* talk to the member, and I close my eyes, thinking about turning around and going home because the entire night is ruined. When I *do* turn, I hear it.

"Hi," she says. "Leaving so soon?"

I turn back, and she's in front of me now.

"No. I decided I didn't want a drink, after all," I lie.

"What *do* you want?" she asks, stepping closer to me.

I look past her at the woman who is now watching us.

"I think what I want isn't an option tonight," I say.

"What do you want?" she asks again.

"You," I say.

She smiles and says, "Then, I'm all yours."

I hold back my smile and say, "What about her?"

"She's here for someone else. I was just at the bar when she walked up."

"So, you're…"

"Going to take your hand and look for a room," she says.

She reaches for my hand just as the music starts. I pay no attention to the people moving around us, trying to find someone or multiple people to be with tonight. I only care about the feel of her hand in mine and how she possessively takes the bag I'm carrying and leads me down the hall and up the stairs to a room with an open door.

"Master bedroom," she says, motioning for me to get inside.

"We won't get in trouble this time, will we?"

"No," she says. "I double-checked."

"You double-checked for *me*?"

She nods and closes the door behind us. Then, she locks it, and I could not be happier or more turned on. I've waited two months for this, and now I get five hours with her.

"Wait," she says suddenly. "I don't want to leave once we're in here. I'm grabbing food and water. Do you want a drink?"

I laugh lightly at her and say, "Maybe champagne."

"I'm closing this door so that no one takes this room. Lock it behind me. I'll knock twice and then two more times."

"So secret agent," I say, smiling at her.

"Don't get undressed yet," she says and leaves the room.

I lock the door behind her, and I'm suddenly nervous. I don't know what to do until she gets back. I pick up my bag and move it closer to the bed, for easy access later. I check my breath to make sure that the mint I popped before I parked my car was still effective. Then, I walk to the mirror over the dresser and check my hair. I lift my boobs up a bit and adjust them in the bra. When I have nothing else to do that I could come up with, I'm just left to stand in front of the bed like an idiot. Finally, she knocks. I open the door and let her in. When I lock it behind her, she places a plate of food on the dresser along with two bottles of water. She pulls two more out of her suit jacket and reminds me a little of a squirrel preparing for winter. I laugh silently at how cute it all is.

I see that she's brought an entire bottle of champagne along with two flutes that she'd stored in her suit pants' pockets. I'm in awe of her – she really *doesn't* want to leave this room all night. That's fine – I don't, either. When I finally get to look around the space, it's huge. The king-sized bed behind me is a nice touch. There's a massive television mounted to one wall, a nice oriental rug between a chair and a matching loveseat opposite it, and there's also a balcony that overlooks the backyard and pool. All I can think is that it's perfect.

"I was hoping you'd be here," she says, uncorking the champagne.

"You were?" I ask.

"Yes," she says as the foam pours out of the bottle and onto the floor.

"Oh, no," I say, laughing.

"They'll have it all cleaned anyway," she says, unphased as she pours some into a flute and more into another. She passes one to me and places the bottle down on the dresser. She turns to me with her own glass and holds it out. "Cheers," she says.

"What are we toasting to?" I ask.

"This," she says. "You look amazing." She leans in and kisses my neck as our glasses clink together. "You smell amazing."

I breathe her in, too, and she smells perfect. I take a sip of my champagne as she continues to kiss my neck.

"You have to take a sip or it's bad luck. You don't know that?" I say.

"Bad luck?"

"To toast and not take a drink," I explain.

She pulls back a little, downs the whole glass, and takes mine from me as well.

"I want all the good luck tonight," she says, placing my still-full glass on the dresser and moving into me. "Tell me what you want tonight, and I'll give it to you."

"I just want the whole night with you. No interruptions," I say.

She smiles softly and says, "Okay."

"And I don't want you to have to ask." I wrap my arms around her neck. "You can just take; you know my safe word."

Her hands are around my back.

"Wall Street," she says.

"I want you to have me any way you want me," I say.

Then, I lean forward, giving her a chance to pull away if she doesn't want this. When she doesn't move, I lean in closer. She leans forward a bit, too. Our lips are millimeters apart, and I can feel her hot breath on my skin. I need more. I close the distance, pulling her fully against me, and deepen the kiss. She gives a soft sound that tells me this is what she wants as well. Her lips taste of champagne, and when her tongue flicks against my own, it does, too. Her hands move to the zipper of my dress, and she pulls it down. Her hands splay across my back as she continues to kiss me. My hands are in her hair and on her neck possessively – she's mine tonight. Her kiss is demanding and exactly what I want, but I also want more. My hands go to her collar, and I push the jacket off her shoulders. She removes it the rest of the way, and I untuck her white shirt. My hands go under it to her skin, pressing to her tight abdomen, and I need her naked.

"Turn around," she says, pulling her lips away.

"I–"

"Turn around," she says again.

I do, and she's wrapping her arms around me and kissing my shoulders. Her hand slips under the hem of my dress, and it's just like the first time – she lowers one strap with her free hand, and her hand is inside my bra, massaging my breast; her lips are on my neck, and her other hand is inside my thong, working my clit hard and fast.

"Fuck," I say, leaning my head back against her.

"I want to," she says. "Tonight, I want to fuck you."

"Yes," I say as she slips a finger inside. "God, yes."

"What's in your bag?"

"Toys and clothes," I say.

"What kind of toys?" she asks, stroking my clit even faster now.

"Oh, fuck," I say.

She nips at my neck.

"What kind of toys?" she repeats.

"A strap-on and a few different vibrators," I say. "And nipple clamps."

"Nipple clamps? You want me to put them on you?"

"I want to put them on *you*," I say. "While you fuck me, I want you to wear them. God, I'm going to come."

"Will you suck on them after to make them feel better?" she asks.

"Hell, yes," I say.

Then, I press her palm flat against me and hold it there. I rock against her hand as her other one squeezes my nipple.

"I'm coming. Fuck, I'm–"

"I don't plan to let you stop coming all night," she says, and I believe her.

She sucks on my neck, and I know she's leaving a mark. I don't care. She's claiming me, and I *want* to be claimed by her. I ride out my orgasm against her firm hand, and then I go slack in her arms. She keeps me up, and her sucking turns to soft kisses before she turns my head to the side and kisses my lips. Her hand slips away and lets down the other strap of my dress. I shimmy it down my body until it's on the floor.

"Oh, wow," she says, looking down the front of my body. "You have no idea what this is doing to me right now."

"What's it doing to you?" I ask.

"Red is my favorite color," she says, walking around to face me and look me up and down. "You are so fucking sexy."

"So are you. Take this off," I tell her, tugging on her shirt.

"Should I put anything *on*?" she asks, undoing the buttons.

"We'll get there," I tell her.

The shirt's gone, and she's not wearing a bra, so I cup her breasts and kiss her neck as she works on her pants. I've never watched her come before, and right now, that's all I can think about.

"Can I taste you?" I ask her, wanting her to know that she can absolutely say no to anything I want to do tonight.

"Yes," she breathes out as her pants fall to the floor.

I look down at her dark-blue panties and give her hips a little shove backward. She ends up sitting on the edge of the bed as I stand in front of her in my red see-through bra and matching thong. I'm still in my heels, so I kick those off and reach for her. She places her lips between my breasts, and I need her mouth on my nipples, so I lower the cup of my left breast and place her mouth there instead. She sucks and flicks. I close my eyes and hold her head there, taking it all in.

It's been two months, and now, I'm worried five hours won't even be enough. She moves to the other breast on her own, lowers the cup of the bra, and sucks on the nipple. Her hands move to thin sides of my thong. She doesn't remove it, though. She just slides her hands inside the bit of fabric and then places her hands on my bare ass, cupping it and bringing me closer to her.

Before I know it, her lips are lowering. She's pushing me back a little, and her mouth is on my thong. She's licking under it, and I'm close to begging her to suck me. Instead, I push her shoulders back. She smirks up at me. I yank at her underwear until it's gone. I pull off her shoes and her black socks, and she's finally bared to me.

"Do *you* have a safe word?" I ask her as I kneel.

"Do I *need* one?" She looks at me.

"I want to do things to you that I want you to be okay with," I say, kissing the inside of her thigh.

"Like what?"

"Go inside you," I say, moving my lips closer to her sex.

"With your fingers?"

"And my tongue," I say.

"Fuck," she says, flopping back down onto the bed. "Yes, fuck me with your tongue all you want."

"If you want me to stop, you'll say what?"

"Just take me," she says. "I need you to just fucking take me."

So, I do. I breathe her in first. Then, I lower my tongue to her sex and lick between her folds. I swipe my tongue over my lips, taking in the taste of her and craving more.

"I'm not stopping until you come," I say.

"It won't take long," she replies.

I can't stop myself – I spread her lips with my fingers and stare blatantly at her perfect pussy. Her clit is already swollen and begging for me to suck on it. She's slick and ready, and I lower my face until my tongue can slip inside. Then, I lift her ass off the bed a little and slip in farther.

"Oh, fuck," she says.

Her hand goes to the back of my head, and she holds me there. I move back and forth as she continues to make sounds. I place one hand over her breast and the other at her clit. I flick it back and forth as I continue to fuck her with my tongue.

"Yes, baby," she says, and I groan because I want her to call me 'baby' again. "Yes, there."

"Say it," I say, pulling out of her. "Say it."

She looks at me and shakes her head.

"Call me *baby* again. I like it."

She nods, and I enter her again and move my tongue faster as I lift her hips a little to slide in as far as I can.

"Fuck, yes. I need you deeper. I need your fingers, please."

I don't want to stop, but I want to give her anything she wants, so I pull my tongue out, slide it through her wetness, and then suck on her clit, bringing my fingers to her entrance and pushing them inside.

"Fuck me, baby," she says.

And I do. I move my fingers hard and fast as I suck her clit into my mouth. I twist her nipple, and she comes way too fast, but it's so hard that she forces my fingers out and sits up on the bed. I look up at her, wanting to keep going, but she stands, pushing me gently back on the floor. She's still breathing hard. I look up at her from my spot on the floor, and I can't wait for whatever she's planning on doing to me. Then, I know what she's planning on doing to me because she's opening my bag and putting it on. She's walking over to me and kneeling.

"Turn over," she says.

I do. I'm on all fours now.

"Are you ready for me?" she asks.

"Fuck, yes. I've been ready for you since the last time. Fill me up," I tell her.

She does.

"Oh, Jesus. Yes," I say, finally feeling full.

She presses to me and pushes deeper inside, her hands grasping my hips and pulling me forward and back.

"Is this what you wanted?" she asks.

"Yes," I say.

"You wanted me to fuck you from behind?"

"Yes," I say, biting my lower lip because it feels so good.

"How does it feel?"

"So fucking good," I say.

"Has anyone else fucked you like this since we met?" she asks.

I open my eyes because I wasn't prepared for that question, but I decide to answer.

"No," I tell her, but I know there's something in my voice that gives me away.

"Did *you* fuck someone else like this?" she asks next.

"Yes," I say.

"Last month?"

"Yes," I repeat as my orgasm begins to build.

"Did you come?"

"Yes," I reply.

"Was it good?"

"Yes," I say.

She thrusts harder.

"Oh, fuck. I'm coming," I say.

Her thrusts are deeper now and hitting just the right spot. I can't hold on any longer, so I scream out in pleasure. I flop onto the floor face first, and she slips out of me. She rolls me over and climbs on top of me, her hands at either side of my head. She's breathing hard, but her eyes are soft.

"Was it because I wasn't there?" she asks.

"Yes," I say.

She nods.

"And it was good, I won't lie to you, but no one has ever made me come how you do," I say, wrapping my arms around her neck. "I mean that. I've spent the past two months thinking only about this."

"I'm sorry I wasn't here," she says, leaning down and pressing into me, her face buried in my neck. "How did she touch you?" she asks softly.

"She didn't," I say, running my hand through her short, now sweaty hair. "I was behind her."

"But she didn't touch you?"

Now wasn't really the time to tell her there were two women present, so I just nod.

"Is it unfair for me to say that I don't like the idea of anyone else at these things touching you?" she asks.

I kiss her temple and smile. I shake my head.

"Get the champagne," I say.

"The champagne?" she asks, lifting up.

"I want you to lick it off me," I say.

She smirks again and stands, still wearing that strap-on and looking fucking sexy doing it.

"Where should I lick it from?" she asks, holding the bottle.

"Dealer's choice," I say, spreading my legs for her.

MONTH 4. PART 2. – WHAT I NEED

(POV Escort)

The past month has been a whirlwind of awfulness, mostly. I'm barely present at work, and I'm sure my boss has noticed – it's only a matter of time before all the sick days I've had to take, to take care of her, come back to bite me in the ass. I can go on short-term leave, but that won't pay me my entire paycheck, and we need the money. The tests, the hospital stays, and the treatments – only so much of it is covered by insurance. The rest is on me now that her savings are all gone, and there's no one else. It makes me want to move back to the old country, as she calls it, where her parents were from. There's universal healthcare there, so we wouldn't be worried about all of this – just the part where she's dying.

My friends didn't go to the party last time, either. They stayed with me in solidarity, and when she came home, they were there with dinners and helped with some cleaning when they could. They really are the best, and they've been with me through so much. I wish I could get rid of my pride and let them pay for this, but I just can't. I'm not there yet. I made good money for the first two events, and I used that to pay off some bills, but now there are more. It's likely I'll need to stay on at the monthly events for the rest of the year, maybe longer.

I decide that while everything around me is terrible right now, the one place that's not is with her. So, while I probably should've stayed home, I waited for her to fall asleep, as I've done before, and then told the home nurse that I was going out and would be back late. She costs a fortune, but she helps when I'm not there, which is what allows me to still go to work *and* to come to these things and make extra money.

"Hi," I say when I see her. "Leaving so soon?"

She turns around and sees me.

"No. I decided I didn't want a drink, after all," she says, referring to the bar.

"What *do* you want?" I ask, stepping closer to her, and she looks over my shoulder.

"I think what I want isn't an option tonight."

"What do you want?" I ask again.

"You," she says.

I get wet.

"Then, I'm all yours."

"What about her?" she asks.

I turn around to see the woman she's talking about.

"She's here for someone else. I was just at the bar when she walked up."

"So, you're…"

"Going to take your hand and look for a room."

I take her hand and the bag she's carrying, curious about what's inside, and walk her down the hall and up the stairs to a room with an open door.

"Master bedroom," I say, feeling lucky for the first time in a very long time.

"We won't get in trouble this time, will we?"

"No," I say. "I double-checked."

I asked earlier if any rooms were off-limits tonight, and I was told no, so this one is fair game.

"You double-checked for *me?*"

I nod and close the door. Then, I lock it – I'm not taking any chances tonight.

"Wait," I say. I'm an idiot. I want her in here all night. "I don't want to leave once we're in here. I'm grabbing food and water. Do you want a drink?"

She laughs, and it's sexy.

"Maybe champagne," she replies.

"I'm closing this door so that no one takes this room.

Lock it behind me. I'll knock twice and then two more times."

"So secret agent," she teases.

"Don't get undressed yet," I tell her, wanting to be the one who undresses her tonight, and I leave.

I see a couple headed this way and say, "Occupied all night."

Then, I go back downstairs and stuff my pockets.

"Eager beaver," my friend says, approaching with her wife.

"Yes, I am."

"So, you found her?"

"She's waiting for me, so I've got to go," I reply.

"Well, if you want to look for us later, we won't mind at all."

"I kind of just want her tonight. Obviously, she's the member, so if she wants to, I'll come find you guys. I've got to go."

I'm sure I sounded rude, and I'll apologize to them later, but I need to get back – I want all night with this woman. I knock on the door with my elbow, looking not at all like a secret agent, and she opens the door. I walk in, and she locks it behind me. I smirk – she doesn't want to be interrupted, either. I place everything on the dresser and un-cork the champagne.

"I was hoping you'd be here," I say.

"You were?"

"Yes," I say as the foam pours out of the bottle and onto the floor.

"Oh, no," she says, laughing a little.

"They'll have it all cleaned anyway," I reply, not at all concerned about the damn carpet in this place. I pour us each a glass and set the bottle back down. "Cheers," I say.

"What are we toasting to?"

"This," I say. "You look amazing." I can't resist telling her how hot she looks. Then, I lean in and kiss her neck, one of my favorite spots on her body. Our glasses join, and

I add, "You smell amazing."

She sips her own champagne and kisses my neck. God, that feels good.

"You have to take a sip or it's bad luck. You don't know that?"

"Bad luck?" I say.

"To toast and not take a drink," she says.

I down the whole glass and take hers from her as well.

"I want all the good luck tonight," I say, putting the glasses down and stepping into her space. "Tell me what you want tonight, and I'll give it to you."

"I just want the whole night with you. No interruptions," she says.

I smile and say, "Okay."

"And I don't want you to have to ask." She wraps her arms around my neck. "You can just take; you know my safe word."

My hands move to her back.

"Wall Street," I say.

"I want you to have me any way you want me."

She leans forward, and fuck... I think she's going to kiss me. We haven't done this yet. Are we even supposed to do this? She waits – she's giving me an out. I don't need an out, so I lean in closer. She smells so damn good. When she presses her lips to mine, I'm lost from the beginning. I think I make a sound. Her tongue meets mine, and we deepen the kiss together. On their own, my hands go to her dress zipper, and I pull it down. I can't help but spread my hands across her back as I revel in this kiss. She's got her hands on my neck and in my hair. It's turning me on. I want more. She pushes my jacket down, and I remove it the rest of the way. She untucks my shirt, and her hands are under it instantly, touching my skin. My muscles are tightening as she caresses me.

"Turn around," I say, pulling my lips away.

"I–"

"Turn around," I tell her again.

She turns, and I want what I had that first time we were together like this – I need it in a way I didn't expect to. I need to remember how good it feels to have her like this, her back pressed to my front. I stroke her while I caress her breasts. She's wearing all red tonight, and it's see-through lingerie. I'm lost in her body, and while I want it all to stay on her, I also can't wait to strip it off and see more.

"Fuck," she says, leaning her head back against me.

"I want to. Tonight, I want to fuck you."

"Yes," she replies.

I slip a greedy finger inside because I can't wait any longer.

"God, yes," she breathes out.

"What's in your bag?" I ask.

"Toys and clothes," she says.

"What kind of toys?" I stroke her clit now.

"Oh, fuck," she says.

I nibble on her neck and ask again, "What kind of toys?"

"A strap-on and a few different vibrators," she says. "And nipple clamps."

"Nipple clamps? You want me to put them on you?"

"I want to put them on *you*," she says. "While you fuck me, I want you to wear them. God, I'm going to come."

"Will you suck on them after to make them feel better?" I ask her.

"Hell, yes."

She holds my palm flat against herself, and she's rocking against my hand now. It's such a turn-on to watch her take what she wants. I squeeze her nipple to reward her.

"I'm coming. Fuck, I'm–"

"I don't plan to let you stop coming all night," I say.

I possessively mark her by sucking on her neck – I want the people here to know that she's mine tonight. I help her ride out her orgasm until it's clear she's done, and I stop sucking on her neck to place soft kisses there instead. I reach for her and turn her face to me so I can kiss her again. Her

92

lips taste like the sip of champagne she took, with a bit of mint mixed in. I help her off with her dress now.

"Oh, wow," I say, looking down at her body. "You have no idea what this is doing to me right now."

"What's it doing to you?"

"Red is my favorite color," I tell her and walk around to face her and look her up and down. "You are so fucking sexy."

"So are you. Take this off." She tugs on my shirt.

"Should I put anything *on*?" I start undoing the buttons.

"We'll get there."

When my shirt is gone, she cups my breasts and kisses my neck. She's working on my pants now.

"Can I taste you?" she asks.

"Yes," I manage out, and my pants fall to the floor.

She shoves me back against the bed and stands in front of me. I kiss her between her breasts, and she lowers the cup of her bra and brings my lips to her nipple. I don't mind at all – I suck as she holds me in place, and after a minute, I move to her other breast, lowering her bra to take it into my mouth. I reach for her thong, wanting to tear it off her but liking the feel of the thin material in my hands. My hands are on her ass now. I bring her closer to me and lower my lips. I push her back a bit because I can smell her now, and I need to taste her again. I lick under the material, and she shoves me back on the bed. I smirk up at her. My underwear is pulled off, along with my shoes and socks.

"Do *you* have a safe word?" she asks as she kneels.

"Do I *need* one?"

"I want to do things to you that I want you to be okay with."

She kisses the inside of my thigh.

"Like what?"

"Go inside you."

"With your fingers?" I ask.

"And my tongue," she says.

"Fuck." I flop back down onto the bed. "Yes, fuck me with your tongue all you want."

"If you want me to stop, you'll say what?"

"Just take me," I tell her. "I need you to just fucking take me."

And I do. I need her to take me. I need this release. I've waited for two months for her to make me feel this good, and with everything else going so badly, I deserve a little good right now. This woman, who should only care about making herself come at one of these things, wants to make me come for some reason, and I'm going to let her. She goes to work on my clit, and I'm already breathing hard.

"I'm not stopping until you come," she says.

"It won't take long."

It's true – I know I won't last long. I haven't come even by my own hand since that night with my friends.

"Oh, fuck," I say as her tongue slips deeper inside me, and she lifts me a little off the bed.

I hold her head in place with my hand, and I know I'm moaning. Hell, I'd be saying her name if I knew it. She's got a hand on my breast now, and her other hand is on my clit while she's basically fucking me with her long tongue.

"Yes, baby," I say.

She groans. It's hot.

"Yes, there," I say.

"Say it," she says, pulling out of me. "Say it."

I look at her, confused.

"Call me *baby* again. I like it."

I nod. I'll call her 'baby' a hundred times if she makes me come right now. Her tongue slips back inside.

"Fuck, yes. I need you deeper. I need your fingers, please."

She pulls her tongue out and brings it to my clit. Her fingers go inside.

"Fuck me, baby," I say.

It's over before I even know it. Her fingers fuck me hard and fast while she sucks, and I can't take it. It's too good. I'm coming, feeling every bit of tension leave my body. The force of my orgasm pushes her fingers out of me, and I take my chance – I stand up and shove her back on the carpet a bit. Then, I go straight to her bag, not caring if I'm not allowed to see something. I pull out her strap-on, put it on, and kneel.

"Turn over," I say.

She does.

"Are you ready for me?" I ask.

"Fuck, yes. I've been ready for you since the last time. Fill me up."

I do.

"Oh, Jesus. Yes," she says.

I grip her hips, push deeper inside, and I pull her against me before pushing her away.

"Is this what you wanted?"

"Yes," she says.

"You wanted me to fuck you from behind?"

"Yes."

"How does it feel?"

"So fucking good," she says.

"Has anyone else fucked you like this since we met?"

I don't know where that came from. My eyes go wide, and I'm lucky she can't see them.

"No," she says, but something sounds off.

"Did *you* fuck someone else like this?"

"Yes," she says.

I swallow, but I don't stop.

"Last month?" I ask.

"Yes."

"Did you come?" I ask, needing to know.

"Yes."

"Was it good?"

"Yes."

I push in deeper, wanting to claim her.

"Oh, fuck. I'm coming," she says.

I fuck her harder. She's mine tonight, at least. As she

comes, I think about how had I not missed that party, *we* would've done this last time. She falls to the floor, and I slip out of her. I roll her over and get on top.

"Was it because I wasn't there?" I ask, knowing the answer.

"Yes."

I nod and swallow.

"And it was good, I won't lie to you, but no one has ever made me come how you do." She wraps her arms around my neck and adds, "I mean that. I've spent the past two months thinking only about this."

"I'm sorry I wasn't here." I press into her, burying my face in her neck. "How did she touch you?" I ask softly, wanting to know and not know at the same time.

"She didn't." She runs her hand through my hair. "I was behind her."

"But she didn't touch you?"

She shakes her head.

"Is it unfair for me to say that I don't like the idea of anyone else at these things touching you?" I ask.

She kisses my temple in a sweet gesture and shakes her head again.

"Get the champagne," she says a second later.

"The champagne?" I ask, lifting up.

"I want you to lick it off me," she says.

I stand quickly, still wearing that strap-on I plan to use again later.

"Where should I lick it from?" I ask after grabbing the bottle.

"Dealer's choice."

She spreads her legs for me, and I make her come with my mouth, tasting the champagne from her belly button, her lips, her clit, and her back when it pools in the dimple above her ass. Later, I fuck her on the bed while I wear nipple clamps for her. The pain is eased when she sucks them after and makes me come again with her mouth. We take a break, but surprisingly, we don't say much. I follow her to the balcony that overlooks the backyard, and wrap a sheet around her, standing behind her and liking this position I now find familiar.

"You're still wearing it," she says.

"I am," I say. "Problem?" I ask, moving my hips forward a bit, bringing the toy between her legs.

"I don't think I can go again," she says. "I've never come so much in my life."

"Are you sure?" I ask, sliding my hand down to where the toy is, grazing her inner thigh.

We both look down at the women below. There are two women in the pool, at least making out if not doing more underneath the water. There are also two women on an outdoor chaise.

"She's sitting on her face," I whisper in her ear.

"I know. I'm watching."

"Do you want me to do that to you?" I ask, moving the toy between her legs as she spreads them for me.

"Next time," she says.

I am so happy to hear her say those two words.

"And this time?" I ask, moving until I can push inside her and press against her.

"Oh. Again?" she asks, moving her hips back.

"Yes, again," I say, rocking into her. "And next time, too," I say.

There's a knock at the door, and it's almost four — that's our warning.

"Don't stop," she says.

"I won't," I tell her.

I grip her hips, and she watches them as I make her come one last time for tonight. It saddens me to think that, but then I remember that she said there would be a next time.

MONTH 5. PART 1. – CAN THIS GO ON

(POV Member)

I'm supposed to be on a retreat for work. It's a team-building thing, and it takes place at some corporate campsite where there will be, no doubt, trust falls and fireside chats about the important moments in our lives and how we all got here. Truthfully, I love my job. It's challenging without being overly stressful, and I get more done in a day than most people, so the fact that I often stay late is more by choice than by necessity. I could choose not to work and go the route of my mother, who has lived off of family money her entire life. She volunteers her time to various charities, which is fulfilling enough for her, but I know it wouldn't be enough for me. I still donate, and I give time when I can as well, but I need to use the strategic part of my brain at least five days a week.

I do *not* need a corporate team-building weekend, though. And I especially don't need it *this* weekend. It's the one time a month that I get to see her; think about nothing other than how good it feels to just give into my desires and let her take me away. Last time might have just been the best night of my entire life. I've never been married, and I don't have kids, so the only other best-night contenders would be graduations or award ceremonies where I took home the prize. My life is pretty boring. Well, it *was* pretty boring. Now, I have one night a month to look forward to where I now it will be anything but.

"So, you're supposed to be at a work thing this week-end?" she asks.

"Yes, a retreat," I say and sip my wine.

"Well, thank you for skipping it for me," she says, smiling across the table at me.

I didn't, I think to myself. I skipped it for *her*.

"I told them I was sick. I haven't been feeling all that well for a few days, and I think I need to get some sleep in my own bed," I lie.

"I know we've had to postpone this a few times – which is my fault – but if you're not feeling well, we can finish dinner and call it a night. We can try again another weekend," she says.

"Actually, that would be nice. Thank you," I say. "I'm sorry. I've been very busy at work, and I don't think I'm getting enough sleep. Plus, my assistant came in with a cold the other day."

"Does she have a kid?" she asks. "I swear, people with children coming in when their kids are sick is one of the main reasons the flu spreads."

I cringe internally at the comment but give her a fake smile.

"She does not. She actually tried to work from home, but we had a meeting get moved up, and she needed to be there for it. She's an MBA student I hired as my assistant while she's working and going to school simultaneously. When she graduates, the plan is that she'll get a position on our operations team. So, I have her sit in on important meetings whenever I can – not to take notes, but to learn. It's my fault she had to come in," I tell her.

That's all true – my assistant *did* come in not feeling well – but I'm feeling fine. My mother has been trying to set me up on a date with this woman for six months. We were supposed to go out right away, but she had some urgent business in China. We've tried again and again, and there's always something; either she can't make it, or I can't. She's attractive, and I can see myself wanting to sleep with her more to see if it would be any good. She seems like a Type A, corporate lawyer with a bug up her ass that might be good in bed, but I can't get beyond this stagnant conversation.

She talks about her work, which is boring, as I'm sure mine is to her as well, and she talks about how she doesn't want to get married or have kids. In fact, she's said that three times since dinner began, and we're just wrapping up our entrées. I get it – she's not looking for a wife or a woman who wants kids. And I'm really not looking for her, so that works for me. I finish my wine and push my plate away. She does the same.

"Maybe when you're feeling better, we can do this again," she says as she takes the check when it arrives.

There's no arguing with her about paying; I've already tried.

"Maybe," I say, knowing there won't be a next time with this woman.

"I'll take you home," she says after her credit card is returned.

Again, I don't waste my time arguing about it. She drives me home after the most boring date of my life and kisses me on the cheek while we sit in the car.

"I'd ask to come in, but you're not feeling well."

Read the room, I think to myself. I am *not* interested.

"I'll call you," I lie and climb out of the car, not wanting to give her a chance to ask me when or talk about a next time.

The only next time I'm interested in is the one I have tomorrow night.

***

When I arrive, she's already there, standing about ten feet away from the door. She smiles when I enter, and I know she's standing there for me. I don't know how I got so lucky to find her on my first time here, but I'm grateful for her; not just for how she touches me and lets me touch her, but because she's just her, and she's wonderful.

"Hi," she says as I approach.

"Hi," I reply back, feeling a little nervous, which I shouldn't be at this point.

"You didn't bring a bag this time," she remarks, noting

that I handed my purse and my jacket to the woman at the door.

This is the second women-only event, and I was happy to receive an email that they would be continuing with these for at least two more months and would then let us know if they'd go on beyond that.

"I didn't, no," I say.

"Any reason?" she asks.

"Honestly," I say as I sigh. "I planned on packing today, but I ended up not having the time. I was actually supposed to be at a work retreat this weekend, but I skipped it. Everyone else is there, though, which means no one is around to respond to urgent emails. So, I had to take a few calls today, and by the time I got done, it was time to go already. I didn't even have time to put on the new dress I bought and the lingerie I picked out for tonight."

She takes my hand and says, "You look perfect. You don't need fancy lingerie to turn me on, you know? You do that just fine on your own."

"I do?" I say, knowing the answer.

"Yes."

"Do they make you wear these suits?" I ask, tugging on her lapel with my free hand.

"No," she says. "Why? Do you not like them?"

"Oh, I do. You're sexy in them. But if you don't have to wear this, why do you?"

"I thought I should dress up for these things, and I'm not really much of a dress girl."

"You should be comfortable. What do you normally wear?" I ask.

"T-shirts, jeans," she says.

"Wear that next time," I say, hoping there *is* a next time.

"Jeans and a t-shirt? I don't think they'll even let me in if I wear that."

"Tell them a member asked for it," I say, stepping in closer to her.

"Okay. If you're sure, I–"

"I'm sure," I interrupt just as the music starts.

I look around, realizing I haven't taken in the house yet. I was told there are eight bedrooms in this one, along with a den, a pool, and a hot tub in the backyard. I don't assume we'll be lucky enough to get the master bedroom again this time, and I didn't make arrangements for us to have anything special, but I'll have to remember to do that for next time. I'm not exactly sure what *special* means, but as she pulls me in the direction of the stairs, I decide to just ask her what she wants later.

"I don't want to presume anything here…" she says as she stares down at our joined hands. "Is there anything *else* you want tonight?" She nibbles on her sexy lower lip a bit. "Any*one* else? There are more people like me here this time if you want–"

"I don't want," I say, running my hand inside her suit jacket and over her breast, which I can feel under her shirt. "When you're just wearing t-shirts with no jacket… Do you wear a bra or no?"

"I usually do, yeah."

"Bummer," I say, smirking at her.

"You prefer me without?" She smiles.

I unbutton her top button and then the second and third, sliding my hand inside and cupping her right breast.

"I prefer you without all of it," I say.

"Want to find a room?" she asks.

"Yes," I say.

"Hey, you two," a woman I recognize says.

She's with her partner from before, and meeting them like this feels kind of strange because I've seen these women naked, having sex, and they've seen me somewhat nude having sex, but I have no idea what their names are or know anything about them.

"Hi," my partner says to her. "Off to a room?"

"Yeah. You guys, too?" the other woman says.

"Yes."

"Find us later, maybe?" the first woman asks.

My partner for the evening looks over at me. I nod, but I'm non-committal. I don't know what the night has in store for us yet, and I don't want to promise we'll meet up with them if we're enjoying ourselves alone.

"We'll walk up with you," my partner says.

We walk up the stairs behind a couple of other women. I notice that the women we know – if we can even call it that – are holding hands. The other two aren't. *We* are, though. We're holding hands like we're on a double date with these two and headed into the restaurant for dinner. Our 'friends' disappear into a room, leaving the door open, and we find one two doors down. It's much smaller than our last, with only a queen bed, small television, and dresser. There's no fancy balcony overlooking the backyard, but there *is* a window that we could look out later if anyone's out there that we want to watch.

"Should I close the door?" she asks as I walk farther in.

I turn back to her and think maybe she's trying to tell me something.

"Do *you* want to keep it open?"

"It doesn't really matter what *I* want."

I walk back to her and close the door myself.

"Can it just be us tonight? Maybe another time, we can leave it open, but I just want you tonight."

"Sure," she says.

"Do you want that, though?" I ask. "I know you don't mind people watching us since we've left the door open before when we were with the other two, but it's different when it's just us, I think."

"I don't know. Maybe." She shrugs a shoulder.

I remove her jacket and say, "You can tell me. You can tell me what you want. I want to know."

"I don't exactly know what I want," she says.

I place my hands on her chest under her half-buttoned shirt and leave them there. Her arms go around my waist and rest on my lower back.

"You don't have to answer this, but maybe start with what you've done with other people that you liked."

"Other people?"

"At these things," I say.

"Other members?" she asks.

"Yeah. I don't know if I should ask about the other people you've been with outside of these things," I say, feeling my face flush. "Doesn't seem fair. But if there's something you've done, and you want to do it with me, I'd like to."

She bites her lower lip as I massage one breast and undo the buttons of her shirt with my other hand.

"You're the only person I've been with at these things outside of that woman you saw me with, but that was all I did with her."

I pull back, removing my hands, and say, "What do you mean?"

"My first night here was the same as yours," she says.

"You—"

"I only sat behind that woman and touched her breasts while the other woman did the rest. I guess they prefer each other," she says.

"I was with them," I blurt out.

"What?" she asks.

"That time you weren't here; that was who I was with."

"Both of them?"

"I was behind," I say, not sure how to explain the rest. "The member was being eaten out by the woman I guess you *work* with. I was behind her."

"Oh," she says, looking into my eyes. "You came from that?"

"She has a vibrator in the dildo," I say, swallowing.

She moves into me with her shirt completely unbuttoned and dangling, leaving me a nice view between her breasts down to her pants.

"That got you off? Or was it fucking her while she

went down on someone else?"

Her hands go to my zipper, which is on the side tonight. She pulls it down slowly.

"It was both," I admit. "And I liked it, but I missed you."

"Yeah?" she asks.

"Yes. I wanted you."

"I wanted you that first night," she says. "I saw you watching us, and I wanted to push her off me and get to you."

"You did?"

"It's why I came to find you right after."

"After she came?" I ask.

"Yes."

"I liked listening to her come. She's sexy," I say.

"She is, but not as sexy as you," she replies, slipping my dress off of me.

"You've really only ever been with me here?" I ask.

"Yes," she says.

"I like that," I reply.

"Me too," she says.

"Does it bother you that I was with them when you weren't here?"

"Yes," she says, shoving me back on the bed.

"How much?"

"Enough that I need to be inside you right now because I want you to forget about it."

I lie back and watch in awe as she pulls my bikinis off my body. She takes off her own pants and underwear, and I don't know where her shoes and socks end up, but my heels end up being tossed somewhere by her.

"Take off your bra," she says.

I do. She spreads my legs wide, stares at me like she can't wait to dominate me, and I know I'm wetter already.

"Have you been with anyone else?" she asks.

"Here?" I ask.

"No, anyone else at all," she clarifies, moving to lie on

top of me. "Who else has touched you?"

"No one," I admit. "No one else. And she didn't even touch me, baby. I've only been touched by you since–"

She enters me with two fingers.

"Oh, yes," I say, head back against the pillow.

"You're not lying to me, are you?"

"No," I say.

She rocks into me and thrusts in deeper.

"Have you touched yourself?"

"Yes," I say.

"How many times?"

"I've lost count."

"Do you think of me when you do?" she asks.

"God, all the time. I think about you all the time."

She thrusts harder, and my hands go to her ass to squeeze. She's moving faster now, and I can feel her sex coating my thigh – she's soaking wet.

"I'm going to make you come so fucking hard," she tells me.

"Yes," I say.

"All night," she adds.

"Yes," I repeat.

But, before I can come, she's coming on my leg. I help her by pressing my thigh up into her, and I open my eyes to watch her. Her eyes are slits, and her mouth is wide open. She's gasping over and over again.

"Take what you want," I tell her. "Take it all, baby."

She rocks as she thrusts, and I come right after her. She falls on top of me, and I just hold her there. My hands run up and down her back, and I kiss her temple and the top of her head.

"Have you been with anyone?" I ask after several minutes of shared silence.

She nods, and I bite my lower lip. I shouldn't have asked...

"The two women we've watched," she mumbles against my skin.

"I thought you said you haven't been with other members," I say.

"They're my friends." She lifts her head up to look at me. "I found out about this from them. It's a long story, but I've watched them before. They're married. They've never touched me before, and I've never touched them, either, but before last month's party, they told me they wanted me like that."

"Oh," I say, looking up at her. "So, you were all together?"

"Not exactly. I touched one of them, and I touched myself during. That was it. I only watched after that."

"Why?"

"I don't know," she says. "I just wasn't ready for everything that night."

"Will you be with them again?"

"Maybe," she says. "I don't want to talk about that, though. I just want to be with you tonight."

"Right," I say softly. "They're here tonight."

"Yes."

"Do you want to watch them?"

"I want *you* again. That's all I can think about right now," she says.

Her fingers are still inside me, and she begins to move them slowly.

"Roll over," I say.

She pulls out seemingly reluctantly and rolls onto her back. I straddle her, rubbing my wetness over her stomach.

"Oh, that's nice," she says, watching me.

"Yeah? Do you want more?"

"Yes."

I move until I'm hovering over her face. She tries to pull me down, but I hold myself up.

"I'm marking you tonight. You're mine," I tell her. "I don't want anyone else to touch you."

"Let me taste you," she says.

"Do you deserve to taste me?" I tease her. "You

touched someone else. You didn't like when *I* did that."

"No, I didn't. And it was quick; I only stroked her clit."

I take her hand from my hip and bring it to my lips.

"With these fingers?"

"Yes."

I suck them into my mouth, and they taste like me.

"Oh, fuck," she says.

"I want these to only taste like me."

"Yes," she says.

I move just enough to slip them back inside my body.

"Now, suck my clit like this with your fingers inside me."

She lifts her head into what must be an uncomfortable position and does just that.

"Make me come," I say.

She groans. I reach behind me with a free hand and stroke her. This gives her more access to me, and her fingers go a little deeper.

"That's good," I tell her. "Harder. Lick my pussy, baby." She does as I demand. "Now, suck me hard." She does. "Oh, fuck. Yes, don't stop. Put your fingers in deeper; I want to be full." She fills me, sucks even harder, and when she moans into my sex, I feel the vibrations. "You like this, don't you?" She groans in pleasure. "Does your clit feel good?" She moans. "Do you need to come?" I feel her nod. "Will you touch only me tonight?" She nods. "Can you promise me you won't be thinking about anyone else?" She nods again. "Then, fucking come for me."

I flick her clit back and forth how I now know she likes. She sucks harder and goes deeper, and I'm rocking my hips against her face – her chin, mainly – until she's coming beneath me. When she comes down, I sit up fully and rock until I come hard in her mouth and coat her fingers with my desire for more. I come down and move until I'm straddling her hips again, rubbing my sex against her skin.

"I don't want you to come until next month," she says.

"What?" I ask, shock clearly written all over my face.

"Tonight, you and I will do whatever we want, but I don't want you to come until the next time I touch you," she says.

"You don't want me to have an orgasm for a month?"

"Yes."

"I touch myself all the time now. I can't stop thinking about sex now that I've met you."

"You can touch yourself all you want. In fact, I like picturing you touching yourself but not letting yourself come."

"There's no way I'll be able to go that long," I tell her, still rubbing myself against her.

"Show me how you touch yourself, and I'll show you when to stop," she says.

"What about you?" I ask.

"What *about* me?" She squeezes my breasts and lifts herself up to meet one of my nipples with her mouth.

"Well, if *I* don't get to come, *you* shouldn't get to come, either," I say.

"That seems fair," she says, pulling on my nipple with her teeth.

"Oh, that feels good."

"Too bad you didn't bring those nipple clamps this time," she says.

"Next time," I say. "And are you really not going to come until next month?"

"I have a feeling I'm going to come a lot tonight."

"You will," I say.

"I'll wait with you," she tells me, kissing up to my neck.

"What about…" I begin but don't finish.

She looks up at me and says, "I only do this once a month. This isn't my day job."

I nod in response to that. She understood what I was going to ask without me having to ask it.

"Now, let's take advantage of the next few hours if we're going to go thirty days without," she suggests.

"I have an idea," I say.

"I'm listening."

"Let's go find those friends of yours," I say.

"You want to watch them?" She rubs my back while she stares up at me.

"No, I want to fuck you while *you* do."

MONTH 5. PART 2. – SHE CLAIMS ME

(POV Escort)

When she appears, I'm standing by the door. She smiles at me when she sees me, and I smile back.

"Hi," I say as she walks over to me.

"Hi," she says.

"You didn't bring a bag this time," I say, noticing her empty hands.

"I didn't, no."

"Any reason?" I ask.

"Honestly, I planned on packing today, but I ended up not having the time. I was actually supposed to be at a work retreat this weekend, but I skipped it. Everyone else is there, though, which means no one is around to respond to urgent emails. So, I had to take a few calls today, and by the time I got done, it was time to go already. I didn't even have time to put on the new dress I bought and the lingerie I picked out for tonight."

I take her hand and say, "You look perfect. You don't need fancy lingerie to turn me on, you know? You do that just fine on your own."

"I do?"

"Yes."

"Do they make you wear these suits?" she asks, tugging on my lapel.

"No. Why? Do you not like them?" I ask.

"Oh, I do. You're sexy in them. But if you don't have to wear this, why do you?"

"I thought I should dress up for these things, and I'm not really much of a dress girl."

"You should be comfortable. What do you normally wear?" she asks.

"T-shirts, jeans," I admit.

"Wear that next time," she says.

I lift an eyebrow at the mention of another next time.

"Jeans and a t-shirt? I don't think they'll even let me in if I wear that."

"Tell them a member asked for it," she says and steps closer to me.

"Okay. If you're sure, I–"

"I'm sure," she says just as the music starts.

"I don't want to presume anything here… Is there anything *else* you want tonight? Any*one* else? There are more people like me here this time if you want–"

"I don't want," she says, running her hand inside my suit jacket and over my breast. "When you're just wearing t-shirts with no jacket… Do you wear a bra or no?"

"I usually do, yeah."

"Bummer," she says.

"You prefer me without?" I smile at her.

She unbuttons my top three buttons and slides her hand inside, cupping my right breast.

"I prefer you without all of it," she says.

"Want to find a room?" I ask as my nipples grow hard.

"Yes," she says.

"Hey, you two," my friend says.

Damn it. Go away, you guys. I want *her* tonight.

"Hi. Off to a room?" I say so as not to be rude.

I love my friends; they're amazing people. I just don't want anything to get in the way of me being with her tonight.

"Yeah. You guys, too?"

"Yes."

"Find us later, maybe?" my friend asks, and I recognize her tone.

She wants *me* to find them later. If we both do, that would be fine, too, but she wants *me* there. I turn to the woman next to me since she's the paying customer. She nods a little, but it's not exactly convincing.

"We'll walk up with you," I say.

Once we're upstairs, they head into a room and leave the door open, as always. We find an open room down the hall that's smaller than the master we had last time, but I don't need much space to make her come.

"Should I close the door?" I ask as she enters the room.

"Do *you* want to keep it open?"

"It doesn't really matter what *I* want."

She walks back to me and closes the door herself.

"Can it just be us tonight? Maybe another time, we can leave it open, but I just want you tonight."

"Sure," I say.

"Do you want that, though? I know you don't mind people watching us since we've left the door open before when we were with the other two, but it's different when it's just us, I think."

"I don't know. Maybe."

She removes my jacket and says, "You can tell me. You can tell me what you want. I want to know."

"I don't exactly know what I want," I say.

She places her hands on my chest under my half-buttoned shirt and leaves them there. I put my hands on her lower back.

"You don't have to answer this, but maybe start with what you've done with other people that you liked."

"Other people?"

"At these things," she says.

"Other members?" I ask.

"Yeah. I don't know if I should ask about the other people you've been with outside of these things. Doesn't seem fair. But if there's something you've done, and you want to do it with me, I'd like to."

I bite my lower lip as she massages one breast and undoes the buttons of my shirt with her other hand. I love her hands on my breasts. Sometimes, I think I might come just from her touching me there.

"You're the only person I've been with at these things outside of that woman you saw me with, but that was all I did with her," I admit.

She pulls back, removing her hands, and says, "What do you mean?"

"My first night here was the same as yours," I say.

"You–"

"I only sat behind that woman and touched her breasts while the other woman did the rest. I guess they prefer each other," I tell her.

"I was with them," she says.

"What?" I ask.

"That time you weren't here; that was who I was with."

"Both of them?" I ask, feeling jealousy pour out of me.

"I was behind. The member was being eaten out by the woman I guess you *work* with. I was behind her."

"Oh." I say, remembering what she told me last time we were together. "You came from that?"

"She has a vibrator in the dildo," she replies.

I move into her. I need her now. I need to touch her over and over until she no longer even remembers coming from fucking someone else.

"That got you off? Or was it fucking her while she went down on someone else?"

I pull her zipper down slowly, waiting for a response.

"It was both. And I liked it, but I missed you."

"Yeah?"

"Yes. I wanted you."

"I wanted you that first night," I say. "I saw you watching us, and I wanted to push her off me and get to you."

"You did?"

"It's why I came to find you right after."

"After she came?" she asks.

"Yes."

"I liked listening to her come. She's sexy," she says.

"She is, but not as sexy as you," I reply and slip that dress off her body.

"You've really only ever been with me here?"

"Yes," I reply.

"I like that," she says, smirking at me.

"Me too," I reply.

"Does it bother you that I was with them when you weren't here?"

"Yes," I reply and shove her back on the bed.

"How much?" she asks.

"Enough that I need to be inside you right now because I want you to forget about it."

I take my clothes off and remove her underwear quickly.

"Take off your bra," I order.

She does and spreads her legs wide.

"Have you been with anyone else?" I ask.

"Here?"

"No, anyone else at all," I say and move on top of her. "Who else has touched you?"

"No one. No one else. And she didn't even touch me, baby. I've only been touched by you since–"

I push two fingers inside her. I need her to remember what I feel like.

"Oh, yes," she says.

"You're not lying to me, are you?"

"No," she says.

I start rocking into her and thrust inside her, feeling her tight warmth and loving it.

"Have you touched yourself?" I ask.

"Yes."

"How many times?"

"I've lost count."

"Do you think of me when you do?" I ask.

"God, all the time. I think about you all the time."

I push in harder, and she puts her hands on my ass. I move faster. My pussy is rubbing against her thigh, and I know it's enough to make me come.

"I'm going to make you come so fucking hard," I tell her.

"Yes."

"All night," I add.

"Yes."

It's all too fast. I'm thrusting and rocking into her, but I come first. Just being inside her this way makes me want to come. I'm sure I'm grunting as I rub over her. She presses her leg up into me to help me ride it out, and I keep coming.

"Take what you want. Take it all, baby."

Jesus, that does it. I'm still coming. It's so good, but I remember I'm still inside her. I return my focus to my hand and push inside, fucking her hard until she's finally coming beneath me. Her teeth bite down on my shoulder, and I can almost feel it in my clit. It's so fucking good that when she's done coming, I fall on top of her. I need a minute to recover. She just holds me and kisses my temple and my head. This part is nice, too.

"Have you been with anyone?" she asks after several minutes of silence.

I nod reluctantly.

"The two women we've watched," I say against her neck.

"I thought you said you haven't been with other members."

"They're my friends." I lift up to look at her. "I found out about this from them. It's a long story, but I've watched them before. They're married. They've never touched me before, and I've never touched them, either, but before last month's party, they told me they wanted me like that."

"Oh. So, you were all together?"

"Not exactly. I touched one of them, and I touched myself during. That was it. I only watched after that."

"Why?"

"I don't know. I just wasn't ready for everything that night."

"Will you be with them again?"

"Maybe. I don't want to talk about that, though. I just want to be with you tonight."

The truth is that I *don't* know. It's not like this thing is real. I don't exactly have any other prospects for sex, and I know I love my friends. I know they're interested in us taking that step.

"Right. They're here tonight."

"Yes."

"Do you want to watch them?" she asks.

"I want *you* again. That's all I can think about right now," I say.

I start moving my fingers that are still inside her again.

"Roll over," she says.

I obey and roll onto my back, wanting to know what she has planned. She straddles me and begins to rub herself all over my stomach.

"Oh, that's nice," I tell her as I watch.

"Yeah? Do you want more?"

"Yes."

Oh, fuck – she's moving over my face. I try to pull her down because I need her in my mouth, and she's resisting.

"I'm marking you tonight. You're mine. I don't want anyone else to touch you," she tells me.

"Let me taste you," I request.

"Do you deserve to taste me? You touched someone else. You didn't like when *I* did that."

"No, I didn't. And it was quick; I only stroked her clit."

She takes my hand off of her hip and moves my fingers to her mouth.

"With these fingers?"

"Yes."

She sucks them into her mouth.

"Oh, fuck," I say.

"I want these to only taste like me."

"Yes," I agree.

She shifts and puts my fingers at her entrance. I push them inside.

"Now, suck my clit like this with your fingers inside me."

I bend my head to get the access I need and suck.

"Make me come," she says.

I groan. Then, she's leaning back, and I can go deeper. She touches my clit, and fuck, this is good.

"That's good," she says what I'm thinking. "Harder. Lick my pussy, baby. Now, suck me hard. Oh, fuck. Yes, don't stop. Put your fingers in deeper; I want to be full."

I do everything she says just as she says it. I fill her up and suck as hard as I can. At some point, I can't help myself and moan; it's all so fucking sexy.

"You like this, don't you?" she asks me. "Does your clit feel good?"

I moan again.

"Do you need to come?"

I nod.

"Will you touch only me tonight?"

I nod.

"Can you promise me you won't be thinking about anyone else?"

I nod again.

"Then, fucking come for me."

She flicks my clit back and forth. I suck harder and go deeper. Her hips are rocking against my face, and I can hardly breathe, but I've never been happier. Then, I come. I moan and grunt my orgasm into her pussy. When I come down, she sits up and takes what she wants from me until she comes, too. She slows her rocking, and I pull out my fingers to fresh wetness, which makes me groan again. This is how much she wants me. She straddles my hips again and continues to rub against my body.

"I don't want you to come until next month," I say.

"What?" she says.

"Tonight, you and I will do whatever we want, but I don't want you to come until the next time I touch you," I say.

"You don't want me to have an orgasm for a month?"

"Yes."

"I touch myself all the time now. I can't stop thinking about sex now that I've met you."

"You can touch yourself all you want. In fact, I like picturing you touching yourself but not letting yourself come."

"There's no way I'll be able to go that long," she says, still rubbing against me.

"Show me how you touch yourself, and I'll show you when to stop."

"What about you?" she asks.

"What *about* me?" I squeeze her breasts and lift up to meet one of her nipples with my mouth.

"Well, if *I* don't get to some, *you* shouldn't get to come, either," she says.

"That seems fair." I pull on her nipple with my teeth.

"Oh, that feels good."

"Too bad you didn't bring those nipple clamps this time," I say, remembering how good they felt last time.

"Next time. And are you really not going to come until next month?"

"I have a feeling I'm going to come a lot tonight."

"You will," she says.

"I'll wait with you," I tell her and kiss up to her neck.

"What about…"

I know what she's thinking. I sigh against her breast and look up at her.

"I only do this once a month. This isn't my day job."

She nods.

"Now, let's take advantage of the next few hours if we're going to go thirty days without."

"I have an idea," she says.

"I'm listening."

"Let's go find those friends of yours."

"You want to watch them?" I rub her back while I look at her.

"No, I want to fuck you while *you* do."

***

"You decided to join us," one of the women says as we walk in.

She closes the door behind us and is on me instantly. We dressed haphazardly to walk down the hall, but she's got my shirt and pants back on the floor in no time. We're kissing as I get her dress off of her, and then she's shoving me back on the bed. My friends are on the other side. They're watching as this woman tops me, takes a second to look over at them as if she's telling them something without actually saying anything, and then she's moving down my body.

"Oh, God," I say when she sucks my clit into her mouth.

"Fuck," I hear my friend say. "Baby…"

"Yes," my other friend says.

I hear movements, so I turn my head to see one of them lying behind the other now, watching us. A hand moves around to start stroking. Hips are moving. I look down at my friend's pussy as fingers move in and out of folds. I can see how wet she is for her wife. Then, I can't see much of anything because I'm closing my eyes to the sensation of *her* lips on my clit. Her teeth nip at it as she reaches up and squeezes my nipples.

"Fuck, yes," I tell her, pushing her head down into me. "Fuck, make me come."

I turn my head again and watch as my friends shift once more. One of them moves down the bed and takes her wife into her mouth. I review the scene in front of me: two beautiful women going down on two other women.

"This is so fucking good," my friend says, looking over

at me as her wife sucks on her clit.

"God, I'm–"

"Not yet," my partner says, lifting herself up.

"Wait, baby. I need your–" I'm about to say mouth when her fingers push deep inside me, and she climbs on top of me. "Yes."

"Tell me," she says. "Tell me what you want."

"Fuck me, baby. Fuck me hard."

And she does. She fucks me like this. Then, she turns me over, gets me on all fours, and fucks me like that, too. She bites on my ass a little before I come and fall onto the bed. Then, she rubs her wet pussy over my ass cheek until she comes. My friends stop to watch us before they stroke each other at the same time and come again.

Before I can say that I need a break, I'm being pulled up and out of bed. She's dressing me because I can't seem to focus on dressing myself. Then, as soon as she's done putting her dress back on, without a word, she's walking me back to the room we left, which is still available. When we enter, she strips us of our clothes, and we get into bed. We're still breathing hard when she presses her head to my chest and her arm over my waist.

"This is nice," I say after a long time.

"Yes, it is," she replies.

Then, there's a knock at the door.

"Almost time," I say.

"Yeah," she says, sounding disappointed.

"Let's just stay like this until we have to go," I say.

"I'd like that."

MONTH 6. PART 1. – MAKING DO

(POV Member)

I find out that she's not going to be there. I read the email letting me know that my request to have a room reserved would either be refunded, or I could transfer the request to another escort.

Another escort? Right, I think. I don't want another one. I want *her*. She told me she'd be here. I've gone an entire month without even touching myself because I know that if I do, I'll have to come. It's been hard not being able to get myself off thinking about her doing the same. That's especially true given the fact that we had amazing sex last time. Well, we've had amazing sex every time, but last time was really fucking hot. I wanted them to know that she was mine – at least for that night, she was mine, and they couldn't have her. When we got back to the room, it was too late to do anything else, but she held me, and I held on to her. That felt just as good as having endless orgasms with her, which tells me something.

Maybe I should go without her. Maybe I *should* find another escort to share that room with, after all. I need to stop associating her with these parties. She won't always be there, and she won't always be mine. I was able to skip the work retreat last time, but one of these months, there will be a work event or something else that I can't get out of. I'll miss a party, and she'll be expected to get someone else off that night. It bugs me just thinking about it, but I need to just get over it already. It's going to happen, and there's nothing I can do about it. She's not really mine, and it's her job to make women come. It's as simple as that.

I cancel my reservation but keep my RVSP. I'll go and

try to meet someone new. I might not do anything, but this is what I need. Maybe I'll just walk around for a bit to see if anyone else strikes my fancy. Maybe I'll just watch and go back home. I don't know yet, but I remember that I'm not supposed to come unless she's the one touching me, and I think she can't possibly mean that I have to wait another month now. Surely, *she's* come either by her own touch or by someone else's. Her friends want to fuck her and have her fuck them. I'm sure they've already done that, and I'm the idiot missing out on all the orgasms I *could* be having.

After a month, I'm so desperate and hard-up, I'm even contemplating calling my Type A date and just getting her off to see what it's like – if she would be less of Type A in the bedroom than she's in the boardroom. It's not worth the complication, though, and even if I let her touch me, I have a strange feeling she won't be able to get me there.

She's called three times since our first date weeks ago now. I didn't answer the first time, but I texted her the second. I'm not a bitch. I told her I was busy and that I'd get back to her. A week later, she called again, so this time, I actually picked up and let her down as easily as I could. I called my mother after that and broke the news that just because the woman is a lesbian, doesn't mean we're going to hit it off. When I told her that the woman didn't want kids, though, my mom agreed that this was a good decision on my part – my mother wants grandkids.

It's the night of the party now, and I'm actually kind of angry with *her*. I hate feeling this way, but I can't exactly help it – I'm upset. We made a plan, and I was looking forward to it. I want her to touch me. I need to come, but it's more than that. I just want to see her. I like her smile and her laugh. I like how she holds me from behind. I like how it felt, lying in bed with her, with her arm around me and my head on her chest. I could feel her heart beating as I stroked her stomach with my fingertips. It felt good, but it also felt right, which is wrong. I shake my head when I enter the house. It's wrong. Stop thinking about her. She's not going to be here. Just get in, have some fun, and go home. She won't know anyway, and she probably doesn't even care because she's had ten orgasms this week or something.

I'm a little later than I'd planned. There's a pro sporting event of some kind in town, and the game must have just ended because traffic to get to this side of town was bad, making me twenty minutes late and without a partner and a room when I arrive. As I stand by the bar, sipping on my cocktail, I think about just going home after the traffic dies down because I'm standing here alone like an idiot. Then, I see the escort I was with last time approach me.

"Well, hello," she says.

"Hi," I reply.

"We have a room upstairs. Would you like to join us if you're not occupied?" she asks.

"You and…"

"You know who," she states.

"Are you sure? You guys seemed pretty content after I left last time."

"Oh, we were," she tells me. "But we liked you there, too." She leans over the bar and orders two drinks. "She's getting ready for me. Sometimes, she likes to pretend like I'm her girlfriend, walking in on her getting off, and I punish her by fucking her. It's pretty fun."

"You guys are always together at these things, huh?" I ask, sipping on my strong drink.

"Yeah. She started coming here about two years ago, and that's about when I first started. I was only doing this to pay off my student loans from grad school."

"Was?" I ask.

"I paid those off a while ago. Now, I just come here for her. I get paid to have mind-blowing sex with a gorgeous woman." She winks. "It's pretty awesome. Plus, now I can finish my Ph. D without having to have a full-time job. I do this once a month and school the rest of the time."

"You just come here for her? What about if someone else wants you?"

"She has dibs; that's how it works. She told me that if I spotted you, though, I should ask if you wanted to join us. She wasn't sure you'd be free since you usually aren't."

"Oh, I am tonight," I say before I think it through.

"Want to watch me go down on her?" she asks. "She's so fucking sexy sometimes."

"Can I ask you a question?" I set my empty glass on the bar as her drinks are placed there by the bartender.

"You've fucked me before – I think you can ask me a question," she says, taking a sip of her drink.

"Do you *like* her?"

"Like her? Yes. Why?"

"No, I mean... Is it more than just sex for you?"

"Oh," she says, looks around, and takes a drink to stall. "Why do you ask?"

"Because when we... finished last time, you two just kind of went all-in with each other, and you seem more intimate than most of the people I've watched here."

"Well, we've been doing this for two years, so we know each other pretty well," the escort says.

"You do? Do you talk?"

"Of course, we talk," she says, laughing a little.

"About more than just sex?"

"Yes. I know a lot about her, actually. She knows a lot about me, too."

"But it's just sex?"

"She's married," she tells me. "To a man. I'm the only woman she's ever been with."

"Really?"

"Yeah," she replies. "I kind of like that, though. Is that weird?"

"No, I don't think so."

"I mean, we've been with other women at these things, but only when we're together. I like how free she is with what she wants. It drives me crazy."

"But you're not into her for real?"

She sighs and says, "Look... Do you want to come up

with us or not? She's probably already about to come, and I want to make sure I'm either there to see it, or I'm there to stop it so *I* can make her come instead."

"Sure. What the hell?" I say.

I have nothing else to do, and I wouldn't mind watching them again. I just have this feeling that there's more to them than just sex. The way this woman is dodging my questions tells me I'm onto something, so I follow her up the stairs and into the room.

"What the hell are you doing?" she says to the naked woman on the bed who has her legs spread wide open.

The member is moving a dildo in and out with her hand while she has a vibrator pressed to her clit.

"Oh, shit," she says, playing the game, and pulls both toys away. "I didn't know you'd be home this early."

"Well, I am," the escort says. "And I brought a guest. How do you think this makes me look?" She places the glasses on the dresser. "She's going to think I don't know how to take care of you. Is that what you want?"

"No," the member says, smirking at her.

"What am I going to do with you?" the escort says.

"What do you *want* to do with me?" the woman asks.

"I want you to watch me get off," the escort says. "And you can't touch yourself."

"But I'm already so close…" the member replies, touching her fingers to her sex. "Hello, by the way." She looks past her escort and makes eye contact with me. "What would *you* like to do tonight?"

"Watch," I state.

"You don't want her to touch you? She's really good."

The escort walks back to me and places her hand on my hip.

"Let me take care of you," she says softly. "I want to."

I take a step back and say, "I'd rather just watch tonight."

She lifts her dress off, and she *is* beautiful. She's wearing an evergreen-colored thong and no bra.

"Baby, you watch me, but don't touch," she says, turning back around to kneel on the bed in front of her partner.

I move to the bed and lie down next to the other member to watch. The escort's hand slowly moves between her own breasts and down to her belly button.

"You're so fucking sexy," the member says with her hands at her sides.

"What do you want to do to me?" her partner asks as she cups and massages her own breasts.

"I want you to sit on my face while she watches me make you come."

"Oh, that sounds nice. But why would I give you what you want? You couldn't wait for me to come home after a long day at work." The escort moves her hips, rolling them around as her hands continue to massage and play with her breasts. "I work hard for us, and you stay at home all day, touching yourself."

"No, baby. I don't. I promise, it was just this time."

"I was going to take you to a nice dinner at *Templeton's*."

"My favorite," the member says.

The escort's hand slips to her sex over her thong, and she begins to rub herself.

"I know. I was going to order that wine you like, and we'd get the filet and that cheesecake you love so much. I planned on us bringing it home so that I could eat it off your body before I take care of you, and you've already taken care of yourself." She cups herself hard and moans.

I swallow. My head is on a swivel. For a second, I return my attention to the woman lying down next to me, who licks her lips at the sight of her partner slipping her hand beneath the thong now, stroking her clit.

"I didn't. I promise, I didn't come, baby. I want you to make me," she says.

"Suck on my nipples," the escort says.

"Yes," the woman says, sits up, and greedily takes a nipple into her mouth.

Then, I notice one of her hands is on my bare calf, sliding up to my knee before it just rests there. It's not an unwelcome touch, and she's not asking for more, so I let it stay there while I lift my dress enough to place my own hand on my inner thigh and start stroking the soft skin there.

"The other one now, baby," the escort says, moving the woman's head to her other breast and holding it there. She makes eye contact with me and says, "Her mouth is remarkable. She can make me come like this if she tries."

I'm touching higher up on my inner thigh now.

"Try, my love," she says to the woman.

The woman groans and sucks harder while the escort continues stroking her own clit. She called the woman 'her love.' She knows her favorite restaurant and wine. I don't even know my usual partner's name. The escort removes her hand from her own panties and places it on her lover's breast instead as the woman continues to suck.

"Oh, God," the escort gasps out. "Yes, just like that, baby. Make me come."

And she does. The escort comes without touching herself; she comes just with this woman's lips around her nipple. My hand moves even higher, and I'm dangerously close to touching myself. The escort pushes her partner flat onto the bed, and I watch as she hovers over the woman and kisses her deeply. Her partner's arms are around her neck. She's holding the escort on top of herself, wanting to kiss her like this – like it matters. The escort's hips start rolling down into her, and they forget I'm here again.

I can't look away. I'm a foot apart from them, and they've completely forgotten about that, but I can't look away from them. I want to come so badly. I want one of them to touch me. I want to touch them. Hell, I just want an orgasm.

I watch the escort's ass as she rolls down into her lover while continuing to kiss her. Her hand disappears between them, and I know she's inside her partner now. She makes her come once this way. Then, she lowers her mouth and takes her that way.

"Oh, I've missed you," the member says while she holds her partner's head in place with one hand and massages her own breast with the other.

I can't help it any longer – I move my hand between my legs and start stroking over my bikinis. I'm so wet that it's easy to feel through my underwear. I feel myself harden at my touch, and I bite my lower lip. I stare up at the ceiling to try to calm my need, and the women next to me aren't helping very much. The member comes hard. Her hips fly off the bed, and her partner pushes her back down. I stare at the ceiling and remove my hand. I have to stop. I stand up and look down at them.

"Sit on my face," the woman tells the escort.

The other woman moves up her body and hovers over her mouth.

"Fuck me with your tongue," the escort commands.

The woman moans and lowers her partner's body until she's sucking on her. I can't keep watching this and not come, so I turn and go. I'm standing with my back pressed to the wall when I see into the room across the hall – it's the friends. They're taking off their clothes. Maybe they were late, too. I watch as they slowly remove their clothing and climb into bed together.

"I love you," I hear one of them say.

"I love you, too," the other one replies.

I watch them make love, and it's beautiful. There's passion there that comes not from lust but from love. It's so sweet, I almost look away because it should be private, but they like it when people watch, so I stand there and do just that until they finish. When the one on top shifts, she notices me standing there just outside the door.

"You can come in," she says.

"I was just leaving," I reply, hooking my thumb in the direction of the stairs.

"She wanted to be here," she says.

"What?" I say.

The woman lies back, and her wife sits between her legs. They're not touching one another, but they *are* naked and pressed to one another, so I walk in slowly but don't intend to stay.

"She wanted to come tonight – she couldn't."

"Oh, okay. Thanks for letting me know," I say and turn to go.

"It's not really my place, but she had a death in the family."

"She what?" I ask, turning back around.

"I won't give you details, but she *did* tell us it was okay to let you know that she wanted to be here and that she plans on coming back next time. Someone really important to her passed away."

"Oh, my God," I say, sitting on the edge of their bed, facing away from them. "I…"

I nearly say that I should be with her right now; that I should be holding her and taking care of her, but I'm not her girlfriend. I'm someone she meets once a month for sex that I'm paying for.

"You care about her, don't you?" the other woman asks.

I turn my head to her and nod.

"We do, too," she says.

"I know. She told me you're friends."

"She'll be back next month."

"Is she okay? I mean, I know she's not. That's a stupid question. Is there anything I can–" I stop myself again. "This is strange. I know you can't tell me, and I understand, but I want to do something. I *need* to do something."

"I don't think we can tell you any more than that. We didn't discuss that with her."

I nod again and say, "Can I do *anything*? Can I send flowers or something? Shit. I don't even know her name."

"You want to send flowers?" the woman asks.

"I don't know what else I *can* do," I say.

They look at each other for a moment.

"Tell us what you want to send, and we'll take care of it," the one sitting behind the other says.

"Roses and lilies. I have cash with me. It's in my purse. Can you... I don't know. Can you put something generic on the card? I don't think I have the right to put anything more than that, but I'd like to sign it, at least."

"With your real name?"

"No, with... Can you sign it from Wall Street?" I ask.

They look at me like I'm crazy. Then, one of them nods.

MONTH 6. PART 2. – IT HAPPENS

(POV Escort)

"Are you sure?" my friend asks.

"I can't go," I say.

"But the nurse will be here."

"I know, but she's worse. The doctors are telling me I should consider hospice care," I tell her.

"Okay. Well, she comes first," my friend says.

"I don't want to miss the event. You know how much I want to go."

"To see her," she says.

"The woman that mounted and fucked you to claim you in front of us," her wife says.

I laugh a little and say, "It was kind of hot, huh?"

"Kind of? It was definitely hot," my friend says. "God, all four of us on that bed – that's something I'd like to do again."

"Me too," I admit.

"You would?" her wife asks.

"Definitely. I liked watching you guys while she was doing what she was doing."

"She was marking her territory."

I chuckle again and say, "I don't mind at all."

"Why *would* you when she does it like that?"

"So… At the risk of sounding like someone that's desperate, when, I assure you, I'm not – is there something *we* can talk about?" my friend asks.

"What do you mean?"

"Well, about the three of us," she says, pointing to me and then to her wife. "We haven't talked about that night since, and then that display at the party really got us going. Is there a chance you'd be up for us taking another stab at all three of us going upstairs one night and enjoying each other?"

"Oh," I say. "You mean tonight?"

"No, I mean any night," she replies. "We know she *claimed* you because you told her what we did, but she's not here, and it's not like she can *really* claim you. You're a free woman. We're two women who want to be with you."

"Maybe. But not for a while, okay?" I reply.

"Because of her," her wife says knowingly.

"Because of her, yeah."

This time, we don't mean the woman I meet once a month. We're referring to the one with the nurse right now, back at the house.

"We understand. Just know that the option is open," she replies and smiles at me.

"I know," I say.

"Well, do you want to stay tonight?" my friend asks. "We were thinking about opening a bottle of wine and taking our time if you're interested."

"Can I make a request?" I ask.

"Your wish," my friend says.

"One of you needs to watch me the whole time."

I get a curious expression from both of them.

"I'm not supposed to come until I do with her," I explain. "Now, it's going to be two months; and I don't know if I can watch you guys and not touch myself. That means I'm going to need one of you to stop me."

"Wait... She *told* you that you're not–"

"No, *I* told her," I interject. "I told her I didn't want her to come until I make her. I told her I wouldn't either, in solidarity. It's been a long three and a half weeks."

"She wouldn't know if you did," my friend remarks.

"I would," I say.

"Should you even watch us then?" my friend asks. "Seems like the opposite of what you should be doing."

"Probably not, but I want to, and I like the idea of getting myself there and not coming until she makes me."

"Okay. Whatever you say," my friend replies. "I'll pour the wine. You two can head upstairs. No one starts without me."

We head upstairs together, and she lies on the bed, spreading her legs for her wife, who will soon walk in the door. I notice she's not wearing panties, and I lick my lips. This is going to be very difficult. When my friend arrives, she's carrying a tray with three empty glasses and a bottle of red on it.

"Oh, fuck. I said slow, baby," she says, looking at her wife and placing the tray on the dresser.

I sit in the chair in the corner of the room and wait.

"I know, but I want one fast. Then, we can go slow. I need you inside me," she says, sliding her fingers through her own folds, and I can tell that she's already wet.

"Hard or soft?" my friend asks.

"Soft, my love," she replies.

I look at my friend, who is cupping whatever she's packing in her pants. I hadn't even noticed she was wearing anything, but apparently, she's had that on since before I arrived. I smirk as I keep my hands at my sides, resisting the urge to get started already.

"I don't think we're going to be able to keep an eye on you if you're over there while we do this. Come onto the bed," my friend says as she unzips her jeans.

"I will. I just want to watch from here first. I won't come," I say.

"Okay."

She unbuttons her jeans and pulls out the dildo, which is purple tonight. It must be new; I've never seen it before. She strokes herself as her wife watches and strokes between her own legs.

"Take off your shirt and bra, but leave your skirt on, baby," she tells her.

Her wife complies until she's topless but still wearing the skirt that's pushed up around her waist.

"Play with your nipple."

She does, and I watch. This is going to be harder than I thought.

"Now, tell me what you want," my friend says as she takes a step toward the bed.

"I want you to fuck me slow and deep until I come," her wife says.

I watch as my friend starts stroking her dildo faster, as if she can feel it.

"And what will you do for me?" she asks.

"Suck you while you touch yourself," she replies.

"Fuck, babe," she says, kneeling on the bed now, still wearing her jeans.

She pulls off her shirt, though, and she's not wearing a bra.

"Suck it now," she says. "And then again, when it tastes like you."

I watch as my friend's wife sits up and takes the toy into her mouth. She grips my friend's ass and sucks on the toy. My friend's hand goes inside the shorts she's wearing, and she starts touching herself. Her head rolls back. Her eyes are now closed. I reach for the button of my jeans and stop myself. My friend presses her free hand to the back of her wife's head and silently asks her to stay there. She moans, and her wife moans as well.

"I don't want to come yet," she says. "But you feel so good, baby."

The woman stops sucking. She lies back down, spreads her legs, and points to her sex.

"Fuck me. Come inside me," she says.

My friend is on top of her now. She pushes at the woman's skirt, turns to look back at me, and smirks. Then, she pushes inside her.

"Yes," her wife says when she's all the way in.

"My clit's so hard, babe," my friend says as she begins to thrust. "I'll come."

"Slow, baby," the woman replies, moving her hands inside her partner's jeans, cupping her ass. "But deep."

My hand moves back to my button, and I undo it, leaving the zipper alone for now. I watch as they move slowly together, and it's so fucking hot. I'm ruining my underwear right now and know it wouldn't take more than a few strokes to make me come, so I have to wait if I'm going to touch myself and pull away just before I do. The moaning starts in earnest.

"Did you put the vibrator in?"

"No, I–" She stops talking, and her hips move a little faster.

"Yeah? Are you already there?" her wife asks, spreading her legs wider.

"Yes," she says. "Fuck, you're so good."

"Suck on my nipple, baby."

My friend leans down, and her wife holds her breast for her as she begins to suck. I unzip my jeans and wait.

"Oh, yes," she says. "Suck, baby. Yes, that's so good. I'm so full. I'm ready. Will you do it for me, baby? Just a little."

"Yes," the woman replies, lifting her lips from the nipple before lowering them back to the other one.

I watch as the woman on the bottom lifts her hips but a little. My friend's hand disappears under her body.

"Oh, fuck! Yes, that's so good. Baby, I'm coming," she says a second later.

"Me too. Oh, God," my friend says.

It's then that I realize that she likely has her finger inside her, too. She's got a finger in her ass, a dildo inside her, and is sucking on her nipple.

"Fuck me," I whisper to myself.

"We want to!" my friend yells as she comes, rocking erratically into her wife.

I laugh a little and stand up. I move to the bed and lie down beside them. I'm on my side, watching up-close now as they come down. I want to reach out and touch them, but I know that if I start that tonight, I'll come, and I promised *her* I wouldn't until I see her. So, I wait. My friend pulls out and kneels. My other friend sits up, pulls her wife to her mouth, and sucks her own juices off the toy that was just inside her. My friend has her hand inside her shorts now. Her eyes are closed again. Her head is back, and her hand is back on her wife's head, pressing the woman into her, begging her to continue.

I sit up and get closer. I watch the toy disappear into her mouth and then emerge a little. I'm kneeling next to them now, and a hand goes to my hip as the woman sucks on her wife. She doesn't do anything, but it makes me feel like I have to touch myself now. When her hand moves away to grip her wife's hips, I slip my own hand inside my underwear.

"Fuck, I can't," I say when I realize how close I am.

"Yes, you can," my friend says. "Touch yourself."

"I'll come," I tell her as I test that theory with a hesitant stroke.

"No, you won't. I'm going to, though," she says. "Fuck, baby. That's so sexy," she says, looking down at her wife. "Don't stop, and I'll come."

Her wife moans, and I allow my clit another stroke.

"God, that's good," I say.

"Yes, it is," my friend says. "Yes, yes, yes." Her hips buck forward, and she comes. "Fuck, yes."

I remove my hand just as I'm about to come myself.

"Jesus fucking Christ," I say.

When my friend comes down, she lies on top of her wife, breathing hard. I lie next to them, my jeans still undone.

"She wouldn't know," my friend says to me.

"I would," I say.

"She pays you for sex. It doesn't mean she owns you," she replies.

"It's my choice, not hers."

"That was before you knew you wouldn't see her for two months. You're really not going to allow yourself to come until then?"

"I'm sure going to try," I say.

***

"That's two events you'll be missing out of six."

"I know," I say.

"You're on contract for the full year, and you're only allowed to miss two. Are you sure?"

"I don't really have a choice. I have to take care of something," I say.

"If you miss any more, your contract for this year is terminated, and you'll have to wait a year after that before you can reapply."

"I know," I tell her.

"Okay… And, by the way, your regular requested special accommodations. We'll have to tell her that you won't be able to make it."

"She did?" I ask, surprised.

"Yes. She requested a room, at least."

"I didn't know."

"How *would* you?" she asks.

"Right," I say. "Well, will she get her money back?"

"We'll offer that or the room with another escort."

I bite my lower lip.

"Of course," I say.

"We'll see you next month," she replies.

An hour later, I'm upstairs with her. We're watching some game show she likes when I ask her what her guess to the question would be. I don't get a response, so I turn to her. Her eyes are closed, and I lean over – she's not breathing.

***

It's two weeks later, and she's gone. The last three years of my life – all the hospital visits, the tests, the hair falling out, the vomiting, the bathing and feeding her – is over. She's gone, and I'd take her back if it meant another fifty years of having to take care of her. Of course, I know that's selfish of me because she was in so much pain, but she's the only parent I've ever known, and it shouldn't have ended this way. She was too young to go, completely healthy before the cancer came. She beat it once, but it came back, and I hate it. I fucking hate cancer.

"Why don't you stay with us for a while," my friend says at the funeral. "We have the guest room. We've made it up for you."

"I have to clean up her house. It's a mess still from when the paramedics came. I haven't even been in there since we left for the hospital."

"Let us take care of that and stay with us," she says.

"Maybe, but not tonight. I should be home."

"Sweetie, you shouldn't be alone."

I walk over to where there are several bouquets of beautiful flowers. There's one from an old friend of my aunt's, another from someone she used to work with, and I nearly break down when I see one from her favorite nurse. Then, I'm confused because I see a massive bouquet of lilies and roses with a card attached that just reads, *'My deepest condolences.'* It's not the message that sticks out; it's the name provided on the card – it says they're from *Wall Street.*

MONTH 7. PART 1. – THE NIGHT IT CHANGED

(POV Member)

I spot the two women over by the bar. The escort has her hand in the member's. If I didn't know any better, I'd think they were a couple at a cocktail party. I *do* know better, though, and I know one of them is married to a man, and the other is being paid to have sex with her. I really don't know why I'm so fascinated by these two, but I find myself wanting to see them here every time I come. I watch as the member removes her hand from the other woman's and, instead, wraps it around her waist and rests her head on the woman's shoulder. The escort's now-free hand moves to the member's ass, and she gives it a little squeeze. I smirk at the exchange while finding it kind of cute.

"Well, hello."

I turn around and see my *kind of* friends. They're also standing there holding hands, but it makes sense for *them* to do it because they're a married couple that attends these things to liven up their sex life.

"Hi," I reply.

"Are you in line for a drink?" one of them asks.

"Oh, no," I say, not really sure why I'm standing here at all.

"Can we–"

"Oh, sure. Yeah," I say as I move out of their way.

"Thanks," the other one says.

"No problem," I say, certain I'm being very awkward right now for whatever reason.

"So, are you looking for someone new?" one of them asks.

"What?"

"I saw you checking out those two," she says, pointing to the two women who were now walking away from the bar.

"Oh, I was just looking," I say.

"But not touching?" the other asks.

"What?" I ask.

"They have people join them sometimes. You're not interested?"

"I'm not here for them," I say. "I think you know that."

"She's upstairs," one of them tells me. "Waiting for you."

"She's here?"

"Yes. She's in a room with the door closed; third one on the left."

"Thank you," I say.

They nod in unison, and I turn to leave. It's been two months since I've seen *her*, and while I'd love for us to finally get to touch one another again, I need to know she's okay first. I hated only sending her flowers, and I'm still not sure if signing them with my safe word was the right call. She'd just lost someone important to her, and I'm writing something like that, but I needed her to know that they were from me. Maybe that was wrong, too. I don't know. I just hope she doesn't hate me. More than anything, I just want her to be okay. I breeze past a couple of women fucking against a wall, and I don't even stop to take in the sexy sight. I'm happy that the women-only event is going to continue because I do like the fact that it's just us gals, so to speak. I arrive at the third door, double-checking that I'm at the right one, and knock twice and then again. I hope she remembers our secret knock. The door opens, and there she is.

"Hi, baby," I say softly.

"Hi," she says, smiling warmly at me.

I walk into her arms and pull her in for a hug. I hear the door close behind me, but I don't pull away to look.

"Thank you for the flowers," she says.

"You don't have to thank me," I reply, breathing her in.

"You didn't have to," she says, squeezing me tighter.

"I wanted to. I didn't know what else to do. Your friends wouldn't tell me much. I understand why. I just wanted to do something."

She kisses my neck and pulls out of the hug.

"Thanks," she says, looking at the floor.

"I don't know what I'm allowed to ask or if I'm allowed to ask anything."

"We're not really here to talk," she says, placing her hands on my hips.

"But we *can*," I say.

"It's been two months," she says. "I want to touch you."

She pulls me flush against her, and my body hums with anticipation. I want her, too, but something feels off.

"I want to touch you, too," I say. "But we don't have to tonight. We–"

"You came here for sex." She pulls back again.

"I came here for you. I always come here for *you*," I tell her.

"Why are you complicating things right now? I'm an escort. You pay me to–"

"Hey," I say softly, taking her hands in mine. "If I wanted just sex with anyone, I'd be in a room with someone else or downstairs in the living room right now – I'm in here with you."

"Well, I'm not exactly the life of the party tonight. It's been two months. You don't just want to fuck?"

I stand there, holding her hands, and say, "Why did you come here tonight?"

"I just told you. I–"

"No, be honest with me. Why did you come here?"

"Because I need money," she says.

"Oh," I say, letting go of her hands.

I should have expected that answer. Still, I'm more than disappointed and also a little embarrassed that I hoped for something more.

"And because I wanted to see you," she adds a long moment later.

I don't say anything.

"I've missed you," she tells me.

"I've missed you, too," I say, smiling a little.

"And I've missed touching you," she says, cupping my cheek with her soft hand.

"I've missed that, too," I reply, leaning into that touch.

"But it's more than that," she says, stepping in closer.

"Tell me." I kiss the inside of her palm.

"I just..."

I lean in and give her a quick kiss, pulling away before either of us has the chance to take it further.

"Come here," I say.

I take her hand again and walk us to the bed. I'm wearing a dress, as per usual, but she's wearing a pair of jeans and a t-shirt just like I asked. She looks adorable and sexy at the same time, and I notice that I can see her nipples through the light-green shirt, which means she decided not to wear a bra with that shirt after all. I swallow at how sexy that is and sit her down on the bed.

"I want to hold you. Is that okay?" I ask.

"But we–"

"I'm not asking as a member who expects something from you. I'm asking as just plain old me. Can I just hold you for a while?"

"Okay," she says.

"Just..." I look down at my tight dress and realize I might not have worn the right thing for this particular night.

I unzip it while she watches. Then, I let it fall to the floor and step out of it along with my heels.

"Oh, wow," she says, placing her hands on my hips

and pulling me closer to the bed. "You're so beautiful."

"I'm only taking it off so I can get behind you and hold you," I say, smiling down at her.

"But… you're wearing red. You know how much I love red," she says, kissing my stomach, and I have to close my eyes because it's been so long.

"I'll come if you keep touching me," I say.

"Good," she says. "I want you to."

"Not yet, baby," I say, moving until I'm sitting back against the pillows, holding my arms out for her.

She looks at my spread legs and the patch of hair between my thighs, licks her lips, and it takes everything in me not to let her do whatever she wants.

"Lie with me," I say.

She stares a moment longer before she stands up and pulls off her jeans and shoes.

"Oh, hell," I say when she also pulls off her shirt, revealing her bare breasts. "You're killing me right now."

"You did it first," she says.

Then, she climbs into bed next to me and places her back against my front. I wrap my arms around her, feeling her warmth against me, and think that it can't get any better than this. I kiss her shoulder and her neck. I kiss her temple and run my hand through her hair. We sit like this for a long time with neither of us saying anything, and it's so nice, I almost forget there are rooms full of people in this house right now, going at it like rabbits.

"It was my aunt," she says.

"Your aunt?"

"She died," she says.

"I'm so sorry," I say, kissing the back of her head.

"She raised me."

"Tell me," I say.

"I didn't know my dad. His name wasn't even on my birth certificate, so he can be anyone, really," she says, settling more against my body. "My mom wasn't even sure who he was, from what I was told. She was into drugs when she got pregnant young, and I got taken away from her when I was six years old. I ended up in foster care for a while. She got me back once, and then I went back. I lived in a house with seven other kids, and I shared a twin bed with a girl twice my age for a while. It wasn't bad – I've heard of a lot worse – but it wasn't home, either."

I kiss her shoulder and wait for her to say more.

"My aunt lived here, and we lived about a thousand miles away. She didn't have much, but when she heard that my mother wasn't going to try to get me back again, she took a bus and came to get me. My mom filled out whatever paperwork you fill out when you give up your kid, and my aunt and I took the bus back here. She was ten years older than my mom and had her life together. We lived in a one-bedroom apartment for a while, just the two of us. Then, she met her husband, and we moved into his house and made it our home."

I can feel her smiling a little even though I can't see it.

"When he died about five years ago, it was just us again," she says. "A few years ago, she got diagnosed with cancer. She called my mom to tell her. They're sisters, after all. I hadn't seen my mother since the day they took me away from her, but my aunt always sent her pictures of me and kept her updated on my life as if she cared. Anyway, she visited when my aunt was sent to the hospital the first time, saw me, and acted like she didn't even know who I was. I didn't have the energy to deal with her – my aunt had cancer, and she was my *real* mother."

"Yeah," I say softly.

"I was dating someone at the time. It was still new. Normally, I wouldn't have introduced someone I'd only been on a few dates with into my chaos, but we were together when I got the call that she'd been admitted. My mom took one look at our joined hands, called me a dyke, and then said she was glad she gave me up. She did that all in one breath while her sister lay dying."

"She sounds awful," I say.

145

"She is," she says. "I wish it was her," she adds.

"Wish what was–"

"I wish the cancer had taken her. My aunt was a good person; she didn't deserve this."

"No, she didn't."

"She beat it once, but it came back worse. I gave up my apartment and moved back into her house. There was no one else to take care of her. My mom sure wasn't going to offer to move here to do it. I have a job – I mean, I don't just do this. She couldn't work anymore, though, and the bills started to pile up."

"That's why you started doing this," I say.

"My friends tried to just give me the money. They're loaded. I said no, and they tried to loan it to me, but I know I'd never be able to pay it back. She's *my* aunt. It's my responsibility."

"Pride is a dangerous thing," I say, hoping I'm not crossing the line.

"I'm here, though," she says. "I thought I'd do this a few times just to get to a point where I could take care of the existing debt, and I'd quit. But... I don't know. I wasn't expecting to actually *want* to come here."

I smile a little and kiss her shoulder again as I move my hands over her stomach.

"Want to come here, huh?" I tease.

"Yes," she says. "It's crazy. I know how this is supposed to work. I'm supposed to show up, someone picks me out of a group of escorts, and we just have sex. My sole purpose is to give someone pleasure at these things until they're done with me or the party is over. That is *not* at all what I thought I'd be doing with my life. Then, I saw you, and we've..."

"Connected?" I ask.

"Yes," she says and laughs as little. "I love *connecting* with you."

I laugh as well and say, "I love *connecting* with you, too." Then, I kiss her cheek. "How *are* you?"

"Right now, I'm pretty good. I can feel how wet you are through that thong of yours."

I laugh again and say, "Not what I meant."

"It's hard, but it'll be okay. At least, I knew this was coming. She also had a chance to take care of her affairs: she left me the house and her car. I've sold the car, but I haven't decided about the house yet. Right now, I'm still living there, but I might sell it for the money and move into an apartment or something. It's hard, being there without her. It's quiet."

"Do you think she'd want you to stay?"

"I don't know. I think she always wanted me to be happy. When I told her I was gay at sixteen, freaking out that she could disown me because I'd only known a mother who wanted nothing to do with me, she just asked if I had a girlfriend. I said yes, and she invited her over to dinner."

"Who is this girlfriend? Should I be jealous?" I joke.

"Well, she *did* feel me up in the backseat of her car after prom."

I laugh and say, "Describe exactly what she did."

"We left the dance early because it was boring. She drove, so we went to her car. She had those tiny bottles of booze. We drank a couple and made out for a while. Next thing I knew, my shirt was open, and her mouth was on my nipple."

I clear my throat and ask, "Where were her hands?"

"One of them was on my other breast, and the other was inside my pants."

"Did she make you come?" I ask, my heart racing inside my chest.

"No," she says. "It was her first time doing anything like that, but it was mine, too, so it was still good. I came later that night, though."

"You touched yourself?"

"I did."

"How?"

"I can *tell* you, or I can *show* you."

"Show me," I say.

"Well, I changed out of my dance clothes and didn't put anything else on. I remember my panties still being wet, but I didn't want to change them yet, so I lay on my bed wearing only my underwear."

"Like you are right now?"

"Yes," she says.

"And then?"

"Then, I slipped my hand inside." She does it.

"Oh, fuck," I say when her hand disappears.

"I'm really hard, baby," she says.

Her head rolls back against me, and I lick my lips, looking over her shoulder as she strokes herself under her panties.

"Did you touch your breasts?"

"Yes," she says, reaching for her left one with her free hand.

I watch for only a second before I place my hand over hers and help her massage.

"Oh, I'll come if I don't stop," she says.

"How fast did you come that night?"

"It took a while," she says.

"Because she didn't get you off how I can get you off?"

"Yes," she says.

"You're so damn sexy right now," I say.

My hand moves on top of her panties, and I feel how she's moving beneath them.

"You're soaking wet, baby."

"It's been two months," she says.

"You waited?" I ask.

"Yes," she says and gasps right after.

"You haven't come in two months?"

"No. And I'm so fucking ready right now. I need–"

"Baby, no," I say, pressing my hand down into hers.

"What? I–"

"I haven't, either," I say.

"What?"

"I didn't come. I've been waiting for you, too," I say.

She turns her head back to me and says, "Really?"

"I wanted to so badly, but I didn't."

"Neither did I," she says.

"Not even with your friends?"

"No," she says.

"Then, don't come right now. Let me touch you," I say.

"I'm rock hard. It won't take much."

"Shh," I say, kissing her lips. "Can you sit up?"

"You're killing me."

I laugh a little and move out from behind her when she shifts. Then, I motion for her to lie back and move myself on top of her.

"I'll make it count, I promise."

I wait for her to make a dirty comment, but she doesn't. She just stares up at me and wraps her arms around my neck.

"I really missed you," she says.

I kiss her slowly, keeping my body up; only our breasts are touching. I know that if I start rolling into her with my hips, she'll come before I've even really touched her. As I kiss her, I think about how much I love kissing her. Her taste, the way her lips move against my own, and the way she kind of nibbles on my lower lip drive me wild, but it all feels intimate. I move my lips all over her body, kissing her everywhere I can while she begins to writhe beneath me and begs me to make her come.

When I lick over her panties, she gasps. I press my lips to the spot and kiss her there. I do it over and over again until she bucks her hips. Then, I sit up and remove my own bra. She stares at my breasts, licking her lips. I hover back over her and drop a nipple into her mouth. She sucks on it, and I rock against her, my sex over her stomach, rubbing against her. I'm not claiming her this time, though. I'm just loving it how good she feels against my core that begs me for release. I move until my other nipple is over her mouth.

She sucks as her hands go to my hips, and she helps me move forward and back.

Before she makes me come this way, I lift up and spread her legs with my own. Then, I remove my soaked thong and toss it aside. She tries to sit up, reaches out her hand to touch me, and I gently shove her back down with a smile. I'm on top of her again, rocking slowly against her, my sex pressed to hers.

"You feel so good," she says.

"How do you want to come first?" I ask, feeling my own orgasm build.

"Like this," she says. "Just like this."

She grasps my ass and presses me down harder.

"Yes," I say.

"Will you come, too?"

"Yes," I repeat.

I move faster and kiss her as she lifts her hips in time with my thrusts. I can actually feel how hard she is, and it turns me on like crazy. When she comes, it's softly. It's so soft, I almost don't know she's coming. I come right after that, though, and fall down into her.

"I needed you," she says.

And she didn't say she needed *that* – she said she needed *me*.

"God, I needed you, too," I say. "Don't move."

I slip down the bed until I'm settled between her legs. I look up at her, give her a soft smile, and lick her pussy.

"Oh, God," she says.

I fill her with two fingers as I suck on her clit. It takes no time at all – she's coming again, and this time, louder. When I move back up her body, she rolls us over and slides her own fingers into me, kissing me deeply as she makes me come with her fingers. After I do, she moves down and takes me into her mouth. I try to make this one last, but it's no use. I've needed her mouth on me for the past two months. I've needed *her* for the past two months. I don't know what that means. It scares me a little, but right now, I can't think about that. All I can think about is her; how gorgeous she is, how amazing she is, and how very little I know about her. She pulls me against her body, and we lie there, her holding me this time. I run my hand over her breasts and stomach while I listen to her heart.

"I like when you call me *baby*," she says after a long time.

"I like it, too," I say.

"Can I know something about you now?" she asks.

"Like what?" I say.

"Anything," she says.

I smile. Then, I start talking.

MONTH 7. PART 2. – I SHOULDN'T GO

(POV Escort)

I stand in front of my mirror dressed in my best. No, that's not right. My *best* suit was reserved for my aunt's funeral, and it's the only one I owned prior to picking up this not-nearly-as-nice one from the department store downtown. I remember staring at it hanging in my closet before the first party. I was planning on wearing it, but I knew she didn't have much longer. I remember swallowing. I remember the tears in my eyes. I remember thinking about how I'd wear it at her funeral one day. I went to the store that day and picked out this suit.

I tuck my white shirt in. It's not the same one I've worn before – I bought a new one since *she's* seen me in the old one. I'd buy a whole new suit, too, but I can't waste any more money. Besides, she told me to wear jeans and a t-shirt. I zip up the bag I'm bringing with me, knowing that I can't just show up in my casual wear – I'd be fired on the spot. Then, I get into my old, trusty car and head to the location where I'm then placed into the SUV and driven to the party.

"Hey. We were wondering if you'd be here," my friend says when she sees me.

"I thought about not coming again, but I need the money," I say.

"And you need to see *her*," she replies. "I think it's about time you just admit that it's not all about the money these days."

"It's been two months," I say.

"And she got you flowers," she replies.

152

"She got my aunt flowers."

"She doesn't even know that you have an aunt," she says.

"*Had*," I correct.

My friend just nods solemnly.

"I'm going to find a room for us," I say. "I don't want to wait until she gets here, and then there's nothing left. There are more women here this time than the last time, I think."

"You're right. These are becoming very popular," she replies.

"If you see her, can you–"

"Tell her where you are?"

"Yes," I say.

I leave my friend and see her wife approach on my way up the stairs. I quickly find a room and text them both where I am, just in case they can let *her* know. I only hope she actually still wants me tonight. I know I want her. It's a strange thing to think that I've spent the past two months thinking of someone, and I don't even know her name. The worst part about it is that my aunt, the most important person in the world to me, passed away after a painful illness, leaving me with debt, a house, and a car, and I have to figure out what to do with all of it. I owe it to her. I would have done anything for her. If only I'd just been born a doctor with the ability to cure cancer, I think as I change out of my suit and into a t-shirt and jeans, tucking my suit away for later. There's a knock at the door, our secret knock. I smile, thinking only of her in that moment. I walk to the door, take a deep breath, and open it.

"Hi, baby," she says, and it's so soft, I almost don't hear it.

"Hi," I reply, smiling at the term of endearment neither of us should really be using.

She walks straight into my arms. I close the door behind her and wrap my own arms around her for a hug. I didn't even know how much I needed this hug.

"Thank you for the flowers," I say.

"You don't have to thank me," she says.

"You didn't have to," I say, squeezing her because I need her closer.

"I wanted to. I didn't know what else to do. Your friends wouldn't tell me much. I understand why. I just wanted to do something."

I kiss her neck and pull out of our hug.

"Thanks," I say, looking down at the floor because I can't quite look at her yet.

"I don't know what I'm allowed to ask or if I'm allowed to ask anything."

"We're not really here to talk," I say because she's given me an out – or, an in, depending on how I look at it.

I don't want to talk about losing my aunt. I don't want to talk about the funeral or anything else. I just want to lose myself in her. I've waited all this time to be in her space again, to have her pressed against me, and I want that more than anything right now. I put my hands on her hips to indicate that I'm ready to take this to the bed or the wall or the door or the floor – whatever she wants.

"But we *can*," she says.

"It's been two months," I say insistently. "I want to touch you." I pull her against me.

"I want to touch you, too," she says. "But we don't have to tonight. We–"

"You came here for sex." I pull back again, annoyed.

"I came here for you. I always come here for *you*," she replies urgently.

"Why are you complicating things right now? I'm an escort. You pay me to–"

"Hey," she says, taking my hands. "If I wanted just sex with anyone, I'd be in a room with someone else or downstairs in the living room right now – I'm in here with you."

"Well, I'm not exactly the life of the party tonight. It's been two months. You don't just want to fuck?"

I know it's probably not the right thing to say, especially to her. I know she's trying to be nice and make sure I'm okay, but I'm vibrating, and I want to stop. I just want to stop.

"Why did you come here tonight?"

"I just told you. I–"

"No, be honest with me. Why did you come here?"

"Because I need money," I blurt out, not meaning to.

"Oh," she says, letting go of my hands.

The disappointment in that one word hits me square in the chest. Then, there's her body language. She's upset. *I've* upset her. I sigh and know I have to be honest. She deserves that.

"And because I wanted to see you," I say. Then, I add, "I've missed you."

"I've missed you, too," she says with a small smile.

"And I've missed touching you," I say, cupping her cheek.

"I've missed that, too," she says, leaning into the touch.

"But it's more than that," I tell her, stepping into her.

"Tell me." She kisses the inside of my palm.

"I just…"

She kisses me on the lips but pulls away before I can deepen it. I've missed those sweet lips more than I thought because all I want to do is press my own back to them.

"Come here," she says.

She takes my hand and walks us to the bed. She sits me down on it and stands in front of me.

"I want to hold you. Is that okay?"

"But we–"

"I'm not asking as a member who expects something from you. I'm asking as just plain old me. Can I just hold you for a while?"

"Okay," I reply.

"Just…"

She unzips her dress, and I watch. It falls to the floor, and she steps out of it and her shoes.

"Oh, wow," I say, placing my hands on her hips and pulling her closer to me. "You're so beautiful."

"I'm only taking it off so I can get behind you and hold you," she says, smiling down at me.

"But... you're wearing red. You know how much I love red," I remind her, kissing her stomach; I've missed this soft skin.

"I'll come if you keep touching me," she says.

"Good," I reply. "I want you to."

"Not yet, baby," she says, moving away from me until she's sitting back against the pillows.

She's holding her arms out for me. She wants me to sit between her legs. I look down at her spread legs and the patch of hair I can see between her thighs. I lick my lips, wanting my tongue to be there instead.

"Lie with me," she says.

I know I'm not getting that chance now, so I stand up and remove my jeans and shirt to match her lack of dress.

"Oh, hell," she says. "You're killing me right now."

"You did it first," I tease, feeling a little bit better already.

I climb onto the bed and press my back against her front. The warmth of her engulfs me when she wraps her arms around my body protectively, as if she has the ability to keep all of the darkness away from me. She kisses my shoulder first, then my neck and my temple. She runs her hand through my hair, and I have to close my eyes to just let this all in. We sit like this for a while, and it's nice. She kisses me occasionally on different parts of my exposed skin, and despite the fact that I'm nearly naked, I've never felt more covered up in my life. It's like she *has* me; she won't let me go. She wants me here, and not only that, but she doesn't just want me for sex. She wants to hold me like this. She wants to talk to me, to learn more about me. That says something, right? I should trust how I feel when I'm with her, no matter how crazy it sounds.

"It was my aunt," I say.

"Your aunt?"

"She died," I reply.

"I'm so sorry." She kisses the back of my head.

I close my eyes again, feeling her surrounding me.

"She raised me."

"Tell me," she says.

"I didn't know my dad. His name wasn't even on my birth certificate, so he can be anyone, really," I settle against her body, needing even more of her now. "My mom wasn't even sure who he was, from what I was told. She was into drugs when she got pregnant young, and I got taken away from her when I was six years old. I ended up in foster care for a while. She got me back once, and then I went back. I lived in a house with seven other kids, and I shared a twin bed with a girl twice my age for a while. It wasn't bad – I've heard of a lot worse – but it wasn't home, either."

She kisses my shoulder, and I smile a little.

"My aunt lived here, and we lived about a thousand miles away. She didn't have much, but when she heard that my mother wasn't going to try to get me back again, she took a bus and came to get me. My mom filled out whatever paperwork you fill out when you give up your kid, and my aunt and I took the bus back here. She was ten years older than my mom and had her life together. We lived in a one-bedroom apartment for a while, just the two of us. Then, she met her husband, and we moved into his house and made it our home. When he died about five years ago, it was just us again. A few years ago, she got diagnosed with cancer. She called my mom to tell her. They're sisters, after all. I hadn't seen my mother since the day they took me away from her, but my aunt always sent her pictures of me and kept her updated on my life as if she cared. Anyway, she visited when my aunt was sent to the hospital the first time, saw me, and acted like she didn't even know who I was. I didn't have the energy to deal with her – my aunt had cancer, and she was my *real* mother."

"Yeah," she says softly.

"I was dating someone at the time. It was still new. Normally, I wouldn't have introduced someone I'd only been on a few dates with into my chaos, but we were together when I got the call that she'd been admitted. My mom took one look at our joined hands, called me a dyke, and then said she was glad she gave me up. She did that all in one breath while her sister lay dying."

"She sounds awful," she says.

"She is," I say. Then, I add, "I wish it was her."

That's bad. I know that's wrong, but it's how I feel. One woman chose her drugs over her child. She chose mental, emotional, and sometimes even physical abuse because it was easier than taking care of her kid by giving up her addiction. For just a second, I think that maybe the addiction gene was passed onto me, but my drug of choice is sex with the woman currently sitting behind me. I toss that idea out because we're not having sex right now. We're just talking.

"Wish what was—"

"I wish the cancer had taken her. My aunt was a good person; she didn't deserve this."

And as bad as it sounds, to wish that my own mother got cancer instead of someone else, my aunt should still be here. My mother hasn't contributed anything to the world. My aunt raised me. She put food on the table, made sure I had lunch for school, took me to practices, and went to all of my games. She helped me pay for college. She told me that love is love and that she just wants me to find it and be happy. She should still be here.

"No, she didn't," she says.

"She beat it once, but it came back worse. I gave up my apartment and moved back into her house. There was no one else to take care of her. My mom sure wasn't going to offer to move here to do it. I have a job – I mean, I don't just do this. She couldn't work anymore, though, and the bills started to pile up."

"That's why you started doing this," she says.

"My friends tried to just give me the money. They're loaded. I said no, and they tried to loan it to me, but I know I'd never be able to pay it back. She's *my* aunt. It's my responsibility."

"Pride is a dangerous thing."

"I'm here, though. I thought I'd do this a few times just to get to a point where I could take care of the existing debt, and I'd quit. But... I don't know. I wasn't expecting to actually *want* to come here."

She kisses my shoulder again and moves her hands over my stomach.

"Want to come here, huh?"

"Yes. It's crazy. I know how this is supposed to work. I'm supposed to show up, someone picks me out of a group of escorts, and we just have sex. My sole purpose is to give someone pleasure at these things until they're done with me or the party is over. That is *not* at all what I thought I'd be doing with my life. Then, I saw you, and we've..."

"Connected?"

"Yes," I say and laugh. "I love *connecting* with you."

She laughs as well and says, "I love *connecting* with you, too." Then, she kisses my cheek. "How *are* you?"

"Right now, I'm pretty good. I can feel how wet you are through that thong of yours."

"Not what I meant."

"It's hard, but it'll be okay. At least, I knew this was coming. She also had a chance to take care of her affairs: she left me the house and her car. I've sold the car, but I haven't decided about the house yet. Right now, I'm still living there, but I might sell it for the money and move into an apartment or something. It's hard, being there without her. It's quiet."

"Do you think she'd want you to stay?"

"I don't know. I think she always wanted me to be happy. When I told her I was gay at sixteen, freaking out that she could disown me because I'd only known a mother who wanted nothing to do with me, she just asked if I had a girlfriend. I said yes, and she invited her over to dinner."

"Who is this girlfriend? Should I be jealous?"

I laugh a little. How did we get here?

"Well, she *did* feel me up in the backseat of her car after prom."

She laughs and says, "Describe exactly what she did."

"We left the dance early because it was boring. She drove, so we went to her car. She had those tiny bottles of booze. We drank a couple and made out for a while. Next thing I knew, my shirt was open, and her mouth was on my nipple."

She clears her throat and asks, "Where were her hands?"

"One of them was on my other breast, and the other was inside my pants."

"Did she make you come?"

"No. It was her first time doing anything like that, but it was mine, too, so it was still good. I came later that night, though."

"You touched yourself?"

"I did."

"How?"

"I can *tell* you, or I can *show* you."

"Show me," she says, and I almost come with how husky her voice just got.

"Well, I changed out of my dance clothes and didn't put anything else on. I remember my panties still being wet, but I didn't want to change them yet, so I lay on my bed wearing only my underwear."

"Like you are right now?"

Oh, we're doing this.

"Yes," I say.

"And then?"

"Then, I slipped my hand inside," I tell her and slide my hand inside my underwear.

"Oh, fuck," she says, watching me.

"I'm really hard, baby," I tell her.

And I am. I'm really fucking hard. I roll my head back against her as I stroke myself, knowing full well that I don't want to come by my own hand, but it feels so good, I can't stop just yet.

"Did you touch your breasts?"

"Yes." I touch my left one with my free hand.

Her hand covers mine, and she's massaging it with me.

"Oh, I'll come if I don't stop."

"How fast did you come that night?" she asks.

"It took a while," I tell her.

"Because she didn't get you off how I can get you off?"

"Yes," I say.

"You're so damn sexy right now," she says.

She slides her hand down to my panties, feeling me touching myself.

"You're soaking wet, baby."

"It's been two months," I say.

"You waited?"

"Yes." Then, I gasp because I'm already close.

"You haven't come in two months?"

"No. And I'm so fucking ready right now. I need–"

"Baby, no," she says, pressing her hand down into mine.

"What? I–"

I'm dangerously close now.

"I haven't, either," she says.

"What?"

I stop.

"I didn't come. I've been waiting for you, too," she says.

I turn back to her and say, "Really?"

"I wanted to so badly, but I didn't."

"Neither did I," I say.

"Not even with your friends?"

"No," I say.

"Then, don't come right now. Let me touch you," she says.

And I cannot wait.

"I'm rock hard. It won't take much."

"Shh," she soothes, kissing me. "Can you sit up?"

"You're killing me," I say, not at all wanting to move.

I just want her to touch me. I'll come if she just touches me. But she's moving, and she wants me to move, so I do. I lie down quickly, and she's on top of me. I know then, as she stares down at me, that I am *not* here for the money.

"I'll make it count, I promise," she says.

I wrap my arms around her neck.

"I really missed you," I tell her.

Her kiss is a slow one. She keeps herself up so that only our breasts touch, and I'm ready to beg for more, but I also want this. I'd be good with just this and how she's kissing me right now. She kisses me everywhere, and I can't stop myself from moving beneath her. I have to beg her to let me come now. She licks me over my panties, and it's so hot. It's what I've been missing. She kisses me there, and she keeps doing it until I'm bucking under her.

She sits up, and I'm about to beg her to go back to doing what she was just doing, but she takes off her bra, and I can see her breasts now. I lick my lips with anticipation. I'm going to have my mouth on them. She must have just known what I wanted. She hovers over me once more, places her nipple into my mouth, and I suck on it gratefully. She rocks against me. Her pussy is pressed to my stomach, and I can feel how wet and needy she is right now. She moves her other breast into my mouth, and I suck and suck as my hands go to her hips, and I slide her forward and back on my stomach. She needs to come, too. I can feel it.

She lifts up and spreads my legs, placing her legs between them. Then, she moves again to take off her thong, and she's naked now. She's gloriously naked and perfect in all her imperfections. I reach out to touch her, but she shoves me back down. Now, her sex is pressed to mine, and she's rocking. Our ever-present connection is more potent.

I know it's not just about sex now.

"You feel so good," I say.

"How do you want to come first?" she asks between heavy breaths.

"Like this," I say. "Just like this."

I press her ass down so I can have more of her.

"Yes," she says.

"Will you come, too?"

"Yes," she repeats.

She's moving faster now. Good; I need her to come, too. She kisses me deeply, and I lift up to meet her hips. I want every bit of her pressed to every bit of me. I can't remember a time when I've wanted someone this badly, and it's not just because I haven't had an orgasm in two months – it's because of her. I don't know how this happened. It should be impossible, but it's not. I know nothing about her except how her body feels pressed to mine, how she tastes and sounds when she comes, how hard she makes me come from just one touch, but I know that I was meant to be in this room with her right now. I was meant to be touched by her.

When I finally come after all this time, I hold in my scream. I want to exist in this moment with her without distraction. I focus on the tingling sensation between my thighs and how it radiates outward up into my belly button, up through my stomach to my nipples, and into my rapidly beating heart. It keeps moving until I can feel it in the lips she's still kissing. I notice it moving down then, past my shaking knees and into my toes. It's in my fingertips now. It's everywhere. *She's* everywhere. Once I register that I'm finally coming down, I realize that she's coming, too, now. I think about the tingles she's feeling. I wonder if they're radiating out just as mine had moments ago. I hold her, and I kiss her, and I hope that she's feeling all that I'm feeling right now.

"I needed you," I say.

"God, I needed you, too," she says.

I let out the breath I was holding.

"Don't move," she says.

She moves quickly until she's settled between my legs. Then, she licks me.

"Oh, God."

She fills me with her fingers and sucks. I'm not sure I can come again this quickly, but soon enough, I am, and I finally let out the scream I'd held back before. I let her know this time how fucking good it feels when she touches me. Then, I roll us over and slide my fingers inside her now. I need to feel her warmth around me like this now. I kiss her deeply, and she comes quickly. After she does, I take her into my mouth and taste her for the first time in far too long. She comes all too fast, but I don't mind. I know somehow that we'll do this again, and I'll get to feel her come over and over. I pull her against me as we lie in bed, me holding her now. She touches my breasts and my stomach, and I just stare at the ceiling, thinking about how I got here.

"I like when you call me *baby*," I tell her after a long time, not worried about her getting scared by the comment.

"I like it, too," she says.

"Can I know something about you now?"

"Like what?" she asks.

"Anything," I say.

"Anything? Okay," she says and laughs a little. "Well, I have two brothers."

"Older or younger?"

"Older, both of them. It's annoying," she says as I run my hand through her hair.

"Big brother protectors?" I guess.

"Yes. But I'll tell you a funny story about that. When I was seventeen, I came out to my parents, but both of my brothers were off at college, and I hadn't told them yet. So, it's around May or June, and they're now home for the summer. I was working up the courage to tell them when I meet this girl. She was beautiful and worked at the mall at one of those kiosks. I finally asked her out after going there nearly every day and buying stupid stuff I didn't need. She says yes, and it's Saturday night. She asked to pick me up since she wasn't out yet, and I agreed. I thought this was a good opportunity to tell them about me, so I told them I had a date that night. They both sat in the living room, waiting for this 'boy' to show up. I swear, one of them had a barbell in his hand. He was pretending to do curls or something while sitting on the sofa. It was really stupid. Anyway, the doorbell rings, and my parents just sit there. I think my dad actually smirked at them. I decided to let them answer the door. My oldest brother tapped the other one on the shoulder, basically telling him he was going to do the talking."

"He was going to give your date a lecture?"

"I think that was the plan, yeah," she says, laughing against my chest. "When they opened the door, one jaw dropped. The other one looked confused as hell. He asked her if she had the right house, and I burst out laughing."

"You were mean to your protective brothers," I say, smiling.

"They were acting like idiots."

"I don't know… I kind of like the idea of them watching over you," I say, kissing the top of her head.

"You think I need watching over?"

"I think we could *all* use a little watching over sometimes," I tell her.

"She's watching over you now. You know that, right?" she says softly.

"I know," I say.

She runs her hand up and down my thigh, and I decide to ask, "So, can I know what you do for a living?"

"Oh, that's a long story," she says.

"It's okay."

"No," she says, looking up at me. "It's not that I don't want to tell you – it's just complicated. I basically run the family business."

"What about your brothers?"

"Neither of them wanted it. My dad started it before

we were born, and now it's this massive corporation. I started in acquisitions and did so well, that he passed it over to me when he wanted to retire early. One of my brothers *does* work there, too, but he's just a department head. He's happy, though. My other brother started his own thing out of college."

"Are *you* happy?" I ask.

"I am right now," she says.

I smile.

"But if you're asking if I'm happy with my job, the answer is also yes – I like what I do. Admittedly, I've not been as focused as I have been in the past. Something – or should I say, some*one* – has been on my mind for a while now."

"I'll kill her," I joke.

She laughs and moves until she's on top of me, straddling my hips.

"I'm going out of the country for the next few weeks," she says.

I stop smiling and say, "You're going to miss next month…"

"I was able to move some things to make it back in time, but there's a chance that I'll have to stick around and miss the next month, yes." She places her hands on my stomach. "I will do everything I can to wrap things up in time for me to get back to you, but I wanted you to know just in case I'm not here. I just…"

"It's okay. I–"

"No, I want you to know that I *want* to be here, too," she says.

"I know."

"If I'm delayed, will you…" She looks to the wall behind us. "Will you be with…"

"Oh," I say.

"Yeah," she says.

"I don't know," I reply honestly. "I *do* still need money, so I can't skip it. Plus, I've skipped two already, and if I miss another, I'll lose the job."

"I understand. I wouldn't ask you to…"

I sit up and place my face between her breasts. I kiss her and wrap my arms around the small of her back.

"Let's talk about something else, okay?"

"Like what?" she asks.

"Like… the things I packed in my bag. Are you interested?"

She laughs and kisses me.

MONTH 8. PART 1. – THE UN-OPENED HOTEL

(POV Member)

This one is different, and I know that. It's different because I'm choosing to make it that way. I have no idea how she's going to feel about this, but I've asked for special accommodations tonight. It's nothing crazy; I just don't want us to be disturbed all night, and this should ensure that. The work trip took the full three weeks and, technically, one extra day, but I was able to make it back with enough time to send the email, make the reservation, and sigh in relief because I'd get to see her again. I'm done telling myself how crazy this whole thing is; I just am. I like her. I like how we are together, how she is with me, and how good she makes me feel in every single way. It's not crazy; it's two people *connecting*. And I want tonight to be special.

It's important because there was a chance I wasn't going to be able to make it, and the last time we saw one another, we touched and talked as if that would be the case. We kissed long. We talked more about our childhoods and marveled at how different they were. We made each other come until the knock on the door, and I kissed her while we stood there just after she changed into that sexy suit. We whispered our goodbye, and more than anything, I wanted to ask her to meet me somewhere. We could have gone to some twenty-four-hour diner and had a bad cup of coffee. We could have gone back to my place and just slept for hours before waking up and having breakfast. We could have done anything, really, but her friends were there right when I opened the door. I chickened out.

Worse than that, I thought about how they seem to want her, too. I was jealous. Not only because I don't want her touching anyone else or being touched by them, which is unfair, but because they already have each other. I wanted them to just let me have her, but that's not how this works. On top of that, they're really nice, and I can't be mad at them. I shouldn't be jealous of them, either. She told me how amazing they've been before and after she lost her aunt, and I know she needs people like them in her life. They're actually *in* her life. I'm on the outside of it all, practically tapping a hole in any floor I'm standing on until I can see her again.

When it's time to go this time, I put on a new dress but don't slip a thong on underneath – there's no point. I have a strapless bra on more for comfort than anything else, and I'm wearing a pair of heels that are a little taller than what I normally wear. I feel sexy, I'm confident, and I just can't wait to see her.

The drive to the new location is a long one – longer than I thought it would be – but I still arrive on time. I'm not worried this time because I've set something up for us, so we'll have our privacy. I'm able to pull straight into the parking lot this time, and I still have to hand my keys to the valet just in case I drink too much, but I can count on one hand the number of drinks I've had at these things because I'm not here for the top-shelf alcohol – I'm here for her.

I enter the lobby of the hotel, surprised to see that it's already bustling. This is the first time the event has been held at a hotel. When I got to the location, there was an extra message about it. The hotel has transferred ownership recently and is owned by someone the company trusts. It's going to be completely redone in a few weeks, but until then, it's still a luxury hotel with all the amenities and no guests. It's not overly large, which is perfect for this event. It has forty rooms, an indoor and outdoor pool, two hot tubs, a sauna, a spa that they've got masseuses on staff tonight for, unless a member wants a special massage from an escort, there's a full bar, and more.

I'm only interested in my room, though. It's mine from

eleven until four in the morning, at least, and I plan to make full use of it. I find her leaning against the bar with her friends. She reaches out for a drink. Then, I see her reach for another. I wonder if she's going to hand it to someone, but she stands there with both drinks in her hands. She laughs at something her friend says. I can't hear it over the noise of the music and other partygoers, but I can see her smile. It's wide and exuberant, and I love that she's smiling like that. I watch as one of the women slides her hand up under her wife's dress and cups her ass. I watch when the said wife begins kissing her wife's neck and slips her own hand under the woman's shirt and onto her back. These two are sexy, and I can see why *she* might want to be with them fully. Maybe she has already; I don't know.

"Well, hello," the member says.

It's the woman who I was technically in bed with twice now. She's without her usual escort.

"Hi," I say.

"Any chance you'll join us tonight?" she asks.

"Us?" I ask.

"You know who I'm talking about," she replies, winking at me.

"Where is she tonight?"

"She's getting changed. I'm meeting her in a room in a minute. She wanted to dress up for me tonight."

"Isn't she always dressed up?"

"She picked out some new lingerie," the woman replies. "And won't let me see it until she's ready."

"That'll be fun," I say.

"It's always fun with her," she says.

"You're always with her, aren't you?" I say, knowing the answer already.

"Yes, and sometimes another, but always her," she replies. "Why?"

"I'm always with someone here, too," I say. "Well, except for the times I was—"

"She wasn't there, though, right?"

"Right. She couldn't make the event."

"Is she here tonight?"

"Yes. I was just going to go over to her."

"Well, better make sure no one else snaps her up if you like her."

"And do you like yours?"

"She's not mine," she says seriously.

"Oh, I didn't mean it like that," I reply, realizing how that must have sounded.

She sighs and says, "It's been two years."

"That's a long time," I reply.

"Can I ask you something?"

"Sure," I say.

"Are you…" The woman takes a step toward me. "When you're not here, are you with women, or men, or both, or neither? I don't know exactly what I'm asking."

"I'm gay," I say, helping her out.

"So is she," she says.

"You're not, though," I say.

"I used to think so," she replies. "Honestly, I wonder now. I've always found women attractive. I even thought about experimenting in college like everyone else, but I didn't. Then I got married, and I figured that was it."

"But?"

"But, when my husband climbs on top of me the three times a month, or so he wants to have sex, all I can think about is her," she replies. "It's the one thing that gets me through knowing that he's fucking his Director of Sales and that I have to wait until the next month to see her."

I nod and say, "You like her."

"I do," she says. "We have a lot of sex." She laughs. "But we talk, too. She's so smart. She's only doing this to put herself through school. We're completely different and wrong for each other, and we met under the strangest circumstances, but no one has ever made me come how she can." The woman pauses. "And no one has ever made me feel how she can, either."

"Does she know how you feel?"

"No," she says, laughing. "And I can't tell her, either. What's the point? I'm still married, and she's young and will find someone else. She'll stop doing this once she's paid everything off, and I'll lose her. At least, I have right now. I'll have the time we had together."

I look over at the bar, and *she's* no longer standing there – she's walking toward me with a smile on her face, and I can't help but smile back.

"Oh, no," the woman next to me says when she notices what I'm staring at. "You too?"

"What?" I look at her.

"Nip it in the bud before you're just like me, getting through the month just to see her again."

"I–" But I can't say anything because it's too late; I'm already there.

"Hi," she says, handing me a cocktail. "I hope this is okay."

I don't even know what the drink is, but I say, "It's perfect. Thank you."

"You're welcome," she says. "So, I hear there's a room reserved for us tonight."

"There is, yes," I reply, smiling at her.

She looks over at the woman next to me and says, "Is it for all of us or–"

"No, not me. I have my own room to get to," she says. "She told me that it's light-blue, like her eyes. I'm going to go find her now."

The member walks off down the hall leading to the elevators.

"What's light-blue?" *she* asks.

"Nothing," I say. "Hi," I repeat, taking a drink.

"We did this part already," she replies, taking my hand with her free one. "Can we get out of here before they all get started?"

"Sure," I reply.

"It's just us tonight?" she asks when we get to the bank

of three elevators.

I tap the card I've been given against the reader.

"Yes. Did you want–"

"No, I like it when it's just us," she says. "Don't get me wrong... I like it when we're with other people, too. There's just something about touching you while other people are doing the same thing that I find a turn-on."

"Me too," I say as the elevator arrives.

"Oh, that's the private one," she says, pointing to the elevator.

"I know," I tell her.

"That's to the penthouse."

"I know," I repeat.

"You reserved the penthouse?"

We get into the private elevator reserved for the penthouse guest and head up.

"I did," I say, pulling her against me.

Her hands wrap around me first; she kisses me, and as our tongues join in, her hand slips under my dress and onto my thigh. It moves a little closer to my sex, and she pulls out of the kiss.

"You're not wearing any underwear."

"No," I say.

"Fuck," she says, pushing me against the elevator wall as it arrives on our floor.

It doesn't matter, though – we're the only ones that can use it, so it can't really go anywhere. She cups me, discovering how wet I already am for her, and her fingers enter me. Her thumb moves to my clit, and she's fucking me against the wall of the elevator. I don't know what she does that no one else has ever been able to do to me, but I'm coming hard, tearing at her suit jacket until it's off her shoulders, and pulling apart her shirt, buttons heading to the floor until I have a nipple in my mouth. I suck on it as I continue to come into her hand. She's panting and gasping. I'm reaching for her pants, which I somehow manage to undo. The entire time I was on my work trip, I dreamed of this moment – of fucking her hard and then touching her slowly.

"Off," I say.

She's still thrusting inside even though I've already come, but she kicks off her pants, and I'm inside her underwear now. I'm stroking; she's leaning against me. My free hand moves to her breast, and I twist her nipple. Then, I coat myself with her wetness and slip inside.

"Yes," she says.

"Like this?" I ask as her own thrusts slow down and then stop inside me.

"Yes," she repeats.

"Pull out, babe," I say.

She pulls out of me, and I flip us around. I tap her leg. She spreads them wider. I push in deeper and flick her clit. I massage her breast while I suck on the other one, and her head goes back against the wall – she's coming. I lift my head up and turn to the side. The walls are mirrored, and I can watch her from this angle now. I can only see my arm and a little of my wrist since my hand is buried inside her panties, and there's something so sexy about this, that I can't stop. I'm not sure if she comes a second time or if it's a really long orgasm, but when she's done, I remove my hand and pull on her until we're out of the elevator and in the room. She's barely able to walk because her pants are around her ankles. I laugh and bend down to help her step out of them. She's still a little wobbly, which is both sexy and adorable, so I decide to push her on the small sofa in the middle of the wide-open room.

"This place is–"

She can't get the rest of the sentence out. I take off my dress and my bra, then sit on her lap, and her arms are around me in an instant. I move her mouth to my breast, and she sucks.

"I love your mouth," I tell her.

She moans.

"Make me come with it," I say.

"Let's go to bed," she replies, pulling back a little.

"No, here. Please, baby," I say.

She nods, and I stand. She lies back, and I straddle her face. Her hands grip my ass and lower me down to her waiting mouth. Her tongue paints my outer lips, causing me to buck forward. Then, she's sliding between my folds, moves inside me, and I'm still so sensitive, I almost come.

"Yes, I missed you so much," I say.

She sucks; she licks. And I come. It's sexy and perfect, and I know this is not what I had planned at all for tonight – this is the *opposite* of what I had planned – but I wouldn't change anything about it now. I lift up and move until I'm straddling her hips again. She wipes her chin and smirks at me.

"Cocky?"

"I can be," she says. "Want me to wear one?"

I laugh at the terrible joke.

"Maybe later," I say. "I didn't bring one, though."

"I did," she says, lifting an eyebrow at me, moving my hips back and forth with ease. "You're still so wet. Let me make you come with it."

"Later," I say, giving her a playful glare.

"Why later? Do you need a break? We just got started."

"Eager, huh?"

"Well, you *did* tear off my shirt, and I think my jacket is somewhere on the floor behind me, so I'd say we were *both* a little eager."

I look up and around the room. It's set up exactly how I asked. I laugh.

"What's so funny?" she asks.

"We were supposed to lead *up* to the sex, not start with it," I say.

"Supposed to?"

I stand up, completely naked, and she sits up, still in her shirt that's hanging open and her panties.

"I had them bring up food, and there's an in-room jacuzzi. There's also a giant TV in the bedroom, apparently, and I ordered a movie I really like."

175

"A movie?" she asks, standing up with me now.

"Yeah, *that* kind of movie," I say.

"Oh," she says, understanding. "You're into that?"

"Not much, but this one has a story, and the women are hot."

"Not as hot as you," she says, pulling me in.

"Nice," I say, laughing.

"I'm serious," she says, kissing me. "But I'm down to watch a movie of two hot women getting it on – as long as I get to touch you while we do."

"That can be arranged," I tell her, wrapping my arms around her neck. "Can you lose the rest of your clothes and join me in the hot tub? There should already be perfectly hot water in there, with the bubbles already going and a bottle of champagne chilling. I asked for chocolate-dipped strawberries, too. Do you eat those?"

"I can't say I've ever really had the opportunity to eat a chocolate-dipped strawberry."

"Oh, I'm going to feed them to you, then," I tell her, sliding her underwear off her body. I kiss her collarbone and pull her shirt the rest of the way off. "I love that you don't wear a bra. Your nipples are so perfect." I lean down and pull one into my mouth.

"We can't go to that hot tub if you're doing this," she says, holding my head in place.

"I was going to do this *in* the hot tub," I tell her, kissing her neck.

***

After we get out of the hot tub, we sit at the small table against the wall of windows overlooking the city. We share the appetizers that were prepared for us and another glass of champagne. We sit there completely naked, not worrying about someone maybe seeing in the windows. Honestly, I don't think about anything outside this room – I can only see her. We talk for a long time until we're up to our college years. She went to state school. I was at an Ivy. We discuss how different those experiences were, and by the time we're up to her first job post-college, it's already so late, that I'm happy to skip the movie and sex the rest of the night if it means more talking and laughing with her like this. There's a sense of dread that has nothing to do with us not having sex again for a month. It's about not seeing *her* until then.

"Bed?" she asks.

"What?" I say.

"Bed?" she says.

"Oh, sure," I say.

"What movie did you order?" she asks as we walk into the room hand in hand.

"Something with a terrible title," I say.

She laughs and says, "That's all of them."

She sits back on the bed, spreading her legs wide. I look. She rolls her eyes. I sigh and move to sit between her legs, and she pulls me against her as I turn on the movie.

"Can we just watch something else?" I ask.

"You don't want to watch what you picked out?" she asks, kissing my shoulder.

"No. Maybe just a regular movie," I say.

"Whatever you want," she tells me.

The hotel's selection is extensive, and I'm able to find a lesbian rom-com. It's not sexy, but at least it's not one of the tragic ones. I lean back against her, and we watch the movie. Occasionally, her hands roam my skin, and her lips press to it. By the time the movie is over, it's three-thirty in the morning, and I can almost feel the time slipping away. She reaches between my legs and gently strokes the hairs there.

"I don't want to leave without touching you one more time," she says.

"Yes," I reply.

"Can I get it?" she asks.

I nod, and she gets up and returns wearing the strap-on we used last time. I lie back with my head against the pillow. She moves over me, and we kiss for a long time; so

177

long that I worry the knock will come any moment. Then, I remember: we have a private elevator leading to this room. They can't knock on the door. They'll probably just call the room if we're not out of it by four.

"Hey," she says softly.

"What?" I ask softly back.

"Are you here?" she asks.

"What?"

"You seem… distracted."

"Oh, no." I hold her face with my hands. "I'm here, baby."

She nods slowly and kisses me again as she moves the toy through my wetness and then inside. We look at each other as she moves inside me. I hold her ass with one hand and her cheek in the other. She's moving slowly at first. Her eyes bore into mine, and I know this isn't sex.

"Are you okay?" she asks, rocking her hips a little faster now.

"Yes," I say. "Don't stop."

"I won't."

"Can you come like this?" I ask, feeling my orgasm build.

"Yes," she says, squeezing her eyes together for a second.

She's already almost there. I am, too. She moves faster, and her head goes to my shoulder. She's rocking erratically now. I come when she presses perfectly against my clit.

"Baby, yes!"

"Oh, fuck," she says a moment later.

We come together, and then I just hold her there, against my body, while she's still inside me. I hold her there, thinking about the other member downstairs and how she warned me not to get too deep – I was right earlier.

The phone rings.

"What's–" She lifts up.

"They can't knock, so they're calling," I explain. "It's three-forty-five."

She turns to see the phone next to the bed and picks it up.

"We'll be down in a minute," she says into it and drops it back down.

I laugh a little, and she falls back on top of me.

"Stay here with me until four," I request.

"Of course."

"No, I mean – stay inside me," I say. "I want to hold on to this."

She kisses my neck and nods.

MONTH 8. PART 2. – ALL ABOUT US

(POV Escort)

I'm told prior to my arrival that she's booked something special for us. I'm not told what exactly, but I *do* know that we have a room reserved just for us. That makes me very happy.

"You're smiling," my friend tells me.

"I am," I say.

"Because you'll be with her in a couple of days?" she asks.

"Well, I don't have much else to smile about, do I?"

"Hey, we're not half bad," she says as she puts on her shirt.

"Yeah, I take offense to that," her wife says as she climbs off the bed and pulls open a drawer to find a new pair of underwear.

"You're assuming my smile is *only* about her. I enjoyed myself tonight, too. I like that thing you did with the ice," I tell them.

"Yet, you still won't participate," she says as she pulls on a pair of pants.

"We said we wouldn't pressure her," her wife says, wrapping her arms around the woman from behind.

"And I'm not. I'm just mentioning that she seems to enjoy herself every time, and we'd love for her to enjoy it more."

"It's true. I'd really love to enjoy *you*," my friend says, staring at me with lust in her eyes. "I love watching you make yourself come, but I'd also like to do it one day."

"I want to," I admit. "I'm not sure what's holding me back, honestly."

"*She* is," my friend says.

"She has nothing to do with *this*," I tell her, pointing

between myself and the two of them.

"She's sexy," my friend says. "I wouldn't mind if you two came into our room and we got to watch *you* this time."

"She got us a room," I tell them.

"It's a hotel," one of them says.

"I know, but she put in some special request. The other rooms are just up for grabs, but I guess we have one."

"Just for you two?"

"I hope so," I say, standing up and buttoning my jeans.

"Maybe next time, then," one of them says. "If you trust her, I do, too. Maybe one day, we could all have one night of real fun."

"It hasn't been fun for you yet?" her wife teases, kissing her neck.

"Oh, I had a lot of fun about five minutes ago," she says, taking her wife's hand and sliding it inside her underwear. "And I could go again if you're interested."

"Always," she says as she strokes.

I stand there and watch.

***

I arrive dressed in my suit, as usual, and discover my friends are already at the bar. They're an interesting couple, to say the least. I don't know that I've ever met a married couple quite like them. They seem to understand each other in a way I've surely never seen before. I know they want to take things to the next level with all three of us touching each other, and there's a part of me that definitely wants to do that, but there's also a part of me that says I only want to do it if *she's* there. I knew I liked watching people before I started coming to these things, but she has opened me up to explore things I never knew I wanted; things I now know I need.

"So, where's your girl?" my friend asks as I walk up to them.

I order myself a drink and then decide to order one for

her, too. I don't really know what she likes to drink, and we don't always have drinks, so I'm definitely guessing, but hopefully, she'll drink whatever I order for her.

"She's not here yet," I tell her.

"Any chance she won't show? Didn't you say she was out of town? Just because she paid for the room thing doesn't mean she'll be here for sure," she says.

"She just doesn't want you to get your hopes up," her wife adds.

"I guess I just worry about you. If you're only with her when you're here, and then she stops coming – well, you know…" she says.

"I know. I understand."

"What are you going to do once you have all that debt paid off?"

"What do you mean?" I ask.

"She means once you have it paid off, you don't have to come here. We've talked about this before. Are you still going to come?"

"I don't know."

"Yes, you do," she says, laughing a little. "You're going to work these events as long as she's coming to them, aren't you?"

"Why not? At first, I was worried and slightly terrified, but I'm getting paid to have sex with an amazing woman who just does things to me. So, why should I stop?"

"What happens when you want her for more than once a month?"

I already do, I think to myself.

"My love, let her off the hook. She's got a big night ahead of her, apparently; special accommodations have been made."

"Think she ordered her a sex swing," my friend offers, and I burst out laughing.

"I hope not," I say.

"Why? They're not bad."

"I've never tried one," I say.

"Oh, now there's an idea," she says, looking me up and down. "Your sexy body in that thing, and the two of us get to–"

"She's here," I say, looking up and seeing *her*. Then, I squint. "She's talking to that member."

My friend turns around and says, "So?"

"So, that's the one she was with," I remind her. "Twice."

"Oh, right. So?" she repeated.

"She's jealous, babe."

"I'm not jealous. I just–"

"Don't want her to use those *special accommodations* on that woman and the other woman she's always with," she interrupts.

"Right," I say, watching the two women talk to one another. "Since she's been with them already... Do you think she wants them to be with *us* tonight? Could that be the accommodation?"

"The other member would have to be okay with it," my friend tells me.

"She probably would be," I say. "I've got to go. I'll see you guys later."

I walk over to them, and *she* looks up at me. She greets me with a smile that makes me feel hopeful, but I'm still wondering if she plans on anyone else joining us – I really wanted it to just be us tonight.

"Hi," I say, handing her the drink. "I hope this is okay."

"It's perfect. Thank you."

"You're welcome," I say. "So, I hear there's a room reserved for us tonight."

"There is, yes."

I look over at the woman next to her and say, "Is it for all of us or–"

"No, not me. I have my own room to get to," she says. "She told me that it's light-blue, like her eyes. I'm going to go find her now."

I watch the other woman walk away toward the elevators, and I might just get my way.

"What's light-blue?"

"Nothing," she says. "Hi." She takes a sip of her drink.

"We did this part already," I reply, taking her hand. "Can we get out of here before they all get started?"

"Sure."

"It's just us tonight?" I ask when we arrive at the elevators.

She presses her card against the reader.

"Yes. Did you want–"

"No, I like it when it's just us. Don't get me wrong… I like it when we're with other people, too. There's just something about touching you while other people are doing the same thing that I find a turn-on."

"Me too," she says with a wicked smile as the elevator arrives.

"Oh, that's the private one," I tell her as I point, thinking she's made some mistake.

"I know," she tells me.

"That's to the penthouse."

"I know," she repeats simply.

"You reserved the penthouse?"

I'm strangely honored. I have no idea how much a membership costs for this private club of sorts, but if I had to guess just based on what I get paid, it has to be a lot. Now, she's also paying for the penthouse suite and whatever else is up there on top of it. I decide to take this as a compliment and get into the elevator with her.

"I did." She pulls me against her.

My hands wrap around her first. I pull her in for a kiss and move my hand under her dress as my tongue seeks out hers. I decide to move in a little closer, expecting to find a lacy thong I can toy with until we can get into the room.

"You're not wearing any underwear," I say, feeling instantly turned on.

"No," she says confidently.

"Fuck," I say and push her against the elevator wall just as it dings to tell me we've arrived.

I don't care. We can go back down to the lobby and return up here again. The doors could open, everyone downstairs could watch me touching her, and I wouldn't stop. I cup her and find her wet and wanting. I waste no time and push my fingers inside. I press my thumb to her clit, and I fuck her against the wall of the elevator. I want her to know that tonight, she's mine. I bite down on her neck a little, letting her know the same thing. She comes hard just a moment later, tearing off my jacket, leaving it at my shoulders. Buttons fly off my shirt as she pulls it apart. I guess I'll deal with that later. My nipple is in her mouth, and I look up at the mirrored ceiling. Damn, this entire elevator is all mirrors, and I just noticed. She's still coming into my hand, and I wonder if she'll ever come down. Before I can think too much about it, my pants are opened, and her hand is inside them.

"Off," she says.

I'm still pushing deep inside her, even though I know she already came, but I manage to kick off my pants. She's inside my underwear now, and she's stroking. Fuck, she's stroking me. It's so good. I lean against her, and she twists my nipple. Then, she slips inside.

"Yes," I say, knowing I need this.

"Like this?" she asks, and I can't keep up my own thrusts inside her, so I stop.

"Yes," I repeat.

"Pull out, babe," she says.

I love when she calls me *babe* or *baby*. It's like I'm not an escort, and she's not a member; we're just two women who love to make each other come. I pull out of her, and she flips us around. She taps my leg, and she owns me now. My head is against the wall, and she fucks me. I start to come, and it's a long one. I could melt against her right now and be completely content, but she pulls out and then tugs on my hand until we're in the room. The elevator hadn't moved. I'm seeing stars from the intensity of my orgasm, and she's pulling on me. My pants are around my ankles, and I think I'm going to trip, but somehow, I manage to keep myself up. I'm pushed down on a sofa in the room. I only have a second to look around, but I notice how big the place is and how nice it looks.

"This place is—"

I stop talking and watch her take off her dress and her bra. Next thing I know, she's sitting on my lap, straddling my hips. I wrap my arms around her, and she's ushering my mouth to her nipple. I don't protest.

"I love your mouth," she says.

I moan because I love her body.

"Make me come with it," she says.

"Let's go to bed," I say, pulling back to look up at her.

"No, here. Please, baby," she says.

I nod, knowing what she wants. She stands, and I lie back, allowing her to straddle my face. Now, I'm gripping her ass and lowering her down to me. I lick her. Her hips move, and I lick more. I slip inside her, and I can feel how ready she already is.

"Yes, I missed you so much," she says.

I suck. I lick. She comes hard in my mouth. She lifts up quickly and moves until she's straddling my hips again. I wipe my chin happily and smile up at her.

"Cocky?"

"I can be," I say, bucking my hips once. "Want me to wear one?"

She laughs.

"Maybe later," she says. Then, she seems to think for a second and adds, "I didn't bring one, though."

"I did," I say.

I have a bag that someone carried up here for me earlier. When I arrived, I was told to make myself available at the bar until she got there. They took the small bag I brought with me, letting me know it would be in the room we've been assigned to for later when I need it. I lift my eyebrow at her and move her hips back and forth on my stomach.

"You're still so wet. Let me make you come with it."

"Later," she says, giving me a playful glare.

"Why later? Do you need a break? We just got started."

"Eager, huh?"

"Well, you *did* tear off my shirt, and I think my jacket is somewhere on the floor behind me, so I'd say we were *both* a little eager."

She looks around the room.

"What's so funny?" I ask her.

"We were supposed to lead *up* to the sex, not start with it," she says.

"Supposed to?"

She stands and is completely, perfectly nude. I sit up. I realize just then that I'm still wearing my shirt, which is open, and my now-destroyed panties.

"I had them bring up food, and there's an in-room jacuzzi. There's also a giant TV in the bedroom, apparently, and I ordered a movie I really like."

"A movie?" I ask, standing up.

"Yeah, *that* kind of movie," she explains.

"Oh," I say, understanding perfectly what she means and being intrigued. "You're into that?"

"Not much, but this one has a story, and the women are hot."

"Not as hot as you," I tell her, pulling her against me.

"Nice," she laughs.

"I'm serious," I say, losing my smile and kissing her because I want her to know that I *am* serious. "But I'm down to watch a movie of two hot women getting it on – as long as I get to touch you while we do."

"That can be arranged," she says, wrapping her arms around my neck. "Can you lose the rest of your clothes and join me in the hot tub? There should already be perfectly hot water in there, with the bubbles already going and a bottle of champagne chilling. I asked for chocolate-dipped strawberries, too. Do you eat those?"

"I can't say I've ever really had the opportunity to eat a chocolate-dipped strawberry."

"Oh, I'm going to feed them to you, then," She slides my underwear off, kisses my collarbone, and then pulls my shirt off. "I love that you don't wear a bra. Your nipples are so perfect." She pulls one into her mouth.

"We can't go to that hot tub if you're doing this," I say, keeping her there with my hand because I love when she does this.

"I was going to do this *in* the hot tub." She kisses my neck.

We finally head toward the hot tub a minute later, my nipple sore from the sucking and nibbling. The bathroom is larger than the old studio apartment I had before my aunt got sick. The jacuzzi could easily fit six people, the shower is separate, and there's also a sauna, apparently. It could fit those same six people, or even a different six, I think as I watch her pour us each a glass of champagne. She hands it to me, and I take a sip. She picks up a strawberry coated in chocolate and presses it to my lips. I take a bite. The chocolate cracks a bit, and I try to gather it all in my mouth. She laughs at me. Then, she steals the rest of the berry for herself. She gives me a quick kiss, takes a drink of her own champagne, and slips into the bubbling water.

It turns out that I *do* like chocolate strawberries, but I like the taste of them on her lips even more. I finish my champagne, which I'm sure is a mistake, and climb into the tub, facing her. We just stare at one another for a long time. Then, she smiles softly, and I smile back. I stretch my legs out. She takes the invitation and moves into me, hovering over me with her hands on the side of the tub, holding her up.

"Well, what did you think of the strawberry?" she asks, and I can feel the warmth of her breath on my skin.

"I want to make you come in here," I say, ignoring the question. "Will you let me?"

"Yes," she says.

I reach between her legs and find her clit, swollen and hard.

"Stay just like this," I say.

She does. Water thrashes as she comes in my hand minutes later. Her lips meet mine, and I can taste the champagne on them now, along with the chocolate and sweet berry. Her taste is intoxicating, and just for a second, I think that maybe all that I feel is real. It's not just sex – though, that's fucking amazing – it's more. Maybe her pheromones are *meant to be* with my pheromones. Maybe we're supposed to be together like this, but also like something else, too.

"You okay?" she asks me when she pulls away from the kiss.

"I'm a little hot suddenly," I say, smiling up at her.

"*You're* a little hot?" She laughs. "I just came, and I think there's more water on the floor than in here now."

"More champagne and more strawberries?" I suggest.

***

After the hot tub, we sit at the small table against the wall of windows overlooking the city. She had appetizers brought up for us before we'd even arrived, so we have more champagne and just talk. We don't talk much about my aunt this time. We discuss pretty much everything else, though. We talk about how different our lives have been and still are. It's hours of talking, and I find myself watching the clock that's above the gas-burning fireplace. I don't want this night to end. I love talking to her, getting to know her, but I don't want to wait another month until I get to touch her again.

"Bed?"

"What?" she asks.

"Bed?" I repeat.

"Oh, sure," she says as if that's not why we're here.

"What movie did you order?" I ask her as we walk into

the bedroom we haven't even used yet.

"Something with a terrible title," she replies.

I laugh and say, "That's all of them."

I sit back on the bed, spreading my legs wide. She stares, and I roll my eyes. When she finally sits between them, I pull her against me. I've decided that I will always love pulling this woman against me like this, holding on to her, and breathing her in. Tonight, she smells only a little bit like herself. Her shampoo is all her, but her skin now smells of the hotel soap we used a little in the hot tub. She also smells a bit of the champagne we've had and even a little like strawberry.

"Can we just watch something else?"

"You don't want to watch what you picked out?" I ask, kissing her shoulder.

"No. Maybe just a regular movie," she replies.

"Whatever you want," I say, wondering what's changed.

She picks something out, and it's a rom-com I've seen before. At least, it's a happy lesbian movie. We watch it together, with her leaning back and relaxing against me. I run my hands over her skin and sometimes offer her soft kisses as we let it play on the large TV. When the movie ends, I know time is almost up for us, so I reach between her legs and gently stroke the hairs I find there, wanting to signal that I need her now.

"I don't want to leave without touching you one more time," I say shortly after.

"Yes," she says.

"Can I get it?" I ask.

After she nods, I climb out of bed and go to the bag, which someone had left in the main room. I slip on the strap-on and go back into the bedroom room, not wanting to waste any time. She's lying down now, so I move on top of her. I know the night is almost over, but I can't keep myself from kissing her. We stay like this for a long time before I notice something – her kisses aren't like they normally are.

She's not keeping up with me. Her hands have stilled on my body, too. I pull back to look at her.

"Hey," I say softly.

"What?" she asks back, looking up at me with beautiful eyes.

"Are you here?" I ask her.

"What?"

"You seem… distracted."

"Oh, no. I'm here, baby." She takes my head in her hands.

I nod, wondering what she was just thinking about, and kiss her again. I move the toy through her folds, gathering her wetness – that's all for me. She's wet all the time, every time we're like this, and it's all for me. I push gently inside, giving her a moment to adjust but not taking my eyes off her as I push and pull and move inside her. She's holding on to my ass, encouraging me with one hand, and her other is cupping my cheek.

"Are you okay?" I ask, rocking my hips a little faster now.

"Yes, don't stop."

"I won't," I tell her.

"Can you come like this?" she asks.

"Yes," I say, knowing I'm already almost there.

I move faster, wanting us to come at the same time. My head is on her shoulder now. I can't keep my hips rocking in rhythm because it feels so good. She's coming now.

"Baby, yes!"

"Oh, fuck," I say because I'm coming now, too.

We come together, and she holds me against her body. God, she just holds me as I breathe against her neck. It's a powerful thing to come like this with someone, but it's on a whole other level that she holds me this way – against her – after and kisses the side of my head as we both attempt to catch our breath. Then, the phone rings.

"What's–" I lift myself up; the mood altered by the obnoxious phone call.

"They can't knock, so they're calling. It's three-forty-five."

I notice the phone next to the bed and pick it up.

"We'll be down in a minute," I say without waiting for someone on the other end of the line to say something back.

Then, I drop it back down, and she laughs. I fall back down on top of her.

"Stay here with me until four," she says.

"Of course."

"No, I mean – stay inside me," she says. "I want to hold on to this."

I kiss her neck, nod, and think I wish that I could hold on to this forever.

***

"So, how was it?" my friend asks as we box up some of my aunt's things at the house. "You've been awfully quiet about the special accommodations."

"She got us the penthouse. It was nice," I say.

"Just nice?" she asks.

"It was perfect," I tell her, smiling.

She sits on the old sofa in the living room and says, "Babe, it's not supposed to be perfect."

"Why not?"

"Because you don't mean perfect like it's perfect sex; the sex you've always fantasized about having, and she gives that to you. I'm sure she does, that's part of it, but that's not *all* of it. You were, like, wistful just then when you said *perfect*."

"So what if I was?" I say.

"It's supposed to be just sex."

"You two don't always just have sex," I say.

"We're married," she replies, pointing to the kitchen where her wife is making us coffee. "We've been together for eleven years. We go there because it lets us experience something we both want, but it's a small part of our life to-

192

gether. We wake up every morning next to one another and have dinner together each night. Yes, we have an amazing sex life, and trust me, I'm grateful for that, but if she told me she wanted to quit going to these things tomorrow, I'd agree, and we'd still be *us*. We'd still be in love and sharing a life together. I love that woman; I'd do anything for her. I'd die for her in a heartbeat." My friend sighs. "You two meet once a month, and it's supposed to just be for sex, for fun. It's supposed to be about her letting that part of herself out one night a month so that she can get through the rest of her life or get some release because her girlfriend can't give her what she wants. It's–"

"I get it," I say, needing to not think about her having a girlfriend.

"Do you?" she asks softly. "I'm not trying to give you a hard time. It's just been, what, eight months now? I know you're going through a lot, honey, but your aunt's gone now. You've taken care of her for so long, you've given up on finding someone. But you're getting things taken care of now. Maybe it's time to put yourself back out there."

"I thought you wanted me to be with you two," I say, crossing my arms over my chest.

"For sex, once in a while," she says, laughing a little. "We're not looking for another member in our marriage. And yes, we still talk about that; doing that with you. We'd like to, but if you're not into it, all you have to do is tell us no. You don't have to keep saying that you're not ready."

"It's not a no, though," I tell her, sitting down next to her. "I think I…"

"It's okay. You can tell me."

I sigh this time and say, "I want her to be there, too."

"To watch?"

"No, I want us all to…"

"Oh," my friend says.

"I don't even know if she'd want that, but I was thinking about asking her if you two are okay with it."

"You want all four of us to be together?"

"Oh, that sounds fun," her wife says as she enters the room with two cups of coffee in hand. "Mine is in the kitchen. Keep talking, though; I like where this is headed."

She disappears after handing us our cups. We laugh a little.

"Well, *she's* up for it," my friend tells me. "Can I ask why you want her there, too?"

"I feel like I need her there; like I shouldn't be with anyone else like that unless she's there."

"Because you think it's breaking some rule or something?"

"We don't talk about it, but I don't think she's with anyone when we're not together, either."

"Well, that's dangerous," my friend tells me. "But you know how I feel about this, so I'll shut up."

"I can't explain how I feel about her. I *do* know that it's not just sex, though."

"You're not asking for my advice, but you need to just hook up with someone. Get on an app, swipe whatever direction you're supposed to, and fuck their brains out. Get her out of your system because she's not real, babe. She's someone that will leave you one day. She'll get bored of the parties or move out of the city. She'll meet someone herself, assuming she hasn't already, and maybe she'll stop coming because she's in love, and they're not into it. It's not meant to last, and you deserve something lasting."

"Okay, are we really talking about a foursome here?" my friend's wife asks as she walks back into the room.

MONTH 9. PART 1. – EXPECT THE UNEXPECTED

(POV Member)

"Hey stranger," I say when I sidle up to her, giddy with anticipation for this night.

Work has been particularly difficult lately, and my mother has pushed yet another lesbian on me, saying she wants grandkids sooner rather than later, and if I want to have them by myself, I need to find someone now. It's funny the first time she brings it up. Then, it's just annoying. I wonder if I'll ever be like this to my own kids, hope not, and then decide to focus on the gorgeous woman in front of me that I haven't seen in a month.

"I was worried you might not come," she says.

"I told you I'd be here." I take her hand.

"You're just late."

"Sorry, I got stuck at home with some work stuff to take care of."

"Isn't it the weekend?"

"Yes, but it was a client thing, so I had to call them. I'm here now, though. Missed me that much, huh?" I tease hopefully.

"Yes," she replies with her perfect smile.

"We should get a room before they fill up," I suggest, nodding toward the stairs.

"Can we talk first?" she asks.

"Of course, we can talk," I say, hoping she knows that we can always just talk – I don't come here only for sex. "We can find the room and talk as long as you want, babe."

"It has to *do* with the room," she says, walking us to the sofa and sitting down.

I sit down next to her. I notice women making out in the corner, but I don't care about them right now. I'm worried about her.

"Is this yours?" I ask when I notice the bag at her feet.

"Yes," she says.

"Can't wait to see what's inside." I squeeze her hand. "What's wrong?"

"Nothing."

"I can tell something's up. Are you okay? We don't have–"

"I'm okay," she interrupts and kisses me. "I just have something I wanted to run by you. If you don't want to do it, we'll find a room."

"Okay. What?"

"My friends," she says.

"You want to watch them tonight?" I ask.

"I want to *join* them tonight," she replies, and I swallow.

I should have expected this. She's not just here for me.

"Oh," I say, pulling away.

"Never mind," she says, taking my hand back. "It was a stupid idea. I–"

"It's not a stupid idea," I say.

And it's not. The whole reason we come here is to let out our fantasies. I know she's technically working, but if she wants to be with them, and they want her, I can't fault her for that. I had my own fantasies. It's why I'm here right now.

"You've been with them before, so…"

"Just that one time I told you about," she says.

"Oh, I assumed you'd…"

"No," she says. "I thought tonight would be a good time."

"I see," I say. "Well, this is unexpected, but they *are* members, so… if they've requested you tonight, and you want to be with them, I can't really argue. I'll just…" I have to force myself to stand because I have no idea where to go from here.

"Where are you going?" she asks, holding on to my hand.

"To figure out how to spend the rest of my night," I reply honestly. "I think I'll just go home. I—"

She stands and presses me against her body.

"You're misunderstanding, babe. I don't want it to be the three of us. I was thinking, it could be the *four* of us."

"All of us?" I ask with wide eyes.

"I haven't been with them because I want you there with me," she says.

"I've never… I mean, the most I've experienced with more than one partner was…"

"Here," she says. "With the two women."

"Yeah," I reply. "And also with you, while we were next to your friends, but we didn't touch them then."

"It's okay if it's a no," she says, running a hand through my hair.

She's so good with me. She just knows when to touch me and how, and not in a sexual way necessarily. She just knows when I need her to pull me against her like she just did so that I know she's there. She knows when to cup my cheek, press her lips to mine gently, and caress my hair so sweetly. She just knows.

"Why do you want me there?" I ask.

"Because I'm not ready to be with them alone," she says. "But also, because it's something I've never done, either, and I wanted to experience it with you."

I put my arms around her neck just as a woman in the corner moans. We both turn our heads to see a woman on her knees in front of another woman. Oh, that's nice, I think. The woman on the floor is a member I recognize, and the woman she's pleasuring is an escort I've seen around a few times, who seems to be thoroughly enjoying herself.

"Why is watching so hot?" I ask, pulling her in closer.

"I have no idea, but it is," she replies, running her hand up under my dress.

Her hand isn't demanding – *she's* rarely demanding. In fact, she's only demanding when I want her to come. She always knows that, too.

"Are you trying to start something right now?" I ask, feeling wetness rush out of me at her touch.

"Would that be a bad thing?" she teases, moving her hand until she's touching me there. "Thong tonight?"

"It's flimsy. I thought you'd be able to move it if you really tried," I tease back.

"Would you like me to move it right now?" she asks.

"Maybe," I say, lifting an eyebrow at her.

"Watch them," she says.

Then, she slips her fingers inside the fabric of my thong, and I just watch the two women as she strokes me slowly. The escort pulls at the spaghetti strap of her dress until she has one breast out. She massages it slowly as she lifts a leg over the other woman's shoulder. I think about how nice it would be to suck on her nipple while the other woman makes her come.

"I'll make you come down here," *she* whispers into my ear. "Then, I'll take you upstairs."

"Yes," I say as she strokes.

She wraps me up in her other arm, and I watch the women. I hear moans and gasps as the other strap is dropped. Now, I want both of the breasts in my hands. I want to squeeze them, twist nipples until she's moaning out. I watch the member's hand disappear inside her, and the escort yells out. I watch that arm move up and down. God, she's thrusting inside her while she sucks on her.

"And I'll fuck you senseless," *she* tells me as she strokes me clit faster.

"What if I want one of them to fuck me, too?" I ask, watching the two women but picturing myself standing behind the escort, playing with her breasts.

"Do you?" she asks and stops stroking.

"I think so. I want you there touching me, too. Don't stop, baby," I tell her.

She starts again. I'm so close.

"What if I want to fuck someone else or they want to fuck me?" she asks.

"Can I watch?" I ask.

"You can *touch*," she says.

"Oh, yes," I say, referring both to how she's touching me *and* to that idea. "I don't want anything unless you're there. What have you done to me?"

"I'm about to make you come," she says, not really answering my rhetorical question.

I hold on to her as I watch the woman against the wall come.

"Oh, fuck," I let out, collapsing against *her* as I come, too.

"I can't believe this is me," I say after I come down. "I've never done this before. I'm a vanilla-sex kind of girl."

"You are *anything* but a vanilla-sex kind of *woman*, babe," she says. "Are you sure about this? We can always stay right here or find another room."

"I'm sure," I say, not feeling entirely sure yet but knowing enough about myself now that I want to try. "I like that I'll be there with you." I smile at her. "You'll have to take your hand out from under my dress, though, since I'll need to walk up the stairs."

"Maybe we should just stay here, then," she says.

When I pull her hand out, I hold it to her lips. She opens her mouth, and I watch her as she sucks on her fingers.

"Now, they'll know you're mine," I say, knowing that when she kisses them, they'll taste me.

"All yours."

We head up the stairs. She holds my hand as we enter the bedroom. The door closes behind us, and she locks it for good measure. This is going to happen.

"Yeah?" her friend asks when she hears the door close and turns to see that it's us.

"Yeah," *she* says.

"We're new to this, too," her wife says. "You two are the first we're going to let…"

"Touch us," *her* friend finishes for her wife. "Well, except that time you had your hands down my wife's pants in the kitchen." She looks at *her*.

"Will you do that again?" the woman's wife asks, licking her lips.

God, she wants *her*. She wants my girl to fuck her, and I can understand why. *She* looks at me as if to ask for permission. I give her a nod because I want to watch this. She kisses me softly and then once more before she turns and walks toward the other woman. She kisses her hard as if she's been holding back something she's wanted. Yes, I'm jealous, but I'm also okay with this. I can tell she's letting something out that she's wanted to for a while, most likely. I smile softly as I watch *her* kiss her. She wanted me here for this. She *needed* me here for this. There's something about that, right?

Her friend moves to them. She's got her hand on *her* back now and her other on her wife's head, encouraging them to continue. When *she* pulls out of one kiss, she goes right into another with her friend. I watch as the first woman she kissed undoes her belt. Without hesitation, I move behind *her*. I'm not ready for anyone to touch *her* just yet – I haven't had my chance. I help undo her pants, let them fall to the floor, and slip my hand inside her underwear. She's so fucking wet, I want to come again just from touching her. I start stroking. I look and notice *her* hand is slipping beneath the dress of the woman in front of her. Oh, yes – she's going to fuck her now. My hips rock into *her* ass. I'm so ready.

"Oh, yes," the woman in front of her says.

"Make her come hard," her friend says to her after pulling out of their long kiss.

She kisses her friend's wife again, and I keep stroking *her* clit. Her friend looks at me with dark eyes, and I nod. She moves behind me, lifts up my dress, presses her still covered sex into my bare ass, moans a little, and then moves her hand around my front, pushing my thong aside – she strokes. I don't know what else she's doing until I feel her pants at my feet. She kicks them away, and she's naked from the waist down now. Her pussy is wet and pressed to my ass cheek.

"I like to come quietly sometimes. I'm going to ride your ass and come while she makes my wife come," she whispers into my ear. "And while I make you come."

I nod because I can't form words, and that sounds so good as I stroke *her*. I moan because her friend is pressing against me, and I can feel how hard her clit is already.

"Fuck, that's good," I say. "Baby, she's making me feel so good," I tell *her*.

"Yes, feel good, baby," *she* says back.

"Go inside. I need you inside," the woman *she's* fucking says. "Oh, I knew you'd fill me," she says.

She must be inside her now.

"Don't stop until I come in your hand," the woman she's fucking says.

"Baby, I'm going to come. Come with me," I say, feeling hard and fast strokes on my clit with the woman behind me fucking herself on my ass and offering me sexy gasps against my neck.

"Fuck," *she* says. "Yes, there."

I stroke her there, and she comes. I love when she comes.

"I'm coming," the woman she's touching says. "Oh, God. Fuck me, yes!" she screams next.

"Fuck, honey. You're so fucking sexy. I can't wait to taste you," the woman behind me says to her wife.

I gasp. I moan. It's all so fucking good.

"Are you coming?" *she* asks me.

"Yes. So good," I say, unable to form complete sentences.

"I get you next," she tells me.

We all come and then come down. We stay there for a while, gathering our breath. My legs are shaking. I've never felt this before, and only part of it is because of the woman who just made me come. It's really because of *her*. I'd never be able to do this without her here, without her assurances, telling me it's okay to want what I want. *She* turns around and kisses me harder than usual. This must be working for her, too. She unzips my dress, and I step out of it. I don't know what else is happening around us, but she kicks off her pants. I undo the buttons on her shirt. I suck on her nipple. She tears her shirt off and presses my face closer. I suck harder.

"Yes. Suck it, baby," she commands.

"Do you want me to?" I ask, stopping to look up at her. "I *can*." I lift an eyebrow at her.

"Yes."

She pushes my head down, and I laugh silently at her eagerness. I toss her underwear aside and suck her into my mouth. She spreads her legs farther apart, and I hear her gasp, so I look up. Her friend is playing with *her* breasts now. Oh, wow. I suck and keep looking. *She* has her head back on a shoulder. Her hand is wrapped around her friend's neck, pulling her in as the woman sucks on her earlobe.

"Inside," *she* says to me.

I suck and push my fingers in deep.

"Oh, my God," she lets out.

She's kissing her friend now. She has her hand in my hair, pushing me into her pussy, rocking her hips into my face, and I want all of her. I want her everywhere and all the time.

"I want you to taste me," the woman she only just fucked says.

"Yes," *she* says.

"And then, I'll taste her," her friend says, placing her hand on top of the one *she* has on my head.

I moan; I can't help it. This is all so erotic and exactly what I never knew I needed. She comes hard; her hips rock into me over and over. Her hand presses me into her harder. She needs me here; I can feel it in how her hand grips my head.

"Oh, my God," she says when her hips finally stop and she loosens her grip on my head.

I stand up and wipe my chin. She kisses me.

"Taste her," I tell *her*, nodding to the woman behind her.

God, I never knew I wanted to watch *her* go down on another woman, but I do right now. The woman I referred to is already on the bed. Her legs are spread for *her*. She touches herself, and it's sexy. Suddenly, I'm being taken by the hand and lowered to the bed by the other woman, next to her wife. I want to kiss her. She's about to have the woman I'm crazy about go down on her, and I'm going to kiss her. I do. The other woman leans over and kisses me back. Her tongue plays with mine, and we both moan, knowing what's about to happen and wanting it. I feel my legs being spread. Then, I have a tongue on my clit. It's not *hers*, but it's still good. I reach for the woman lying next to me. I cup her breast and play with her nipple. She does the same with mine.

"Yes, there," I say as the woman sucks on my clit.

I look over at *her*. Her eyes are open, and she's looking back at me, not at the woman she's sucking. I nod.

"Shit. Yes," the woman next to me says. "Harder."

She looks at me as she gives the woman what she asks for.

"Inside," I say to *her*.

"Oh, that's good," I say when the woman sucking on me slides inside.

I hadn't meant for her to do that, but I'm not protesting. Her fingers are almost as long as *hers*, and they manage to find a good spot. I watch *her* the entire time, though, as I hear the moans and other sounds the woman next to me makes.

I know my girl is giving it to her good, but I need her to know something, so I mouth, "You're mine," to her.

She nods. She understands. She is mine, and I am hers. We both come around the same time; the woman next to me comes a little before me. I see *her* stand up only for a second before the woman lying next to me rolls on top of me and kisses me hard. Damn, she's a good kisser. I wrap my arms around her neck and pull her down as I spread my legs for her on instinct.

"Are you going to make me come now?" I hear someone ask.

"I was thinking about it," *she* says.

Oh, she's going to fuck her friend now.

"You're an amazing kisser," the woman currently kissing my neck says.

"So are you," I say, pulling her mouth back to mine.

"This is how wet you get? Fuck," *she* says.

"Wait," the other woman says, and I hear rustling.

"Babe," the woman says to her wife. "I'm going to fuck you."

"I want you to fuck me," her wife says back, but she's looking down at me when she says it.

"Will you make her come with your mouth while I do?"

"Oh, yes," she says, winking at me.

"I don't know if I can come again just yet," I say.

"You can just feel good – you don't have to come. But she's amazing with her tongue," the other woman says.

"It's true," the woman on top of me says. "I bet you taste good."

She slips down my body, and now, I'm able to see it all; to see *her*. She's standing behind her friend, who's wearing a strap-on. Her friend enters her wife, and her wife licks my sex. *She* slips her hand inside the woman's shorts and strokes her clit for her.

"Make me come. I'm so hard," the woman says to *her*.

"I can tell," she says back.

I don't hear anymore. The tongue slipping inside me feels too good, and I can't focus on words anymore until I hear her speak loudly.

"Make her feel good," *she* says.

"She is, baby," I say, playing with my breasts now. "I'm going to come."

The woman with her head between my legs moans, either because of how good it feels for her to be fucked by her wife from behind or because she's about to make me come. It could be both.

"Fuck, I'm going to come," the woman fucking her wife with the dildo says, thrusting harder. "Babe, she's making me come so hard. God, I knew you'd be good at this," she says to *her*.

"I'm just getting started," *she* says. "Take that thing off, and I'll let you sit on my face. I'll show you how good I am with my tongue."

"Yes," her friend says, thrusting wildly.

"I'm coming!" her wife yells.

"Don't stop!" I yell because I'm so close.

I push her head back down to my pussy.

"Yes," the woman fucking her wife says, rolling her head back against *her* shoulder as she slows and then stops her thrusting.

Her wife comes down quickly, and I come down as *she* watches me. She winks at me, which is adorable and cocky, all wrapped in one. I lick my lips and taste her.

"I love you," one of them says to her wife, who is now standing facing her.

"I love you, too," the woman replies, kissing her.

She ends up on top of me, and I spread my legs for her. We're both naked and sweaty, and it feels so good to have her on top of me again.

"How are you?" she asks, looking concerned.

"So good," I say, because I am.

She kisses me softly, taking her time. I move her hand to my sex – I need her. She presses inside me, which is exactly what I wanted. She rolls down into me as she curls inside.

"I missed you," I tell her.

"I miss you all the time," she says.

When I come, she's kissing me. I bite her lower lip a little, and she groans. When I'm done, she falls on top of me, like she usually does, and, for a minute, I forget there are two other women in the room with us.

"So?" one of them says as she lies down next to us.

"Yeah, so?" the other one asks, lying down on top of her wife.

"That was…" her wife says to her.

"Fucking amazing," her wife replies.

"Yes," she says, laughing a little.

"I want you alone now," she whispers into my ear. "The rest of the night."

"Okay," I say.

"Okay, what?" the woman above her wife asks.

"This was really fucking great," I tell them, smiling and then laughing a little.

"Agreed," *she* says, mumbling against my skin.

"But, I think she's ready for it to just be us now," I tell them, rubbing *her* back up and down slowly.

She nods, and I kiss the side of her head and laugh a little.

"Yeah, babe?" I ask.

She nods again.

"We're going to get dressed and go grab some food. We usually take a break anyway. Why don't you guys keep this room? We don't mind *not* having privacy anyway," she says, slipping off of her wife. "Come on, my love. Let's carbo-load and grab a drink."

"I could use some water," her wife says, standing up.

"I think those two we like were downstairs earlier. Want to watch them for a bit?"

"That sounds good," she says.

They dress.

"Say goodbye, babe," I tell *her*.

"Goodbye, babe," she says without lifting her head off of my shoulder.

Her friends laugh.

"We'll see you guys later, maybe," one of them says as she closes the door behind them.

"Are you okay?" I ask her.

"I'm so tired," she says against my skin.

I laugh and say, "Do you need a nap?"

"No," she says, lifting her head up to look at me. "Can we just lie here for a while, though?"

"Why don't I go get us some water, at least? Then, we can lie here as long as you want."

"In my bag," she says.

"What?"

"I brought bottled water in my bag," she says.

"You thought of everything, didn't you?"

"I didn't want to have to leave the room," she says, sitting up and then moving off the bed to retrieve the water. "I brought protein bars, too, if you're interested." She winks at me.

I laugh.

MONTH 9. PART 2. – ANTICIPA-TION & PARTICIPATION

(POV Escort)

I wish I could call her. Hell, I wish I had her damn name. I want to ask her ahead of time, but then, again, it's probably best that I don't. It should be done face to face. I know she's the paying *client*, but we've pretty much always had a reciprocal relationship. When I want something, she's game. When it's all about me for a while, she's up for it and then some. I smirk, just thinking about how much we fit in the bedroom. Then, my smirk changes to a soft smile when I think about how we fit when we're out of the bedroom, too. We spent hours talking last time and even the time before that, and as much as I want to take advantage of every moment we have together once a month to have sex, I'd go a whole night without touching her if it meant we were having good conversation and I could hear her laugh.

"Thanks for this," the man says. "We needed a car for our daughter but didn't want to get something new. She's sixteen – she's going to hit a parking meter or something." He laughed as I handed him the keys.

"No problem. All yours," I say.

He holds up the paperwork and nods. Then, I watch him drive away in my aunt's car. Honestly, I'm glad to be rid of the thing – I had to take her to the hospital in it far too many times. My car works fine, but it's much smaller, and there were days when she needed to lie down in the back seat. There were days she was throwing up in the back seat while I drove her to the hospital. The car's been cleaned top to bottom, and I took an extra five hundred off when he told me it's for his daughter, so hopefully, it'll make a nice starter car for her, and she can have fun in it. Well, not *too* much fun, I think, recalling the time I spent in a back seat with someone's hand down my pants.

The house is next. I turn and look at it, still unsure if I'm keeping it or selling it. It's true that I need the money. The house won't sell for much, but she only had a few years left on the mortgage, so most of what I get is mine and the government's once taxes come due. If I get that money, I can pay off all the debt in full and move on with my life. That just means selling this house, the only place that's ever felt like home.

On the other hand, I can keep working parties until the debt is paid off and keep the house. I can turn it into my place now. It needs a lot of updating, but I could keep going to the events to afford all the repairs and changes I want to make. I could start with new hardwood floors and getting rid of the wallpaper in the dining room. That'll probably add up. The master bedroom and bathroom would be next. I could finance all of those things by attending some parties. I'd also get to be with *her.*

I need to go inside now and start getting ready. I'm bringing my bag tonight in case she doesn't bring hers – I like having options when there are five hours where we can explore. Tonight, I decide to go with a pair of gray slacks I bought recently. They're not exactly expensive, but they look like it, at least. I have a new gray suit jacket, and I had to replace the white button-down she tore apart last time. I didn't mind. The pants and jacket have pinstripes that make me look more sophisticated, I think. I run my hand through my hair with only a comb and some water. I don't like when it has product in it. I want her to be able to feel it soft. I like when she tugs a little on it, and I have considered growing out a little longer to get her more to work with.

When I arrive, I look around and see several women I recognize. It's crazy – I've been doing this for almost a year now, and I've only talked to a few other people. I'm usually so wrapped up in *her* that I don't have time. We're in a house this time, so I sit on the sofa next to the escort I know *my* girl has fucked. It's strange. I'm both jealous *and* turned on by this.

"Hey," she says, looking up at me.

"Hi," I say back, placing my bag at my feet.

"Coming prepared tonight?" she asks.

"I like to be, yeah," I say.

"Me too. I put my bag in a room already. You might want to do that, too. I usually just hide it in a closet and hope for the best. If I don't end up with that room, sometimes, the door is open, so I can run in and grab it. If not, we have fun in other ways, and I grab it before I go."

"Not bad advice," I reply.

"So, your girl coming tonight?"

"Yeah, she'll be here," I say, liking her being called *my girl* by someone other than me. "Yours, too?"

"She's always here," she says, smiling. "Every month. She's never missed a month."

"She's married, though, right?" I ask.

"Yeah," she says, her smile falling.

"And he doesn't know she comes here?"

"If he does, *she* doesn't know that he does. He travels for work a lot, so he's usually out of town when one of these things is going on. And if he's not, she has a bunch of prepared excuses. Her sister has been 'sick' several times; her brother has needed her to babysit his kids the other couple of times; work has needed an emergency weekend trip. He either buys it, or he doesn't listen enough to notice."

"Doesn't sound like a good marriage. What do *I* know, though?"

"He's fucking someone who works for him." She tells me and rolls her eyes. "He has this perfect wife at home, and he's fucking someone else. Who *does* that?"

I watch her as she shakes her head with a look of disgust.

"You don't like him much, do you?" I say.

"What's to like?"

"Right," I say.

"You can't say anything about what I told you. It will get me in trouble, probably fired, and then I'd…" She fades out as her expression turns serious.

"You wouldn't be able to see her again," I finish for her.

"Yeah," she says softly. "How'd you know?"

"Because I understand," I admit.

"Your girl?"

"She's not really *mine*, though, is she?"

"No, she's not," she says.

"Do you wish yours was really *yours*?" I ask.

"I don't know if we'd fit outside these walls. We don't just have sex – I know that much – but she's a wealthy, older, married, established woman, and I'm a Ph. D student who worked sex parties to pay off my student loans and keep myself from going into massive debt before I've even earned my degree."

"Worked?" I ask, noticing the use of past tense.

"Yes, I'm all paid up. Working these events for two years did that for me. Now, I work them for two reasons: I don't have to have another job, which means I can finish up my dissertation faster, and because *she's* here."

I nod at her just as the front door opens and two women enter. I don't pay attention to them since I don't recognize them, but I check the clock on the wall, and it's eleven on the dot.

"They'll be here soon," I say.

"And we get five hours," she replies, standing up. "Make the most of them if you can."

She sounds almost defeated as she walks to the foyer where she stands there, waiting. It's not long before her member enters and smiles wide at her.

"I've missed you," the woman says and wraps her arm around the escort whose name I still don't know.

"I've missed you," the escort replies. "Shall we?"

"Let's," she says, taking her hand.

I stand and watch them walk up the stairs together, hand in hand. The music starts. It's two after eleven, and I worry that maybe she's not able to make it, after all. I see my friends walk in. They nod at me and head straight up the stairs to find a room. I nod back.

"Hey stranger," *she* says.

I turn a little and find her standing in front of me.

"I was worried you might not come," I reply.

"I told you I'd be here," she says, taking my hand.

"You're just late."

"Sorry, I got stuck at home with some work stuff to take care of."

"Isn't it the weekend?" I ask.

"Yes, but it was a client thing, so I had to call them. I'm here now, though," she says. "Missed me that much, huh?" she teases with a smile.

"Yes," I say, smiling back.

"We should get a room before they fill up," she says, nodding toward the stairs.

"Can we talk first?" I ask.

"Of course, we can talk," she says as if I should know that. "We can find the room and talk as long as you want, babe."

"It has to *do* with the room," I say, walking us to the sofa and sitting down.

She sits down next to me. There are two women in the corner of the room making out against a wall. I focus my attention only on her, though.

"Is this yours?" she asks.

"Yes," I tell her.

"Can't wait to see what's inside," she says, squeezing my hand. "What's wrong?"

"Nothing," I reply.

"I can tell something's up. Are you okay? We don't have—"

"I'm okay," I interrupt and lean in to kiss her on the lips. "I just have something I wanted to run by you. If you don't want to do it, we'll find a room."

"Okay. What?" she asks.

"My friends," I say.

212

"You want to watch them tonight?"

"I want to *join* them tonight," I say.

"Oh," she says, pulling her hand away.

"Never mind," I say, taking her hand back. "It was a stupid idea. I—"

"It's not a stupid idea," she says. "You've been with them before, so…"

"Just that one time I told you about."

"Oh, I assumed you'd…"

"No," I say. "I thought tonight would be a good time."

"I see," she says. "Well, this is unexpected, but they *are* members, so… if they've requested you tonight, and you want to be with them, I can't really argue. I'll just…" She stands up.

"Where are you going?" I ask, grasping her hand so she can't pull away entirely.

"To figure out how to spend the rest of my night," she says. "I think I'll just go home. I—"

I stand up and pull her against me.

"You're misunderstanding, babe. I don't want it to be the three of us. I was thinking, it could be the *four* of us," I tell her.

"All of us?" she asks.

"I haven't been with them because I want you there with me," I confess.

"I've never… I mean, the most I've experienced with more than one partner was…"

"Here," I finish for her. "With the two women."

"Yeah," she says. "And also with you, while we were next to your friends, but we didn't touch them then."

"It's okay if it's a no."

"Why do you want me there?"

"Because I'm not ready to be with them alone," I say. "But also, because it's something I've never done, either, and I wanted to experience it with you."

She wraps her arms around my neck as I hear moans. We both turn our heads to see a woman on her knees in front of another woman.

"Why is watching so hot?" she asks me, pulling me in tighter.

"I have no idea, but it is," I say, running my hand up under her dress.

"Are you trying to start something right now?" she asks.

"Would that be a bad thing?" I ask back, moving until I meet her sex with my hand. "Thong tonight?"

"It's flimsy. I thought you'd be able to move it if you really tried," she teases.

"Would you like me to move it right now?" I ask.

"Maybe," she says.

"Watch them," I tell her.

Then, I slip my fingers inside the fabric. She's wet for me already. Her head is turned in the direction of the other women.

"I'll make you come down here," I whisper into her ear. "Then, I'll take you upstairs."

"Yes," she says as I stroke.

Her legs are already a bit wobbly. I wrap her up with my other arm to keep her from falling.

"And I'll fuck you senseless," I say.

"What if I want one of them to fuck me, too?" she asks.

I stop stroking for a second and ask, "Do you?"

"I think so," she says. I want you there touching me, too. Don't stop, baby," she adds as I continue my strokes.

"What if I want to fuck someone else or they want to fuck me?" I ask her.

"Can I watch?"

"You can *touch*," I say.

"Oh, yes," she says. "I don't want anything unless you're there. What have you done to me?"

"I'm about to make you come," I say.

She holds on to me tightly as the woman against the wall comes.

"Oh, fuck," she says, collapsing against me as she comes hard.

Her hips move into my hand, and I stroke until they stop.

"I can't believe this is me," she says a minute later. "I've never done this before. I'm a vanilla-sex kind of girl."

"You are *anything* but a vanilla-sex kind of *woman*, babe," I say. "Are you sure about this? We can always stay right here or find another room."

"I'm sure," she tells me. "I like that I'll be there with you." She smiles at me. "You'll have to take your hand out from under my dress, though, since I'll need to walk up the stairs."

"Maybe we should just stay here, then," I joke.

When *she* pulls my hand out, she brings it to my lips, and I open my mouth. She watches as I suck my fingers.

"Now, they'll know you're mine," she says.

I'm happy to nod and say, "All yours."

We walk up the stairs, me with my bag in one hand and her hand in the other. My friends are in the fourth room on the left, just past the bathroom. From the looks of it, they're just getting started, so I walk in with her at my side and close the door behind us, locking it and then turning around.

"Yeah?" my friend says when she hears the door close and turns to see that it's us.

"Yeah," I say.

"We're new to this, too," her wife says. "You two are the first we're going to let…"

"Touch us," my friend finishes for her wife. "Well, except that time you had your hands down my wife's pants in the kitchen." She looks at me.

"Will you do that again?" her wife asks.

I look at *her.* She nods, and I lick my lips. Then, I kiss her. I can't believe she's not only okay with this, but by her darkening eyes, I can tell she's also into it. She wants this, too. I press my lips to hers again quickly before I walk over to a woman I've known for years and kiss her hard. My friend watches me as I make out with her wife. Then, she moves into us, holding on to the back of her wife's head, encouraging her. Her other hand slips under my suit jacket and presses into my back. I pull back from the kiss with her wife and turn to my friend, who pulls *me* in for a kiss. Her wife reaches for my belt and undoes it. Then, I feel arms around my waist. It's *her*. She's helping the woman in front of me undo my pants. They fall to the floor, and I feel *her* fingers slip inside my underwear. My eyes are closed as I kiss my friend, but I'd know *her* sure fingers anywhere. I reach up under the dress of the woman in front of me, find her not wearing any underwear, surprisingly, and begin stroking her.

"Oh, yes," she says.

My friend pulls out of our kiss and says, "Make her come hard,"

I nod and return to kissing my friend's wife as *my* girl keeps up her fast strokes on my clit. My friend disappears. I don't turn around, but I hear my girl moan a second later. Oh, she's being touched now. Her moans are right in my ear. Her fingers are on my clit, and I'm going to come too fast.

"Fuck, that's good," I hear *her* say. "Baby, she's making me feel so good," she adds.

I pull out of the kiss and say, "Yes, feel good, baby,"

The woman in front of me says, "Go inside. I need you inside."

I waste no time. I push two fingers inside her and leave my thumb on her clit.

"Oh, I knew you'd fill me," she says, wrapping her arms around my neck loosely. "Don't stop until I come in your hand."

"Baby, I'm going to come. Come with me," *my* girl says.

"Fuck," I say. "Yes, there."

She strokes my clit so hard that I come with my head

against the other woman's shoulder as I'm thrusting inside her.

"I'm coming," she says as I thrust harder. "Oh, God. Fuck me, yes!" she screams.

"Fuck, honey. You're so fucking sexy. I can't wait to taste you," my friend says to her wife.

I hear gasps and moans in my ear.

"Are you coming?" I ask *her* as I come down.

"Yes," she lets out softly. "So good," she adds.

"I get you next," I tell her as I continue to thrust into the woman in front of me.

My friend's wife begins to come down, and I come down. *My* girl comes down. We all stay where we are for a second, gathering our breath and, likely, our thoughts. The room already smells like sex, and we've only just gotten started. I pull out and turn around to see *her* standing there, looking thoroughly fucked. I kiss her hard and unzip her dress. She steps out of it, and I feel my jacket being pulled off me. I pull out of the kiss and watch my friend pull off her wife's dress as she stands behind her now. I kick off my pants, and *she* undoes the buttons on my shirt. Her lips meet my nipple. I throw off my shirt and pull her head to my breast tighter.

"Yes. Suck it, baby," I tell her.

"Do you want me to?" she asks, stopping to look up at me. "I can." She lifts an eyebrow at me.

"Yes," I say, pushing her head down.

She removes my underwear, and I know I need her mouth. I can hear my friends behind us, but I can't see what they're doing. Then, I feel her mouth on my clit, sucking me into her. There's a hand from behind me on my breast, playing with my nipple. That means one of my friends is behind me, my head is on her shoulder, but I have no idea who it is. I have my hand wrapped around the back of her head as she sucks on my earlobe. It's too much, but it's also exactly what I need at the same time.

"Inside," I say.

She pushes her fingers deep inside as she sucks.

"Oh, my God," I say.

My friend turns my head enough so that we can kiss. Without them all helping me stand, I would have fallen over by now. I have one hand in my girl's hair, pressing her face into my pussy. My hips rock into her faster and faster with each one of her thrusts. My other hand is holding on to the head of the woman behind me, the same woman I fucked only a minute ago.

"I want you to taste me," she says when she pulls away from the kiss.

"Yes," I say.

"And then, I'll taste her," my friend says, placing her hand on top of mine that's on my girl's head.

I hear the woman moan; I feel it on my clit. She likes that idea, and I love what she's doing to me. I come hard, hips bucking into her mouth and holding hard onto her head because I need her to keep me there a little longer.

"Oh, my God," I say when I finally come down.

She stands up and wipes her chin. It's so damn sexy. I kiss her.

"Taste her," she says, nodding behind me.

I look around and see the woman already on the bed, her legs spread wide. She's touching her clit and beckoning me with her eyes. I watch my friend take *her* hand and lower her onto the bed next to her wife. We both stand in front of them and watch as they lean into each other and kiss. I hear *her* moan.

"This is the…"

"Best night of our lives?" my friend says.

I nod. We kneel at the same time, spreading their legs wider. We lean in, and I lick the woman in front of me first. She moans. I look up, and she's still kissing my girl. Their hands found their ways to nipples. They twist and play. I look over at my friend, whose face is buried between *her* legs, and yet again, I am both entirely way too jealous and completely turned on. I lick and suck her wife as her hand moves to the back of my head. Her other one is likely on my girl's body somewhere, but I can't see because my eyes are closed – I'm focused on making her feel good. I'm also focused on listening for *her*. I want to hear her sounds. I want to know that she's being taken care of.

"Yes, there," *she* says.

I open my eyes, and the woman I'm currently eating out has her own eyes closed and head back. Her mouth is open, but she's not making any sounds. I look over at *her*. Her eyes are open, and she's looking at me. She nods, and I suck harder.

"Shit. Yes," the woman I'm fucking says. "Harder."

I look at my girl as I suck harder.

"Inside," my girl says, and I don't know if she's talking to my friend or to me.

I decide it's maybe both, and I slip inside.

"Oh, that's good," she says.

My girl and I don't lose eye contact as she gets fucked by someone else and I fuck someone else. I see her mouth the words, "You're mine," to me, so I nod – I am hers. No matter how good these women make us feel or how good we make them feel, we know we belong to each other only, just like they belong to each other only. When they come around the same time, I stand. The woman I just fucked rolls over on top of my girl. They make out as my friend and I stand there watching. I move behind my friend and play with her breasts.

"Are you going to make me come now?" she asks.

"I was thinking about it," I say.

She moves my hand lower between her legs.

"This is how wet you get? Fuck," I say as I easily glide around.

"Wait," she says.

I remove my hand, and she walks over to her own bag, pulls out and then puts on her strap-on. I think about doing the same thing, but then she's standing in front of me again.

"Babe," she says to her wife. "I'm going to fuck you."

"I want you to fuck me," her wife says.

"Will you make her come with your mouth while I do?"

"Oh, yes," my friend's wife says.

"I don't know if I can come again just yet," *she* says.

"You can just feel good – you don't have to come. But she's amazing with her tongue," my friend says.

Once everyone is in position, I'm again able to stare into her eyes as the woman goes down on her, my friend slips her dildo inside her wife, and I stand behind her, stroking her clit.

"Make me come. I'm so hard," she says.

"I can tell," I say. "How long have you wanted this?" I ask into her ear.

"A long time," she says. "I've wanted your hands on me for a long time."

"And?"

"They're so good," she says, thrusting into her wife.

"Make her feel good," I say to her wife, referring to my girl.

"She is, baby," *she* says, playing with her own breasts. "I'm going to come."

I hear the woman with her head between *her* legs groan. Then, the woman I'm touching groans.

"Fuck, I'm going to come," she says, thrusting harder into her wife. "Babe, she's making me come so hard. God, I knew you'd be good at this," she tells me.

"I'm just getting started," I say, feeling confident now. "Take that thing off, and I'll let you sit on my face. I'll show you how good I am with my tongue."

"Yes," she says, thrusting wildly.

"I'm coming!" her wife yells.

"Don't stop," *my* girl tells her, pushing her head back down to her pussy.

"Yes," my friend says, rolling her head back against my shoulder as she slows and then stops her thrusting.

Her wife comes down quickly. My girl comes down

slowly. I watch her, and she watches me. I know we should all take a break. This is too much for the amount of time we've been doing this, but the look in her eyes tells me she's far from done. I wink at her. She licks her lips, and I know they taste of me.

"I love you," my friend says to her wife, who is now standing, facing her.

"I love you, too," she replies, kissing her.

I move around them to find *her*. She moves back until her head is against the pillow and spreads her legs for me. I climb on top of her, realizing I have no idea how we all got naked. Somehow, all of our clothing is in a pile on the floor, and I have no recognition of it, but I feel her naked body pressed to mine, and I am grateful.

"How are you?" I ask her.

"So good," she says wistfully.

I lean down and kiss her softly. I hear moaning behind us but don't stop kissing her. She takes my hand and brings it down to her center. I move inside her at her request and slowly rock into her.

"I missed you," she says.

I don't know if she means since the last time we were together like this, naked and pressed together, with me inside, or if she means because it's just us right now when before it was the four of us.

"I miss you all the time," I admit, knowing that it's the truth.

MONTH 10. PART 1. – IT'S MORE

(POV Member)

"And then, he tells me that he doesn't believe in bisexuality. He thinks it's something people make up because they're gay and don't want to admit it," she says.

"Well, that's awful," I tell her.

"I know. I couldn't believe my sister thought he'd be right for me. She's no longer allowed to set me up," she states firmly.

I laugh and say, "So, my mom thinks you're gay. She actually told me she met a woman at church with a gay daughter that would be good for me."

"Interesting, because I've never met your mother," she says, laughing.

"What is it with parents?" I ask.

"Are yours talking to you about kids yet?"

"Yes," I say, sipping my coffee.

"Mine have been on me about it for years," she says. "My dad actually told me that if I just married a man, it would be easier. We could make it happen *naturally*. He's not sure bisexuality exists, either, I don't think."

I laugh and say, "Well, I'm sure it exists."

"And it doesn't bother you that I date men, too?" she asks, taking a drink of her own coffee.

I almost ask if it would bother her that I go to sex parties once a month and don't intend to stop anytime soon, but I don't.

"No," I reply as we arrive at my car.

"Well, this was fun," she says.

"It was," I agree.

"So, I passed the pre-first-date coffee trial?" she asks.

"Yes," I say and laugh. "Sorry, my mom's set me up before, and it never works, so I'm a little more cautious now."

"No problem. I get it. Does this mean you'd like to go on a real first date with me, though? I'd like to buy you more than just a cup of coffee; maybe a nice dinner with some wine."

I nod.

"I'll call you," she offers. "Maybe we can do something this weekend," she adds.

I should say yes – she's great. Surprisingly, my mom might have actually introduced me to someone likable, someone I could possibly *really* like, even. She's a beautiful doctor that volunteers her time for a local clinic when she's not at the hospital. She has a sister and three brothers. She keeps up with current events, is obviously very intelligent, and she's had me laughing during a much longer coffee date than I'd intended. She has a very nice smile, and as she takes my hand and pulls me in just a little, I feel her soft skin and think that this has potential.

"I have plans this weekend, but maybe next," I say instead.

"You can just say no," she says.

"It's not a no," I reply. "I really do have plans this weekend."

"Okay. Then, next weekend. I'll call you on Monday, maybe, and we can set something up." She leans in and kisses my cheek.

She smells really good. I close my eyes to breathe her in but open them before she has a chance to notice as she pulls away.

"I'll talk to you then," I say.

On my drive back to the office, I think about my date. She's pretty amazing. I like the idea of going on a date with someone I actually like. Then, I think of *her*, and I sigh, climbing out of my car. I did it again – I put *her* ahead of something that might actually be real.

"So, I have your next meeting out in the hall. He's early. Should I make him wait, or are you ready?" my assistant asks.

"It's fine," I say.

It's better that I have less time to think about my personal life right now. I have meeting after meeting until it's well after six. I only had coffee for lunch, so I ask my assistant to order me something for dinner. She does, and I eat at my desk. By the time I'm finished, it's after eight, and I'm more than ready to head home. I get there by nine and run a bath for myself. I add some soothing bubbles and sink into it. I grab a quick snack after and go to bed. Pulling out my laptop, I go to the website to check if there are any messages. There's one, and I worry they're going to tell me that she can't make it to the event. Instead, they tell me that they're offering VIP-members or members seeking that status a chance to have special accommodations this weekend.

Member,

Our location for this month's women-only event is no longer available. While we will still host the main event, which you are welcome to attend, we will also be hosting a women-only event at a different location. Please click the link below to view the information. Due to the last-minute change, we were only able to secure so many rooms. If you are interested, please click the RSVP link below, and we will ensure you have a reserved room due to the last-minute change. If you would like to attend the main event, please reply to this email directly, and we'll have a room for you as well as a complimentary bottle of champagne and appetizers sent to your room directly. If you'd like to cancel, please reply directly, and we will offer you either a percentage off your membership for the remaining term or a credit for special accommodations in the future. If you have any questions, please let us know.

Member Services

I read the email again before clicking on the link to

check out the location. Smiling at what they were offering, I click on the RSVP link and then email them separately, requesting a certain someone join me in my room if possible. Then, I close the laptop and smile as I fall asleep.

***

"Welcome," the woman in the gravel parking lot says.

"Thank you," I reply, handing my keys to the well-dressed man next to her.

"You're in cabin six," she says. "The main party is in cabin one, but you're not required to join that unless you're interested. We've set up your cabin with a wood-burning fire, champagne, and wine, as well as some food options. More can be found in the main cabin if you'd like. We'll be by at three-forty-five, like always."

"Thank you," I repeat.

"Cabin six is just over there," she motions with an open hand. "You can take the golf cart if you'd like."

It's only about fifty yards away.

"I think I can walk," I say.

"Very well."

I leave them there and walk to my cabin. Tonight's location is a cabin resort on a lake. It's likely most beautiful at sunrise and sunset, but the lake is lit up around the shore, so I can see at least some of the beauty just fine at eleven at night. I completely forgot to ask if my one actual request had been met. If it hasn't, I'll have to head to the main cabin, but I'm already almost here, so I decide to check first. There are two steps leading to the door of the beautiful log cabin. The lights are on inside, and I can see some flickering, likely from the fire. Before I can open the door, it's opened for me, and there she is.

"You're here," I say.

"Where else would I be?" she asks.

She's wearing a t-shirt and a pair of worn jeans, and she looks perfect. I walk into her arms, and she closes the door behind me. She pulls me in for a hug. I hug her back and kiss her neck.

"So, this is pretty nice, huh?" she asks, running her hands up and down my back. "We get this all to ourselves, and no one will interrupt."

"Just us?" I say, looking into her eyes.

"My friends decided to go to the main party if that's what you're asking," she says.

"Are you disappointed?" I ask.

"How could I be disappointed?" she asks back. "I'm here with you. We have a beautiful fire going in this spacious cabin; there's champagne and wine if you want. Plus, I snagged some chocolate-covered strawberries from the main cabin, and they brought us other stuff, too."

I smile at her and kiss her quickly.

"I'm really happy you're dressed like *you* tonight," I say.

"I was hoping you would be," she says.

"You manage to make a t-shirt look sexy," I tell her, running my hands over her chest.

"Hey, I have an idea if you're up for it," she says.

"What's that?" I ask.

"Well, we have a fire." She nods over to it. "And this is a fancy place. It turns out, they stock stuff in a minibar, but it's unlocked. I checked with the boss, and she says it's all fair game."

"Okay..." I say, giving her a confused expression.

"They have stuff for s'mores," she says.

"They do *not*," I say, laughing.

"They do. Plus, there's peanut butter. Want a peanut butter s'more?" she asks.

"Are *you* doing the cooking?" I ask.

"Like I can trust a fancy lady like you to make my s'more," she teases.

I laugh and say, "I can honestly say I've never made one, so you're right to trust yourself more."

"You've *never* made a s'more?" she asks, pulling back

to look at me in disbelief.

"Babe, I've never had a reason to make a s'more. We never went camping as a family, and I'm not exactly an outdoor girl if you haven't noticed," I say.

"I'm going to teach you how, then," she says, running off into the kitchen.

I laugh and watch her. She gathers up whatever she needs, stops to set it all on the counter, pauses to fill two glasses with red wine, and then hands me one of them.

"You watch. I'll cook," she says, kissing me.

"No problem," I say. "You're nice to watch."

She smirks and gets to work. I sit on the sofa and drink my wine as she opens things. She puts the marshmallows on the end of the metal skewers and turns to me.

"Come over here so I can show you," she says.

"But your ass looks good in those jeans, and I have the perfect view."

"If you're over here, you can kiss me," she says.

I stand and look down at the rug in front of the fireplace.

"I didn't exactly dress for sitting on the floor," I say.

"You can take it off," she says, looking up at me. "I really wouldn't mind."

My dress is of a tight variety. I pass her my wineglass, unzip it, and let it fall to the ground.

"Better?" I ask.

"Definitely," she says, licking her lips.

"You don't have to make me snacks to get me into bed," I say as I sit down on the rug next to her.

"Really? I was hoping to impress you."

"You're already impressive," I tell her.

She doesn't say anything. Instead, she hands me the skewer, and we roast our marshmallows. When she pulls hers out, I do the same. She squishes it between two graham crackers already loaded with chocolate and peanut butter and passes it to me. Then, she takes the one I roasted and repeats everything.

"Are you ready?" she asks, holding hers up.

"Sure," I say.

We take a bite, making a big mess, and laugh as we eat. She makes us each another, and we talk a little about the change in location and how it ended up being a change for the better. Then, she packs up the stuff and places it on the table to worry about later.

"Oh, you have chocolate on your–" She points at my chest.

"I do not. I–"

Her lips land between my breasts, and I am confident there was never any chocolate there. She lowers me to the rug. Her lips move to my collarbone and then my neck.

"Smooth," I say as she climbs on top of me.

"What? I didn't want it to go to waste," she says.

I laugh a little and let her kiss me wherever she wants to kiss me. Her hand roams over my stomach and my chest until she's reaching under my back. I lift up. She unclasps my bra, and we pull it off together. Her lips move across my breasts before landing on a nipple. She's still fully clothed, and I'm only in a thong.

"Can you–"

"Yeah," she says, knowing what I mean.

She sits up a little and takes off her shirt.

"There they are," I say, cupping her breasts. "I've missed them."

"They've missed you," she says.

"Have they not been taken care of by anyone else in my absence?" I ask.

"No, no one has taken care of them," she says.

"Not even…"

"No, babe. I haven't been with them since that night," she says.

"Did I–"

"They've been in Europe for their anniversary for the past three weeks, but even if they *had* been here, I don't want to be with them alone, babe. I only want all four of us to be together. Can we not talk about them now, though? I just want to talk about us tonight," she says.

"Of course," I say. "I'm sorry, I didn't mean–"

She kisses my forehead and says, "You don't have to apologize for anything. I just missed you. Last time was fun, but we only got a little time together after they left."

"I know. You're right," I say, pressing my lips between her breasts. "Let me make sure they know how much I love them."

I kiss my way over to her nipple.

"You know how you could *really* show you love them?" she asks.

"How?" I ask back.

"Let me fuck you from behind while I wear nipple clamps," she says.

"I didn't–"

"I bought some," she interrupts. "I've been thinking about the things I want to do with you all month, and that keeps coming to the top of my list."

"And after?" I ask, licking a nipple.

"You can suck on them," she says, breathing a little harder.

"And?"

"And fuck me however you want."

"Oh, I like the sound of that," I say. "How do you want me, baby?"

"On all fours. Keep the thong on," she says.

"Whatever you want," I tell her, licking the other nipple.

I roll over on all fours, suddenly very turned on. It takes her longer than I expect it to, but she walks back over to the rug. I turn my head to see her kneeling behind me. She's wearing the nipple clamps. She's also stroking the dildo she's wearing, as if she can feel it, while she stares at my ass. I lower my body to the floor to allow her to see a little more.

"Like this?" I ask.

"Yes," she whispers as she strokes herself.

"Do you want me to touch you first?" I ask.

"No, I just like looking at you. I've never wanted to just look at someone before, how I look at you. When I'm by myself, I come so fast thinking about you."

"Yeah? Tell me," I say.

"I've fucked myself with this thing picturing your fingers inside me."

"I want to see that," I say.

"Can I–"

"Whatever you want, baby," I repeat my earlier words. "I'm yours. Fuck me however you want."

"Shit, that's so sexy," she says.

I watch her slip her hand inside the shorts she's wearing while the other one still strokes the toy.

"What else is sexy?" I ask.

"Touch yourself," she says.

I reach between my legs, push the thong aside, and waste no time.

"I'm so wet," I say.

"Fuck," she says.

"Should I go inside?"

"Yes, get ready for me," she says.

"How big are you?" I ask.

"Big enough to make you come hard," she says.

"I better use three fingers, then," I tell her.

I reach deeper until I slip three fingers inside with ease.

"Are you tight, babe?"

"I'm tight," I say.

"And you want me to open you up?" she asks.

"All the way, baby," I say as I move my fingers inside and out.

"Fuck, I'm going to come," she says.

"Don't, baby. Come inside me, please."

"You want me to come inside you?" she asks.

"More than anything. Fuck me until you come inside me. Make me come hard."

"Move your hand," she says.

I do. I shift forward again and then turn back to the front, facing the window with the curtains pulled back. Technically, anyone walking past this cabin would see us like this, but we're far enough away that that's unlikely.

"Oh, fuck," I say when she pushes inside me.

She tears at the thong until it's loose and hanging and no longer in the way.

"Full, babe?"

"Yes, so deep, baby," I tell her.

She doesn't go slow; she thrusts hard, and it's so good.

"God, yes," I say. "I need you. Make me come," I add, holding on to the edge of the rug.

"Tell me to fuck you."

"Fuck me," I say.

"Yell it."

"Fuck me!" I yell louder.

"God, you're so sexy. I fucking love your body," she says. "Play with your breasts."

I take one hand and squeeze my breast while the other keeps me up.

"Yeah! How does it feel?"

"So good," I say.

"I'm going to come soon," she says.

"Scream when you do, babe. Let me hear how much you love fucking me."

"Oh, wow. That's—" She thrusts harder and faster. "Fuck! Yes! Yes! Yes!" With each push inside me, she repeats the word until she's falling on top of me.

I haven't come yet, but it's more than fine because she's clearly spent, and her orgasm was so intense that the dildo slips out, and she's pressing me into the rug.

"I like you on top of me," I say, my head turned toward the fire.

"I'm sorry. I couldn't hold back."

"Never apologize for that."

"Did you…"

"Not yet," I say.

"Well, fuck. I wanted…"

"Babe, stay there until you're ready. Then, try again," I say.

"Really?"

"Yes. In fact… We can make tonight *your* night. Whatever you want, you get."

"That's not really how this–"

"Shut up. Not tonight. Not right now. Right now, we're just two people renting a cabin for the night, okay?"

"Okay," she says softly.

She gets up a little and kisses down my back slowly until she kisses my ass cheeks and spreads my cheeks.

"Is this okay?"

"Yes," I say.

"Can I…"

"Yes," I whisper.

She kisses me there – no one's ever kissed me there before. Her hand slips between my thighs, and she cups my front.

"I'm really close. It won't take long," I tell her.

"It can take all night, for all I care," she says.

She kisses the spot again. Then, I feel her glide her other hand through my wetness. While one strokes me, the other moves to my ass. She slips a hesitant finger inside.

"Oh," I say.

"Okay?"

"Yeah," I say.

She doesn't go in deeper or move her finger, so I rock my hips down against her hand and the floor as a result. I come quickly, and the finger inside me makes it more intense than I would've ever imagined. After I come down, she kisses the inside of my thighs, lifting me until she can lie down underneath. I ride her face until I come again.

When my tremors dissipate, she gets up quickly and is behind me again. She's inside me. I'm rocking back against her as she holds my hips. It takes no time at all, and I'm coming again.

"God, I love you," she says.

My eyes go wide. I'm sure she doesn't mean that; it's in the heat of the moment.

"Fuck, I'm coming," she says a second later.

Yes, that's what it is – she's coming. She loves me because I make her come like this; that's all it is. When we both come down, she rolls me over, takes off the toy, and climbs on top of me.

"Hi," I say.

"Hi," she says back, her eyes all wistful and gorgeous. "These clamps are killing me, by the way."

"Should I take them off and kiss your nipples to make them feel better?"

She smiles and nods.

***

After we make each other come a few more times – once with me straddling her on the sofa and her toy buried deep inside me – we lie on that sofa, nude, just holding on to one another as the fire burns.

"Can I ask you something?" she says, running her hands up and down my back.

My eyes are closed, and I'm very close to falling asleep, but I know I need to stay awake. I *want* to stay awake. I don't want to miss a single moment with her.

"Yes," I say.

"Have you been with anyone since last time?"

"No," I say.

"Have you *wanted* to be with anyone?"

"Not exactly," I say.

"What's that mean?"

"I went on a date," I say.

"Oh, right." She tenses up beneath me.

"It was just coffee," I say.

"But you like her?"

"She's nice. We don't really know each other yet," I tell her.

"When will you see her again?" she asks.

"Maybe next weekend; I don't know," I say. "Have *you* been dating?" I ask.

"No," she says. "I've been trying to figure out my aunt's stuff."

"Of course," I say. "Have you?"

"Have I what?"

"Figured it out?"

"Yeah. I've decided to keep the house, and I'm making plans to fix it up now."

"That's great," I say.

"I think I'm finally starting to feel okay for the first time in a while," she says.

Then, I realize that if she's feeling okay, if she's moving on and done figuring things out, that means she's ready. She's ready to start dating.

"Can we just stay like this for the rest of the night?" I ask.

"Whatever you want," she says.

MONTH 10. PART 2. – THE CABIN

(POV Escort)

"Didn't you guys just get back?" I ask.

"Last night, yeah," my friend says.

"And don't you have to reacclimate to the to time zone?"

"The answer is no, isn't it?" she asks.

"I thought I'd just see you guys at the party."

"We're going to the main one this time, and I assume you're going to the all-women one that they had to change," she says.

"That's the plan. I've been requested," I say, smiling into the phone.

"You've definitely got it bad, girl," my friend says, laughing. "We were hoping we'd see you before then. We got this amazing lube in the red-light district. I think we bought the whole shop after we tried it – it makes everything more intense."

"Sounds like fun."

"It is. I wanted to try it out on you," she says.

"Maybe some other time," I reply.

"Are you saving yourself for her?"

"Not saving, no," I say. "I just like it when I don't come for a few days, and then she's the one making me come – it's so intense."

"So is the lube I just told you about," my friend tells me. "Come over tonight. The wife has the hot tub ready to go, and I'm pulling out the massage oil... I can relax you before I make you come."

"Really, that sounds very nice, but–"

"I thought we were good... We're good, right? The timing of the last party and then our trip wasn't great, but if we need to talk about what happened or–"

"No, I'm more than good with what happened. It was great."

"Yeah? Are you sure? I don't want it messing up our friendship."

"It won't. It's not."

"But you're not interested in doing it again?"

"I am, just not before the party."

"We can switch up our plans and go to the whole cabin thing if you want. I can see why you're so into her – she's really hot, and when she comes, she explodes. It's sexy as hell."

"It is, yeah."

"Can I tell you something?" my friend asks.

I turn off the TV I wasn't really watching anyway and say, "Sure."

"I'm touching myself right now, thinking about your hand down there," she says.

"Really?" I ask, sitting up on the sofa in the living room.

"Yes," she says.

I notice it now, her breathy tone.

"Is it good?" I ask.

"Yes, but not as good as when you did it," she replies.

"What does your wife think about that?" I ask.

"She wants your fingers back inside her, and I want to watch you make her come."

"Jesus," I say mainly to myself. "Where is she right now?"

"In the bedroom. She needed to unpack a few *things*," she replies mischievously. "I'm out back by the pool."

"Where's your hand?"

"In my bikini," she says.

"Would she be okay with this?" I ask.

"She told me to call you."

"She did?"

"Yes," my friend says, and it sounds like she's close.

"When she comes outside, have her sit behind you and touch you," I say.

"I'm going to come before she gets out here," she says.

"Your fingers found all my spots."

"Do you have that lube on you right now?"

"Yes," she says. "I can feel it in my toes."

"Then, come," I say.

"Tell me again, and I will," she replies.

"Come for me," I tell her.

"Fuck," she says.

Then, it's silent. I wait. This is the first time we've ever done this before. There's a sound on the other end of the phone.

"You made her come, huh?" her wife says.

"She made herself come," I reply, wondering if I'm in trouble now.

"She's a little jet-lagged and has been horny for hours," she says. "I'll take it from here."

I laugh a little and say, "Have fun."

"When can *we all* have fun again?"

"I don't know. Maybe at the next party."

"You're going to the main one?"

"No, I mean, the one after that. If she wants to," I add.

"Ah, *her*," my friend's wife says. "Babe, give me a minute." She laughs and then tells me, "She's taking off my shorts. I guess I should hang up before she goes down on me while we're on the phone."

"Wait," I say before I can stop myself.

"You want to listen, don't you?"

"Yes," I admit.

"We could FaceTime you, and you could watch since you don't want to come over."

"Just let me hear it, please."

"Babe, I'm putting your phone on speaker; she wants to hear you make me come with your mouth."

I hear a groan followed by more sounds. Likely, she placed the phone on the table or the ground.

"Do you want a play-by-play while I can still talk?" she asks.

"Yes," I say, leaning back.

I unbutton my jeans and unzip my fly. Then, I listen.

"My shorts are on the ground. Her lips are... Oh, lower."

Fuck, I think to myself.

"She's walking me over to the hot tub."

I wait.

"She's no longer wearing her bikini. Damn, you're so sexy, baby. She's in the hot tub. I'm trying–" She stops for a second and then says, "Oh. She wants me on the edge of it. I think she's going to eat me out while my legs hang in the water."

"Yes, I am," I hear my friend says.

I've seen them do this before, so I can easily picture it. I slide my hand into my jeans, but not inside my panties just yet.

"Baby, yes," my friend's wife says.

"Shit," I say, reaching quickly inside my underwear now.

"Her tongue is... there. Oh, I love when you get like this."

"How is she?" I ask.

"Like she's going to devour me all night long."

"I will," the other woman says.

"Did you like fucking me at the party?"

"Me?" I ask.

"Yes. Did you like fucking me?"

"Yes," I reply, sliding my fingers around my clit.

"Which part did you like the best?" she asks.

"All of it," I say.

"Did you like fucking my wife?"

"Yes," I say.

"Did you like how we touched you?"

"Yes," I reply.

"Then, why aren't you here so we... Oh, yes!"

"Yes," I say again. "Come for me."

"I am," she replies. "Fuck, I'm coming, baby. Don't stop!"

I rub my clit hard and fast as I try to catch up.

"God, I'm coming, too," I say.

"You're touching your–"

"Yes," I interrupt.

"We want you," she says. "We want you again. Fuck, yes!"

I think about buttoning up my jeans and rushing to their house on the other side of town. I see my car keys on the table by the door, and I lick my lips at the thought of rushing over there just to make them both come and let them make me come in return, but I don't.

"How was it?" I ask when I hear how shallow breaths begin to slow.

"Really fucking good," she replies. "This one wanted to fuck me on the return flight, but I made her wait. She needed to earn it."

"I earned it," the other woman says. "And I want to keep on *earning* it all night."

"I think it's your turn," my friend's wife replies. "Are you coming over?" she asks me.

"Maybe next week," I say.

"Baby, you'll make me come again," she says to her wife.

"Good," her wife replies. "We're hanging up now."

"Okay," I say. "Have fun tonight."

"We will. There will be ice cubes."

"Fuck," I say again, remembering the last time I saw them use ice cubes.

I hung up before they could.

***

"You're here," she says.

"Where else would I be?" I ask, smiling at her as I hold the cabin door open for her.

Her dress is red tonight because she's trying to kill me, apparently, but it's not her usual, more flowing number. It's tighter. It's so tight that I think she *is* actually trying to kill me. She's so damn beautiful, and she's now walking into my open arms. I close the door behind her and pull her in for a long hug. She kisses my neck, and I have a moment where I picture us doing this for real: she comes home from work, and I greet her at the door like this.

"So, this is pretty nice, huh?" I ask, running my hands up and down her back, trying not to think about the vision of a life I *don't* have in order to focus on the time I have with her tonight. "We get this all to ourselves, and no one will interrupt."

"Just us?"

"My friends decided to go to the main party if that's what you're asking," I say.

"Are you disappointed?" she asks.

"How could I be disappointed? I'm here with you. We have a beautiful fire going in this spacious cabin; there's champagne and wine if you want. Plus, I snagged some chocolate-covered strawberries from the main cabin, and they brought us other stuff, too."

She kisses me and says, "I'm really happy you're dressed like *you* tonight."

"I was hoping you would be," I reply.

"You manage to make a t-shirt look sexy," She runs her hands over my chest, perking up my nipples.

"Hey, I have an idea if you're up for it," I say.

"What's that?" she asks.

"Well, we have a fire." I nod to it. "And this is a fancy place. It turns out, they stock stuff in a minibar, but it's unlocked. I checked with the boss, and she says it's all fair game."

"Okay…"

"They have stuff for s'mores," I tell her.

"They do *not*," She laughs.

"They do. Plus, there's peanut butter. Want a peanut butter s'more?" I ask.

"Are *you* doing the cooking?"

"Like I can trust a fancy lady like you to make my s'more," I tease her.

She laughs and says, "I can honestly say I've never made one, so you're right to trust yourself more."

"You've *never* made a s'more?" I ask, pulling back.

"Babe, I've never had a reason to make a s'more. We never went camping as a family, and I'm not exactly an outdoor girl if you haven't noticed," she says.

"I'm going to teach you how, then,"

I run off excitedly to the kitchen while she laughs at me. I grab what I need to get started. Then, I stop at the counter because I realize I haven't gotten my girl a drink yet. I'm not sure if she wants wine or champagne, but I decide to take a chance on red – I've had it open and breathing since I got here anyway. I pour our glasses and walk one over to her. She smiles at me, which makes everything worth it.

"You watch. I'll cook," I say, kissing her.

"No problem," she says. "You're nice to watch."

I smile at her and go to the fire with my supplies. It's been a while since I've made smores, but they're not exactly difficult. I get everything ready to go, turn around, and see that she's made herself comfortable on the sofa.

"Come over here so I can show you," I say, laughing a little.

"But your ass looks good in those jeans, and I have the perfect view."

"If you're over here, you can kiss me," I say.

She stands up instantly, and it makes me laugh a little again.

"I didn't exactly dress for sitting on the floor," she says.

"You can take it off," I reply, looking up at her. "I really wouldn't mind."

She passes me her wine, and I watch as she unzips her dress and lets it fall to the floor.

"Better?" she asks.

241

"Definitely," I say, licking my lips because I want them on her.

"You don't have to make me snacks to get me into bed," she says as she sits down on the rug.

"Really? I was hoping to impress you."

"You're already impressive," she tells me.

I wish I could actually believe her, but I am totally un-impressive. I have a dead-end job that I'm lucky I haven't lost yet, a college degree I'm not even using, no family I can count on now that my aunt is gone, and a house I don't really want to live in, but it just makes the most sense for me to keep it. I've spent most of my life there, and I can make it my own, I guess. It *is* home. I just never thought I'd be there forever. I have no money saved. What I *do* have, I've recently been spending on sex toys and clothes for par-ties like this one instead of applying it to the debt I've col-lected. Oh, yeah, there's that, too – the debt. Compared to her, I am the most unimpressive person on the planet.

I hand her the skewer, and we roast our marshmallows. We sit there silently together, and it's nice. I pull mine out of the fire probably a moment too late, but I don't mind them a little too done. She pulls her out right after me. I make a s'more with the one I roasted and hand it to her because I don't want her to think hers is terrible since hers stayed in the fire a little longer than mine. Then, I do the same to the one she roasted and take that one for myself.

"Are you ready?" I ask.

"Sure," she says.

We take a bite and make a total mess as we laugh. I make us each a second s'more because we might as well en-joy them while we can. We talk as we eat, and it feels like we're here on vacation – a couple that's maybe celebrating their anniversary. I decide I should pack up everything be-cause it gives me something else to think about. I put it all on the table and turn back to her. She's a goddess.

"Oh, you have chocolate on your–"

"I do not. I–"

I kiss between her breasts and lower her to the rug. I kiss her collarbone and then her neck.

"Smooth," she says as I climb on top of her.

"What? I didn't want it to go to waste," I lie.

There was no chocolate there. She laughs as my hand begins to skate over her skin. I lift her up a little and unclasp her bra. We remove it, and I kiss her breasts.

"Can you–"

"Yeah," I say.

I lean up and take off my shirt.

"There they are," she says, squeezing my sensitive breasts. "I've missed them."

"They've missed you," I say.

"Have they not been taken care of by anyone else in my absence?"

"No, no one has taken care of them," I tell her.

"Not even…"

"No, babe. I haven't been with them since that night," I say, deciding not to tell her about that strange but very nice phone sex call.

"Did I–"

"They've been in Europe for their anniversary for the past three weeks, but even if they *had* been here, I don't want to be with them alone, babe. I only want all four of us to be together. Can we not talk about them now, though? I just want to talk about us tonight," I say.

"Of course. I'm sorry, I didn't mean–"

I kiss her on the forehead and say, "You don't have to apologize for anything. I just missed you. Last time was fun, but we only got a little time together after they left."

"I know. You're right," she says, pressing her lips between my breasts. "Let me make sure they know how much I love them," she adds and sucks on my nipple.

"You know how you could *really* show you love them?" I ask.

"How?"

"Let me fuck you from behind while I wear nipple

clamps," I state.

"I didn't—"

"I bought some. I've been thinking about the things I want to do with you all month, and that keeps coming to the top of my list."

It's true – I've had probably a hundred orgasms since I last saw her. I've touched myself in the shower with my hand *and* with my shower head. I've touched myself in nearly every room in my house with my fingers and with my vibrators. I've even gotten my dildo out a few times and fucked myself with it while I thought about her. Hell, I got off in the parking garage at work just last week, picturing her on all fours in front of me.

"And after?" she asks, licking my nipple.

"You can suck on them," I say.

"And?"

"And fuck me however you want."

"Oh, I like the sound of that. How do you want me, baby?"

"On all fours. Keep the thong on," I say.

"Whatever you want." She licks my other nipple.

She's on all fours now, and I stare at her for a long second before I practically run to my bag, which I left in the bedroom of this place. I put on the strap-on first. Then, I find the nipple clamps and attach them, feeling the pain and pleasure at the same time. I return to the living room, and she's still there, on all fours, just like I told her. She's waiting on me, and I can't help it – I stroke the toy with my hand as if it's an actual appendage. She lowers her front, and now I can see her pussy. She's already wet.

"Like this?" she asks.

"Yes," I say.

"Do you want me to touch you first?" she asks, watching me.

"No, I just like looking at you. I've never wanted to just look at someone before, how I look at you. When I'm by myself, I come so fast thinking about you."

"Yeah? Tell me."

"I've fucked myself with this thing picturing your fingers inside me."

"I want to see that," she says.

"Can I–"

"Whatever you want, baby. I'm yours. Fuck me however you want."

"Shit, that's so sexy," I say.

I know this isn't how things are supposed to go. She's the member; she's the one who's supposed to tell *me* what *she* wants. But maybe this *is* what she wants – me, to take her this way. There's something about all this that just gets me going. I slide my hand inside my shorts and touch my hard clit as I stroke the toy with my other hand.

"What else is sexy?" she asks.

"Touch yourself," I say.

She pushes her thong aside, and I can see her fingers moving through her wetness.

"I'm so wet," she says.

"Fuck," I say.

"Should I go inside?"

"Yes, get ready for me," I tell her.

"How big are you?" she asks.

"Big enough to make you come hard," I say.

"I better use three fingers, then."

Then, she fucks herself with three fingers as I watch, mesmerized.

"Are you tight, babe?"

"I'm tight," she says.

"And you want me to open you up?" I ask.

"All the way, baby," she says.

"Fuck, I'm going to come," I say because I can't hold on any longer.

"Don't, baby. Come inside me, please."

"You want me to come inside you?" I ask.

"More than anything. Fuck me until you come inside me. Make me come hard."

"Move your hand," I say.

She removes her hand, and I shift the thong to the side a little. I push inside her all the way, not wanting to wait.

"Oh, fuck," she says.

The thong is in my fucking way. I pull at the fabric hard until it's a limp, loose mess and no longer a worry.

"Full, babe?" I ask.

"Yes, so deep, baby," she says.

My hands are on her hips, and I'm rocking hard into her, wanting her to feel me everywhere.

"God, yes. I need you. Make me come."

"Tell me to fuck you."

"Fuck me," she says.

"Yell it."

"Fuck me!" she screams.

"God, you're so sexy. I fucking love your body," I say. "Play with your breasts."

She squeezes her breast with one hand while she tries to keep herself up with the other.

"Yeah! How does it feel?" I ask.

"So good."

"I'm going to come soon," I say.

"Scream when you do, babe. Let me hear how much you love fucking me."

"Oh, wow. That's—"

Just her saying that makes me come.

"Fuck! Yes! Yes! Yes!" I fuck her hard as I come into her.

It's probably too hard, but she doesn't say anything, and after I come, I fall down on top of her, which causes her to fall flat to the rug beneath us. I slip out of her and try to gather my breathing. I always end up falling on top of her, which is kind of embarrassing, but when I touch her, it's so good that I can't hang on a moment longer without being pressed totally against her.

"I like you on top of me," she says.

"I'm sorry. I couldn't hold back."

"Never apologize for that."

"Did you…" I ask.

"Not yet."

I open my eyes. I didn't even get her there. What's wrong with me?

"Well, fuck. I wanted…"

"Babe, stay there until you're ready. Then, try again," she tells me.

"Really?"

"Yes. In fact… We can make tonight *your* night. Whatever you want, you get."

"That's not really how this–"

"Shut up. Not tonight. Not right now. Right now, we're just two people renting a cabin for the night, okay?"

"Okay," I say softly.

After a minute, I shift and begin kissing up and down her back. She's a little sweaty, and I like tasting the salt on her skin. I lick my lips as I kiss down to her ass and spread her cheeks.

"Is this okay?" I ask, hoping she gets it.

"Yes," she says.

"Can I…"

I've never really wanted to do this until right now.

"Yes," she whispers.

I kiss her there. Then, I reach between her legs and cup her sex.

"I'm really close. It won't take long," she says.

"It can take all night, for all I care," I say.

I kiss her there again. I stroke her clit, too. With my other hand, I move into her folds and gather what I need. Then, I move it back to her ass and wait. She doesn't say anything, so I push my pinky finger just a little inside.

"Oh," she says.

"Okay?"

"Yeah."

She starts rocking her hips against my hand, and it doesn't take long – she comes almost too quickly for me, and I'm not done. I move under her, bring her down to my mouth, and she sits on my face. Then, she comes again almost just as fast. I still need her, though, so I get behind her, lift her hips, and when she moves back into me, I slip the toy inside her. I fuck her until I hear her come for the third time.

"God, I love you," I say.

Oh, my God! Did I just tell her that I love her? I think about stopping what I'm doing, but that would make it worse, so I keep thrusting until a minute later, when I start coming.

"Fuck, I'm coming," I say, hoping she'll forget about what I just said.

When we both come down, I roll her over to look into her eyes, and there doesn't appear to be worry or concern there. I remove the strap-on and climb on top of her.

"Hi," she says.

"Hi," I say back. "These clamps are killing me, by the way," I add, trying to change the subject.

"Should I take them off and kiss your nipples to make them feel better?"

I smile and give her a nod.

***

Later, we move to the sofa, where she puts the toy back on me. I laugh as I watch her try to slip the shorts on me while I'm sitting down. *She* laughs at herself before she climbs onto my lap.

"How are those nipples?" she asks, wrapping her arms around my neck.

Mine are around her back. I kiss between her breasts as I rub her skin.

"Sore, but good," I reply.

"So, no more playing with them tonight?"

"Not tonight, babe," I tell her. "But you do have me at full attention here. Are you planning on doing anything with this?" I look down.

"Oh, yes," she says. "I was hoping I could put it inside me."

I nod. She smiles, reaches for it, and moves it through her wetness before she pushes it inside.

"I was also hoping you'd kiss me until I come."

I press our lips together as she starts moving her hips. This orgasm takes a while, and I don't know if it's because she's come so much already that her body needs longer, if she's dragging it out on purpose, or if it's just not the best angle, so it's taking her longer.

"You feel so good inside me," she says when she pulls out of our kiss.

Yeah, I think she's dragging it out. A bead of sweat falls between her breasts. I lick it and then move to her nipple to suck on it.

"Kiss me," she says.

I move my mouth back to hers, and she kisses me, sucks on my tongue, and nibbles on my lip until she starts moving faster. I kiss her until she comes. Then, I watch.

"Yes. Oh, baby. Yes, this one is…"

"What? Tell me."

"This one is the best," she says as she rocks.

I look up at her. Her eyes are closed, but there's a tear falling down her cheek. I wipe it away with my thumb and keep watching. She crashes into me a few seconds later, her head on my shoulder, breathing hard.

"Are you okay?" I ask her.

"Yes," she says and sniffles. "I just need…" She lifts up to let the toy come out. Then, she stands. "I'll be right back, okay?"

"Can I get you anything?"

"No, just a minute," she says.

She disappears into the bathroom, and I'm left wondering what's going on. I take off the shorts, tossing the whole thing to the floor to worry about later. A minute later, though, she returns with a smile on her face. It looks a little forced, but I don't say anything. I lie down on the sofa and open my arms.

"Can I ask you something?" I say as I hold her.

"Yes," she replies.

"Have you been with anyone since last time?" I ask, swallowing and wondering if she can feel it.

"No," she says.

"Have you *wanted* to be with anyone?"

"Not exactly," she says.

"What's that mean?" I ask next, my heart beating wildly now.

"I went on a date," she says.

"Oh, right."

"It was just coffee," she says.

"But you like her?"

"She's nice. We don't really know each other yet," she replies.

"When will you see her again?" I ask, knowing I have no right to.

"Maybe next weekend; I don't know. Have *you* been dating?" she asks.

"No, I've been trying to figure out my aunt's stuff."

"Of course. Have you?"

"Have I what?"

"Figured it out?"

"Yeah. I've decided to keep the house, and I'm making plans to fix it up now."

"That's great," she says but sounds off.

"I think I'm finally starting to feel okay for the first time in a while," I say.

That's not entirely true. I don't know that I want the house, but I don't have many options. Oh, and I can't date anyone because I only want *her*. I can't even get it on with my best friends without her, and they want me. They want me so much, they text me almost daily asking if I'm coming over. I've been saying no because I want her; I only want *her*.

"Can we just stay like this for the rest of the night?" she asks.

"Whatever you want," I say.

I've got to stop putting this woman ahead of everything else in my life. My friends want to fuck me; I should just let them. I should go on a date with a woman and do what my friends suggested – fuck her until I get this woman out of my system. Then, I hear it – her breathing has slowed. She's sleeping. She's sleeping on top of me while I hold her. I smile and kiss the top of her head. I pull the throw blanket that's over the sofa on top of us and try to wrap it around her with my one free arm. She doesn't stir until the knock on the door at three-forty-five.

"Shit. I fell asleep," she says and sits up quickly.

"You're beautiful," I reply.

She leans back down, smiles at me, then kisses me softly, and I know I'm not going to do any of those things I tried to talk myself into earlier.

"*You're* beautiful," she says.

MONTH 11. PART 1. – A FIRST

(POV Member)

"Mom, he's going to be fine," I say into the phone.

"You don't know that. Your father is healthy, but this is surgery."

"He's having his gallbladder removed. It's a common procedure," I tell her.

"Honey, anything could happen."

"I'm sure it will be fine. How is Dad doing?"

"He's okay. He's better at this stuff than I am. I've called your brothers. They're going to be here."

"Okay."

"The surgery is Saturday morning. It's the earliest they can get him in."

"Saturday?" I ask.

"Yes, Saturday morning. Then, we'll all be at the hospital for him when he gets out."

"Right," I say, thinking about what a horrible person I am.

I'm not thinking about my father, who's going to have surgery; I'm thinking about the sex party that's also *this* Saturday. I can still make it. It doesn't start until eleven. I can leave the hospital by then.

"The boys are going to stay at the house that night. I thought you'd stay, too. We could make a night of it."

"At the house?"

"Yes, I could use a distraction. They won't let me stay with your father at the hospital, and visiting hours will be over at seven. I thought we could do a late dinner and then spend some time together so I don't go out of my mind before we go back to the hospital on Sunday to check on him."

"Of course," I tell her. "I'll pack a bag and stay the night."

It's the right thing to do.

"Oh, before I let you go… How did your date go?"

"Mom…" I say.

"What? I'm allowed to ask; I'm the mother."

"She's nice," I say.

"Nice?"

"She's great. I'm sure she'll make a great girlfriend for someone; maybe even a wife one day, if that's what she wants."

"Oh, honey, no. What happened?"

"Nothing happened. We went out for dinner."

"You just told me that she's great."

"She *is* great."

"Is there no chemistry? Did she do something or–"

"She's just not the one for me, Mom," I tell her.

"She's a doctor who comes from a good family."

"All that's true. I can't really explain it, Mom. It's not there for me."

"I give up," she says. "You're on your own. But I want grandchildren."

"You already have grandchildren," I say, laughing.

"I want them from you, too," she says.

I laugh again, roll my eyes, and we finish our call. I think of that dinner date and how amazing the woman really was. She was kind and sweet and made me feel like all of her attention was on me, despite the fact that she's a busy doctor with patients and was technically on call, so she couldn't drink the wine she still insisted we order so that *I* could enjoy it. She also held my hand as we left the restaurant and then kissed me sweetly when she dropped me off on my doorstep. The problem was that later that night, when I was in bed, getting myself off, I wasn't thinking about her.

I can't believe I'm going to miss this month's party.

"God, she's going to think I don't want to be there because I'm dating someone," I say to myself. "Fuck."

Not knowing what to do, I continue to work until dinnertime. Then, I pack up and head home. I have no other option – I need her to know why I'm not going to be there.

I pick up my computer, log in, and find the messaging center. I type out my email, hit send, and wait. When I hear back the next day, they accept my request to pass along my message, but not that the other member will get back to me. I take my chance anyway. I send the email and wait again. The waiting is the worst part, and I'm back to taking my personal laptop to work again so I can check incessantly to see if they respond. I'm at home when I finally get an email.

Hey,
It's me. My number is below. You can call me whenever.

It's not signed, but I know it's *her*. She gave me her number, and now, I have to dial it. I agonize over this for hours, though. Do I just call, like she says? Do I text first? Yeah, I should text first. What the hell should I text her? I'm lying in my bed, staring at my phone, unable to do anything with it. I start picturing all of our moments together, and instead of helping me come up with what to message, they turn me on so much, I make myself come. Then, I take a cold shower. Finally, I lie back down and send a quick message of 'Can I call you' just to finally get it done. A second later, I get a response. I smile and call.

"Hello?" she says.

"Hi," I say.

"Hi," she replies.

"Well, *we're* making progress," I joke.

God, I'm nervous. This woman has touched every single part of my body, and I'm nervous just to talk to her on the phone.

She laughs and says, "Sorry. I don't exactly know how to do this."

"Neither do I," I say. "I just knew I needed to talk to you."

"How's your dad?" she asks.

I smile at how thoughtful she is and say, "It's his gallbladder. They say he'll be fine, but my parents have been together since they were sixteen years old, and this is the first health scare he's really had. My mom is terrified he's going to go into surgery and not come out. The doctors assure me it's a standard procedure, but I want to be there for her – and for him, obviously."

"Of course. I'm sure it will be fine."

"Yeah." Neither of us say anything for a moment. "So, I have your number now."

"And I have yours," she says, sounding happy.

"That's a good thing, right?

"What do we do now?" I ask.

"Well, we could just *talk*," she says.

"I guess we could," I reply, laughing. "Is that okay? Did I interrupt anything?"

"No, I'm at home. Where are you?"

"Home," I tell her.

There's another long silence.

"Baby?" I say, trying to make it as normal for us as I can.

"Yeah?" she replies.

"I miss you."

"I miss you," she says.

"Are you going to the party?" I ask.

"I have to, or I'll lose the job," she says.

"Yeah," I say, thinking about some other member touching her and hating it.

"I'll just ask my friends if I can hang out with them all night."

"*Hang out* with?" I say.

She laughs and says, "I don't participate unless you're there. I'll just watch."

"That sounds nice," I say.

"Do you ever think about that night?"

"Yes," I say.

"Would you want to do it again?"

"Yes," I repeat.

"Me too," she says.

"I miss your hands on me," I tell her.

"Fuck, me too."

"I shouldn't ask you for this," I say, knowing that it's wrong.

"Ask," she says.

"This is crossing a line… We've already crossed one with me calling, but this–"

"Ask," she says louder this time.

"Will you meet me somewhere tomorrow night?"

"Where?" she asks.

"I don't know. I was thinking about a hotel or something," I say.

"Yes, name it," she says.

I smile to myself, running my fingertips along my inner thigh, thinking about her doing it instead.

"You don't have to," I say, giving her an out.

"I want to."

"It's just us. There's no company to–"

"I want to," she repeats.

"I'll make a reservation," I say. "I can text you the details."

"Yes," she says.

"And you're absolutely sure?" I ask.

"You're alone right now, right?" she asks.

"Yes."

"The woman you…" She pauses. "The woman you're dating; she's not–"

"We're not dating. We went on one date after the coffee thing. She's nice, but I can't right now."

"Can't what?" she asks.

"Think of anyone but you," I tell her.

"Can you do something for me?"

"Yes."

"Touch yourself with me right now."

"Oh," I say. "Really?"

"Yes, please. Just talking to you has me so turned on."

"Me too," I say. "Your voice is so sexy on the phone."

"So is yours. I need to hear you come."

"You *can* tomorrow night," I tease.

"Now, babe."

"Jesus. You really need it, don't you?" I ask.

"Yes," she says.

"Are you already–"

"It won't take long," she says.

"Damn. One second." I shift until my hand is inside the shorts I threw on after my shower. "Okay."

"Yeah?"

"Yeah," I say.

"What are you wearing?"

"A pair of shorts and a shirt."

"Bra?"

"No."

"Panties?"

"Yes," I say.

"Are you over or under?"

"Under," I say, stroking myself.

"How wet are you?" she asks.

"Very," she says. "I just did this to myself about an hour ago."

"You did?"

"Yes." I stroke harder.

"Were you thinking about me?"

"Yes."

Fuck, she's got me so turned on, I can't find the spot I need. I'm too wet and slide around until I can finally find what I need.

"What was I doing to you?"

"Actually, I was sucking on your clit."

"Jesus," she says. "Did you make me come?"

"Don't I always?" I ask, smirking.

"Yes, you do. I'm going inside for a second."

"Oh, yes. Fuck yourself, babe." I slip inside myself as well and listen to her for a minute. "So good."

"Are you close?" she asks.

"Yes," I say, moving back out to my clit that needs me to touch it.

"Me too," she says.

"Baby, I'm coming," I say when my orgasm builds so quickly, I didn't even see it coming. "Oh, God. Yes," I say as I stroke fast and hard until I can't anymore, and I crash back against the pillow with my palm still cupping my own pussy.

"I want to scream your name," I say to her.

"I want you to always scream my name when you come," she tells me.

"God, this is *definitely* crossing the line," I say.

"Hey."

"Yeah?"

"Tomorrow night?" she says.

"Yes?"

"Will you tell me your name? Your real name?" she asks.

"Will you tell me yours?"

"Yes," she says.

"Did you come?"

"Not yet," she replies.

"Oh, babe. How hard are you right now?" I ask, cupping myself a little harder.

"Very."

"Come for me, then," I say. "And I'll tell you my name tomorrow night."

Then, I listen for a few more minutes until she comes and I hear her perfectly sexy sounds and picture her perfectly sexy face how it always looks when she comes. When we hang up, I make the reservation. I text her the hotel information, and we keep texting all night. I find myself laughing at her replies. We come again, texting back and forth dirty messages that get me too turned on to sleep unless I placed my vibrator where I needed it. She tells me she comes, too, but I have no way of knowing if that's true or not. I finally say goodnight via text when it's actually morning, and I know I'll get to see her in about twelve hours.

***

I arrive at the hotel early and head to the desk to check in. They give me my key card and tell me they've got the champagne chilling in my room for me as well as the wine and strawberries I've requested. I thank them and turn around to nervously wait for her to arrive. Right on the dot, she walks into the lobby, looking sexy and gorgeous. She's wearing a pair of steel-gray dress slacks and a navy button-down that she's left untucked. Her hair is a little longer than it was the last time I saw her, but not by much. She talks to the man standing there as she looks around, confused. I know why. I told her I would text her the room number, and I didn't. She doesn't even have my name to give the man to find me. I decided I wanted to meet her down here first. I swallow hard as I walk over from the side.

"Are you waiting for me?"

She turns to me and says, "I found her."

Yes, yes, she did, I think to myself. I walk up a little closer.

"Hi," I say.

"Hello," she replies.

"You look nice," I tell her.

"You look *beautiful*," she says. "You always do, though."

I smile and say, "I thought we could grab dinner in the restaurant first. Is that okay?"

"Dinner?" she asks.

I worry.

"Is that not okay? It–"

"It's fine. I'm nervous, too, by the way."

"Yeah?" I say, laughing a little.

"Definitely," she says.

"I don't know what I'm supposed to say or do. I just want us to be here tonight; just the two of us."

This is it. This is the thing we haven't talked about yet that we need to bring up before anything else happens.

"I want this to be *your* choice. Do you want to be here with me?" I ask.

"Of course, I do."

"No, I mean, if I'm not…"

She nods.

"You mean, if you're not paying me?" she asks.

I swallow. Please don't let this change anything for her. "Yes."

"I didn't come here for money," she says. "I want what you want tonight."

"And you're sure?"

"Yes," she says again.

"I might ask that, like, ten more times tonight. Sorry," I tell her, wincing a little at the awkwardness.

She laughs, takes my hand, and entwines our fingers.

"You don't have to apologize. I want this as much as you do," she says.

She seems a little awkward at dinner until the appetizer comes, and we lean over to share it. Then, she settles in. This is the first time we've been somewhere in public together where sex isn't an option. At the parties, sex is everywhere. People can fuck each other in any room, in front of people or behind closed doors. If we tried anything here, we'd be kicked out and, likely, arrested. It makes this dinner matter more to me, knowing that we're just enjoying a meal together without the possibility of anything else. Well, at least, for a little while. Eventually, I hope we go up to the room I've reserved for us, but that can wait. We talk for well over an hour as we eat and drink our wine. She makes me laugh more than anyone I've ever met, and I once dated a stand-up comedian in college. When the bill comes, she offers to pay, but it's easier to just sign it to the room, so I take it instead.

"I got us a room," I tell her.

"Do you want to go up?" she asks.

"This place is on the lake. Do you want to go for a walk first?" I ask.

"Yes," she says.

I take her hand once we're outside. We walk for a bit until she stops to take in the sunset. I stand next to her and watch, too. She lets go of my hand but only to go behind me and pull me back against her in that way that only *she* can do.

"Why do you feel so good?" I ask.

"Why do *you*?" she asks back.

I laugh a little, and she kisses my temple sweetly. Then, I tell her.

"Who's that?" she asks.

"My name. That's my name," I say.

She kisses my neck and pulls me in tighter. A second later, she whispers *her* name into my ear.

"Take me upstairs?" I say.

She nods, and we walk hand in hand back inside and toward the elevators. When one arrives, we climb in with an older couple. I use my room key to get us to the higher floors and press the button.

"It's not the penthouse. Don't be disappointed," I whisper to her.

"I'm not," she replies, pulling me back against her. "That would be impossible tonight anyway."

I smile at her.

"Newlyweds?" the woman standing with her husband on the other side of the elevator asks.

"Sorry?" she says.

"Are you newlyweds?" the woman asks.

"Oh, we–" she starts.

"Sure," I say. "We're here on our honeymoon."

"That's nice, dear," the woman says. "Thirty years for us." She points to the man next to her.

"Something for *us* to aspire to," I say, smiling as I do.

The couple gets off on the ninth floor, and she turns to me.

261

"We're married now?" she asks playfully.

"Why not? We'll never see them again anyway," I reply.

"Well, if this is our honeymoon, I plan to spend the entire thing in the bedroom," she teases, leaning in and nibbling on my lower lip.

That just does things to me. When the elevator arrives, I pull us out of it because I want her hands on me.

"Let's go," I say.

When we're finally in the room, I watch her as she takes it all in.

"Oh, wow," she says.

She's so cute. I smile as she looks around at the room.

"Is this okay?" I ask, knowing the answer already.

"Are you kidding? Can I move in?" she says, walking in past me to look around more. "Holy shit! The view," she says, pointing out the sliding glass doors.

I laugh silently and walk behind her. I press against her, placing my hands on her chest from under her arms, resting them above her breasts. I place my chin on her shoulder and breathe in her scent.

"Do you want to watch it from the balcony?"

"This is good," she says.

"There's wine and beer or sparkling–"

"Babe, *this* is what I want." She places her hands on top of mine. "Just this."

"Okay," I say, smiling.

We stand there for a while, just watching the sun move through the sky. Neither of us says anything for a long time.

"You're so beautiful." I finally have to break the silence because I can't hold it in any longer. "I've missed you so much."

"I've missed you, too," she replies.

"What does that *mean*?" I ask.

She kisses my fingertips one by one.

"I don't know," she says when she's done.

"May I?" I place my hands on her belt.

"Yes," she replies.

I unbuckle it for her. Then, I unbutton each of her shirt buttons slowly. Once I open it up, I move my hands to her chest to run them up and down, feeling her solid body in front of mine. She's not a dream. She's reality.

"I think this is more than just sex for me," I say.

"But we're still going to have sex now, right?" she asks.

I laugh and pull her shirt off, pressing against her back again.

"Yes," I say.

"It's more than sex for me, too," she says.

I undo her pants.

"So, tonight…" I trail off.

"Is a date?" she asks.

I nod and kiss her shoulder. When her pants fall to the floor, I move my hands to her stomach and run them over her skin as she takes care of her shoes.

"A *first* date," I say.

"If it's a first date, should we even be doing this? I'm a pretty traditional girl. Normally, I don't put out on the first date," she replies.

I take my own hand and touch myself, gathering my desire for her. Then, I reach around and show it to her. Without hesitation, she takes my fingers into her mouth and sucks on them.

"We don't have to, but you should know how much I want you," I whisper in her ear. "And how ready I am for you."

"You taste so good," she says, moving my fingers in and out of her mouth, caressing them with her soft tongue.

"I want you," I say.

"I want you, too," she replies.

"I want you to take me slowly."

"That might not be possible." She lowers my hand to her panties and slips it inside. "I'm already soaked for you."

"Oh, God," I say, pressing my body fully against hers and stroking her clit.

"I'll come," she says.

"Good."

"Baby, I'll come too fast. Let me take you to bed," she says, removing my hand.

She turns around, and we're facing one another for the first time since we walked into the room.

"I love your eyes," she says, cupping my cheek.

"Yours aren't half bad, either. I love how dark they get when you're turned on, but how light they were in the lobby earlier when you just saw me."

"Can I take this off?" she asks, her hand slipping under the strap of my dress.

I nod. She walks behind me and finds the zipper on the back. She kisses my skin as she unzips me. When the dress falls to the floor, she walks back around.

"Slow," she says.

I nod with a smile. She takes her time with my bra, kissing every spot it vacates as she removes it. She kneels and does the same as she pulls down my underwear. She kisses my sex, but avoids where I need her. I massage her scalp with my hand and play with her short hair as she slowly kisses every inch of my inner thighs. When she stands again, she walks me back to the bed and nods for me to lie down. I do. She removes her own panties and then slides on top of me.

We kiss for the longest time. My lips are swollen and, likely, a little bruised, but I don't care. Her hands stay in the *safe* zones, so we don't accidentally come when we're not ready for that yet. Her lips roam my body until I ask her to roll onto her back so I can climb on top and give her the same attention. Her skin is what I've craved since the last time we were together. It's soft and smooth, and I love how it tastes on my tongue.

"We should…" she fades out.

I look up at her.

"What, babe? We should what?"

"I mean, we only have…"

I move back up her body and look down at her.

"We've got all night. No one's going to knock at three-forty-five this time." I kiss her. "No one is going to kick us out at four." I kiss her again. "The door is locked. No one can interrupt this." I place my hand on her heart. "You're mine. I'm yours."

She smiles up at me with hazy eyes.

"I might be in love with you," she says.

I wasn't expecting that, but I smile and lower myself to kiss her again. I roll my greedy hips into her sex, loving how wet she is for me. She gasps, and I listen as she moans out my name. We rock together. My clit is ready to come, and it won't take long. I wait for her, though. When she comes, she yells my name. I yell hers in return. Then, I fall on top of her, knowing we're going to do this again and again all night.

"I might be in love with you, too," I whisper into her ear.

She tightens her hold on me and kisses my cheek.

MONTH 11. PART 2. – THE NIGHT IT ALL CHANGED

(POV Escort)

"How do *you* know she's not going to be there?" I ask them.

"The website messaged us saying that she requested to message us privately. Normally, even members can't contact one another unless it's through the company. They do that to protect our anonymity, but if a member requests it, the company reaches out to the other member and asks if it's okay. We said okay," my friend says. "She asked for your number," she adds.

"She wants my number?" I ask.

"I guess she wants to explain to you directly why she can't be there."

"Can I read the email?" I ask.

"Sure," my friend says, passing me her phone where she's already got it pulled up.

I read.

Hi,

I know this is unconventional. For that, I apologize. Thank you for agreeing to accept my message in the first place; I know you didn't have to. Anyway, I don't exactly know what to do here because I think I should just leave it – that's probably the right thing to do – but I need her to know that I won't be there this weekend. Mainly, I need her to know why I can't be there. It's not by choice. My father is in the hospital. He's having surgery on Saturday, and it should be fine. It's not major, but my mother wants all the kids there, and I need to make sure she's taken care of. I know that's probably too much infor-

mation, but I need her to know that it's not because I don't want to be there. She'll understand this, but if you can tell her that it's not because of what we talked about last time, I'd really appreciate it. I'd really love to explain it to her myself, so if you could maybe just ask her if it's okay for me to have her phone number, I'd love to call her and tell her. I know that's a stretch and that outside of a few nights together, you don't really know me, but I promise I just need to tell her why. If there's an email address or something else she'd be comfortable with, I'd take anything. And if she's reading this because you're sharing it with her – I miss you.

The message isn't signed, but those last three words stick out to me and make me smile. I pass the phone back to my friend and meet her wife's eyes.

"What do *you* think I should do?"

"Whatever you want," she replies.

"Maybe make a new email or something and give *that* to her instead," my friend says. "Safer that way."

"She'd only have my phone number. Plus, I don't think I have anything to worry about," I reply.

"It's up to you," she says, taking her wife's hand. "We're just passing along the message. For what it's worth, I *do* think it's cool that she's reached out to us to let you know ahead of time. She didn't have to do that."

"What did she mean about the thing you talked about last time?" her wife asks.

"She's dating someone," I say solemnly. "They'd had a coffee date before the last party. I don't know if it's still going on or not, but it's probably that."

"Why would that–" My friend glares at me. "What exactly did you two *do* last time?"

"What we always do," I reply. "We had sex."

"And?" she asks.

"And, what?"

"Why would she care if you thought she was skipping the party to be with someone she's dating?" her wife asks.

I swallow.

"What happened?" she presses further.

"Nothing. I mean… something, maybe. I…" I sigh. "When I was…" I look down at the floor. "When I came, I accidentally told her I loved her."

"You did *what*?!" my friend shouts.

"It was a heat-of-the-moment thing. I didn't mean it like that. It was more that I love how she makes me feel, how she makes me come, and–"

"You told her you love her?" my friend asks.

"What did she say?" her wife asks.

"Nothing. She was a little busy."

"She didn't hear you or she just didn't acknowledge it?"

"I don't know. I came, and I was kind of loud, then I kind of dropped on top of her, and we stayed there for a minute, but she didn't bring it up or anything, so maybe she didn't hear me."

"Well, if she didn't hear you, why would she be worried about you thinking she's skipping this thing to fuck someone she's dating?"

"I don't know," I say. "It just felt different last time."

"Well, you *did* tell the woman paying you for sex that you love her," my friend says.

"Hey," I say back. "You don't have to be an asshole about this."

"It's the truth, though, sweetie," her wife says. "I know *she* pays the company, and *the company* pays you, but she *is* paying you for sex once a month."

"I know that," I reply.

"Do you?" my friend asks.

"Do I understand that she's paying me?"

"Do you love her?" she asks.

I stand up and say, "I don't really know her."

"But it bothers you that she's with someone?"

"She's allowed to be with whoever she wants. That's always been true."

"But it bugs you now," her wife says. "Is that why you're not with us by yourself?"

"Don't make this about that," I reply, crossing my arms over my chest.

"It's a good question," my friend says. "Do you feel like you'd be cheating on her if you let us touch you or if you touched us?"

I look away from them toward the front door, needing to escape.

"Can I have your phone back?" I ask.

"Why?"

"Please," I say, holding out my hand.

She unlocks it and passes it back to me. I type out my message, hit send, and hand it back to her.

"I should go."

"Why?" my friend asks. "We're not trying to beat up on you here. We're just trying to talk to you."

"I know. I just need to get some air. Can I call you guys later?"

"Of course," she says.

I leave their house, climb into my car, roll down the window, and let the cool air hit me as I drive off to nowhere in particular. After a few hours and a near empty gas tank, I decide it's time to go home. I drop my keys on the table and look around the living room. All I can see is my aunt sitting on that sofa, crying over the husband she'd just lost. I'm comforting her. Then, she's on the floor in the fetal position because the pain of her cancer overtook her. Next, she's holding a trash can in front of her as she vomits into it one night. I see her pulling at a piece of her hair as it began to fall out. I'm no longer able to see the good times we had here when I was growing up or home from college; a new coat of paint or new tile in the bathroom won't change that for me.

I run up the stairs to the guest room I've been living in since I started taking care of her and close the door behind me. I know now that I can't stay here. As easy as it

269

would be just to fix it up and try to make it my own, I know it never will be. It will always remind me of the hard times more than the good ones now. I need to make a new start somewhere. I pull out my laptop, open the browser, and start looking for apartments. I'm nearly done paying off the bulk of what's owed, so I can sell this place and afford a nice one-bedroom somewhere. It's time I start putting my life back together.

After a few hours of narrowing down my search to three places to go check out in person, my phone beeps. I assume it's either my boss or my friends. My boss probably wants to make sure I won't miss my shift tomorrow. He checks in about once a week still just to make sure I'm showing up, despite that fact that I haven't missed a day or been late since I lost my aunt. My friends probably want to make sure I'm okay. I pick it up to look at the screen. It's a text from an unknown number.

"It's *her*," I say to no one.

Her message is simple, and I reply yes. Then, the phone rings. I'm nervous. I wait until the third ring. Then, I answer.

"Hello?" I say.

"Hi," she says.

I bite my lower lip. Her voice – I've missed her voice.

"Hi," I reply.

"Well, *we're* making progress," she teases and laughs.

I laugh a little and say, "Sorry. I don't exactly know how to do this."

"Neither do I," she says. "I just knew I needed to talk to you."

"How's your dad?" I ask.

"It's his gallbladder. They say he'll be fine, but my parents have been together since they were sixteen years old, and this is the first health scare he's really had. My mom is terrified he's going to go into surgery and not come out. The doctors assure me it's a standard procedure, but I want to be there for her – and for him, obviously."

"Of course," I say. "I'm sure it will be fine."

"Yeah," she says. Then, there's a silence before she adds, "So, I have your number now."

"And I have yours," I reply, smiling.

"What do we do now?" she asks.

"Well, we could just *talk*," I say.

"I guess we could," she replies, laughing a little again. "Is that okay? Did I interrupt anything?"

"No, I'm at home. Where are you?"

"Home," she says.

We say nothing for a long moment. There's a tension here, but it's not an awkward one; it's a pleasant one.

"Baby?" she says.

"Yeah?" I say back, smiling at the term of endearment.

"I miss you."

"I miss you," I say.

"Are you going to the party?" she asks.

"I have to, or I'll lose the job," I say.

"Yeah," she says, sounding disappointed.

"I'll just ask my friends if I can hang out with them all night."

"*Hang out* with?"

I laugh and say, "I don't participate unless you're there. I'll just watch."

"That sounds nice," she says.

"Do you ever think about that night?"

"Yes," she says.

"Would you want to do it again?"

"Yes," she repeats.

"Me too," I say.

"I miss your hands on me," she says.

"Fuck," I say, shifting on the bed. "Me too."

"I shouldn't ask you for this," she says.

"Ask," I say.

"This is crossing a line... We've already crossed one with me calling, but this–"

"Ask," I repeat.

"Will you meet me somewhere tomorrow night?"

"Where?" I ask.

"I don't know. I was thinking about a hotel or something," she says.

"Yes, name it," I say.

"You don't have to," she says.

"I want to."

"It's just us. There's no company to–"

"I want to," I say again.

"I'll make a reservation," she says. "I can text you the details."

"Yes," I say, pushing the laptop off to the side of the bed.

"And you're absolutely sure?" she asks.

"You're alone right now, right?" I ask.

"Yes."

"The woman you..." I bite my bottom lip. "The woman you're dating; she's not–"

"We're not dating. We went on one date after the coffee thing. She's nice, but I can't right now."

"Can't what?" I ask.

"Think of anyone but you," she says.

I close my eyes and say, "Can you do something for me?"

"Yes."

"Touch yourself with me right now."

"Oh," she says. "Really?"

"Yes, please. Just talking to you has me so turned on."

"Me too," she replies. "Your voice is so sexy on the phone."

"So is yours." I undo my pants. "I need to hear you come."

"You *can* tomorrow night," she says.

"Now, babe."

"Jesus. You really need it, don't you?" she asks.

"Yes," I say, touching myself.

"Are you already–"

"It won't take long," I interrupt.

"Damn. One second," she says, and I hear some rustling on the other side of the phone. "Okay."

"Yeah?"

"Yeah," she says.

"What are you wearing?"

"A pair of shorts and a shirt."

"Bra?"

"No."

"Panties?"

"Yes," she says.

"Are you over or under?"

"Under," she says.

"How wet are you?" I ask.

"Very," she says. "I just did this to myself about an hour ago."

"You did?"

"Yes," she says, breathing faster now.

"Were you thinking about me?"

"Yes."

"What was I doing to you?"

"Actually, I was sucking on your clit."

"Jesus," I say. "Did you make me come?"

"Don't I always?" she asks.

"Yes, you do," I say. "I'm going inside for a second."

"Oh, yes," she says. "Fuck yourself, babe."

I slip two fingers inside. I know I won't come like this, but it feels good to be filled while I picture *her* fingers there.

"So good," she says.

"Are you close?" I ask.

"Yes," she says.

I put my fingers back on my clit and rub it fast.

"Me too," I say.

"Baby, I'm coming," she says.

I stop, and I listen. I'm so hard. I know I need to come, but I can't yet – I have to listen to her moans and gasps first. I need to hear her make herself feel good.

"I want to scream your name," she says as she comes down.

"I want you to always scream my name when you come," I tell her, stroking myself slowly.

"God, this is *definitely* crossing the line," she says.

"Hey," I say.

"Yeah?"

"Tomorrow night?" I say.

"Yes?" she says.

"Will you tell me your name? Your real name?"

"Will you tell me yours?"

"Yes," I say.

"Did you come?"

"Not yet."

"Oh, babe. How hard are you right now?"

"Very."

"Come for me, then," she says. "And I'll tell you my name tomorrow night."

I do.

***

When she said hotel, she meant five-star resort. This place is massive and super fancy. The door is opened *for* me. When I walk in, someone is there to greet me to see what I need. I was only given the address. She was supposed to text me the room number, but I've checked my phone ten times while I sat in the back of my Uber, and nothing.

"I'm just waiting for someone," I tell the man who asked me the question.

"Are you waiting for me?" a voice says from my left.

I turn, and she's standing there dressed in a short, flowy, white-and-green sundress. Her hands are clasped a little nervously in front of her. Her hair is down and framing her beautiful face. I actually have to take a step back because she takes the breath out of my body.

"I found her," I tell the man.

He nods, I think. I don't actually know because I'm

only focusing on her. She walks up closer to me and smiles.

"Hi," she says.

"Hello," I say.

"You look nice," she says, looking me up and down.

"You look *beautiful*," I tell her. "You always do, though."

She smiles shyly now and says, "I thought we could grab dinner in the restaurant first. Is that okay?"

"Dinner?"

"Is that not okay? It—"

"It's fine," I say. "I'm nervous, too, by the way."

"Yeah?" she says, laughing a little.

"Definitely," I reply.

"I don't know what I'm supposed to say or do," she says. "I just want us to be here tonight; just the two of us."

I don't exactly know what she means by that, so I give her a confused expression.

"I want this to be *your* choice. Do you want to be here with me?"

"Of course, I do," I say.

"No, I mean, if I'm not…"

I get it now, so I nod.

"You mean, if you're not paying me?" I ask.

"Yes."

"I didn't come here for money," I say. "I want what you want tonight," I add.

"And you're sure?"

"Yes," I say again.

"I might ask that, like, ten more times tonight. Sorry," she says.

I laugh. Then, I take her hand and entwine our fingers.

"You don't have to apologize. I want this as much as you do," I say.

We walk through the lobby, and she leads me down the hall and into the restaurant, where she's made a reservation. I'm definitely out of my element here. My friends have taken me to nice restaurants before, but I've never been on a date in a place like this. Shit. Is this a date? Are we on a date? I don't ask the question out loud as the waiter pours our water and then brings us the wine she asked me to pick out like I actually know what I'm doing. I pointed at something. The waiter nodded at me, and I assumed that meant I'd made a good choice. We talk as we share an appetizer, and we talk some more as we eat our entrées. I love making her laugh – her whole face lights up. We share a dessert, which is way too rich for me, but I like how she eats the rest of it when I only take a couple of bites. I don't like when women order only salads on dates and then just move their forks around their plate.

"I got us a room," she says when she's signed the check after I offered to pay.

"Do you want to go up?" I ask.

"This place is on the lake. Do you want to go for a walk first?" she asks.

"Yes," I reply, loving that idea very much.

Outside, she takes my hand again, and it's like we met through friends at work or something and we're here on our anniversary. There are lights strung up outside, but they're not on because the sun is only just setting. I stop us to stare out at the sun and the water. I move behind her and press my back to her front, wrapping her in my arms.

"Why do you feel so good?" she asks.

"Why do *you*?" I ask back.

She laughs a little, and I kiss her temple. Then, she says something.

"Who's that?"

"My name. That's my name," she says.

She just told me her name. I close my eyes and say it over and over in my head. It's beautiful, just like her. I kiss her neck then, pulling her in tighter against me. Then, I whisper my name into her ear.

"Take me upstairs?" she asks.

I nod. We walk hand in hand back inside and toward the elevators. When one arrives, we climb in with another couple. She places her room key over the reader above the buttons and presses floor seventeen.

"It's not the penthouse. Don't be disappointed," she whispers to me.

"I'm not," I reply, pulling her back against me again. "That would be impossible tonight anyway."

"Newlyweds?" the woman standing with her likely husband on the other side of the elevator asks.

"Sorry?" I say.

"Are you newlyweds?" she asks.

"Oh, we–" I start.

"Sure," she says. "We're here on our honeymoon."

"That's nice, dear," she says. "Thirty years for us." She points to the man next to her.

"Something for *us* to aspire to," she says.

The couple gets off on the ninth floor, and I turn to her.

"We're married now?" I joke.

"Why not? We'll never see them again anyway," she replies, smiling at me.

"Well, if this is our honeymoon, I plan to spend the entire thing in the bedroom," I tease, leaning in and nibbling on her lower lip.

The elevator dings, and the doors open.

"Let's go," she says.

She pulls me by the hand out of the elevator down the hallway. Room 1743 is ours. She uses the key and pushes the door open. We're inside in an instant, and the door slams closed on its own behind us. I look around.

"Oh, wow," I say.

It's true that it's not the penthouse, but it's still a very nice room. There's a small living area with a minibar and sofa with a coffee table in front of it that looks more expensive than all of *my* furniture combined. The bed is a king, and it has some of the most comfortable-looking bedding on it I've ever seen.

"Is this okay?" she asks.

"Are you kidding? Can I move in?" I joke, walking in past her to look around more. "Holy shit! The view," I say, pointing out the sliding glass doors at the lake and sunset we can now see from much higher now.

Then, I feel her behind me. I close my eyes as I feel her body press against me. Her hands go to my chest from under my arms and rest above my breasts. Her chin goes to my shoulder.

"Do you want to watch it from the balcony?" she asks.

"This is good," I reply, not wanting to move from this spot right now.

"There's wine and beer or sparkling–"

"Babe, *this* is what I want." I place my hands on top of hers. "Just this."

"Okay," she says softly.

And we stand there for a long time, just watching the sunset. Neither of us says anything. I think about all the moments we've shared together, and all of them were amazing, but just being still with her right now – this is the best one of all.

"You're so beautiful," she says. "I've missed you so much."

"I've missed you, too," I reply.

"What does that *mean*?" she asks.

I bring her hands to my lips and kiss the fingertips one by one until I've kissed all ten of them.

"I don't know," I say.

She lowers her hands to my belt and asks, "May I?"

"Yes," I say.

She unbuckles it. Then, her hands move to my shirt. She unbuttons each button slowly, and once my shirt is open, her hands move back to my chest. She runs them up and down, grazing my breasts and making my nipples grow hard. I swallow when she stops to massage them.

"I think this is more than just sex for me," she says.

"But we're still going to have sex now, right?" I ask.

She laughs and pulls my shirt off, pressing herself

against me again once it's on the floor.

"Yes," she says.

"It's more than sex for me, too," I say.

Her hands move down to my pants, and it doesn't take long for her to unbutton and unzip them.

"So, tonight…" she fades.

"Is a date?" I ask.

She nods as she kisses my shoulder. My pants fall to the floor, and her hands move to my stomach, rubbing it as I kick off my shoes and flick the pants away.

"A *first* date," she says.

MONTH 12. PART 1. – END OF THE YEAR

(POV Member)

"I hate this," she says.

"I'll be back tomorrow night," I reply.

"It's been two weeks."

"I know."

"We've had one date," she says.

"One perfect date," I reply, smiling at her.

"I want another one," she says.

"So do I, babe," I tell her. "I'm sorry it's taken so long. I really thought we'd have this whole account sorted, but I have a flight booked for tomorrow afternoon, and I won't miss it, I promise."

"That's cutting it pretty close," she says.

"I know. I can just meet you there," I say.

"I thought we were going to go together," she says.

"Can we, really? You're still *technically* working," I reply.

"Yeah, working out ways I'm going to make you come."

"Babe, I'm at work," I say, blushing.

"Well, you should have thought about that before you called me. You know how hard-up I am for you."

"I'm hard-up for you, too," I whisper as I look down the empty hall. "I can't wait to see you."

"I'm thinking about doing something tonight," she replies.

"Yeah? What's that?"

"FaceTiming you while I touch myself," she says.

"Yes," I say, clearing my throat a little too loudly.

She laughs and says, "You really like that idea, huh?"

"It's been too long," I say.

"I know. We've both been busy, but you're all mine tomorrow night."

"I am," I say as my client walks toward me. "I have to go. I'll call you tonight when I'm back at the hotel."

"Get naked first," she says.

"Babe," I say, laughing.

Our first date only ended after a late check-out. We kissed in front of her car for another ten minutes before I finally had to go. I'd moved all of my meetings to the afternoon and took the whole morning off to be with her. God, was that worth it or what?

We'd made plans to connect after my dad's surgery, but he'd had some complications and had remained in the hospital for a few extra days, terrifying my mother in the process. Everything is fine now, but I helped her with him when he got home just to make sure, and that butted up against a work trip that I hadn't planned on. We'd had to cancel not one but two of our planned dates, which I hated doing, but I knew I needed to be there for my parents. I also knew that we were about to drop this pain-in-the-ass account, and I needed to be there to do it in person. Because this is a long-term contract with many details involved, several lawyers from both sides across the table were also present there to argue their points. It's taken longer than I would have thought, but once this is done, I should be able to avoid work travel for a while, meaning – I can focus on *her*, on *us*.

The flight home is a turbulent one, but I calm my nerves with a stiff drink and thoughts only of her. Phone sex is helpful but isn't enough anymore. The parties aren't enough anymore, either. I want her all the time, not just once a month or on a date or two between them. We've talked a lot since that first date. Hours and hours have been spent on the phone. We both love the parties and want to keep going, but I hate the idea of any other member touching her. I know that's hypocritical, but she says she doesn't want anyone else unless I'm there with her and want it, too.

We agree on that. Tonight is the last night of her twelve-month contract. It's also the last night of my membership unless I renew. She told me before that she had watched her friends have sex a couple of times and would still like to do that. I told her I think that's hot and have no problem with it. I asked her if I could watch people, too, and she said yes. Then, there's her getting herself off while I watch on my laptop while we FaceTime. We've been on one date, but I feel like we've been together for a whole year by now. I'm sure to most people, it's crazy and wouldn't work, and while it's still new, I know that it can, so I hope that it will.

"Well, hello," she says, smiling at me when I walk through the door.

"Hi," I say, smiling back.

"May I take your coat?" she asks.

"Are you on coat duty tonight?" I ask, looking confused.

"No." She shakes her head. "Just for you."

She removes my jacket and holds it over her arm. Then, she takes my hand, and we walk to the walk-in closet they're using for the coatroom. She closes the door behind us and pushes me back against the wall behind a row of coats and jackets. Mine ends up probably somewhere on the floor, but her hands are up my dress, slipping off my thong, so I don't care.

"What if someone walks–"

"Do you care?" she interjects as she kisses me.

"No," I say and realize at the same time.

I push her head down. She takes my thong and tucks it into her pocket. Then, her head is under my dress, and her mouth is on my pussy.

"Oh, I've missed you," I say.

She sucks on my clit hard, needing to make me come quickly, apparently. The door opens, and the woman who *is* in charge of the coats sees us. *She* doesn't stop. The woman hangs up the coat in her hand, pauses for only a moment, and then leaves, closing the door behind her.

"Fuck me," I say.

She makes me come hard. Then, she stands up and looks at me proudly.

"Can I have you all to myself for the next hour or so?" she asks.

"You get me all night," I tell her, wrapping my arms around her neck.

"There are a couple of women upstairs already that were wondering if we might join them later," she says.

"Oh, really?" I tease, pulling her in for a kiss and tasting myself.

"Yes," she says, cupping my ass under my dress. "I have this image in my head of me wearing a strap-on, fucking one of them, while you're riding my face."

"That's quite an image," I say, kissing her neck.

"Is it okay?"

"Why wouldn't it be?" I ask, sucking on her earlobe.

"Well, we're…"

"Dating?" I ask, smiling against her neck.

"Yes," she says, moving her hands out from under my dress and wrapping them around my waist instead.

"I love how insatiable you are. I don't want to stop that. Plus, I like it, too," I say. "I'd love to ride your face while you make one of them come."

"Shit. Really?" she asks, pressing her hips into me now.

"Are you…" I look down.

"I put it on right before you got here."

I cup her.

"Jesus, babe," she says.

I unzip her pants and slide it out.

"Make me come with it first," I say.

"Here?" she asks.

"Yes," I say, pulling on it until she gets the point.

She takes it from me and glides it over my still sensitive clit. Then, she lifts my leg with her free hand, holds it up, and pushes inside me.

"Fuck me, how you'll fuck them later."

"Oh, no, baby." She thrusts up. "I save all the best stuff only for you."

I smirk at that. Her hands press my own against the wall now. I keep my leg against her hip as long as I can as she fucks me hard against this wall behind the row of coats. The door opens again. I hear it close a minute later, but I don't open my eyes to see who it was or if they watched us.

"Fuck, yes," I say when I come.

Then, I yell her name.

"Upstairs," she says.

"Yes," I agree when she pulls out.

We stop off in a bathroom where she cleans the toy and I watch. Then, she tucks it back into her pants, and we make it up to the rooms. Only one door is open tonight, and it's the one we want. Her friends are already naked on the bed. I shove *her* onto it next to them. They look up but don't say anything. I close the door behind us and unbutton and unzip her pants again. Then, I tug the shorts down to her ankles so she can kick them off for now, and I spread her legs and lick her pussy.

"Yes," she says. "I need you."

"I'm here, baby," I reply, sucking on her clit.

"You two are so sexy," I hear one of the other women say.

I make my girl come in my mouth.

"Good, baby?" I ask, licking her thigh.

"So good," she says.

Then, I put the shorts back on her body. She strips off her shirt while I tear off my own clothes.

"You want to fuck someone?" I ask.

"Yes." She moves back until her head is on the pillow.

"My love? Can I let her fuck me?" one woman asks.

"Only if I can watch," the other says.

"You can rub my clit," she replies.

I move to straddle *her* face. I'm turned around this time to face the other woman who slips onto *her* toy.

"Oh, yes," she says.

I lean forward and kiss her.

"Fuck," her wife says as she moves behind her and starts rubbing her wife's clit with one hand and her own with the other.

"Lower yourself, babe," *she* says.

I lower my sex to her mouth. Her hands wrap around me and land on my thighs. I kiss the woman *she's* currently inside while the woman moves up and down on the dildo. That woman plays with my breasts, and I play with hers. When I'm about to come, I lower my mouth to her waiting nipple, which she brings to it. She holds my head there as I suck, and she comes first. I come next, sucking on her nipple until I have to scream out *her* name. Her wife comes next. I reach down into *her* shorts and massage her clit while the woman is still coming down from her orgasm from the toy.

"Yes," *she* says. "Make me come, baby."

And I do.

***

"Well, now that you two are dating, what changes?" her friend asks later as I lie in front of *her*, and she lies behind her wife.

We're lying side by side, facing each other. *Her* arm is around me. She's currently gently stroking the hairs between my legs, occasionally dipping into my wetness and circling my clit – just enough to drive me totally crazy.

"Nothing," she says. "Well, I don't think."

I smile as she kisses my shoulder.

"We like doing this," I say.

"We like it, too," the woman closest to me says just as her wife strokes her clit like *she's* doing to me. "Oh, yes."

I move closer to this woman, bringing *her* with me. Then, I kiss her, and she kisses me back. *She* strokes a little faster. Then, her hand is moving, and she enters me from behind.

"Fuck, babe," I say.

The woman in front of me cups my sex and starts stroking my clit.

"Yes, baby," her wife says.

I open my eyes to see that her leg is over her wife's thigh. She's pressing her sex into her wife's ass, rocking into her. I reach behind me for *her* leg. She takes the hint, and I feel her wetness on my ass cheek.

"Your body is perfect for me," *she* whispers into my ear.

I kiss the other woman as her wife does what *she's* doing to me right now and enters her from behind. I place my hand on the woman's clit, and we get each other off as our partners get themselves off against our bodies.

"I think we could make this a regular thing," the woman in front of me says as she comes down.

I keep stroking until I don't feel any more tremors.

"Rules?" *she* asks.

"We all have to be into it," her friend says.

"And we all have to be here," *she* says. "All four of us."

I smile.

"Deal," her friend says.

I roll over to face *her* and say, "Want to find our own room now?"

"Yeah, let's go." She kisses my nose.

We dress quickly and say goodbye before we leave.

"Hey, if you left now, who would notice that you're gone?" I ask.

"Well, normally the guy that takes me back to my car, but we parked in the lot behind the building tonight."

"Can you escape?" I ask.

"I guess. Why? You don't want to find a room?"

"I do," I say, pressing against her. "At my place."

"I've never been to–"

"I know. I don't want a knock at three-forty-five, babe."

"Hi, you two," the member and her usual escort walk

down the hall toward us.

"Oh, hi," I say.

"We didn't see you here last time," the member says to me.

"I had a family emergency," I reply.

She wraps her arms around me possessively, and it's adorable.

"We're taking off," the escort says.

"You can do that?" *she* asks.

"I no longer work here," the woman says, smiling.

"I've agreed to let her make an honest woman out of me," the member says, smiling wide, too.

"What?" I ask.

"I only came here tonight to tell her that I've officially separated from my awful husband. I have my own place now, and I'm taking her to it."

She pulls the now-former escort against her side.

"We're going to give it a shot," the woman says.

"Crazy, huh?" the member asks, looking at me and then looking over at *her*.

"Yeah, crazy," I say sarcastically. "Good luck."

"Thanks," they say together and walk down the hall hand in hand.

"Crazy," *she* says. "I mean, what are the odds of a couple finding love in this place?"

I pinch her shoulder.

She laughs and says, "I do, you know."

"What? Think it's crazy?"

"No," she says, pressing her lips to mine for a second. "Love you."

"Oh, baby," I reply, cupping her chin. "Can tonight be your last night, too?"

"Working?"

"Yes."

"You want me all to yourself?" she teases.

"Yes, unless we're with them or doing something together, I want you all to myself."

"I want *you* all to myself, too," she replies, kissing my forehead.

"How are you with the whole money thing? Can you afford to quit?"

"Let's escape so they still pay me for tonight. Then, I'll be good. My contract is over, and I don't have to renew."

"Or, you *could* renew," I say.

"I'm confused," she says.

"As a member," I reply.

"Member? I can't afford—"

"I'll pay. It'll be a very nice gift for myself."

"Me being a member here is a gift for *you*?" she asks.

"Definitely," I say.

***

When we arrive at my place, I pull into the garage. She parks her car in the driveway, and we head inside. I hadn't planned this, but now that we're here, it seemed stupid not to think about what would happen at the end of the night. I guess neither of us is used to this yet.

"I have no food. I've been gone for three weeks," I say when we walk into the kitchen.

"We can order in," she says.

"Whatever you want."

"Whatever I want that *delivers* at two in the morning," she says.

"I might have a frozen pizza," I say.

"I'm game," she replies. "Can I get the tour while it cooks?"

"Of course," I say.

I get the pizza in the oven and take her by the hand.

"So, you've seen the kitchen. There's a formal dining room, which I never use. I have a living room, of course, and the informal dining room, too, which is where I usually eat," I say as I motion to it. "Do you want to see the back-yard?"

"I want to see your bedroom," she replies, nibbling on my neck.

I laugh and say, "I think you're going to like this, actually."

I open the back door and pull her through it.

"Grill, wet bar, very expensive and underutilized patio furniture, pool, and hot tub."

"Holy shit, babe," she says. "That's a waterfall."

"And if you play your cards right, I'll let you touch me under it," I say.

She lets go of my hand. I watch as she takes off her shirt and her pants. I laugh as she kicks everything along with her underwear off and onto the cement-tiled ground.

"Let's go," she says softly.

"What about the pizza?" I ask.

"We've got time." She reaches out for me.

I realize that she's right. We've got nothing but time now. Tomorrow is Sunday. I can wake up next to her. We can have breakfast together and make love all morning if we want. We can watch the morning news or a movie while we snuggle in bed. I take off my dress and remember that she still has my thong in her pocket. I laugh a little but take her hand, and we enter the water together.

"Shit, it's cold," I say.

She pulls me into her, and I wrap my legs around her.

"I've got you," she says, just like she did that first night.

I place my head on her shoulder, wrap my arms around her neck, and close my eyes as she spins us in the freezing water. She's rubbing my back and kissing my bare shoulder. Before I know it, she's walked us back to where the water falls over the fake rocks and into the pool.

"Are you ready?" she asks.

I bury my face in her neck and mumble, "Yes."

She walks us under the freezing water. I yelp a little until we're on the other side of it. Then, she pulls my face to hers and kisses me. We stay like that for a long time, just kissing, with my legs wrapped around her and her hands caressing my back until I'm finally warm. I feel my sex rubbing against her stomach before I realize I'm even doing it.

"So, you *are* ready?" she says, laughing.

"I need you," I tell her.

With one arm still wrapped around me, she brings her other hand to my sex and slides inside. Her thumb presses into my clit, and I move against her.

"God, yes," I say. "I can't believe I get you like this all the time now."

"Every night if you want," she says, kissing me.

"I want," I reply. "Fuck, I want. I want you all the time."

"I'm here. I'm here, baby." She thrusts deeper.

I come and say, "I love you."

She stares into my eyes. Then, a slow smile takes over her face.

"How is this possible?" she asks.

"I have no idea," I tell her, laughing before I kiss her again.

"Can I stay the night?"

"I just told you that I love you. Of course, you're staying," I say.

She kisses me again and says, "You really want me to join the club as a member?"

"We'd go together," I say as she slips her fingers out of me. "We could watch. We could participate if we want. We could just touch each other. If you don't want to, though, I'd understand – it's different for you. I'll cancel my membership now if you–"

"It's not that. I just can't believe you really want to do this with me. You just…" She kisses my throat. "Babe, you just get it. You get *me*. I don't even know that I got *me* before all this, but *you* do."

"You get me, too," I say. "That first night, you knew what I needed without me saying a word. You touched me; you held me; you let me go when I was scared."

"Are you scared now?" she asks.

"I'm terrified." I laugh. "But for an entirely different reason now."

"Why?" she asks, looking concerned.

"Oh, sweetheart," I say, cupping her cheeks with both hands. "Because I *love* you. That's very scary."

"How can I make it *less* scary?"

"Just be you," I say. "Wake up next to me every morning."

"That sounds nice," she says, pressing her face into my chest. "I can do that."

"Should we go inside and have a two AM snack before I show you my room?"

"Can we stay naked?"

"Yes," I say, laughing. "We can even take a long, hot shower after we eat."

"Oh, I like the sound of that."

"I have a rain shower, and there's extra room inside." I climb off of her. "In case you maybe wanted to suck me hard and make me come one more time tonight."

"Only one more time?" she asks.

I smile at her, the woman I love.

MONTH 12. PART 2. – CON-TRACT ENDS

(POV Escort)

"I hate this," I tell her.

"I'll be back tomorrow night," she says.

"It's been two weeks."

"I know."

"We've had one date," I say.

"One perfect date," she says.

She's right, but still.

"I want another one," I say.

"So do I, babe. I'm sorry it's taken so long. I really thought we'd have this whole account sorted, but I have a flight booked for tomorrow afternoon, and I won't miss it, I promise," she tells me.

"That's cutting it pretty close," I say.

"I know. I can just meet you there," she says.

"I thought we were going to go together," I say.

"Can we, really? You're still *technically* working," she replies.

"Yeah, working out ways I'm going to make you come," I say, picturing a few.

"Babe, I'm at work," she says, sounding so damn adorable and shy.

God, I want her.

"Well, you should have thought about that before you called me. You know how hard-up I am for you."

"I'm hard-up for you, too," she whispers. "I can't wait to see you."

"I'm thinking about doing something tonight," I say.

"Yeah? What's that?"

"FaceTiming you while I touch myself," I say.

"Yes." She clears her throat pretty loudly after.

I laugh and say, "You really like that idea, huh?"

"It's been too long," she says.

"I know. We've both been busy, but you're all mine tomorrow night."

"I am. I have to go. I'll call you tonight when I'm back at the hotel."

"Get naked first," I say.

"Babe," she says, laughing.

I've packed up everything in the house. I sold a lot of stuff, donated some, and threw out the rest. The house was bought by a young couple looking for a starter home, so I'm hopeful they'll take care of the place for me; for her. My apartment is on the other side of town now. I was able to afford a decent place. I didn't want to go crazy, but the house sold for the asking price, which meant I was able to pay everything off and still have enough for rent for the first few months while I figure out if I want to keep my day job or actually go for something I really want that will pay more.

I haven't spent much time with my friends lately. That's partly because we've all been busy with other things but also because my time has been taken up with calls with *her*. We haven't used the term *girlfriend* yet, but it's serious enough that we're talking about things we will and won't do together and with other people from now on. I like that. I like that I can talk to her about what I want, what she wants, and what we want together. I've never had this before, and I want to protect it.

"Are you naked?" I ask when she FaceTimes me later that night.

"Yes, as per your request."

"Prove it," I say, staring at her beautiful face through my phone.

She turns her computer a little, and I can see her there, lying on her side, naked.

"Oh, yes," I say.

"And you?" she asks.

"Let me change to my computer. Hold on," I say. It

takes a minute, but we're connected to my computer now. I drop my phone and turn it. "There."

"Fuck, you're hot," she says.

"So, should we talk about your day at work or—"

"No, you should touch yourself," she interrupts. "I'm so horny, babe. I need you inside me."

"Get it out," I say.

"Already?"

"Get it out," I repeat, squeezing my thighs together.

She moves off the bed, and I get to watch her cute ass as she rummages through her luggage. She holds it up and moves back to the bed.

"Does it need lube?"

"Doubt it. I've been waiting for this all day," she says, moving the dildo she brought with her to her sex.

"Stroke your clit with it," I say.

"I am," she says.

I watch.

"Are you swollen?"

"Yes."

"Want me to take care of you?"

"Yes."

"Pretend my lips are there, baby. I'm kissing your clit."

"Fuck," she says, rubbing the dildo a little faster as I watch.

"Do you want me to suck on it for you? Make it feel good?"

"God, yes," she says.

I reach between my own legs and tell her, "Go inside, but do as I say, okay?"

"Yes," she says.

She spreads her legs a little, and I watch the toy disappear.

"Oh, Jesus," she says. "I'm so tight."

"And ready for me to fuck you?"

"Yes," she says.

"Pull it mostly out. Just leave the tip in."

"Baby, I want to come."

"You will," I say.

I stroke myself slowly as I watch her.

"Back in again."

She grunts.

"And out."

"I need it," she says, but I don't know that she's talking to me.

It's sexy as hell.

"Tell me what you need."

"I need you to fuck me hard until I scream your name and beg you to stop."

"Oh, my God," I say, not expecting all that. "Baby, you deserve to make yourself come." I rub my clit harder and say, "Fuck yourself while I watch."

The toy moves in and out.

"Move the computer, baby. I want to see between your legs."

It takes her a second, but the computer moves, and I have the perfect view.

"I'm going to come so fucking hard. You are the perfect woman," I tell her. "Make it good, babe."

She moans. Then, she's grunting hard.

"Let me see you rub your clit. Pretend it's my lips sucking on you. I want to suck on you so hard."

"Yes! Fuck! Yes! Oh, there! God," she says as her hips thrash uncontrollably.

I watch her hand rub her clit while the toy pushes deep and comes back out again as she comes.

"I'm coming," I say, closing my eyes to focus on my own orgasm now.

I am the luckiest girl on the planet.

***

"Well, hello," I say, smiling at her when I see her come in.

"Hi," she says, smiling back at me.

"May I take your coat?" I ask.

"Are you on coat duty tonight?" she asks, looking confused.

"No, just for you."

I take her coat off and drape it over my arm. Then, I take her hand and walk her to the coat closet. I quickly close the door, move into her, and press her to the wall as coat hangers and the jackets hanging from them shake behind me. My hands move up her dress, and I remove her thong quickly.

"What if someone walks–"

"Do you care?" I ask and kiss her.

"No."

She pushes my head down, telling me what she wants. I put her drenched thong in my pocket, lift her dress, and suck on her how I've wanted to do for weeks now.

"Oh, I've missed you," she says.

I hear the door opening behind me, but I don't stop. Then, I hear it close.

"Fuck me," she says.

It doesn't take long – she comes hard as she presses my face to her pussy and rocks her hip against me, prolonging the orgasm. When she finally lets go, I stand up and look at her just-fucked expression.

"Can I have you all to myself for the next hour or so?" I ask.

"You get me all night," she says, wrapping he arms around my neck.

"There are a couple of women upstairs already that were wondering if we might join them later," I say.

"Oh, really?" she says, kissing me.

"Yes," I say, cupping her tight ass under her dress. "I have this image in my head of me wearing a strap-on, fucking one of them, while you're riding my face."

"That's quite an image," she tells me, kissing my neck.

"Is it okay?" I ask, worried I might be going too far

since we're technically dating now.

"Why wouldn't it be?" she asks, sucking on my earlobe.

"Well, we're…"

"Dating?" she asks.

"Yes," I say, moving my hands out from under her dress and wrapping them around her waist instead.

"I love how insatiable you are. I don't want to stop that. Plus, I like it, too. I'd love to ride your face while you make one of them come."

"Shit. Really?" I ask, pressing my hips into her.

"Are you…" she looks down between my legs.

"I put it on right before you got here."

She cups me unexpectedly.

"Jesus, babe," I say.

She unzips me and pulls it out.

"Make me come with it first," she says, stroking it a little.

"Here?" I ask.

"Yes," she says.

I take the toy from her, unbuttoning my pants to give myself more flexibility in how I move. Then, I glide it over the clit I just had in my mouth. I lift her leg with my free hand and push inside her.

"Fuck me, how you'll fuck them later," she says when I'm all the way in.

"Oh, no, baby." I thrust my hips. "I save all the best stuff only for you."

I press her hands against the wall behind her with my own. I thrust hard and fast, giving her everything I've got because she's so fucking sexy, and I have to hear her come.

"Fuck, yes," she says when she does.

She yells my name. I thrust until she finally taps my shoulder.

"Upstairs," I say against her shoulder.

"Yes," she says as I pull out of her.

I clean the toy in the bathroom, tuck it back inside my

pants, and we head up to the only open room. My friends are already naked on the bed, kissing one another, and I think about how much I need to come right now. *She* shoves me on the bed next to them, and within a few seconds, she has everything but my shirt off me. Then, she spreads my legs and licks me.

"Yes," I say. "I need you."

"I'm here, baby," she says, sucking.

"You two are so sexy," I hear one of my friends say.

I come faster than I expected.

"Good, baby?" *she* asks as she licks my thigh with that remarkable tongue of hers.

"So good," I say.

She slides the shorts back on me, and I take off my shirt, watching as she starts stripping in front of me.

"You want to fuck someone?" she asks me.

"Yes." I move back until my head is on the pillow.

"My love? Can I let her fuck me?" my friend's wife asks.

"Only if I can watch," my friend says.

"You can rub my clit," her wife replies.

My girl straddles my face, but she's turned around to face the other woman who slides down onto the toy between my legs.

"Oh, yes," the woman says as she settles onto it.

"Fuck," her wife says.

"Lower yourself, babe," I say to *her*, craving her taste on my tongue again.

She lowers herself, and I know things are going on above and around me, but I can't see anything. I can only feel, hear, smell, and taste her as she rocks against my mouth, making herself feel good. Then, I hear the familiar sound of someone coming, and it's the woman currently lowering and rising on the dildo between my legs. Then, *she* comes, and that's always the best – listening to her tell me how good I make her feel when she yells my name. I hear my friend come last, and I think that I'm going to have to come again soon because the dildo is pressing into my clit. Before I can say anything, *her* hand is in my shorts.

"Yes," I say. "Make me come, baby."

I slap her ass, encouraging her on, and start licking at her clit again while she strokes mine. I come only seconds later, sucking on her clit through my orgasm.

***

"Well, now that you two are dating, what changes?" my friend asks later as *she* lies in front of me and my friend lies behind her wife.

We're lying side by side, facing each other. My arm is around *her*. I'm gently stroking the hairs between her legs, occasionally dipping into her and circling her still swollen clit, which I can't get enough of, and likely, never will.

"Nothing," I say. "Well, I don't think."

I kiss her shoulder, letting her know that's her cue to correct me if I'm wrong.

"We like doing this," *she* says.

"We like it, too," the woman closest to *her* says just as her wife strokes her clit like I'm doing to *her*. "Oh, yes."

My girl slides over closer to my friends, and I move with her. I watch as she kisses the woman in front of her, and I make eye contact with my friend, who's behind her. After the initial round we all shared, this woman knelt between my legs and made me come with her mouth. I made her come after that, with my fingers, which she said she needed. Our girls watched us and gently stroked each other until they came, too.

Now, I stroke *her* while she kisses the woman in front of her. I move my hand until I can slip inside from behind because I want to feel her warmth all around me.

"Fuck, babe," she says.

The woman in front of *her* starts stroking *her* clit for me.

"Yes, baby," her wife says.

My friend now has her leg over her wife's thigh. She's pressing her pussy into her ass. I feel *her* reach for my leg, so I smirk as I watch my friend and do the same, rubbing my wet sex over *her* ass.

"Your body is perfect for me," I whisper into her ear.

She kisses the woman in front of her while I fuck her and that woman rubs her clit. I watch my friend start fucking her wife, which gives *her* a chance to stroke her wife for her. They get each other off as we get ourselves off against their bodies.

"I think we could make this a regular thing," my friend's wife says as she comes down.

"Rules?" I ask.

"We all have to be into it," my friend says.

"And we all have to be here," I say. "All four of us."

"Deal," my friend says.

She rolls over to face me and says, "Want to find our own room now?"

"Yeah, let's go." I kiss her cute nose.

Then, we get dressed and leave the room.

"Hey, if you left now, who would notice that you're gone?" she asks.

"Well, normally the guy that takes me back to my car, but we parked in the lot behind the building tonight."

"Can you escape?" she asks.

"I guess. Why? You don't want to find a room?"

"I do." She presses against me. "At my place."

"I've never been to–"

"I know. I don't want a knock at three-forty-five, babe."

"Hi, you two," the member and the escort walk down the hall toward us.

"Oh, hi," *she* says.

"We didn't see you here last time," the member says to her.

"I had a family emergency," she replies.

Why are they talking to us? We were about to leave. I

want to see her house. I want to make love to her in her own bed for the first time. I wrap my arms around her possessively. I know it's silly – we just fucked two other women in a room together – but I don't want anyone else to touch her tonight. She's mine, and I want to go home with her now.

"We're taking off," the escort says.

"You can do that?" I ask.

"I no longer work here," the woman says, smiling.

"I've agreed to let her make an honest woman out of me," the member says, smiling wide, too.

"What?" *she* asks.

"I only came here tonight to tell her that I've officially separated from my awful husband," the member says. "I have my own place now, and I'm taking her to it."

She pulls the now-*former* escort against her body.

"We're going to give it a shot," the former escort says.

"Crazy, huh?" the member asks, looking at *her* and then looking over at me.

"Yeah, crazy," *she* says sarcastically. "Good luck."

"Thanks," they say together and walk down the hall hand in hand.

"Crazy," I say. "I mean, what are the odds of a couple finding love in this place?"

She pinches my shoulder.

I laugh and say, "I do, you know."

"What? Think it's crazy?"

I swallow.

"No," I say, pressing my lips to hers for a second. "Love you."

"Oh, baby," she replies, cupping my chin. "Can tonight be your last night, too?"

"Working?"

"Yes."

"You want me all to yourself?" I tease.

"Yes, unless we're with them or doing something together, I want you all to myself."

"I want *you* all to myself, too." I kiss her forehead.

"How are you with the whole money thing? Can you afford to quit?" she asks.

"Let's escape so they still pay me for tonight. Then, I'll be good. My contract is over, and I don't have to renew."

"Or, you *could* renew," she says.

"I'm confused," I say.

"As a member," she replies.

"Member? I can't afford–"

"I'll pay. It'll be a very nice gift for myself."

"Me being a member here is a gift for *you*?" I ask.

"Definitely," she says.

***

"I have no food. I've been gone for three weeks," she says when we walk into her massive kitchen that looks brand new.

"We can order in," I say.

"Whatever you want."

"Whatever I want that *delivers* at two in the morning," I say, rethinking it.

"I might have a frozen pizza," she says.

"I'm game," I reply. "Can I get the tour while it cooks?"

"Of course," she says.

We put the pizza in the oven, then she takes me by the hand, and we start walking around the downstairs.

"So, you've seen the kitchen. There's a formal dining room, which I never use. I have a living room, of course, and the informal dining room, too, which is where I usually eat. Do you want to see the backyard?"

"I want to see your bedroom," I say, nibbling on her neck.

She laughs and says, "I think you're going to like this, actually."

She opens the door and pulls me through it.

"Grill, wet bar, very expensive and underutilized patio furniture, pool, and hot tub."

"Holy shit, babe," I say when I see it all. "That's a waterfall."

"And if you play your cards right, I'll let you touch me under it," she says.

I let go of her and take off all my clothes.

"Let's go," I say.

"What about the pizza?" she asks, as if I care about the stupid pizza right now.

"We've got time." I reach out my hand to her.

She takes off her dress and laughs. Then, she takes my hand, and we enter the water together.

"Shit, it's cold," she says.

I pull her into me, encouraging her to wrap her legs around me.

"I've got you," I tell her.

Her head goes to my shoulder, and her arms are now around my neck. I spin us around a bit in the water, so happy that I get to hold her like this, in her own house. I rub her back and kiss her bare shoulder for a second. Then, I walk us back to the waterfall.

"Are you ready?" I ask.

She buries her face in my neck, which tells me she trusts me, and mumbles, "Yes."

I walk us under the water, hearing her yelp at how cold it is, and then we're on the other side of it. I kiss her, and I could kiss her like this forever. I hold her and rub her back until I notice she's rubbing something else against me.

"So, you *are* ready?" I say, laughing.

"I need you," she tells me.

I slip inside, still holding her up with my other arm, and she moves against me.

"God, yes. I can't believe I get you like this all the time now."

"Every night if you want," I say, kissing her.

"I want. Fuck, I want. I want you all the time."

"I'm here. I'm here, baby." I thrust deeper, and she comes.

"I love you," she says.

That's the first time she's said it just like that, and I stare at her to make sure she means it; that it's not just because of the orgasm. When I know that it's true, I smile.

"How is this possible?" I ask.

"I have no idea," she says, laughing and then kissing me again.

"Can I stay the night?" I ask.

"I just told you that I love you. Of course, you're staying," she says.

I kiss her again and say, "You really want me to join the club as a member?"

"We'd go together," she says as I slip out of her. "We could watch. We could participate if we want. We could just touch each other. If you don't want to, though, I'd understand – it's different for you. I'll cancel my membership now if you–"

"It's not that. I just can't believe you really want to do this with me. You just…" I kiss her throat. "Babe, you just get it. You get *me*. I don't even know that I got *me* before all this, but *you* do."

"You get me, too. That first night, you knew what I needed without me saying a word. You touched me; you held me; you let me go when I was scared."

"Are you scared now?" I ask.

"I'm terrified." She laughs. "But for an entirely different reason now."

"Why?" I ask, worried now.

"Oh, sweetheart," she says, cupping my cheeks with both hands. "Because I *love* you. That's very scary."

"How can I make it *less* scary?"

"Just be you. Wake up next to me every morning."

"That sounds nice," I tell her, pressing my face to her chest. "I can do that."

"Should we go inside and have a two AM snack before

I show you my room?"

"Can we stay naked?" I ask.

"Yes," she says, laughing. "We can even take a long, hot shower after we eat."

"Oh, I like the sound of that."

"I have a rain shower, and there's extra room inside." She climbs off of me. "In case you maybe wanted to suck me hard and make me come one more time tonight."

"Only one more time?" I ask, knowing I want her far more than just one more time.

She smiles at me and says, "The bedroom is really big, so there's a possibility I'll let you have me on every surface of it."

"Make that every surface in this house, and you have a deal."

She laughs and says, "Not all tonight, though. Let's pace ourselves. We've got time now."

And she's right – we've got time.

EPILOGUE. PART 1. – MEMBER

I walk in and see them against the wall. The music just started, and they're already making out like they can't get enough of each other. I am constantly amazed by how turned on I get when I watch other people – but especially these two – have sex. I walk up behind them and watch. There are other women in the room, too. Some are just sitting or standing, talking, likely lining up their options and plans for the night. I see three women over by a window. One has her hand in the pants of another woman, and the third is kissing the one being touched while she fondles the other woman's breasts. I can see her twist a nipple hanging out of the woman's dress, and I suddenly feel grateful that I didn't wear a bra because my own nipples are hard and pressing into my dress, begging to get out. I move until I'm next to the two women I *really* want to watch.

I don't say anything. I just watch as the one leaning against the wall unzips her wife's pants. She cups her hard before pulling it out of the woman's pants, stroking it, and then moving it between her thighs as a signal that she wants to move things along.

"Hey. I didn't think you were coming tonight," I say.

The woman with the dildo attached to her body stops kissing her wife and turns to me.

"We changed our mind," she says, looking down at how her wife is rocking her hips into her body. "Fuck, babe."

"We either need to do this now or get upstairs. I'm so hot for you," her wife says, kissing her neck.

"Why does it have to be *or*?" she asks and then looks at me again. "Are you watching?"

"For a minute, at least," I say.

She smirks at me, lowers the strap of her wife's dress, and sucks on her nipple. I gasp, knowing how good that nipple tastes and thinking about sucking on her other one while her wife fucks her, but I can't. I watch instead. Her wife is still trying to get her to move inside.

"Babe, fuck me already," the woman says.

"So needy," she says to her wife and lowers herself down to her knees.

I watch as she removes her wife's panties and lifts her dress, moving her head under it. Then, I watch as she eats her pussy. The woman still standing is holding her wife's head against her. Her head is back. Her eyes are closed. I listen as she starts to make those sounds I've heard before, and they get me going. I cup my own breasts and lick my lips.

"I can help you with that if you want," I hear from behind me.

I turn around and say, "I'm okay, but thanks."

"Are you sure? Your nipples are poking through your sexy dress. I can make them feel better," she says, reaching for my hip.

I don't protest when she pulls me in a little, but I continue to watch the woman next to me as she comes. When her wife stands, she puts the toy firmly in her hand, moves into her wife, and thrusts inside her.

"Oh, God," I say.

Then, I realize the woman still holding my hip is massaging my breasts *for* me now – I hadn't even noticed that I'd dropped my hands to my sides.

"Can I suck on them?" she asks.

"If you really want to," I say.

"Oh, I do," she says, and I believe her.

I lower the straps of my dress and release my breasts as I drop the garment to my hips. I press her face to my right breast and watch the women next to me as they have hot sex against the wall while this stranger sucks on one nipple and then the other.

"Harder," I tell her.

She moves her hand from my hip to my abdomen, and I feel it moving lower. I place my own on top of it and shake my head.

"Not there," I say. "Suck."

She sucks on my left nipple until I can't take it anymore.

"Yes! Yes!"

"She's coming," I say.

"You can come, too," the woman sucking on my nipple says as she moves to begin kissing my neck.

"Oh, I will," I say, pulling away from her. "See you around."

"What? I thought…"

I wink at her and move to the staircase, moving my dress back into place as I walk. I take the stairs slowly, enjoying the tingling that's building between my legs. My nipples are on fire, begging to be touched more, but I know I don't want that woman to take care of them – I have other plans tonight.

Finding an open door, I stand there and watch – my, how the times have changed. I watch as the member and the former-escort-and-now-girlfriend-to-the-member lie in bed, massaging each other. It's hard to believe that I've known them for almost two years now. That's how long I've been coming to these parties. In fact, tonight is my second membership anniversary.

"You can join us if you want," the former escort says when she sees me standing in the doorway.

"I'd rather watch for now," I say.

"Are you sure? She's ready," she replies, running her fingers through her girlfriend's folds. "Aren't you, baby?"

"I'm always ready for you, my love," the woman says, gasps, and then bucks her hips.

"Oh, I like when you do that," her girlfriend tells her.

"Will you make me come?"

"Yes," she replies.

I feel hands wrap around my waist from behind.

"I saw you downstairs," a voice says.

"Yeah. So?" I reply.

"I watched that other member touch you, and it turned me on."

"Oh, yeah?"

"Why didn't you bring her up here? Take her to bed?" she asks, slipping her hand under my dress a little presumptively.

"I was interested in watching for a while," I reply.

"*Was?*" she asks, sliding her hand over my thigh.

"I'm getting turned on," I say.

"I can see why. They're very sexy," she says, and her hand moves to my sex.

I think about stopping her, but I'm too far gone to protest – I need to come. I lower the straps of my dress again and massage my breasts. She takes that as permission, moves my thong aside, and finds my clit.

"Oh, yes," I whisper and practically fall back against her.

I was even more ready than I thought.

"You're hard," she says. "And wet," she adds.

"I told you I was turned on," I reply, watching the two women in front of me.

"I can take care of it for you."

"Yes," I say.

"I can do more than just finger your clit; I can suck on your clit while you watch them," she says.

"Just this," I say, breathing hard. "Just make me fucking come already."

She strokes faster, and my hips move against her hand. Oh, hell… She's right – I want more than just this; I'm about to burst. I can't believe I'm even considering this, but I need more.

"Fuck. Go find us a room," I say, removing her hand from my sex.

"What?" she asks.

"I want you to fuck me. Go find us a room," I repeat.

"We can just–"

"No, I want a room. Get in there, turn off the lights, get on the bed, and put something on if you have it. Take off all your clothes, too."

"No problem," she says.

"We don't mind company," the former escort says as she strokes her girlfriend.

"Baby, focus. I want your mouth," her girlfriend tells her.

"You love my mouth," she replies.

I stay as she moves down the woman's body and takes her with her mouth. I want to touch myself, but I know I have someone waiting that should be able to take care of my throbbing sex. I turn just as a door closes down the hall. I make my way there, wait a minute to allow her to do as I requested, and then push open the door, closing it behind me.

"Are you ready?" I ask her.

"Yes."

"Are you wearing something for me?"

"Yes. I'm touching it right now."

"Do you want to fuck me with it?" I ask.

"Yes," she says. "I want to suck you, too, though."

"One thing at a time," I reply.

I remove my thong but keep my dress on. My breasts are still hanging out, and I just walked down the hall like this, but I don't care. I need it; I need to be fucked. I can only just make out the form of a naked woman on the bed, but as I move closer, I can see a hand stroking a dildo, and I smirk – she did just as I asked. I move up the bed, straddling her hips. She removes her hand, and I slip it inside me.

"Fuck, yes," I say.

"Can I come?" she asks.

"If you make me come, you can come," I tell her.

I lift my body up and lower it back down.

"I need it deep," I say.

"You want me to fuck you deep?"

"Yes," I say.

"Roll over, then. I'll fuck you deep," she says.

"Earn that," I reply.

I rock my hips fast, needing to come right now. I find her hand on my hip and move it to my sex, silently asking her to stroke my clit.

"Yes," she says, flicking it with her thumb. "How does my cock feel?"

"It's fine. Make it better," I order.

Her hips buck up into me.

"That!" I yell.

She does it again and again.

"Yes! I'm coming," I say.

I grasp her breasts in my hands and hold on to them as I rock harder and faster, coming undone on top of her.

"Oh, fuck," she says, and I realize she's coming, too.

"Does it feel good?" I ask.

"Yes," she says.

"Do you want to suck me now?" I ask.

"Oh, fuck!" She's lifting and lowering me now, likely trying to prolong her own orgasm but bringing me to the precipice of another. "God, that's good."

"I want you to suck on my clit," I say as I slip up and off her.

"Fuck, I was—"

I move until my sex is over her mouth.

"Touch yourself while you make me come again," I say, lowering onto her face.

She doesn't hesitate. I feel her lips engulf my clit, and suddenly, there are actual stars in my eyes. I close them and rock my hips. I open them minutes later to turn my head and watch her hand work inside the harness she's wearing. She's moaning. Her hips are rising and falling, and I'm about to come in her mouth. I press my hands to the wall behind the bed and fuck myself against her face.

"Yes! Yes! Yes! Don't stop!"

She moans and vibrates my clit until I come and then come down.

"Did you come?" I ask her, lifting off her and rolling to the side.

"God, yes," she says.

"Do you want me again?" I ask.

"Can I *have* you again?" she asks.

I move until I'm on all fours, and I lift my dress, baring my ass to her.

"Make me come fast," I say. "I want it deep."

"Fuck, I love my job," she says, moving until she's behind me, positioning my hips where she wants them.

Then, she's inside me. Her thrusts are slow but so deep. My hips move back to meet her, and it's so damn good. This is exactly what I needed tonight and what I've craved all day. I practically scream as she makes me come. When I fall down, she slips out. I roll until I'm on my side. I feel her come up behind me, the toy still attached. She slips it between my legs but makes no attempt to go back inside. Her lips move to my neck. She kisses there, lowers them to my shoulder, and bites down.

"Fuck! Don't do that," I say.

"Why?" she asks.

"Because I don't want my fiancée to see any marks. Might give it away that someone else fucked me, don't you think?" I say.

"I didn't know you were engaged," she says.

"Does it matter?" I ask.

"No," she says.

"Good. Do you need to come?" I ask.

"Yes, but–"

"Take it off," I say.

She doesn't reply, but I hear her shuffling behind me. Then, I hear a thump on the floor.

"Spread your legs," I say and move until I'm between them.

She fucked me good. She at least deserves another orgasm in return. I lick her pussy, and she gasps.

"Oh, I didn't expect–"

"Just let me," I say.

"Okay," she replies.

I lick her a few more times. Then, I reach for her hand and put it on the back of my head. She takes the hint and presses me into her. I start to suck.

"Oh, your mouth is…"

I suck harder.

"Yes, there," she says, rocking her hips into my face. "Fuck me."

I listen and push two fingers inside her.

"Curl them," she requests.

I do.

"God, I'm coming. Fuck. Already?"

I laugh silently at that last comment and continue to fuck her until she comes and then comes down.

"Can you handle more?" I ask her, kissing the inside of her thigh.

"How much more?" she asks, still catching her breath.

"Those women I was watching in the other room… I want to go back and join them."

"Yeah?"

"Yes. I want you to fuck them with me," I say, sitting up.

"Will *they* be okay with that?" she asks.

"We've done it before."

"Okay. Yeah, I'm in," she says.

"Don't get dressed," I tell her.

I get off the bed, let my dress fall to the floor, and leave the room, knowing she'll follow me. When I enter the other room, I turn around to see her walk in behind me. She closes the door, and I press her up against it.

"Hi, baby," I say, smiling at her.

"Hi," she says, smiling back at me.

I lean in and kiss her hard on the lips.

"I thought we were pretending all night," she says.

"Did I ruin it?" I ask, running my hands up and down my fiancée's naked body.

"We just had hot sex, so no, I'd say you ruined nothing," she replies.

"Hello, again," the member tells us. "Are you finally going to join us now?"

"I was hoping I could watch her make your girlfriend come," I say, pointing to my fiancée.

"Oh, that sounds good. Any chance you'll make me come while you do?" the woman asks.

"I like that idea," *she* says.

"Take good care of her," I reply, kissing her lips.

I run my hand over her chest, looking at my new piece of jewelry on my ring finger.

"I will," she says, winking at me.

I watch as she climbs onto the bed on top of the other woman. We've done this a few times with them now, expanding the pool of people we also have sex with only recently to include them. It turns out, we both enjoy this part of our life together way too much to stop at only sleeping with our friends. These two also seem to like being with *us*, so it works. *She* kisses that woman as I stand beside her and stroke her hair. We've been together for a little over a year now, and we've been coming to these parties every month as members. When I look at the other woman, she's stroking her clit as she watches my fiancée push her fingers inside her girlfriend.

"How is this so sexy?" she asks as I climb on top of her.

"Can I take over?" I ask, moving my hand to her sex.

"Oh, yes," she says.

I hear *her* grunt as she thrusts, so I turn to watch *her* watching me as she fucks the woman underneath her. I enter the other woman, and we fuck them together, looking at each other. The two women beneath us turn to each other and kiss. They play with each other's nipples and come at the same time. It's incredibly sexy.

"Will you let me eat you out?" the girlfriend says to *her*.

"Yes," *she* says.

I kneel behind the woman sucking on my fiancée's clit, and I fuck her with my fingers as her girlfriend watches us. Then, I look over at the woman. She plays with her breasts and touches herself a little until *she* comes. Then, the woman I'm fucking comes, and I smile down at *her*. I know it's time.

"Want to go?" I ask her.

She nods.

"Come back for more next month?" the member asks us as we stand to go.

"Maybe," *she* says.

"We'll be here," the member replies as her girlfriend rests her head on her chest.

"Home?" I ask when we pick up our clothes from the floor of the other room.

"Yes, please," she says, looking tired.

"Did you have fun?" I ask, wrapping my arms around her neck and pulling her into me.

"I watched that woman downstairs suck on your nipples, and I got so hard, babe," she says. "I wanted to fuck you right there."

"Did you touch yourself?" I ask.

"No, I wanted to wait until I had you up here," she says, wrapping her arms around my waist. "This was fun. I like role-playing."

"I liked pretending like I was breaking the rules. It made it hotter," I say.

"Want to do it again sometime?" she asks.

"This weekend?" I ask. "When they come over, you can be with them, and I can walk in on the three of you and act surprised."

She laughs and says, "But then you'll join us, right?"

I laugh and say, "Yes, baby."

We walk downstairs and find the two women we were just talking about sitting on the sofa, talking.

"Hey, you two," one of them says.

"What happened to skipping tonight?" *she* asks, sitting down next to them.

"We changed our minds," the other one says. "We left her lame work party early." She rests her head on her wife's shoulder. "I thought *you* went upstairs," she says to me and then turns back to my fiancée, "And I didn't even know *you* were here."

"I slipped in," *she* says.

"*Yes*, you did," I say, and our friends laugh.

"We were thinking about heading out," our friend says.

"Yeah, we are, too. We had fun, but we're ready for home."

They look at each other.

"I know we're coming over next weekend, but if we're all leaving now, maybe we could go to your place, open a bottle of wine, and have sex until the sun comes up," one of them says.

"Baby?" I ask.

She runs her hand up my leg and under my dress. Then, she moves it to my sex and slowly drags a finger through my wetness. My thong is tucked away in her pocket.

"Yeah, I think that sounds like a really good idea," *she* says.

A few minutes later, we get into *our* car and drive to *our* house. Our friends arrive moments after. We all walk in together, and I turn on the lights as we walk through the hall and into the kitchen. *She* opens a bottle of wine. I watch her pour it. She's gotten really good at picking out wine recently.

"So, how does it feel to be engaged? We haven't really celebrated yet," one of them says as she brushes her wife's hair behind her ear and kisses her neck.

"I have a feeling we're *about* to," I reply.

"It's amazing," *she* says, smiling at me as she hands me my wine.

"Should we drink our wine first?" one of them asks.

"I think you guys have already kind of started," *she* says.

"Oh, yeah. Sorry," our friend says.

I look down and notice her hand is already under her wife's dress.

"I was out of town for work for a week. Tonight is the first night we've had together, so I'm a little–"

"Handsy?" I say.

"Horny," her wife corrects.

"Do you want to watch while I touch her here?" she asks.

"Yes," I say, drinking my wine.

She takes my hand, and we move to the sofa. They follow us and stand in front, with the table between us. *She* kisses my neck and runs her hand over my dress. I watch as the women in front of me make out, offering us little sounds as our soundtrack. When *her* hand unzips my dress at the side, I know I'm not just going to watch.

"Can't wait?" I ask her.

"No," she says, sucking a nipple into her mouth.

I hold her there as I watch one of the women in front of us finger her wife under her dress.

"Can I see?" I ask.

The woman holds up her own dress. She has panties on, but I can still make out the hand moving inside them. Her arm wraps around her wife's neck, pulling her in closer.

"So sexy," I say.

A hand moves between my legs, and I spread them wide. She strokes me until I come.

"More wine, my love?" the woman asks her wife when she comes down from her orgasm.

"Yes," she says. "Then, let's go swimming. We can all take a shower together after."

They don't wait for us to say anything before they grab their glasses from the kitchen and then disappear out our back door. *She* climbs on top of me, settling between my hips.

"I love you," she says.

"I love you, too," I reply.

"They'll be out there for at least a half-hour. Want to go to bed?"

"Will you hold me?"

"Always, baby," she says, kissing my lips. "Always."

EPILOGUE. PART 2. – ESCORT

When I walk in, I head to the bar first. I grab myself a drink and down it quickly. I should probably take my time with it, but I'm anxious. I know what's going to happen tonight, and it has me ready and wired. I see a few other members I recognize and stop to chat with them for a moment. Then, the music starts, and it's as if the first note shuts down all conversation. Women who weren't even standing near one another move toward one another. A woman who was sipping a glass of champagne approaches an escort and nods her head toward the stairs without words. Then, there are the two women I know, already making out against a wall. I watch them from my position against the opposite wall. There are others in the room already removing clothing, but I watch them.

Then, I watch *her*. She talks to them for a second, and when she starts massaging her breasts, I swallow because I know how good they feel in my hands, in my mouth. Another woman walks up behind *her*. My instinct is to go there now and stop whatever is about to happen because she's mine. That's not why we're here tonight, though, and we both know that we belong to each other. That's all that matters. So, I watch.

The woman touches *her* hip and pulls *her* back against her body. My friend comes as her wife fucks her with her mouth against that wall. Then, my friend thrusts inside her. The woman behind *her* is massaging *her* breasts now. I press my hand to my sex over my pants and watch as she touches my fiancée. I press my palm into my center and feel the pressure start to build. They say something to one another that I can't hear. *She* drops her dress to her hips. Then, she lowers the woman's face to her breast, and the woman sucks. That woman's hand moves lower then, and it nears *her* sex. I rub my own harder over my pants. *She* stops the woman's hand, and I lick my lips.

"Yes! Yes," my friend yells as she comes against the wall.

The woman touching *her* moves her mouth from her nipples to her neck. *She* waits another moment and pulls away from her. I watch as she walks to the stairs, covering her breasts with her dress again.

I love watching her like this. She's gone from being touched by me for the first time while watching two other women have sex and running out of the party right after, to letting me watch her get touched by someone else in a living room full of people, with her breasts on full display and, theoretically, all eyes on her. *I've* gone from being nervous about my first night here, to watching the woman I'm going to marry be fondled by a stranger in front of other people because it turns me on so much.

I wait for a second. Then, I follow her up. She stands in an open doorway, and I stand back and listen.

"Oh, I like when you do that," someone in the room says.

"Will you make me come?"

"Yes," she replies.

I walk into the room and see the former escort and member. The two women have been together as long as we have now, though they're still girlfriends, and I've recently proposed, making sure to put a ring on *her* finger the first chance I got. She's the one, and I suppose I've always known it. From the first moment I saw her watching them, I knew I was supposed to know her. This time, I wrap my arms around her from behind just like that first time.

"I saw you downstairs," I say.

"Yeah. So?" she replies.

"I watched that other member touch you, and it turned me on."

"Oh, yeah?" she asks in her teasing tone that always makes me rock hard.

"Why didn't you bring her up here? Take her to bed?" I ask, slipping my hand under her dress, ready to claim her now.

"I was interested in watching for a while," she replies.

"*Was?*" I ask, sliding my hand over her smooth thigh.

"I'm getting turned on," she says.

"I can see why. They're very sexy," I say, looking up at them.

I move my hand to her sex. She lowers the straps of her dress for *me* this time. When she starts massaging her breasts, it makes me want to rub myself against her just to get off already. Instead, I move her soaked thong aside and find her clit ready and waiting.

"Oh, yes," she whispers and leans against me.

"You're hard," I say. "And wet."

"I told you I was turned on," she says.

"I can take care of it for you."

"Yes," she says.

"I can do more than just finger your clit; I can suck on your clit while you watch them," I say, wanting to taste her.

"Just this," she says, breathing hard. "Just make me fucking come already."

I stroke faster because I love when she's demanding and in charge; it's almost enough to get me off. She rocks her hips against my hand, and it feels like she's about to come.

"Fuck. Go find us a room," she says, pulling my hand out, which surprises me.

"What?"

I know her sounds. I know how close she is.

"I want you to fuck me. Go find us a room," she says.

"We can just–"

I want to finish what we were doing first, and then we can go, but if she wants me to fuck her in a room, I'm finding the damn room.

"No, I want a room. Get in there, turn off the lights, get on the bed, and put something on if you have it. Take off all your clothes, too."

"No problem," I say.

"We don't mind company," the former escort says as she strokes her girlfriend.

"Baby, focus. I want your mouth," her girlfriend tells her.

"You love my mouth," the woman replies.

I want to stay and watch what's about to happen, but I take off down the hall, finding the room I want and walking in. I strip quickly, knowing she's not that far behind me. Then, I slip it on and lie flat on the bed. The lights are off, per her demands. She opens and quickly closes the door behind her. I'm about to be the happiest woman in the world, I think to myself.

"Are you ready?" she asks.

"Yes."

"Are you wearing something for me?"

"Yes. I'm touching it right now." I stroke it up and down.

"Do you want to fuck me with it?" she asks.

"Yes," I say. "I want to suck you, too, though."

"One thing at a time," she tells me in the sexiest voice.

I hear her moving, but I can't see exactly what she's doing, which makes it all the better. She's on the bed now. I stop stroking when she straddles me. I can see she's still wearing her dress, but I'm guessing she took off that ruined thong already. So, I push the toy inside.

"Fuck, yes," she says.

"Can I come?" I ask.

"If you make me come, you can come," she says, lifting up and lowering herself back down. "I need it deep," she adds.

"You want me to fuck you deep?" I ask.

"Yes."

"Roll over, then. I'll fuck you deep," I say, wanting to

be behind her.

"Earn that," she says, and I nearly come.

She starts rocking, and I can feel it against my clit, which is ready to burst. She finds my hand with her own and puts it on her sex. I stroke her.

"Yes," I say, flicking it with my thumb. "How does my cock feel?"

"It's fine. Make it better," she orders.

I lift my hips up and down and up again.

"That!" she yells. "Yes! I'm coming."

She holds on to my breasts and rides out her orgasm.

"Oh, fuck," I say because I'm coming, too.

"Does it feel good?" she asks.

"Yes," I say.

"Do you want to suck me now?" she asks.

"Oh, fuck!" I'm lifting and lowering her on my dildo now, pressing her down into the toy and against my clit, trying to prolong this intense orgasm. "God, that's good," I say.

"I want you to suck on my clit," she says and lifts up and off me.

"Fuck, I was—"

Then, she's hovering her pussy over my mouth, and I'm licking my lips because I want it so bad.

"Touch yourself while you make me come again," she says as she lowers onto my face.

I suck on her instantly. She rocks. I move my hand inside the harness and stroke myself. I was so close to a second orgasm before; I know it won't take long. She's moving so fast and so hard that I can barely breathe, but I don't care.

"Yes! Yes! Yes! Don't stop!"

I moan. She comes. Then, she comes down. I come hard, pressing my palm to my clit and massaging it to make it last.

"Did you come?" she asks, lifting off of me and rolling to the side.

"God, yes," I say.

"Do you want me again?" she asks.

"Can I *have* you again?" I ask.

She's on all fours now. I watch and lick my lips as she lifts her dress and shows me her sexy ass.

"Make me come fast," she tells me. "I want it deep."

"Fuck, I love my job," I say, keeping up with our game tonight.

I move until I'm behind, positioning her hips right where I want them. Then, I fuck her. It's slow at first, but it's also deep because my girl loves deep. It doesn't take her long – it rarely does when she's this turned on. She falls forward, and I slip out. I look down at the toy and see how wet she is for me. I want her again but know she needs a break. She rolls to her side. I move behind her and press the toy between her legs because I love looking down and seeing it disappear between her thighs. I kiss her neck for a minute. Then, I nibble on it.

"Fuck! Don't do that," she says.

"Why?" I ask, smirking.

"Because I don't want my fiancée to see any marks. Might give it away that someone else fucked me, don't you think?" she says.

"I didn't know you were engaged," I lie, still smirking.

"Does it matter?"

"No," I say.

"Good. Do you need to come?" she asks.

"Yes, but–"

"Take it off," she says.

I toss the toy to the floor.

"Spread your legs," she says.

I do, and she moves between them. Then, she licks me, and I gasp.

"Oh, I didn't expect–"

"Just let me," she says.

"Okay," I say, not arguing.

She licks me again and again, then reaches for my hand and puts it on the back of her head. I push her into me, and she sucks.

"Oh, your mouth is…"

She sucks harder.

"Yes, there," I say, rocking my hips into her face. "Fuck me."

She pushes her fingers inside me.

"Curl them," I say.

She does, and it's the perfect spot.

"God, I'm coming. Fuck. Already?"

I can't believe I'm coming this quickly. I wanted it to last, but it's too late – I'm gone.

"Can you handle more?" she asks a moment later.

"How *much* more?" I ask, catching my breath.

"Those women I was watching in the other room… I want to go back and join them."

"Yeah?" I ask.

We hadn't talked about that, but it *does* sound good to me.

"Yes. I want you to fuck them with me," she says, sitting up.

"Will *they* be okay with that?" I ask.

"We've done it before."

"Okay. Yeah, I'm in," I say.

"Don't get dressed," she tells me.

It's true; we've been with these two a few times now. Once, we watched them for hours while we took care of each other before I watched *her* fuck the now-former escort from behind as she sucked on her girlfriend's clit – just like they'd done the first time they were together without me. The second time, we all got each other off once, rotating partners for hours until we were all too spent to go on. The third time, I fucked all three of them first, and then they all made me come. It was a *really* good night.

When I enter the room they're in right after *her*, she turns around, closes the door, and presses me up against it.

"Hi, baby," she says, smiling at me.

"Hi," I say, smiling back at her, a little confused.

She leans in and kisses me hard on the lips.

"I thought we were pretending all night," I say.

"Did I ruin it?" she asks adorably, running her hands up and down my naked body.

"We just had hot sex, so no, I'd say you ruined nothing," I reply.

"Hello, again," the member says to us. "Are you finally going to join us now?"

"I was hoping I could watch her make your girlfriend come," *she* says, pointing to me.

"Oh, that sounds good. Any chance you'll make me come while you do?" she asks.

"I like that idea," I say.

"Take good care of her," she replies, kissing my lips.

Then, she runs her hands over my chest again.

"I will," I say, winking at her.

I climb on top of the former escort. I still don't actually know her name. We've never exchanged them, and we don't intend to, either. I kiss her. *She* is next to the bed now, running her hand through my hair. I push my fingers inside the woman I'm on top of and curl insider her.

"How is this so sexy?" the woman next to us asks as I fuck her girlfriend.

"Can I take over?"

That voice belongs to the love of my life, I think as I rock into the woman I'm on top of. I begin grunting as I fuck her. I turn and see *her* fucking the other woman. We fuck them together, watching each other as we make them come. The two women turn their faces toward each other and kiss before they come at the same time.

"Will you let me eat you out?" the former escort says to me.

"Yes," I say.

She kneels behind the woman now sucking on my clit. I watch *her* as she puts her fingers inside the woman I just fucked with my own. Our eyes stay connected as the woman between us comes. Then, I come hard against her mouth.

My gorgeous fiancée pulls out of her, smiles down at me, and I know what she wants now.

"Want to go?" she asks.

I nod.

"Come back for more next month?" the member asks us as we stand to go.

"Maybe," I say.

"We'll be here," the member replies as her girlfriend rests her head on her chest.

"Home?" she asks when we pick up our clothes from the floor of the other room.

"Yes, please," I say.

"Did you have fun?" she asks, wrapping her arms around my neck and pulling me into her.

"I watched that woman downstairs suck on your nipples, and I got so hard, babe," I tell her. "I wanted to fuck you right there."

"Did you touch yourself?"

"No, I wanted to wait until I had you up here," I say, wrapping my arms around her waist. "This was fun. I like role-playing."

"I liked pretending like I was breaking the rules. It made it hotter," she says.

"Want to do it again sometime?" I ask.

"This weekend?" she asks. "When they come over, you can be with them, and I can walk in on the three of you and act surprised."

I laugh and say, "But then you'll join us, right?"

She laughs and says, "Yes, baby."

We walk downstairs and find the two women we were just talking about sitting on the sofa, talking.

"Hey, you two," one of them says.

"What happened to skipping tonight?" I ask, sitting down next to them.

"We changed our minds," the other one says. "We left her lame work party early." She rests her head on her wife's shoulder and then says to *her*, "I thought *you* went upstairs.

And I didn't even know *you* were here," she says to me.

"I slipped in," I say.

"*Yes*, you did," she says, and our friends laugh.

"We were thinking about heading out," our friend says.

"Yeah, we are, too. We had fun, but we're ready for home."

They look at each other.

"I know we're coming over next weekend, but if we're all leaving now, maybe we could go to your place, open a bottle of wine, and have sex until the sun comes up," one of them says.

"Baby?" she asks.

I run my hand up her leg and under her dress. Then, I move it to her pussy and drag a finger through her wetness.

"Yeah, I think that sounds like a really good idea," I say, knowing she can go again by the time we get home, and so could I.

A few minutes later, we get into *our* car and drive to *our* house. Our friends arrive moments after. We all walk in together. *She* turns on the lights as we walk through the hall and into the kitchen. I open us a bottle of wine.

"So, how does it feel to be engaged? We haven't really celebrated yet," one of them says as she brushes her wife's hair behind her ear and kisses her neck.

"I have a feeling we're *about* to," *she* replies.

"It's amazing," I say, smiling at her as I hand her a glass of wine.

"Should we drink our wine first?" one of them asks.

"I think you guys have already kind of started," I say, smiling at them.

"Oh, yeah. Sorry," our friend says.

Her hand is already under her wife's dress, which is to be expected. Despite their years of marriage, they still can't keep their hands off each other. I hope that's us after years of marriage as well.

"I was out of town for work for a week. Tonight is the

first night we've had together, so I'm a little–"

"Handsy?" *she* says.

"Horny," her wife corrects.

"Do you want to watch while I touch her here?" she asks.

"Yes," *she* says, drinking her wine.

I love her. I take her hand, and we move to the sofa. They follow us and stand in front, with the table between us. I kiss *her* neck and run my hand over her dress. She watches as the women in front of us kiss and make sounds. My eyes are closed, but those sounds drive me wild, so I unzip her dress.

"Can't wait?" she asks.

"No," I say, sucking a nipple into my mouth.

She holds me there.

"Can I see?" she asks.

I don't know what she means, so I turn my head to look. I watch as my friend holds up her dress, and now I can see her wife's hand moving inside her panties.

"So sexy," she says.

She's right. I move my hand between her legs, and she spreads them for me. I stroke her softly, knowing she's probably a little sore, but I don't stop until she comes.

"More wine, my love?" the woman asks her wife when she comes down from her orgasm as well.

"Yes," she says. "Then, let's go swimming. We can all take a shower together after."

They don't wait for us to say anything before they grab their glasses from the kitchen and then disappear out our back door. I climb on top of her, settling between her hips.

"I love you," I say.

"I love you, too," she replies.

"They'll be out there for at least a half-hour. Want to go to bed?" I ask.

"Will you hold me?" she asks.

"Always, baby," I say, kissing her sweet lips. "Always."

When our friends finally come inside, it's well after

four in the morning. We were nearing sleep and not up for anything else with them, so they showered by themselves and went to sleep in one of our guest rooms. We don't have many rules in our relationship when it comes to sex, but we do have one, and it's important.

"Are you too sore?" I ask her.

"Never," she replies.

The one rule is that no matter how we start the night, or who we're with, at the end of the night – or, as is often the case, in the morning – we always end up with each other. I'm the last person to touch her; she's the final person to touch me. Then, we go to sleep holding on to one another. I roll on top of her, kissing her lips first and then her neck. She's so soft, I could kiss her forever. And I plan to.

"Take me slowly," she says.

"I know just what to do," I say, kissing her again.

"You *always* know just what to do," she replies.

I kiss her entire body, every bit of skin. She rolls over for me so I can make sure not to miss a single spot. By the time her hips are pressing down into our high-thread-count sheets, I know it's time. I reach between her legs and move inside from behind. I've already pulled out her favorite vibrator, so I move it between her legs, pressing it against her clit. I turn it on and let her do the rest.

"Oh, fuck," she says into the mattress.

"Good?" I ask.

"I'm going to come," she says.

"You just started," I reply, moving in and out slowly.

"Baby, there. I'll come," she says.

She rocks hard, and I move a little faster. Then, she yells my name. I smile as I bring her back down. She stays where she is, and I roll to the side. She rolls onto her side, takes the vibrator, turns it off, and slips the small device into my mouth a little so I can taste her.

"Put it on me," I say.

She moves it between my legs and turns it back on. She sucks on my nipple, holding the thing in place.

"Wow. Tiny but mighty," I say, forgetting how strong this thing is when it's turned up all the way.

"Do you want me inside you?" she asks.

"Yes," I say.

I hold the vibrator now, and she moves her fingers down and inside. My hips buck.

"You're ready for me," she says, curling them.

"Yes," I repeat.

"Good. Come for me, baby."

I do. She turns off the vibrator, tosses it somewhere, and climbs on top of me, rubbing our pussies together.

"I love you," she says.

"I love you," I reply, pressing her ass down so that she's as close to me as possible.

"I *cannot* come again," she says, laughing.

"*I* can," I say, lifting my hips.

"God, I love how insatiable you are," she says, rolling down into me.

"Enough to let me get off like this?" I ask.

"Enough to do that, fall asleep next to you, and let you wake up in a few hours with my face between your legs."

I groan and say, "That sounds like actual heaven."

She smiles down at me and says, "Two years ago…" She rocks her hips. "I walked into a party thinking I was the craziest woman on the planet, with fantasies that no one else had." She rocks again. "And I saw you on a bed, playing with that woman's breasts. Oh, fuck," she says as she closes her eyes. She's getting turned on again. "I had to leave the room because your eyes were so intense – I couldn't look at you, but I couldn't look away from you, either."

"You're going to come with me, aren't you?" I ask.

"Yes," she says, rocking. "And you found me, touched me, held me, and made me feel like everything was going to be okay. Baby, touch me."

I move my hand between us and cup her, slipping my index finger into her folds and lightly stroking.

"And now, we're here. Yes, there."

"Like this?" I ask, stroking her while the back of my palm presses into me.

"God, I'm so lucky. I'm going to marry you," she says.

Then, we come together, each saying the other's name as we do.

www.ingramcontent.com/pod-product-compliance
Lightning Source LLC
Chambersburg PA
CBHW030639260626
47157CB00007B/2401